THE DEVIL'S CLAW

THE DEVIL'S CLAW
A JENNIFER DOREY MYSTERY

Lara Dearman

CROOKED
LANE

NEW YORK

Copyright © 2018 by Lara Dearman

All rights reserved.

Published in the United States by Crooked Lane Books, an imprint of The Quick Brown Fox & Company LLC.

Crooked Lane Books and its logo are trademarks of The Quick Brown Fox & Company LLC.

Library of Congress Catalog-in-Publication data available upon request.

ISBN (hardcover): 978-1-68331-456-1
ISBN (ePub): 978-1-68331-457-8
ISBN (ePDF): 978-1-68331-458-5

Cover design by Blacksheep/Orion Books
Book design by Jennifer Canzone

Printed in the United States.

www.crookedlanebooks.com

Crooked Lane Books
34 West 27th St., 10th Floor
New York, NY 10001

First North American edition: January 2018
Originally published in Great Britain by Orion Publishing Group, November 2017

10 9 8 7 6 5 4 3 2 1

For Andrew, Lily, Charlie and Lena

P'tit a p'tit l'ouaise fait sen nic
Little by little the bird builds her nest

Edgar Macculloch, *Guernsey Folk Lore*

Prologue

She is looking forward to going out. It has been so long since there has been anything to look forward to. Her new top is black and made of a satiny material. It feels cool against her skin and it has short sleeves and a low neckline. It is a cold night but she will take a jacket. When she gets to the bar, she will take it off and let her friends see.

It is time to let them see.

The scars run from the inside of her elbow down to her wrist. She traces her finger along one. It is palest pink now, almost silver, and very, very fine. Because she never cut deep . . . just often.

Her hair is long and curly and needs a wash but she brushes and braids it. The braid hangs over her shoulder. It looks cute: a little girl's hairstyle. Boys like that sort of thing. She remembers reading it in a magazine. You have to be young enough to pull it off, though. And thin. And pretty. Lucky for her she is all three.

It is getting late. Mum offers to drive her but she says no. It is just an excuse to check up on her. She'd rather walk, she says, but when she gets outside it is colder than she'd thought. After walking for five minutes she decides to turn back. She will put on a jumper and tell Mum she'd like a lift. But then the car pulls alongside her. The window slides down. She doesn't need her mum after all.

*

A rush of cold air brings her round. She can't see properly. Her head is throbbing. She is in the car but it is not moving. She blinks, tries to clear her vision. She remembers. He had a gun. He had a gun and he hit her with it. He hit her so hard she blacked out and now there is blood in her eyes and in her mouth and she tries to open it, to scream but she can't. It's stuck fast and before she can figure out how to unstick it, he is there.

He is opening the door.

Her wrists are bound with silver tape. It shines in the moonlight. She was scared, before he hit her, before she blacked out. She was scared, but too polite to try to get out of the car.

He is pulling her out.

She is terrified. He is going to rape and kill her. She is going to die because she was too polite.

He is standing in front of her. He is smiling. And he is making noises.

He is humming.

She screams with her mouth shut, screams until her throat burns, pushing the sound through her nose and flailing her arms, uselessly, and he pushes her against the car and squeezes her throat until the pathetic noise she was making is silenced, replaced by a soundless trail of snot and blood.

He is stroking her hair. Fingering the pretty braid, the one she thought the boys would like. She whimpers. He leans in, puts his cheek next to hers. She feels his breath, damp and warm on her skin.

He is whispering.

Hush. Hush now. I'm going to help you.

He leads her through the night and she stumbles and she cries and then he pushes her.

Down.

Into the darkness.

1

Jenny

Thursday, 6 November

It was the same motorbike. She knew before she even saw it. There was something tinny about the sound of it, a high-pitched whine underneath the regular thrum and growl of the engine. She checked the rear-view mirror as he rounded the corner and came into view. Neon orange bike, rider dressed all in black, dark helmet, reflective visor pulled down. Definitely the same one. He followed her until they reached Grande Rue. Like he'd done every morning that week. As she stopped at the yellow line indicating to turn right, towards town, he undertook her and peeled off to the left, towards L'Ancresse.

It was like that on Guernsey. You ran into the same people all the time. There was a joke about it: something about sixty thousand people clinging to a rock. At twenty-four square miles it wasn't quite a rock, but it was not far off. There was something unsettling, though, about this bike. Something threatening. She followed it.

She kept her distance until she reached the crossroads at L'Ancresse. To the left the road ran wide and straight to St Sampsons. Ahead a narrow track led to the rubbish dump at Mont Cuet. To the right were the common and the sea. The rider looked over his shoulder as she drew up behind him at the yellow line and although she could only see the reflection of her own car in his visor, Jenny felt sure that he was smiling at her. Goading her. He revved the bike's engine. Fumes poured out of the exhaust. He turned back to face the road and then released his brake, swerving dangerously as he headed towards the sea, tires screeching, one last glance in her direction before he disappeared from view.

She was gripping the steering wheel so tightly her fingers hurt and her hands were sweating. She was being ridiculous. He was probably just some kid showing off. There was no reason for anyone to be following her. Not here. She wiped her hands on her jeans, opened a window to let in a rush of cool air, swung the car around and headed to work.

The drive into town took her south along the coast. The beaches on this side of the island were rocky, swathes of smooth, black pebbles in place of sand, the odd larger rocks protruding from amongst them, their peaks stained green and white with seaweed and dried bird shit. Buoys marking crab and lobster pots dotted the sea, their bright red surfaces faded to a milky pink by years of sunlight. Closer to shore, small fishing boats bobbed about, clanking and creaking against their dock lines; *The Lady Katherine, Margot's Dream,* grand names at odds with the humble appearance of the weather-battered vessels, hulls peeling and streaked with rust. Across the Channel the sky was cloudless, weak rays of early November sunshine promising a fine day ahead. A brisk breeze whipped at the sea's surface, sending spray over the wall and on to the windscreen of her car.

As she approached St Sampsons, the traffic became heavier, the rural lanes of the Vale, her home parish, giving way to the car-clogged roads of the town. She drove, stop-start, one eye on the clock, towards Bulwer Avenue and St Peter Port, past a mismatched strip of offices and apartment blocks. New crimes against architecture stood next to the faded remains of grand hotels, now empty and waiting to be converted into more offices and apartment blocks, or as the developer's hoarding crowed:

**LUXURY CONDOMINIUMS WITH SWEEPING
VIEWS OF THE ENGLISH CHANNEL AND THE
ISLANDS OF HERM AND SARK.**

Nice if you could afford it, which she couldn't. She'd thought London was expensive until she'd moved back and found out the best she could get here was a pokey bedsit in a dilapidated house on one of the least salubrious streets in town. Which was why, eighteen months after she'd returned, and at the grand old age of nearly thirty, she was back in her old bedroom, living with her mum.

The traffic slowed to a crawl beyond a low wall. It was high tide, and from here it looked as though she could just reach out and touch the sea. When she was little, it had held endless wonder. Home to mermaids and hidden cities, smugglers and treasure and the giant squid that her dad said he often glimpsed but never caught. She loved his stories. She would sit on his knee while he played euchre with his friends and listen to the gruff fishermen talk about their boats and the latest fishing regulations or some amateur who had got into trouble on rough seas and needed rescuing. If she were lucky, one of them would tell her a proper story, about a pirate, maybe, whose ghost sailed on the winds around the harbour. Then her mum would come along, shaking her head, telling them all to stop filling the poor girl's head with silly stories and didn't they know they were going to give her nightmares? But they didn't give her nightmares. On the contrary, they filled her thoughts with colour and light and she dreamt of heroes rescuing drowning men, of pale ghosts on phantom ships, tall black masts on glittering oceans.

It was different, now. Now there were no mermaids or pirates or ghosts. Now it was just water, black and uninviting and hemming her in.

It occurred to her she should get out, see if there was anything worth reporting up ahead. Even a minor accident might make page three on a slow news day.

And on Guernsey, most days were slow.

Instead, she checked her reflection in the sun-visor mirror. Summer's tan was fading. She looked pale, and her eyebrows, unruly at the best of times, were currently threatening a complete rebellion. Her hair, damp from her morning swim, was thick and blonde. She wore it loose around her shoulders, but it was too short. She was growing it. She ran her hands through it, pulling at the ends, as if doing so would encourage it back to where it had been. Before . . . She tucked it behind her ears, fingers brushing against the small scar at the nape of her neck. It had healed badly, leaving an itchy, raised welt. It would fade, the doctor had said kindly, given time. She'd known he had been referring to more than just the scar.

The car in front slowly rolled forwards. They gathered pace and she rounded the corner into town just in time to see a skittish-looking heifer being led down Vale Road by a welly-clad handler and a laughing policeman, to good-natured toots and waves.

She should have got out. A quick snap might have made front page.

The *Guernsey News*'s office was part of the Admiral Park development, on the outskirts of the main town of St Peter Port. Surrounded by a soulless collection of glass-fronted office blocks and on a busy main road carrying traffic to the brand-new Waitrose around the corner, the *News*'s office had only two things going for it location wise: ample parking and, beyond the steady stream of cars outside, sea views. Inside, however, it had many advantages. Open plan, bright and airy, a huge atrium filled the place with light on even the dullest of days. Floor-to-ceiling windows lined the sea-facing wall and on the opposite side of the room, glass-walled offices reflected the light from outside on to the office floor. On bright days, at high tide, ripples played on every surface.

At the back of the office, in a separate room, also walled with glass, were the printing presses. Anyone in the office by 6 a.m. could feel the floor vibrate and hum as the day's paper rolled off the press before being stacked and tied into bundles ready for delivery to newsagents and supermarkets across the island. Jenny loved the smell of a freshly printed newspaper: the ink, sharp and metallic on the soft paper, the scent fading, like the news, as the day wore on.

She had missed the morning meeting so went straight to her desk. Covered in piles of crumpled papers and tooth-edged pages torn from notebooks, it looked like chaos, but she had a system and could find what she was looking for in a matter of moments. In the corner, next to her screen, was a picture of her dad, Charlie. Taken nearly ten years ago, he was standing next to his fishing boat, the *Jenny Wren,* just after she'd had a new coat of paint. He was smiling, his hat pulled down over his eyes to shield the glare from the sun. Later that day he'd taken them to Herm, a tiny island three miles off the east coast of Guernsey, and they'd had a picnic lunch on Shell Beach – tinned salmon sandwiches and a flask of lemon tea with milk – and they'd all got sunburnt. It felt like a lifetime ago.

She checked her emails. One from Sarah, asking if they were ever going to meet up for a drink – it was a rare occasion that Jenny's friend managed to ditch the kids and make the fifteen-minute journey into town for a glass of wine. Jenny replied confirming she would love a drink and a catch-up if she could ever make it out of the office before 9 p.m., what with Sarah usually being collapsed on a sofa half asleep by that time of night.

Her police source (a second cousin, an affable Detective

Constable called Stephen who relished meeting her for a coffee and giving her titbits of information) had sent her some photos of 'strange' graffiti at Moulin Huet. She was about to open it when another message caught her eye. It was the address. Unfamiliar. Could be spam. But she knew before she clicked on it.

BITCH

She closed it quickly, not wanting anyone else to walk past and see it. Because it felt shameful, somehow, to be called names. People might think she deserved it. She knew who it was from. Or at least, she knew what it was for. To remind her. That they were watching. She didn't know how closely. The biker, for example. She told herself she was being paranoid. But was he a message too? She wouldn't have thought she was worth that much effort. She moved the email into a folder she'd called *Fairfield Road* and stopped herself from pulling at her hair again, turned her attention to a Post-it someone had stuck on her phone.

SEE BRIAN.

Perfect. She screwed it up and put it in the bin.

Elliot, the new reporter, was pacing around on his phone. He was talking to someone about the Save The Islander campaign, an anti-immigration movement protesting the recent influx of foreign workers. It was a story Jenny had wanted, but it had been given to Elliot as some sort of initiation into the world of small-island politics. He was about Jenny's age, she guessed, late twenties, maybe thirty, local, but had grown up in the UK due to some complicated family background she hadn't figured out yet, and had only recently returned to the island. He was friendly. And good-looking in a wholesome, Boy Scout way; square-jawed and clean-shaven, neatly dressed, slim-cut shirt tucked into jeans, sleeves rolled up over toned arms. She wasn't the only one who had noticed. The two interns were always blushing when he talked to them and she'd caught Marjorie, the semi-retired filing and photocopying lady, giggling at one of his bad jokes and then making him a coffee, bringing it to his desk like it was the nineteen-bloody-fifties. It was hard to hold it against him, though. He was annoyingly likeable.

He stopped as he walked past – he did that a lot – and perched at the end of her desk. She could see a small patch of stubble, missed in the morning shave, just below his left ear, and she imagined running a finger along his jaw, feeling rough stubble and then smooth skin. She felt herself blushing. She was as bad as the interns. Worse, even. At least they had the excuse of adolescence.

'You should watch out,' he said, 'Brian's on the warpath.'

'What's he moaning about now?'

'Not enough decent stories coming in. I swear Mark left the meeting with tears in his eyes.'

Nothing new there. Nobody could understand how the mild-mannered Mark had made it as news editor, but one could only assume it was because he was such a pushover. It left Brian free reign to run the paper his way.

'He wants to see you.'

'Hmm?'

'Brian. He wants to see you. I left you a note. As soon as you get in he said.' He winked as he left.

A wink, Jenny thought, could be either cheesy or lecherous. Elliot somehow managed to make it charming.

Brian Ozanne looked up from his laptop and gave a thin-lipped smile. As editor of the island's only daily newspaper he fancied himself a minor celebrity. He must have been at least sixty, but looked years younger, with his thick, glossy hair and skin that glowed just the right shade of sun-kissed brown. Jenny strongly suspected Grecian 2000 and a spray tan. A photograph of his wife took pride of place on the desk. Brian organised an annual Cancer Research fundraiser in her memory. Everyone in the office took part in sponsored silences or wearing pyjamas to work or shaving off beards and moustaches. Brian oversaw the whole thing personally, pushing everyone to raise more, to beat last year's fundraising record, and then he matched whatever was raised. Which was all well and good, except he insisted, every year, on a double-page spread in the *News,* complete with interview and a picture of him, primped and preened, presenting the cheque to a charity representative. It was nauseating.

'So, Jennifer.' He leant back in his chair, hands steepled under his chin. 'How do you think you're getting on?'

This was a typical Brian question and would no doubt lead to a dressing-down of some sort. But Jenny thought she was getting on just fine. So that's what she told him.

'Very well, thank you, Brian. I've made some good contacts, produced some good copy. Mark seems pleased with my work.'

'Of course. Everything you produce is good quality. Nobody is denying that. This is not an issue of quality, no, no, no.' He shook his head. 'This is about *quantity.*' He paused. 'Frankly, Jennifer, you're just not producing enough.' He raised a hand to stop her interrupting. 'I know you work hard, you put in the hours. But you're going to have to work smarter. To increase your output. And, as of this morning, we're down a features reporter. One of the girls is on sick leave so you can pick up the slack. Starting with the firework display at the castle this weekend. Take a photographer with you, get some nice pictures. Everyone likes fireworks.' He picked up his BlackBerry and started replying to a message, a sign, Jenny presumed, that the meeting was over.

It was pointless to argue with Brian. He had been editor of the *News* for thirty years, as he constantly reminded everyone. He was also a bit of a prick on a power trip and not in the habit of negotiating. If Jenny wanted to keep her job and, right now, though she wasn't entirely sure she did, she needed to keep him happy. She turned to leave.

'And, Jennifer?'

'Yes, Brian?'

He was still looking at his phone. 'I had a call yesterday. Came through on my direct line which is quite unusual, my calls usually go through Rose, as you know.'

Jenny nodded, wondering if Brian was about to try to pin a switchboard error on her.

'It was someone asking about you. A young man.'

'Who?' The question caught in Jenny's throat and Brian looked up, eyes narrowed.

'I've no idea. As I told the caller, I'm not your social secretary. Kindly make sure it doesn't happen again.'

Jenny barely managed a nod.

She sat back at her desk and stared at her screen. Opened the folder, *Fairfield Road*. There were ten emails in there now, including today's. She scrolled through them.

BITCH

BITCH

BITCH

BITCH

BITCH

BITCH

BITCH

BITCH

BITCH

BITCH

2

Matt

Friday, 7 November

The road to Pleinmont Point was closed to cars, so Matt pulled his old Fiesta into the nearest parking spot opposite the Imperial Hotel and turned off the engine. He wound down the window and lit a Marlboro. Waves broke loudly on the shore below. From here the West coast stretched out, one long sandy beach after another, Rocquaine, Vazon, Cobo, until the rocks and pebbles took over in the North. He finished his cigarette, undid his ponytail and let his long, lank hair hang about his face. His ears were too big so they looked better covered, but there was nothing he could do about his forehead. It shone with acne and there was a trace of the concealer he'd experimented with in his hairline.

Nerves. Over a girl. Pathetic.

Outside the night was cold. Along the sea wall they gathered in small groups, illuminated by torches they rested on the wall. Black clothes, black coats, black boots, with studs, chains and buckles.

He made his way to the spot beneath the trees where his friends met every Friday. Lauren was already there, sitting next to a portable barbeque, listening to Neon Fly and swigging from a can of Breda. Her breasts strained against her tight black top. He wondered if she did it on purpose, if she knew her T-shirts were

12

too small. She probably did. She was what his dad would call a cock-tease. Not a slut. A cock-tease. It was different.

Matt sat down next to Sam.

'Hi, Matt.' Lauren smiled at him. Her lips were full and soft. Blow-job lips. She had a smudge of lipstick on her teeth. She handed him a beer. He mumbled a thanks, cheeks burning, and took a swig. Sam was talking about how shit his life was, how much he hated college, how much he hated his dad. Someone had changed the music. Slipknot. A band of cloud was rolling in. It was going to rain. Matt pulled up the collar of his coat.

'Anyway, gonna love you and leave you, mate. Lauren and I were just about to go for a walk.' Sam got up, held his hand out to Lauren, and pulled her to his side.

'Here, help yourself.' He handed the remains of the spliff to Matt and Matt watched them go.

Fucking bastard. Sam knew he liked Lauren. Matt had talked about nothing else for weeks. He rubbed his eyes, pulled his hair back, wound the elastic round so tightly his scalp hurt. He gripped his beer can, felt the thin sheet of aluminium give way beneath his fingers. He squeezed, crumpling the can, and threw it as high as he could. Beer sprayed out as it flew through the air before bouncing off the Tarmac across the road and landing at the feet of a heavily pierced kid.

'Hey, watch out, dickhead!'

'Sorry,' Matt mumbled.

He drank four more cans and finished the spliff, texted a mate who was trying to persuade him to come into town, but Matt was well over the limit now and needed time to sober up before he drove, so he played *Infinity Blade* until the low battery warning came on. He chucked the phone on the grass beside him and lay on his back, gazing up at the sky, which looked trippy, because even though it was night and it should have been black, the low-lying cloud shone white in the moonlight, and the birds – or were they bats? – he wasn't sure if birds slept at night – were black flitters across the sky. They made him feel dizzy, so he closed his eyes, lulled by the rhythmical thrashing of death metal and the shushing of the sea.

It was quiet. He sat up. The barbeque had burnt out, an orange glow barely visible beneath the flaky white coals. He felt around for his phone, switched on the torch. Lauren and Sam's stuff was there, but there was no sign of them. Nearly everyone else had left. A couple, leaning against a car bonnet, were groping each other unenthusiastically, his head buried in her neck while she fumbled with her phone and his crotch simultaneously. Matt looked away, aroused and embarrassed.

Further up the road there was a hunched shape against the wall making groaning sounds. Matt got up, shook his head, took a couple of deep breaths and stumbled over. He had done a first-aid course at St John's Ambulance a couple of years ago, part of a long-since-abandoned Duke of Edinburgh Bronze Award, and he always felt a certain responsibility in these kinds of situations. He crouched in front of the shape. Just a kid, couldn't be more than fourteen. Puke splattered the Tarmac where he'd collapsed. Matt nudged him with his boot. Nothing. He nudged again, harder, until the kid mumbled a 'leave me alone' and rolled over, straight into a pool of his own sick.

Matt stepped away and looked around. Beer cans and chip papers blowing in the wind, fag butts ground into the Tarmac, puddles of vomit. He'd liked it here when he was a kid. Used to bring his kite. There was always a good breeze up near Fort Pezeries. Look what they'd done to the place! It was disgusting. And Sam was probably littering the cliffs with his used johnnies right this minute. Now seemed as good a time as any to tell him to fuck right off. With a galvanising sweep of his greasy hair, he set off into the night.

He walked away from the car park towards Pezeries Point, shining his phone in front of him, following the Tarmacked road until he came to the National Trust meadow, which was a short cut to the fort where he guessed Sam and Lauren were. So he left the safety of the solid Tarmac and stepped on to the thick, springy grass, which put an unwelcome bounce in his step, throwing his ankles in unexpected directions. He walked, unsteadily, nearly tripping when a rabbit ran out from the undergrowth, and it stopped, frozen, eyes glowing white. He swept his phone round so he could try to work out exactly where he was. A sign to the right of him warned of a sheer drop down to the sea below. That sobered him up. He figured wandering around on the cliffs in the dark was a bad idea so cut back to the road and followed it to Fort Pezeries, a ruined castle or fortress – he wasn't sure what the difference was. The outer walls had been restored and you could climb up and walk along them. They'd be in there, fucking against one of the cannons probably. Or maybe Lauren was giving Sam head while he leant against the armoury wall, looking out over Rocquaine Bay. Matt stopped. Listened. Waves smashing against rocks. The nervous peep-peep of an oystercatcher. The rustling of bracken.

Something else.

Twigs breaking.

Rabbits. Overrun with rabbits this place. He remembered finding one up here once, thinking it was tame, reaching down to stroke it, only to find it was blinded by myxomatosis, its fur covered in open sores. He'd known he should kill it, to put it out of its misery, but he couldn't do it and he'd let it limp, unseeing, into the undergrowth. He felt sick at the recollection. What the fuck was he doing? He needed to go, back the way he'd come, although he'd wandered off the path and he wasn't sure which way that was, and suddenly everything was plunged into darkness. Shit. He pushed the power button on his phone, but he knew it was pointless. He walked a few steps, tripped over a rock, sticking straight out of the ground, then another one. A circle of rocks. He knew where he was.

Le Table des Pions, or the Fairy Ring as everyone called it, was a rough table hewn into a grassy plateau, surrounded by a ring of stones. On one side, dense foliage of bracken and gorse formed a natural windbreak, and on the other, flat, grassy headland led to sheer cliffs and beneath them, the sea. Built as a picnic spot for officials who'd inspected the island's roads hundreds of years ago, locals preferred the other stories surrounding the place. About witches. And the Devil. The Devil came here, disguised as a goat or a wolf or a big, black dog and danced with witches. There was a tunnel somewhere here too. Not a real one, at least not as far as Matt knew, but according to legend all of the Devils' cronies used tunnels to get around. The entrances were caves in the cliffs, which led deep underground. Stories. But Matt could not get the image of shadows lurking in dark caves out of his head. He imagined them swarming out on to the beach, right below here, and climbing up over the cliffs, finding him and then tearing him apart, piece by piece, and though he knew that it was the pot making him paranoid, he wanted to go. A thicker band of cloud rolled in and extinguished the pale moonlight. He turned, tried to get his bearings.

More twigs snapping. *More rabbits.*

Whispers. *Just the wind.*

Except . . . There was laughter too, he was sure of it. Rough, hacking laughter.

He remembered his lighter and felt for it in his pocket, hand shaking.

The noise again. Manic, high-pitched, more a scream than a laugh now. He held it aloft, swinging it wildly through the air, but he could only keep it lit long enough to see something pale in the middle of the ring, edges blurred. He thought, for a moment, that he might actually piss himself.

He wanted to call out, to see if Sam and Lauren were nearby, but he was afraid to make a noise. He felt, instinctively, that he should be silent. He steadied his hand, held the lighter in front of him, unlit, as if it might offer protection somehow. Fire! Witches were scared of fire. He shook his head. *There were no fucking witches.* But there was something. There was something in the circle. He'd had a glimpse of it. And he had a feeling, a horrible, ice-cold feeling, that it was something terrible, something worse than he'd ever seen before. He took a step closer. Sparked up.

The figure was flat on its back, arms and legs outstretched. Matt could barely breathe. Bile stung the back of his throat and he coughed, then put his hand to his mouth, desperate to muffle the sound. He wanted to run, but forced himself to step closer, closer, to lean forwards, to bring the flame down, so that he could really see.

It was grotesque. Limbs and head unnaturally large, tight bindings wrapped its wrists and ankles, which ended too suddenly, due to the complete absence of any hands or feet. Most striking though, was its hair. Carefully fanned out around the swollen head, the reflection of the flame on each peroxide blonde follicle created an unholy halo effect. Matt let out a garbled sound, half sigh, half laugh and sank to his knees.

It was a guy, trussed and stuffed and ready for a bonfire. The head, made from a hessian bag packed with straw, was a woman's, the face drawn on cartoon style; large bright blue eyes with exaggerated eyelashes, rouged cheeks and full red lips, smiling up at him. It was wearing a long-sleeved white top and, on the right arm, somebody had slashed four lines, three vertical, one horizontal underneath. Straw poked out from the cuts, and strands of it littered the grass around him.

Noise, from behind. Matt staggered to his feet, swung around.

'What the fuck are you doing, man?' It was Sam, holding a torch. He looked dishevelled, and Lauren leant into him, bracken in her hair.

'It's a guy.' His voice was high and hoarse. He cleared his throat. 'Scared the shit out of me.'

Sam sauntered over to inspect it, shrugged his shoulders.

'Probably just some weirdoes left it there, trying to fuck with people. Come back and have another beer.' Sam and Lauren left arm in arm. A lone sea gull flew over them, a flash of white, its hack-hack-hacking cry unleashed into the night.

Matt crouched back beside the guy. It seemed a shame to let it go to waste. He held his lighter to the end of its right leg and watched as the trouser hem shrunk and retreated, each thread luminous for an instant before it melted away. The flames, fed by the fabric, grew quickly. He watched as the body of straw and newspaper shifted and twisted, as if it was fighting against the flames and the face, smiling up at him, with those big blue eyes locked on his, looked almost as if it was trying to tell him something and, for a moment, he wanted to save it.

But it was too late. The fire consumed it all.

3

Jenny

Saturday, 8 November

She walked into the kitchen in her pyjamas, a faded plaid shirt and wide-legged trouser set she'd had for years, her hair a tangled mess, dark circles under her eyes. It was just past six, but Margaret was already standing at the kitchen sink, dressed smartly in a woollen skirt and a printed blouse, sleeves rolled up to the elbows, pulling on a pair of bright yellow Marigolds. She refused to use the dishwasher. It was a waste, she said, no point running a whole machine for a couple of bits and pieces. There was no point in a lot of things these days, not according to Margaret, certainly not in anything that made life easier, and definitely not in anything frivolous or fun. Not since Charlie had died. She plunged her hands into the soapy water, clinking together cups and plates as she pulled each piece out and swiped at it with a sponge, lending the task a focused, frantic energy.

Margaret Dorey had energy in abundance. Before, she'd had so much to do. Charlie needed a packed lunch, a flask of tea, a T-shirt ironed or a missing sock found. He would leave his breakfast dishes and she would clear them away. She would do the laundry and then plan the evening meal before mid-morning so she could go to the shops if she needed anything. Now she only had Jenny.

19

She rose early and dressed fastidiously, perhaps taking even more care over her appearance than she had before, telling Jenny that she wasn't going to let herself go, just because she was a widow. She kept the house immaculately clean and tidy. And she walked. Constantly. Up and down the house at all hours of the day and night, fidgeting and sighing, polishing a smudge off of a picture frame, rearranging ornaments on the mantelpiece, making endless cups of tea and then only drinking half of them as she became distracted by any number of mundane chores. It was maddening to an observer. Jenny imagined it must be even worse for Margaret.

Jenny poured some juice and sat at the table over a folded copy of the *Daily Mail*. She picked it up and flicked through the first few pages before throwing it back down with an exaggerated sigh.

'I don't know how you can read this rubbish.'

'I like to know what's going on in the world.'

'Well, you're not going to find out in there, are you?' Jenny knew she sounded petulant. 'I'm sorry. I'm tired.'

'Did I wake you again last night, love?' Margaret turned. She looked younger than her fifty-five years but they were quickly catching up with her. Her black hair was streaked with silver, the lines around her eyes were deepening and her face drawn. She'd lost so much weight. Not just from her body. It was like something that had been anchored deep within her had just floated away. Jenny had first noticed at Charlie's funeral. She had taken Margaret's arm to keep her from stumbling. She had been frail. Birdlike. Lightness and bones.

'It wasn't you.' Jenny said. 'Bloody kids letting off fireworks in the middle of the night again.' She was not about to tell Margaret that she was having trouble sleeping. That, recently, she had been waking in the middle of the night, gripped with a cold, damp fear she had not felt for many years. Margaret found enough to worry about without Jenny adding to the list.

Margaret turned back to the dishes. 'You got any plans for the weekend, love?' she asked. 'I saw Sarah in town the other day, with the little ones. She's looking well for having three, I must say. She said you two were going out for a drink. That'll be nice. You should be getting out more, you know. Have a bit of fun, meet some people.'

'I know plenty of people, Mum. Don't worry about me. And I am going to meet Sarah for a drink. As soon as I've got time. I've got to go into the office today. I'm covering the firework display up at the castle – after a quick swim.'

'Not in the sea again? Why can't you go the pool like normal people?' She wore her exasperated look, reserved for what she considered Jenny's most hare-brained ideas. It was a look Charlie had often received and it made Jenny smile.

'The pool's for wimps, Mum, you know that.' Jenny finished her juice and dropped the empty glass in the sink. 'Why don't you come with me to the fireworks? I haven't got much work to do and we could get something to eat when I'm finished. You never know, bit of fresh air, glass of wine – you might actually get some sleep afterwards.'

Margaret hesitated. 'Tonight? I'm not sure. Aunty Pat mentioned she might phone.' She avoided socialising these days, making excuses whenever Jenny suggested that they go for a bar meal or to the cinema or do anything that they used to do as a family.

'Really? You spoke to her what, three days ago?'

'All right, Jenny!' She bristled.

'Think about it?'

Margaret shook her soap-covered hands over the sink and peeled off the gloves, hanging them over the tap to dry.

'I'll think about it. Now you best get to Pembroke before the crowds. I hear it gets busy down there at the crack of dawn in November.'

'Very funny, Mum.'

Margaret knew full well that Jenny hadn't seen a soul on the beach for weeks.

Overlooking the rocky bay of Bordeaux, the crumbling walls of Vale Castle were decorated with strings of colourful lanterns. Behind them, through an arch of stone, people filled the castle grounds. Masked jugglers and fire-eaters paraded through the throng and the yells of excited children rang out over the buzz and hum of the crowd. Behind a row of metal barriers, a mountain of broken pallets and driftwood was assembled next to a small stage; the bonfire awaiting its guy. Next to it, a group of teenagers in band T-shirts huddled in a corner, swigging from a coke bottle and smoking roll-ups. Jenny smiled. It felt like only yesterday that she had been one of them and, for a brief moment, she almost expected to recognise old friends' faces, before she remembered that they were all grown-ups now and half of them were probably at home with their own kids.

It was a perfect evening, the weather an autumn cliché. The only clouds in the starlit sky came from the tall chimney of the power station, just visible behind them, whispering its steady stream of fumes into the night.

Jenny looked over at Margaret. She had actually come out. Not only that, she looked relaxed. Happy, even. Her cheeks were pink from the chill. Jenny, feeling a wave of affection, linked her arm through her mother's and pulled her close. She could smell the wool of her coat, and underneath the faintest hint of washing powder and perfume, comforting and familiar.

'Glad you could fit me into your busy schedule. Won't *East-Enders* be missing you?'

'You leave me alone, Jennifer Dorey,' Margaret sniffed. 'You know I like fireworks. And I know you're right, I do need to start getting out a bit more. As do you. I'm old; I've got an excuse. And, anyway, it's Saturday. *EastEnders* isn't on.'

They sat on a raised stone ledge near the entrance and ate hot dogs. A fiddler and a flautist played nearby, collecting coins in an open violin case.

'Do you remember when dad did fireworks in the back garden?' Margaret asked.

'Yes. No fire safety then, was there? Lucky we didn't all get our heads blown off.'

'It was the Catherine wheels that worried me. He never nailed them in right. You never knew which direction they were going to fly off in. And the bonfires! They were always completely out of control, sparks flying all over the place. I was terrified the house would burn down.'

'I used to hide in the shed while he lit the rockets.' Jenny added. 'I'd look out of the window until I saw that he was safely out of the way and then run out just in time to see them light up the sky. It was brilliant.' She rested her head on her mother's shoulder.

Deputy Ferbrache, one of the parish's elected representatives, portly and bristling with self-importance, pushed his way through the crowd. Jenny had spoken to him recently about a beach clean-up initiative but he had spent most of the time talking about his recruitment company. Most of the island's deputies had a day job which they tried to fit their government duties around. It explained a lot about the way things worked on Guernsey, which was, as a rule, haphazardly or not at all. Deputy Ferbrache was followed by a small girl, beaming with pride, the winner of the best-dressed guy competition, and her mother, who was carrying the child's creation. It was a shocking pink froth of string, straw and ribbons with tumbling black hair. Jenny had interviewed them all for her report.

Deputy Ferbrache welcomed everyone. Congratulations to little Lily for her fabulous guy, wasn't it fantastic? They all clapped and cheered as Lily was presented with a gift voucher for Machon's Toy Store. Time to light the fire! More cheering as the deputy took the guy and climbed the wooden ladder at the side of the pyre, throwing it on top. Loud applause and then suddenly, with a bang, flames licked the wood. A gentle shifting and cracking as the fire took hold. Within minutes it blazed, bathing the onlookers in its warmth and its flickering light. Wisps of smoke wove through the crowd, carrying with them the sweet smell of cedar and pine.

The guy was the last to catch, the nylon and straw concoction burning easier and brighter than the wood below, an angel on a Christmas tree, dry flesh twisting and melting to the cheers of the audience. With the bonfire at full strength, the fireworks began. Standing nearby, a small boy wrapped up in a duffle coat, hat and scarf began to cry. Jenny started towards him, but a fat, jolly-looking woman wearing a premature Christmas jumper suddenly scooped him up.

'Can you hear that?' Margaret said.

'Hear what?

'Somebody's screaming.'

'Everybody's screaming.'

But Margaret had turned her back on the crowd. 'Not here.'

Jenny told her mother to stay put. It was much darker outside of the castle walls. She took her torch from her bag and switched it on. It was small but powerful. She kept it with her but rarely used it, preferring to avoid situations where she might need it.

The next scream came from the beach. Jenny's chest tightened. She was scared, but not as scared as whoever was down there. She ignored the paved pathway which meandered down to the road, running instead straight down the grass-covered hill, ploughing through thick gorse bushes, thorns tearing at her jeans, but at least they slowed her descent enough that she avoided falling off of the steep bank at the bottom of the hill and on to the road.

More screaming. Definitely a woman. Less urgent, Jenny thought. But still terrified. She ran across the main road, pushing her way through the dense row of pine trees on the other side, on to a sandy path edged with large, granite boulders. She could follow this path round to the slipway, but quicker to go straight over. She pulled herself up on to a boulder, struggling to hold on to her torch as she tried to find a footing on the smooth rock. She slid down the other side and stumbled as she landed on soft, dry sand.

A woman stood sobbing halfway down the beach, where the sand firmed up before giving way to the pebbly seabed. Bathed in the amber glow from the power station behind them, she was dressed in running clothes, a body warmer zipped over a long-sleeved top and tight leggings, a woollen bobble hat on her head, the pompom glowing white, a tail on a frightened rabbit.

'I just fell over her. Just fell right over her. Didn't see her,' she whispered, and stared down at a shape at her feet. Jenny shone her torch on it, flooding it in bright white light.

It was a woman. Twenty, maybe younger. She was beautiful and soaking wet – and dead.

4

Michael

Detective Chief Inspector Michael Gilbert was not one for tears. He'd cried in the hospital when his baby daughter Ellen had been handed to him, wrapped in a yellow blanket, her face scrunched and red, her tiny arms struggling against the swaddling. He'd wiped his eyes with the heel of his hand before Sheila or the midwife could see. Eighteen years later he'd cried at her death. Only a little. And not when he'd first heard the news. Then he'd been cold and dry. Numb, he supposed was the right word, although it had taken him years to realise this, to accept he'd been suffering from shock, not a lack of emotion. It was surprising, then, that he was shedding big, fat tears at the death of a stranger. He didn't bother to wipe them away this time. It was dark and there was nobody watching.

He managed to articulate a couple of gruff instructions, clearing all the gawpers who had gathered on the headland, waving their phones in the air as they tried to get footage of whatever was going on below them. They should have been moved straight away, Michael thought. Last thing they needed was pictures of a dead girl floating around the Internet. He told the flapping detective constable who had been first on the scene, and was in the process of trampling over any evidence, to get some police tape up and secure the area. And then he looked at her properly.

She was beautiful. Not more than twenty, by his reckoning.

So pale. White skin. Blue lips. She was wearing short sleeves. There were lines on the inside of her right arm. He crouched down next to her. Scratches. No, deeper. Cuts. Definitely deliberately done. They looked fresh. He took out his phone, snapped a picture close up. He felt around in his pocket for a pen, used it to gently move several strands of hair from her face. He took a few more pictures. Then he stepped back and looked around for a coat of some sort. It was far too cold for her to have been out without one. As if on cue, a chilly breeze lifted the bottom of his jacket and blew a handful of dried leaves across his shoe. She looked so cold. And so uncomfortable, the pebbles beneath her so hard. He wanted to wrap her up in a soft, yellow blanket and take her home to her mother.

There were two witnesses. One of them was hysterical, a late-night runner in all the latest gear. She garbled out a statement before nearly fainting and was carted off in an ambulance with an aluminium sheet wrapped around her as if she'd just finished a marathon. The other one was much more interesting. An angular-featured woman, attractive, although not pretty exactly. Striking, was probably the word, tallish and blonde, thick, sun-streaked hair pulled back in a ponytail, sharp, intelligent eyes. She gave a short but detailed statement. Jennifer Dorey. The journalist. Charlie Dorey's daughter, if he wasn't mistaken. He didn't mention it. She'd had enough to deal with for one night.

With the tent up and Forensics inside, Michael took a walk down to the shoreline. The tide was creeping in. They would have to work quickly.

He looked out at the boats moored in the harbour, black shadows on the water, edges defined by weak moonlight. The girl could have been out on one, he supposed, fallen in, drunk maybe, and then washed up on the shore. Teenagers sometimes used empty boats for hook-ups. They'd had many a boat owner call in with

27

reports of empty beer cans and used condoms found on deck on a Sunday morning. That was in town, though, where you could just jump over the marina gates and walk on to a boat. Here you'd have to drag one in. And there were plenty of secluded spots around the castle for a quickie – why go to the bother? Perhaps she'd been on a boat elsewhere and gone overboard. A possibility. Late-night fishing trip, perhaps, although she definitely wasn't dressed for it. And someone would have called it in, there'd have been a search and rescue underway, and he certainly hadn't heard about one.

Unless she had been alone. And there were only a few reasons a young woman would be anywhere near the sea, all alone, on a cold night like this.

Suicide. There were more than people knew about. Or at least, more than they liked to think about. Up to four or five, some years. Mostly middle-aged men, but they had a fair amount of teenagers too. He thought it might be something to do with the transition: child to adult, young to old. Difficult times. Drowning was a popular way to go. He supposed there was something fitting about it, for an islander to give themselves to the sea. And he imagined it might sit well with a teenage girl's propensity for the dramatic.

He pulled his coat around himself. There were far more comfortable ways to go. Warmer ones at least. He'd thought about them. The first body he'd seen after Ellen's had been swinging in the kitchen door frame of a cottage in St Martins, some bloke whose wife and kids had left him. Bloody fool, Michael had thought, killing himself when his family were only a couple of miles away, when he could have still loved his kids, held them and spoken to them, watched them grow. Michael had raged around the station for days afterwards, not realising, until he'd been ten pints into one of his increasingly regular benders, that what he was feeling was not anger. It was envy.

He walked back up towards the tent where it was now as light as day under the police lamps. Mostly rough gravelly sand and pebbles, a strip of soft sand at the top, banked up against the grassy headland. Not a tourist spot, this beach. It was small and scrubby and too near the rubbish dump. You could smell it, on a warm day, when the wind was blowing in the right direction, sweet and gassy. He'd come here with Ellen, when she was little and every time they'd had a whiff of it, he'd ask, 'Was that you?' and she'd fall about laughing. He smiled. Proper locals' beach this was. A fisherman's harbour, nothing fancy. Nothing like the town marinas, next to the shops and the nightlife of St Peter Port, or the Beaucette Yacht Marina, a little further along the coast from here, with its lobster restaurant and champagne bar. But it was pretty, here. Quaint. He caught a glint of green amongst the stones. Sea glass. He bent down to pick it up. It was a good one, the size of a fifty-pence piece, silky and cool to the touch. He rubbed it with his thumb and then slipped it into his pocket.

Forensics were nearly finished. He could hear them zipping up their bags. He poked his head in.

'How's it going, lads?'

'Just about done. We've bagged up a couple of cigarette butts and we're going to get her moved if you're all done here?'

He looked at her again and was struck by how peaceful she looked. As if she'd just lain down for a rest, with every intention of getting back up again. She certainly hadn't been in the water for long.

He thought, for the second time that night, of Charlie Dorey. Of what the sea could do to a person. People thought a body floated, but it didn't, not right away. It would sink until it hit the ocean floor, only resurfacing after days of decomposition, bloated with gas. By the time it reached the surface, the flesh would be green and peeling, loose around the hands and feet. Degloving, they called it. And those were just the bits that hadn't been eaten. Nibbled at by the same fish someone might find on their dinner plate later that week.

He felt almost grateful, then, that this corpse had eyes in its sockets and flesh on its bones.

5

July 1959

*T*he dried cow shit caught him on the side of the face, just above his right eye. It didn't hurt. He turned. There were more of them than usual, seven – no, eight – the youngest no more than ten years old, the oldest perhaps fifteen. He kept walking. He knew they would follow him.

A sharp pain at the back of his head, the force enough to make him stumble, fall to his knees. A rock. There were no rocks in the field. They'd come prepared. He could feel the blood running down the back of his neck. He got up and carried on. More rocks, but none of them landing a blow as effective as the first. One to the shoulder, one to the back, he hardly felt them. He walked. He never ran. They were shouting:

'Dirty Jerry! Your mother is a whore. She should have called you Fritz!'

By the time he got to the gate at the end of the field they were bored. He walked the rest of the way home alone, blood on his collar and piss in his pants.

Mother scrubbed at the shirt half-heartedly. Her hair was in rollers and she'd already done her face. She'd painted her lips a deep, dull red, the same shade as his school jotter. A cigarette hung from them, the lipstick bleeding into its white filter, flakes of ash floating into the sink as she shook her head. It was never going to come out, she said. 'Nasty little buggers, why are they always picking on you? They're jealous, that's what it is, wish they were clever enough to have got a scholarship like you. Poor boy, look at you, never hurt anyone.' She gave up and 'left it to soak'.

He would clean it properly and put it to dry when she was gone.

She knew why they did it. It was nothing to do with the school he went to. She'd had enough of it herself. It was the women who were worst. He'd seen them spitting and sniping as she walked past. There but for the grace of God, that's what Mother said. They'd all been at it, all of them, sanctimonious cows, she said. He knew that she considered herself unlucky. Stupidity played a larger part than luck where she was concerned. She'd been stupid enough to provide everyone with proof. Proof she was a whore with her little blonde-haired, blue-eyed Jerry-bastard baby.

She stood in front of him, pulling the rollers out of her hair. It was a new one tonight, she said, and she thought this one had 'prospects'.

He doubted it. He couldn't imagine who would possibly want her. She would never tell him her age – it was rude to ask, she said. But he had found her birth certificate in the box in the bureau. She was old. Nearly forty. Her eyes were going wrinkly and her chin was starting to sag. Just a little, but if he had noticed, so had she. That was probably why she'd seemed a bit depressed recently. It must be bad enough being a slut. Being an old slut must be unbearable.

She kissed his head before she left. 'Don't wait up for Mummy, darling, now will you? I might be a bit late.' He said nothing, which clearly unsettled her. She was a talker, and was only quiet when she was miserable, so she would take his silence as a sign of unhappiness. 'Don't let them upset you, darling, now will you? You're such a bright boy, so talented, so handsome. They're just jealous,' she said. 'And things are on the up, you know? This one, the one I'm seeing tonight, he has prospects, I said that, didn't I? It will be a fresh start, for both of us.'

Lies. All of it. There was no escaping what they were.

He reached under his mattress for his journal. It was a large, leather-bound book grandfather had given him before he'd hanged himself. Everyone said it was the shame of a traitorous daughter that made him do it; it was too much for him to bear.

It wasn't. Grandfather had always been strange. He heard voices and spoke to people who weren't there. It was a blessing when he died, even Mother said.

He wrote carefully the events of the day, from the moment he woke that morning up until his mother leaving the house. He wrote in detail, describing how the cowpat had hit him, the outfit his mother had worn out, the amount of blood he estimated he had scrubbed from his collar (two teaspoons). When he had finished he turned to the back of the book where he had started a new project.

He was creating a profile of all of the attributes he believed came from his father. He'd already listed intelligence, strength, good looks, fair hair and skin, all of the things that made him so different from the stupid, short, dark, island children who taunted him.

He had moved on from the obvious and had started noting the more subtle things. His fingers, for example, were long and flexible. It must be why he was so good at playing the piano – having tried it first at school he'd persuaded his mother to buy an old one he'd seen for sale at the church hall and he now practised for an hour every day. He'd noted 'long fingers' and 'musical ability' next to each other. This evening he added 'accidental urination'.

He had been thinking a lot about this problem. Why did his strong, fit body let him down so regularly? Perhaps it was a problem his father suffered from. Perhaps he pissed his pants the day he *landed on Guernsey, wondering what he would find there, expecting a bloodthirsty army, finding instead his mother's welcoming cunt.*

He didn't hate her for it, though. There were many things he hated his mother for, but fucking a Nazi was not one of them.

6

Jenny

Sunday, 9 November

A knock at the front door; Margaret startled. Who could it be, she wondered, so late on a Sunday? She wiped her hands on the front of her trousers as she walked out of the room. Jenny took the opportunity to scrape the remains of her untouched dinner into the bin. She had hardly eaten since the night before and even Margaret's lasagne, usually a favourite, had failed to whet her appetite. She managed to finish her wine, though, draining the glass before she put it in the sink. A break from tradition in the Dorey household, wine on a Sunday night, but Margaret had decided this evening that a glass would do them both good. Margaret returned, followed by a man in a crumpled suit. Jenny recognised him from the night before. DCI Gilbert. He was tall and broad, his large frame filling the room, his barrel chest straining against his shirt buttons. Margaret introduced him and offered him a kitchen chair, asked him if he'd like a cup of tea. He nodded, a grateful expression lighting his careworn face.

'That would be lovely, Mrs Dorey, thank you.'

Margaret retrieved the best china from the top shelf of the cupboard and hastily rinsed the dust off.

The ends of DCI Gilbert's jacket sleeves were fraying and

he pulled at a loose thread before he placed his elbows on the table. He smiled at Jenny.

'How are you feeling, Jenny?'

'Fine, thank you. A little tired. It was gone midnight when I left the station.'

'Yes, sorry we kept you so late. You did a good job though, eh? Very detailed statement. There are just a couple of things to go over, some forms we need you to sign.' He looked apologetic as he handed a manila folder to her. She skimmed through the paperwork. A copy of her statement, a disclaimer, information about counselling services. Michael discussed the case with Margaret. He had a thick Guernsey accent, all guttural consonants and elongated vowels, the obligatory, questioning 'eh' at the end of his sentences.

'Such a waste,' he said. 'These youngsters don't look after themselves and look what happens, eh?' He shook his head and picked up his tea. He had tufts of hair on his knuckles and his hand trembled slightly as he bought the dainty cup to his lips.

'So you think it was an accident?' Jenny asked.

He raised his eyebrows as he drank and then carefully placed his cup back on the saucer, avoiding her eyes.

'Possibly,' he said. 'She might have been messing around on a boat, or on the rocks and fallen in. No witnesses, mind you. Nobody saw her down on the beach, or at the bonfire, either.

'I'm afraid,' he looked up at Jenny, 'that we can't rule out the possibility that this was a deliberate act on the young lady's part.'

'Suicide?'

'Now, Jennifer . . .' DCI Gilbert reached over and patted her shoulder awkwardly. 'Don't you worry about any of this. It must be difficult for you, with what happened to your dad, eh?' He looked to Margaret. 'And for you, Mrs Dorey.' She nodded, eyes down.

'My father's death was an accident. I don't really see how that's relevant to any of this.' Jenny handed the folder back.

'Well, you've been through a lot, that's all. Anyway, we'll have all this sorted out as quickly as possible, there shouldn't be any reason to bother you with it again. Although I presume you'll be taking a professional interest?'

She nodded. 'When will you be releasing details? Her name?'

'Probably late tomorrow. The world and his wife will know who it is by then, but we trust the *News* not to print until we release the details officially. Out of respect for her family. Thanks for the tea, Mrs Dorey. You look after Jenny here. See she gets some rest, eh?'

Margaret was showing him out of the room when he stopped and turned back to Jenny, handed her a card.

'You give me a call. If you want to talk about anything. Not just police stuff.'

His name, Michael Gilbert, and a phone number on one side. On the other,

Christian Friendship Society
Support, Sharing, Friendship

Margaret came back into the kitchen, smiling and began to clear away the cups. 'Well, he seems very nice.'

'I'm not convinced.' Jenny showed her the card he had given her. Margaret shook her head.

'You're just like your father, Jennifer.'

'It's not just that. He seems to have made his mind up about the whole thing already. And I'd seen all those papers before. There was no reason for him to come here – he's wasting his time here having a cup of tea when he should be out investigating this case.'

'Perhaps he wanted to check on you, see how you were doing. Don't look at me like that.'

'Like what?'

'Like you find it impossible to believe someone would do that.

As for the investigation, he's a chief inspector, I'm sure he knows what he's doing.'

'But they'll have to do a post-mortem, surely? I mean, it probably was an accident or a suicide, but it could have been anything. A violent boyfriend? A random psychopath? This place is unbelievable. There was a dead girl found on the beach last night and nobody seems to care how she got there!'

'Jenny, enough. I've had enough. I don't want to hear any more of this.' Margaret left the room, pulling the door behind her with such force that the cabinets shook and the glasses and crockery inside tinkled against each other.

Everything black. She fumbled, feeling around for her lamp, and for a moment, for one terrifying split second, she was fifteen again and she was trapped, the walls, cold and wet, closing in around her, piercing shrieks ringing in her ears.

Short, sharp breaths. Accept the fear. Let it in.

I'm not afraid of the darkness.

Only what it hides.

She found the wire, pressed the button.

Click. Light.

That was close.

She opened her door wider. She always left it open at night. Just enough to allow the light from the hallway in. It was a compromise she'd made with herself. She wouldn't sleep with the light on in her room, like a child, frightened of the monsters under the bed, but she'd leave one on in the hallway, set her door ajar. She flicked the switch on and off. Nothing. Bulb blown.

She sat on the bed and tried to shake off the residual panic, that lingering feeling of imminent danger that took her right back there, to that cold, black, terrifying space in her memory where her lungs and her heart and her brain worked against her so she could no longer breathe or think and the prospect of death seemed real and imminent and the bottom of her stomach fell away. Because real fear does that. Hits you in the gut.

Her last panic attack had been ten years ago. No, eleven. She'd been eighteen. Her first term at Sussex university. She'd been doing well. Using tricks learnt in therapy, she had nearly (but not entirely) got over her fear of the dark. It was the move that triggered it, the stress of meeting new people, the new environment, the tiny, dingy rooms at Lancaster House, the university's traditional campus halls, unfit for habitation really. Her corner unit had been slightly bigger than most of the others but colder too, as two of the walls were exposed to the elements. They were freezing to the touch during those first months and beads of moisture clung to the walls whenever she ran the tiny fan heater, which had cost a week's worth of her maintenance grant. Black mould bloomed on the ceiling and strips of glossy, magnolia paint peeled off in the corners and around the window. She would pick at it, pulling it off like dry skin. A chest infection knocked her for six after only a couple of weeks and even a month or so after that she was feeling tired and wheezy.

A Saturday. A quiet day at Sussex. There were so many Londoners there, so close to home they thought nothing of hopping on a train and going back for the weekends. She'd had a drink at the Falmer Bar with a couple of other international students: cheap rum and warm coke. The barman had been chatting her up, incredulous when she'd told him that, yes, students from Guernsey were technically international and, no, she didn't speak French. She would have stayed there and talked to him, he was cute and funny, but the plan had been to get the bus into Brighton. Students usually avoided Saturday nights in town, they were too expensive and the likelihood of running into a pissed-up townie looking for a fight was high. A good DJ must have been playing for them to have considered the trip a risk worth taking. Maybe it had even been Fatboy himself . . . ? She couldn't remember, because by the time they'd reached the bus stop on Lewes Road, Jenny's cough had started up and she'd not felt up for going out after all. So she'd walked back alone, across campus. Not far.

It had been dark and quiet, just the wind rustling dry leaves, carrying with it the sounds of laughter and music from the flats at East Slope. She'd felt depressed. Not just sad or sorry for herself, but heavy inside, weighed down with it all. She was tired and sick and didn't want to go back to her crappy, cold room, to lie there, alone, filling her lungs with air that was thick with the smell of damp and decay – she couldn't bear the smell. That's when it had gripped her. A cold hand reaching inside, freezing first her stomach and then spreading its fingers upwards, twisting and squeezing her heart and chest until her breathing became so laboured that her vision blurred and she'd crouched down, instinctively, knowing from previous attacks that she needed to be close to the ground. She'd tried to call out but had managed only rasping cries and soon the pain in her chest became so great that she'd felt sure she was going to die, that her heart could not possibly be strong enough to withstand it, not this time.

One of the night guards had found her, hours or minutes later – she'd had no idea how long she'd been there, lying on the grass, panting, like a wounded animal. He'd helped her back to halls and told her with a wink, to lay off the wacky baccy. She'd slept for thirteen hours. The next morning she'd called the doctor, asked for an appointment as soon as possible. The receptionist, clearly used to dealing with students who deemed a missed contraceptive pill or a toe stubbed in a drunken accident a medical emergency, demanded a list of symptoms. Jenny had hung up. She'd gone for a run across the South Downs instead, the first of many. She'd been fine since then. Well, not fine. But that was the last of the panic attacks.

It was disconcerting then, eleven years later, to feel on the edge again. To feel that an attack was even a remote possibility. But it had been. She needed more exercise. That had been the first step on her road to recovery all those years ago. Swimming, every day, or, when she was too far from the sea, running until her chest felt it would burst.

She had an hour before it would be light enough to go out. In the corner of the room, nearly covered in a pile of half-clean clothes, was a large cardboard box, edges sealed with shiny, brown tape.

It had taken her months to unpack her things when she moved back from London. She had sorted out the essentials, her clothes and wash stuff. She needed those even if she wasn't staying. Then slowly, as the weeks went by, she had put her books on the shelves, her photographs on the wall, some tacky souvenirs friends had bought back from their travels on the dressing table, until finally, eleven years after she'd left home, she had made the room her own again.

Apart from the last box. It had been eighteen months and she hadn't opened that one. It looked bigger now, somehow. Looming, almost. She knew she'd been avoiding it, not wanting to be reminded of what it held. And she knew that avoiding something was the best way to ensure it grew bigger and more powerful and would eventually eat her up from the inside. She moved the clothes and ripped the tape off, releasing a fine, cardboard dust into the air.

Inside, there were copies of nearly everything she'd ever written, from her first article for the *Badger* ('*Rogue Landlords Exploit Sussex Students*') to her last London piece about a campaign to save a Hackney landmark. Her last *published* London piece. Her last piece in London had been about a young Romanian woman. She'd never finished that one.

She searched through the box until she found it. Five thousand wasted words. There was no point reading them again. It wouldn't change anything. But she read it anyway. Because after seeing that girl's body on the beach last night, it was impossible not to think of Madalina.

7

March 1961

*H*e towered over them all. It gave him a quiet thrill, walking past them, their taunts and violence reduced to malevolent glares and whispers, which gave way as he held their gaze, unyieldingly. Only a few of them bothered waiting for him any more and on some days there were none at all. School would be over for most of them in a couple of months and then they'd all move on to other things; they'd take menial island jobs, growing or labouring, and a few years later they'd all marry their island cousins and have screaming island babies, the whole tedious cycle destined to be repeated over and over again.

He walked straight past his house and on to Les Sages farm. He'd been helping old Joe Le Measurier for a few months, shifting and carrying, shovelling shit, feeding the sheep. It was hard work but he liked it. He liked pushing himself, feeling his muscles strain, forcing his arms to support too much weight so that they trembled and shook when he offloaded. He would rub his biceps, encouraging the blood to flow beneath the skin, knowing the aches were making him stronger.

He found Joe in the field, kneeling down at the backside of a ewe, which was lying on its side, belly distended, tongue out, panting and rasping. He knelt beside him.

'What's wrong with her?'

'Lamb's stuck. Breech. And it was too big. It's dead already. Thought I'd have one last go at getting it out, try to save her.'

Joe was short and muscular, his skin weathered and tanned. He had rolled up his sleeves and his hands and arms up to his elbows were covered in blood and mucus.

'Cor chapin!' Joe stood, rubbing the small of his back. 'N'faut pas faire lè cotin dèvant què lè viau set naï.' He sighed. 'Or the lamb, in this case. I'm getting too old for this, boyo.' Joe was a kind man with kind eyes, which usually twinkled under his thick white eyebrows. Joe shook his head. 'Nothing else for it,' he said, and walked to the house.

He stayed where he was. It was unseasonably warm and he loosened his shirt collar, let the sun fall on the back of his neck. The sheep's eyes were bulging and edged with pink, the pupils dilated. She looked at him. It was clear she was in pain, but she was not afraid. He stroked her head, combing his fingers through the coarse wool between her ears, pulling it back, away from her eyes so they stretched and widened. His fingers were waxy with wool grease, earthy and sweet-smelling. She kept looking at him, stoic and dull and he knew, in that moment, what true beauty was. It was this sheep. Dying but oblivious. And the other sheep, which stood, nibbling the grass, bleating softly to their lambs, unaware and unconcerned. How perfect it would be, he thought, to live a life momentarily, where pain meant only pain and joy meant only joy and there was no fear of death or of God. It was beautiful and clean and simple and free. He felt a euphoria he had never before experienced.

A hand on his shoulder.

'Didn't know you were so soft-hearted, lad.'

He put his hand to his cheek. It was wet with tears.

'I'm sorry.' He got up quickly.

'Don't mind me. It's always hard. But the animals don't know it's coming, eh? Not sure if that makes it better or worse. Stand back.'

Joe raised the rifle and fired. It was louder than he'd expected and it made his ears ring. Joe told him to get a wheelbarrow and bring the animal round the front and then come in for a 'p'tite goute.'

'I've a nice whisky open. Looks like you need one.' Joe gave him another pat on the shoulder.

The hole in the sheep's head was right between her eyes. It was surprisingly neat and there was very little blood. She was still looking at him.

He let himself in quietly, hoping she was already asleep. A half-empty bottle of gin on the table, only one glass. No company tonight. There had been no talk of 'prospects' for a long time, and it was only thanks to the few shillings a week he was earning at the farm that there was food on the table every night. Even then, there was never enough. If she had an ounce of intelligence she would have realised there was an easy way to make her lifestyle more lucrative. He'd hinted at the idea only a few weeks before. She had shouted at him, judge not lest ye be judged, and then cried, made ugly, cow-like sounds. He had watched her, impassive. He was not judging, he said, just hungry.

He washed his face and hands in the sink, dried himself with a thin, stale-smelling dishcloth. He took a couple of slices of bread from the larder and the last scraping of beef dripping, made a sandwich and sat on the threadbare sofa to eat it. The floorboards creaked above him. She was awake. He licked the grease off of his fingers and then washed and dried his plate and returned it to the cupboard.

He went over to the piano. He couldn't afford to buy new sheet music, but Joe had given him a pile of yellowing paper, which had belonged to his sister. She'd played for the Jerries during the war. Joe had said it like he said everything, calmly, matter of fact. He wondered if it was an acknowledgement, a nod to his own start in life.

It was all German, obviously. Beethoven, Wagner, Strauss. If mother had known anything about music, she might have found it disconcerting. He started with Beethoven's Piano Concerto No. 3. Mother's bedroom door clicked open.

'I didn't hear you come in, darling. You're so late I thought you were staying out.' That girlish voice, too thin for a grown woman.

He kept playing. The door clicked shut.

She came out again as he walked up the stairs. She was wearing a pale blue gauze nightdress with puffed sleeves, a row of tiny silk roses embroidered along the frilled neckline. He could see her large nipples and the whiteness of her heavy breasts through the thin fabric and below, the faint triangle of her pubic hair. He thought about all the men who had climbed on top of her, grunting and fucking while she squealed just like the pigs he had seen doing it on the farm and he felt it. The weakness. She put a hand to his cheek and stroked his face and his breathing quickened and he leant in towards her until he could smell the gin on her breath. 'My beautiful boy,' she said. 'So big and handsome.' She stood on her tiptoes, swaying slightly, pulled his head down even further and kissed him, her lips landing just above his nose. He smiled and kissed her back.

Right between the eyes.

Right where the bullet should go.

8

Jenny

Tuesday, 11 November

They had a name and a photograph.

Amanda Guille. Eighteen years old. A student at the College of Further Education, she'd been studying Health and Social Care. The picture on the front page was a school photograph. A pale blue background, head turned towards the camera, hair scraped back, maroon and gold striped tie. Fuller of face than the girl Jenny had seen on the beach, and so much younger looking, although the picture was only a year old.

Jenny was leading the coverage. Brian was delighted, joking that she had taken the idea of being first on the scene a little too far.

'It's perfect, you can give the whole thing a personal angle, nothing too macabre mind, not yet, don't want to upset the family. Give 'em a couple of days to calm down and then let's get them in for an interview.' He was practically rubbing his hands together. It was distasteful, but they all felt the same. There was a buzz in the office and it was impossible to deny the excitement in the air.

Jenny's piece was on page three. Brian had insisted they include a photograph of her, to put a face to the name. They'd taken one of her at her desk looking suitably serious.

She didn't like it, seeing herself in the paper. She was used to her words being out there, but you could choose your words, shape and manipulate them, tell the story you wanted people to read. A picture was different. A moment captured. Vulnerabilities exposed. *She* felt exposed. She was feeling anxious. Seeing the body, being on a big story again – it was natural, she told herself, to feel unsettled.

Her phone rang and the receptionist told her there was a man in the lobby asking to see her. She checked her diary. No meetings scheduled. She glanced at her emails, at the folder: *Fairfield Road*. Perhaps they'd seen her picture in the paper, decided she was over-stepping somehow. Perhaps they thought she needed a face-to-face reminder. *Stupid*. As if someone would come to the office. They'd grab her in a side street or break into her car and lie on the back seat waiting for her to get in or maybe they'd go to her house, trick Margaret into letting them in and Jenny would come home to find one of them holding a knife to her mother's throat. She put her face in her hands. Slowed her breathing. *Stop catastrophising.* She tucked her hair behind her ears and straightened her jacket.

A man in skinny black jeans and a long black coat was sitting in the reception area, slumped forward on the faux-leather sofa, picking at the nails of his nicotine-stained fingers. He wore ear-phones, the tinny whine of his music audible from across the room. The receptionist, a heavily made-up agency temp, raised her over-plucked eyebrows and nodded her head towards him before returning to her magazine.

He looked up and she relaxed.

A boy, not a man, pale-faced and spotty. He needed a good wash and a haircut. He pulled out his earphones and tucked his hair behind his ears.

'Can I help you?'

'I don't know. Maybe.' He stood. 'I'm Matt. It's about the girl. Amanda.'

*

'I'm afraid I don't understand. I thought you said this was about Amanda Guille?'

'Yeah, it is. Sort of. I dunno. It's just, it looked like her.'

She had pulled a chair over to her desk and he was leaning forwards, elbows on knees, looking down at his hands.

'What looked like her?'

'The guy. I found a guy.'

'And it looked like Amanda?' A trace of the frustration she felt escaped into her voice.

'Do you wanna hear this or not?' He looked up at her, challenging, defiant.

'OK! OK. Carry on.'

He continued, talking into his lap now, avoiding her eyes, describing a guy he'd found at Pleinmont. She shifted in her seat, scribbled some notes. All the black, the long hair covering his face, his death-metal T-shirt covered in skulls and blood. It was a bit macabre. Perhaps he was looking for something to be depressed about, some connection to Amanda, some reason to go to the funeral, to immerse himself in the pain and sadness. Perhaps he needed help. She should call someone. Social Services. Or his parents.

It was weird, he said. It was lying in the middle of the Fairy Ring. He'd thought it was a person, then realised what it was, but it had been creepy. It had blonde hair and blue eyes, just like Amanda, and cuts on its arm.

'What?'

'Like you wrote in your piece. You said she had marks on her arm, scratches or something.' He was angry now and raised his voice. 'So did the guy. Slashes in the fabric and all the straw was spilling out. Don't you think it's a bit weird, the night before this girl turns up dead, someone puts a straw woman that looks just like her in the middle of the Fairy Ring? Fuck me, nobody fucking listens.'

47

Jenny was not writing any more.

'What do you mean, nobody listens?

'I told the police this morning, straight after I read what you wrote. They just laughed at me, but I'm telling you, this shit is freaking me out.' He reached into his pocket and pulled out a packet of Marlboros, began flicking the lid of the box open and closed.

'What did you do with it, Matt?

He shifted awkwardly.

'I burnt it.'

9
Michael

It was bloody madness, every time something out of the ordinary happened on this island. He closed his eyes, took a deep breath in and tried to focus.

He picked up the *News*. Obviously the story was front-page. It would be for days to come. Not every day a young girl's body gets washed up on the beach. But then the *News* had to go and do what they always did and *sensationalise* the whole thing. Which was all well and good, he liked a good story as much as the next man, but it just made everything so much more difficult for them. And they were hardly off to a very good start. There was just him and a couple of detective constables on the case, including that young bloody plod who had clomped his boots all over the sand before they'd had time to cordon off the area. Stephen Marquis, his name was. Skinny, carrot-topped lad with a face full of freckles and a nervous twitch.

There were, as he predicted, no suspicious circumstances so far. Amanda Guille had failed to meet her friends on Saturday night although her parents didn't know that. They'd assumed she was staying the night with one of them and only became worried around lunchtime when they hadn't heard from her. About the same time they saw the *Channel News* report about the body.

It was terrible dealing with the parents. And nobody knew better than him what it felt like. He'd taken them to identify the body, to a room in the hospital, just like the one the detective who had dealt with Ellen's death had taken Michael to, all those years ago. They didn't have to go inside, not like Michael had. These days they had a window between the relatives and the body. Just a simple pane of glass, but it served so many purposes, Michael thought. It was a cold, clear cushion between the living and the dead, a hard surface to beat hands against, a resting place for heads too heavy with grief to hold steady.

Amanda's mum was the first to break, doubling over, howling until she had no more breath in her lungs and her husband put his arm around her, dragged her back, away from the view of the body, before he started crying, quietly. There was no one to comfort *him,* not at that point. His wife was too consumed with her own grief to notice his. Michael had given his shoulder a squeeze, deeming any gesture, however futile, better than none at all. Then he had left them, told the family liaison officer to give them five minutes and then take them some tea and help them out of that godforsaken place.

Maybe they had a chance. More than likely not. He didn't like to be a pessimist, but the statistics spoke for themselves. Michael and his now ex-wife, Sheila, had joined a support group for bereaved parents after Ellen's accident. There had been five couples in it, including them, and they were all divorced now. *All* of them. Some of them lasted a few years. He and Sheila only managed two. Maybe they would have divorced anyway. Maybe none of those marriages were supposed to last. More likely it was the deaths that did it for them. He didn't mention this to Amanda's parents. They had enough on their plates.

With all that to deal with, the investigation, the traumatised parents, and his own unavoidable emotions surrounding the death of an eighteen-year-old girl, he could have done without the bloody lunatics. Call after call from all the usual suspects, all the curtain twitchers, the gossips, the busybodies. He looked at the list of notes from the day's calls.

'Around nine p.m. on Saturday evening I heard a car accelerating and playing very loud rap music, which you don't often hear around here.'

That was from a lady in St Martins. A good four miles from where Amanda was found.

'I think you'll find there are greenhouses in the vicinity of Vale Castle where there are foreigners employed illegally and I have said for a long time that there would be trouble if nothing was done about this.'

Anonymous, that one. Bloody Anonymous always had a lot to say for himself.

If the phone calls weren't bad enough, they'd had a kid in this morning talking about a Guy Fawkes or some nonsense. Michael had popped his head around the door to the interview room to see what all the laughing was about. They'd stopped, of course, as soon as they'd seen him. Nobody on the force had shared a joke with him for a long time. They shared plenty of jokes *about* him but that was a different story. The lad had been in a right state, gabbling about a straw figure he'd found up at Pleinmont. Michael could tell just by looking at him he was one of those Gothic types who spent their time smoking tea leaves and Oxo cubes, or whatever the local dealers could dupe kids into buying these days. Looked like some of the real stuff had snuck in somewhere along the line. He felt sorry for the lad. He'd told them take his statement but the sniggering started up again before he'd left the room.

He rubbed his eyes. It was time to go home. He took one last look through Amanda's file. She had a record. Nothing serious, couple of run-ins for underage drinking and an odd incident when the parents called the police because they found what they'd thought was cannabis in her school bag. Trying to frighten her into going straight, he supposed. Social Services had been involved. He would ask her parents about it when he spoke to them next. He would have to be careful. To consider how he phrased things. Because words could stick with you, just like pictures. He imagined it was the same with all bereaved parents; when you closed your eyes at night, the last thing you saw was your child. On good days, you might see them laughing as they reached for a bit of sea glass, or running towards you, arms wide open, after a day at school. On bad, you'd see them on a mortuary slab. And when it was quiet, as it was right now, the words would come back. The voices. They'd go round and round in your head.

I love you, Daddy . . . So sorry . . . Don't worry, Daddy . . . So sorry . . . It's about your daughter . . . I love you, Daddy . . . It's about Ellen . . . So sorry . . .

I'm afraid she didn't make it.

10

Jenny

It was ridiculous.

It was ridiculous but she couldn't stop thinking about it. Nearly everybody else had left for the day. Brian was in his office talking to Elliot, loudly, the sounds of their voices carrying across the office. She could see them, through the glass walls, Elliot standing, gesticulating, Brian, arms folded, looking up at him, shaking his head. She couldn't make out what they were saying, but there was definitely a disagreement of some sort going on. The cleaner had arrived, a slim lady in her thirties. She muttered and sighed as she cleared mugs from desks, stopping at Jenny's and pointing to her half-drunk coffee.

'You finished?' She was pretty but careworn, with limp hair and tired eyes, the faintest hint of an Eastern European accent.

Jenny nodded. 'Thank you. You're new here?'

'Yes.'

'Where are you from?'

'Latvia.' She gave the desk a cursory wipe.

'Do you miss it?'

'No. Why? Should I?' She glared at Jenny.

'No, just interested. Do you have family, back home?'

'Some. Are you writing about this?'

'About what?'

'This immigration stuff. This local jobs for local people.'

'No, my colleague is covering that. I'm just interested.'

'There is a meeting I saw. Save the Islanders or something. That Tostevin man. All the people who don't want us here.'

Deputy Tostevin was a bigot. A small-minded man whose motto was 'Guernsey for the Guernseyman'. Whatever that meant. He was popular, had been a member of the States of Guernsey, the island's government, for years. It was depressing. Jenny said so. The woman shrugged and moved on to the next desk. There was something about her, her vulnerability thinly veiled behind a mask of indifference. She reminded Jenny of Madalina.

Her phone pinged. Sarah was on her way to the bar. Jenny was about to pack up when Elliot came storming out of Brian's office. He kicked a stray chair out of his path on the way to his desk, sending it spinning in Jenny's direction.

'Jesus! What's wrong with you?'

'Mind your own business!' He spat the words at her.

'Suit yourself.' She turned back to her screen. She wanted to go, but she could see him, angry, shaking a little, looking at her. She stared at the document she'd been working on. Her interview with Matt, typed up in Times New Roman, neatly spaced, black and white, in the hope it would make more sense that way.

'I'm sorry.'

She looked up. He stood over her. 'This place drives me crazy sometimes.' He sat on the edge of her desk. Sweat pricked through his shirt under each arm and she could smell it, sharp and acidic, underneath the artificial scent of his deodorant.

'No problem. I know the feeling.' She smiled, tried to look at ease, unsure if she was nervous because of his behaviour or just because he was there. She turned away, self conscious, remembering her un-plucked eyebrows and the fact that she'd been rubbing her eyes and probably had mascara all over her face.

He was staring at her. Still angry, although she sensed he was trying to get it under control. He ran his hands through his hair. He did that sometimes. A nervous gesture, she thought.

'See you tomorrow, Jenny.'

'See you tomorrow.' When she was sure that he'd gone, she sat back in her chair, relaxed her shoulders. He had made her uncomfortable. No, more than that. The way he'd kicked the chair and then turned to her, the rage on his face. It was only for a moment, but she'd been frightened.

She switched off her computer and pulled a brush through her hair, checked her reflection in her screen, dabbed a tissue at the circles of smeared make-up under her eyes. She rummaged around in her handbag and found her perfume. She'd worn Opium since she was a teenager when her mum had given her a half-used bottle and, despite paying little attention to fashion or make-up, stuck by her Granny Dorey's adage that one wasn't properly dressed without a spritz of scent.

She walked past Brian's office on the way out. Through the glass doors she could see him, phone glued to his ear, deep in conversation, brow furrowed.

Hugo's Wine Bar was busy for a Tuesday evening. Or maybe it wasn't. Maybe it was always like this. She glanced at the menu. There was no proper food, only tapas and sharing platters or individually priced portions of artisan cheese. Everything was painted in muted tones, creams and browns, lots of exposed woodwork. The chairs were leather wingbacks and the tables resembled writing desks, a nod to the author the bar was named for. Passages from *Toilers of the Sea* were painted on the ceiling in elaborate, cursive writing. He'd written it in Guernsey, of course, *'where dwells the noble little race of the sea'*. She craned her neck to make out the end of the quote.

'Well Halle-bloody-luia! It's Jennifer Dorey in an after-work drink shocker.'

Jenny rose to give her friend a hug. 'Hey, it's not just me. How long has it been since you managed to ditch domestic bliss?'

'Too bloody long. Harry's finally sleeping through the night so fingers crossed Simon will manage without me for a couple of hours.' She shook her head in mock exasperation. 'Right. Where's the wine?' She gestured over to the waiter and ordered a bottle of red.

Sarah was a typical Guernsey girl, olive-skinned with thick, dark hair and, at just under five feet tall, a good six inches shorter than Jenny, even in a pair of heels. She'd returned to the island straight after university, landed a well-paid job in a bank, married a local boy from the same school year, and proceeded to buy a house and fill it with children – three at the last count. Sarah gave a quick update on the kids and the house and the husband and then looked at her.

'Anyway. What's going on with you? Bit of a celeb now, aren't you? Tell me all about it.'

Jenny told her.

'It must have been horrible, seeing that girl on the beach,' Sarah said, taking a swig of her wine. She fixed Jenny with her brown eyes, so dark they looked black under the dim lights of the bar.

Of course it was upsetting, Jenny said, but she was fine. She told Sarah about the visit from DCI Gilbert, and about Matt and the guy.

'So, you don't like the policeman because he's religious and some pothead found a guy at Pleinmont. Ever think you might be looking a little too hard for something interesting to write about? Or that maybe you've read one too many Miss Marple novels for your own good? You were obsessed with them when we were kids, do you remember?' Sarah snorted a laugh into her wine glass and then downed half of it in one sip.

'Yes, I remember. I like to read, very funny. But it's strange, don't you think? This guy, or whatever it was, had marks on its arm, just like the scratches on Amanda.'

'Couldn't this kid be making it all up? Bit convenient that he burnt the thing, isn't it? He could have imagined it all. Or maybe he has issues. He's attention-seeking. Or he was high.' She nodded to herself. 'That's the most likely scenario. You know all the kids that hang around up at Pleinmont are smoking weed and doing pills and God knows what else.'

'You sound like my mum.' Jenny teased. 'Kids these days, getting up to all sorts of no good.'

'Maybe. You know I'm right, though.'

It made sense. It probably happened all the time. Cranks and timewasters showing up every time something like this happened. Which wasn't often. Jenny remembered a body had washed up years ago, when Jenny was at school. Another young woman. That had been a suicide. It had been front-page news for days and there had been some criticism about mental health services on the island. Now that was an angle, a sensible one. She finished her drink. Sarah waggled the bottle in front of her.

'One for the road?'

Sarah filled her glass. Jenny sank back into her chair sipping the wine. It was rich and warm and relaxing.

'So, you're definitely all right?' Sarah asked. She wasn't going to let it go.

'I've told you. I'm fine.'

'Only, you've got that look about you.'

'What look?'

'Tired. Stressed. Anxious. I know you, Jenny. I know how you get.'

'It's been a rough couple of days.'

'Rough couple of years, more like.' Sarah paused. 'Are you ever going to tell me why you really came back?'

'You know why I came back. Dad died. Mum needs me.'

'I know that's the official story. But what happened in London? That had something to do with it too. It frightened you. I've only ever seen you like that once before. And we both know what happened after that.'

Jenny drained her glass. It was good to come back, after what had happened. She'd needed to get away from the city. At least, she'd thought she did.

'I've told you all this before.' She was in no mood for an impromptu therapy session.

'You said you'd had a run in with some bad people. Hardly an explanation.'

'That's exactly what happened. I was working on a story. There was a woman who was being exploited, forced to work, kept in permanent debt by a gang. I tried to help her. I failed.'

'What happened?'

'They found out what I was doing, threatened me, told me to keep my mouth shut.'

'And the woman, who was she? What happened to her?'

'Her name was Madalina. I don't know what happened to her.' Jenny shook her head. 'I do know what happened to her. I just can't prove it.'

'What?'

'He killed her.'

'Who did?'

Jenny played with her hair, twisting the ends through her fingers, then she pulled it aside, stretching the scar at the nape of her neck, feeling it stretch and burn and turned to show Sarah.

'The same person who did this.'

Margaret, fretting about where Jenny had been and why she was so late, opened the front door before her daughter could get her key in the lock. She looked at the space on the driveway where the car should have been, asked where it was, and before Jenny could answer, set about panicking, convinced that she'd had an accident.

Jenny locked the door and slid the security chain into the track.

'I went for a couple of drinks with Sarah after work. I told you we were meeting up this week. I left the car in town and took a cab home.'

Margaret's frown relaxed slightly, but her face remained pale and strained. She fluttered down the corridor. Of course, she said, Jenny had mentioned she was going out, but she'd forgotten and when it got so late she'd been worried. She put the kettle on, offered Jenny tea.

'We lost track of time. I sent you a text.'

Sarah had tried her best to get Jenny to tell her more about Madalina but Jenny had distracted her, only temporarily, knowing Sarah, with another bottle of wine and some gossip about school friends. Now, as Jenny sat at the kitchen table, the room spun a little and the bitter taste of alcohol burnt the back of her throat.

Margaret picked up her handbag from the back of the chair and scrabbled around for her phone, jabbing at the screen when she finally found it, shaking her head as it failed to come to life.

'I'm useless,' she sighed. 'Always forget to charge the damn thing. At least you're all right.'

'I'm fine.'

Margaret smiled too brightly and reached for the cups. She asked Jenny was it just her and Sarah, because wasn't Sarah's husband in a band? Perhaps Sarah could introduce Jenny to them? Margaret had seen their pictures in the *News*, a couple of them were nice-looking, she said, bit long-haired and scruffy, but that was all part of the look, she supposed.

'I'm a bit old to be a groupie, Mum.'

'Of course you are. I'm not saying that. It just might be nice for you to meet someone. So you're not on your own.' Margaret poured the boiling water into the teapot and Jenny could see her hands shaking as she set the kettle back on its base. Jenny went to her side.

'Sit down. I'll do this.'

She finished making the tea, brought the cups to the table and set them down.

'You need to stop worrying, Mum. I'm not on my own, am I? I've got you. Unless you're planning on going somewhere?'

'You know what I mean.' Margaret said. 'Surely you must think about it, seeing Sarah with her family? And that poor girl washing up like that – doesn't it make you think? How precious life is, how short?' She sipped at her tea through tightly pressed lips and Jenny could see the tension in her face.

'Mum! Stop it.'

Margaret rubbed her eyes and shook her head.

'I'm sorry, love. It's having you home here again. Of course you don't need me fretting. But I'd like to know you were settled, that you had someone looking out for you.' She reached out her hand and stroked Jenny's hair, tucked it behind her ears.

'It's nearly grown back. But you look different, you know. Around your eyes, I think that's where I see it most. You look at people differently. London changed you: the city, the work, those awful people. What they did to you. It's a cliché, isn't it, to worry about the scars on the inside? But I do, Jenny.'

Jenny took her mother's hand in her own and gently placed it back on the table.

'Mum. It's been a long day. And I'm a bit drunk. You look exhausted too. Let's get some sleep.'

Margaret brushed Jenny's cheek with her lips before going to bed and Jenny felt it again. That lightness. Even her mother's kisses were light these days.

She lay in bed looking at the shadows on the ceiling. The wine should have made her sleepy but there was too much to think about. She tried to still her thoughts, to calm the disquiet she felt rumbling in her stomach. Sarah was probably right. Matt was just attention seeking. And DCI Gilbert, he was probably right too. Amanda's death was likely to be an accident. Or a suicide. And it was only natural that Margaret would be upset by a body washing up on the beach, only natural she would worry about Jenny. She'd been through a lot. They both had.

She closed her eyes. She saw Amanda. She had looked so perfect, lying there. As though she'd been for a swim and then fallen asleep on a bed of stones. Nothing like when her dad had been found. She screwed up her eyes and tried to dispel the image. She tried so hard not to think about it, about what he must have looked like. Although she knew that it would have appealed to his sense of humour – that the fisherman ended up fish food.

11

August 1961

*M*other was dead, her face twisted unnaturally, mouth frozen in a grimace, eyes fixed on the ceiling. Too much alcohol, too many pills. An accident. She surely lacked the nerve to have done it on purpose.

As he got closer to the bed, the smell hit him, sour and damp. Piss. The wetness spread over the sheet covering her. He pulled it back to expose her body, flimsily clothed in one of those girlish nightdresses she loved. He lifted it, pushed it up around her neck and over her face. Her breasts sagged, shapeless, towards the soft spread of the belly in which he once grew.

How many men had used her to service their weakness? Had his father been the same? Had he fucked her once and left like all the others? Or had he come often, tempted time and again by her pliant body and her soft, breathy voice?

He placed his hand on her breastbone and stroked her, tracing down to her stomach. Her skin was cold but soft and textured. It was a miracle, really, that she had given life to him. That he had sprung from this weak, flawed body.

Sparse, black hairs grew around her naval and thickened as they spread down towards her underwear. Her only asset in life had been what lay hidden beneath that slip of yellowed cotton. And *now she was dead and powerless and all she had to show for a life-time of whoredom was him. He pulled back the sheet in disgust.*

There had to be a funeral. The parish insisted on it. There were few mourners, even fewer that he recognised. Unsurprising. Mother had only a handful of acquaintances and no real friends that he knew of. Family, of course, were nowhere to be seen. He listened to the vicar's words with a detached interest but was unmoved until he found himself in the cemetery staring down at the wooden box in the ground.

Ashes to ashes, dust to dust.

He threw in his handful of dirt. He wondered if the coffin would rot quicker than Mother's flesh, or if by the time his dirt touched her she would be nothing more than bones and it would settle into empty sockets or the hollow of her rib cage. He felt his eyes moisten then, at the thought of her heartless, fleshless, hollow rib cage. He could cast off the burden of shame she had forced him to carry. No more questions from well-meaning neighbours about the state of her health. No more sideways glances when he accompanied her on a walk around the village, her dress stinking of gin and moth-balls, lipstick bleeding into the fine, powder-filled lines around her mouth. He was free. As her heart shrivelled and dried, so his seemed to fill, beating with a new strength and he experienced another of those rare moments of exquisite joy. He wiped the tears from his cheek and kept his smile hidden until he'd left the graveyard.

He returned home to find a man sitting on the front door-step. He did not look like Mother's usual type, although there was something familiar about him. He wore a blazer and smart trousers, round, black-rimmed glasses giving him an air of intelli-gence. He introduced himself. Uncle Peter.

When Mother had been drunk, she had slurred Uncle Peter's name, cursed him for forsaking her. She'd loved the melodrama of it all. Uncle Peter inherited when Grandfather died, the island laws leaving it to the eldest son to ensure things were distributed fairly on the death of a parent, or not, as they felt fit. Uncle Peter had not felt it fitting to provide for his Jerry-bag sister, a sister whose existence he had sworn to forget the moment she told them she was carrying a Nazi baby in her belly. He wondered if Uncle Peter was thinking about the fact that this was the very same Nazi baby standing in front of him right now.

He rose from the step.

'I was expecting a child,' he said. 'Stupid. You must be fifteen now?'

He nodded.

'Nearly a man. But not quite.'

Uncle Peter felt some remorse, it seemed. Not at Mother's death, nor at the fact that he hadn't seen or spoken to her for more than fifteen years, but that he had neglected to provide for his nephew who should not be suffering for the sins of his parents. He wished to make amends. To provide for him so that he could finish his education.

'Your mother aside, you're from a fine family. You've done well, to get a scholarship.' Uncle Peter said. 'You shouldn't waste the opportunity to make something of yourself.'

Mother's death turned out to be a wonderful thing in more ways than one then. Not only was he free from her cloying, grasping touch, and her cheaply perfumed, gin-soaked scent, he now had the opportunity to continue his studies.

It was a fresh start.

A new beginning.

12

Michael

Wednesday, 12 November

The wind rattling the windows woke him early. He stood in the back doorway wearing a dressing gown wrapped tightly over fleece pyjamas and a pair of thick socks (slippers made him feel old) and watched the apple tree. Its branches swayed violently in the wind and one in particular was in the perfect position to fly off and smash into his garden shed. He sipped his coffee and turned back into the kitchen. The tree was probably older than he was. It had weathered enough storms. It was a wonder either of them were still standing.

Two years after Ellen died, the end of 1999 – that had been his lowest point. He and Sheila were married but she was getting sick of him. She'd spent the first year after the accident in a state of permanent emotional agony, and then suddenly, just like that, she'd woken up one morning, done her face and started to get on with her life again. She'd been having therapy. That probably had something to do with it. She'd wanted him to go but he didn't want to talk to anyone. How could talking about it make it better? She'd dragged him along to a couple of sessions anyway, tried to get him to discuss his lack of empathy towards her, his lack of emotion about the whole thing. Bloody empathy and emotion. Presumably she meant that twisted ball of throbbing pain in his chest which constantly threatened to burst out of him, choking him and everyone around him, which he pushed, further and further inside of him every waking minute, knowing he couldn't survive if he let it out. But he didn't want to talk about it. He chose the slow, steady, onwards and downwards approach, followed it all the way to the bottom of a bottle and stayed there.

New Year's Eve. Everyone had been talking about the millennium bug, how they were all going to be plunged back into the dark ages, a sort of electronic Armageddon. All the lights were going to go out, planes were going to fall out of the sky, the banking system was going to crash and they were all going to starve because, apparently, you needed a bloody computer to eat these days. He'd barely been sober for a year. At some points he'd been less drunk than others; mostly, but not always, when he was at work. He'd become an expert at disguising his not-so-stale alcohol breath with a combination of chewing gum and Fisherman's Friends. He'd also found that the energy drinks which Ellen had taken to drinking while doing her A levels were especially effective at countering the fatiguing effects of several late nights too many at his local boozer.

Which is where he was that particular 31 December, same as most nights, although it was busier, due to the occasion. He'd waved his empty glass at the barman. People were laughing and shouting. It was a shit pub and most of the clientele were colourful characters, to say the least. They all knew Inspector Gilbert. Some of them even bought him a pint. Sheila was out at a dinner party. He'd been invited but said he was working. She'd known he was lying and he'd known she was happy that he was.

He'd joined in the countdown to the new millennium with gusto, secretly hoping that the doomsayers were right and that everything was going to stop at the stroke of twelve. A fresh start would have been a fine thing, in his opinion. It was a predictable let-down when the music kept playing past midnight and the TV signal remained uninterrupted.

When he'd got home she'd been sitting in her favourite chair, reading a book. She'd smiled when she saw him. Not the dead-eyed upturn of the facial muscles he had become familiar with. A real smile. The corners of her eyes crinkled. She was wearing a black velvet evening dress, which showed off her trim figure and her legs. She had looked so young. She *was* young he had thought, with a rush of emotion. Only forty. Young enough to have another child, even. Why had they not talked about that? Maybe it was something she spoke about with the therapist. He would ask her. It was a new year. It could be a new start for them.

Sheila had agreed. It was time for a new start. She'd said some words. Lots of them, about love and time and healing and about Ellen, and she'd smiled and reached out and touched him, stroked his face, like she used to, when everything had been good, and the words floated around them and none of them made any sense until the bit where she'd picked up her things and left.

So the doomsayers were right. All the lights had gone out after all.

At first, it seemed like a terrible thing had happened. But, quickly, he realised that not much had really changed. He went to work and did a good job, even better than before, if anything, because with nobody to go home to he put in longer and longer hours at the office, which had the knock-on effect that he was spending less time at the pub. He threw himself into every case he was assigned, gaining a reputation as someone who would leave no stone unturned. It made him unpopular at the station – everyone knew there was no getting away with doing half a job around Inspector Gilbert. He was promoted. Chief Inspector. Worked more. Slept less. Spent his days off drunk. Only now he didn't have to bother pretending to be sober and there was nobody to nag him when he fried himself a couple of eggs every morning and ate more than one bag of crisps every night.

He had been actively encouraging a heart attack. He knew, despite the web of black thoughts he spun each night, that he would never have had the courage to end his own life. A massive coronary, however, to rip the pain out of his chest and obliterate it and to take him to Ellen, wherever she was, would be perfect.

When it happened, then, he had been surprised by the force with which he fought it, his body seemingly working against his darkest desires, crawling to the phone in the middle of the night, his fingers dialling the magic numbers, his voice rasping his address to the operator with his dying breath.

He'd regretted it when he woke up. Alive. Tubes coming out of every orifice, pissing into a catheter, a jolly, rough Filipina bed-bathing him like a child every couple of days. They'd told him he was lucky. He had laughed. Properly. Like he hadn't done in years. When he left, after several weeks, finally able to urinate unaided and wipe his own arse and with a scar, which ran from the bottom of his throat to the top of his stomach, they had given him an armful of leaflets. *Eat Right For Your Heart, Need Help with A Drinking Problem? Get Fit, Have Fun!* He'd put all of them in the bin outside of the hospital, except for one.

Looking for Answers? Drop into the Christian Friendship Society: We can help you. Call in and find Support, Sharing, Friendship.

He'd called in. And he'd found all three.

So, here he was. Detective chief inspector, no less. Drinking coffee in a thunderstorm and heading up an investigation into a young girl's death. He had to talk to her parents this morning. Grim job. He tipped the last of the morning's coffee down the hatch and nodded at the huge black cumulonimbus hovering over his back garden.

Mysterious ways. He worked in mysterious ways, for sure.

Amanda's parents lived in a small bungalow on a neat, private housing estate in the Vale parish. On the surface, each house appeared different to the next, this one with a rose window, the next with a porch, but behind these external affectations, they were all the same really. Like people, he mused. The same parcel of flesh and blood and muscles and nerves and brains, just wrapped up seven billion different ways. The thought depressed him. The weather didn't help. Oppressive clouds lingered above him and the air was quick with cold; it tickled his lungs with each breath. He opened the garden gate. A few bunches of withered flowers were propped against the front fence and a sad-faced teddy bear held a message written on the back of a postcard.

RIP AMANDA HEAVEN HAS A NEW ANGEL NOW

Perhaps. Although his belief in some form of God was steadfast, he was not one of those late-to-the-party believers who came to faith because of a desperate fear of the nothingness that inevitably followed an irreligious life. In fact, he was very uncomfortable with the idea that one's deeds, good or evil, would be rewarded or punished after the fact. In his opinion, a lack of accountability at best encouraged laziness and, at worst, was downright dangerous. He would bring it up at the next Friendship meeting. They all enjoyed a good debate, which had surprised him. He'd expected everyone to be prescriptive in their beliefs. It was all part of their plan to suck him in, Sheila had said during one of their infrequent telephone conversations (she tried to be a good ex-wife, telling everyone how amicable their divorce was), but she was wrong. They'd simply opened their arms to him and he'd welcomed their embrace.

He stood on the steps a moment, thinking about an appropriate greeting before knocking. He adjusted his coat collar and smoothed his hair as he waited.

Amanda's father opened the door. He looked worse than the last time they'd spoken. He'd had a few days to let the news sink in – enough time for the lack of food and sleep and the sadness to have an effect. He stepped aside to let Michael in. A door to the side creaked open and a small boy, about six years old with scruffy brown hair and freckles all over his face, poked his head around it, then shuffled out into the corridor. He had a soft toy wedged under his arm, a smiling donkey. Michael smiled and raised his hand in a wave. The boy frowned back at him.

'Go and play with your Lego, Toby.' His dad patted him on the head. 'I'll take you to the playground in a little while.'

'I don't want to go to the playground.'

'To the shop, then. We'll get a new puzzle.'

Toby shook his head and held the donkey to his chest, clutching it tightly. 'I don't want a puzzle.'

'Is that a Guernsey donkey you've got there?' Michael crouched down and pointed at the flag embroidered on the side of the toy. 'I used to have one like that. Don't think they make them any more.' He smiled, ruffled the boy's hair as he got back up. Toby said nothing, went back into his room and shut the door.

His dad leant against it, hand kneading his forehead. 'They were close. I don't know how he's going to cope.'

'Children are resilient.' Michael knew it was a platitude. He followed Amanda's father into the living room.

They sat on the too-soft sofa scattered with velvet cushions, drinking weak tea, which always made Michael feel sick but he didn't want to appear rude. As if Mrs Guille would care if he wasted his tea. It was from her that Amanda had inherited her looks. While her husband was squat with a soft, round face, she was taller with delicate features behind taut, sallow skin and a smattering of freckles, like her son. She sat opposite Michael, poker straight, hands folded in her lap and left her own tea untouched.

He started with the pleasantries and the routine questions, checking that the family liaison officer was doing a good job, asking how they were getting on (stupid question) and did they have anything they wanted to ask him, to talk about? They sat, nodding and shaking their heads. They had nothing to tell him, no answers, no questions beyond did the police know what happened to their daughter yet? How could he tell them they might never know? Not really. *A tragic accident.* That was the easiest way to present it. Better than it being an obvious suicide. Suicides were the hardest for parents to accept. He felt a twist in his gut at the thought and wondered, again, about Ellen.

'Just a couple of things I'd like to go over with you both, if you're up to it?'

They both nodded.

'Whatever you need.' Mr Guille murmured.

'Amanda had had a couple of run-ins with the police.' He looked up and smiled reassuringly, 'Nothing serious, of course, usual teenage stuff. I just noticed that on one occasion, about six months ago, it was you, Mrs Guille, who called us?'

She must have been prepared for the question. She didn't miss a beat.

'Yes. I found cannabis in her bag. It was a shock. I've never had anything to do with drugs, inspector, I didn't even know what it was at first. I suspected, of course, but I had to ask John and even he wasn't sure.' She looked at her husband. 'She was a bright girl. Could have gone to university. But she wouldn't focus. She got in with this crowd. They're not bad kids, just lazy. They have no ambition. I wanted better for her. That's why we called the police. We just wanted to teach her a lesson. Wanted her to know it was serious. That she could ruin her life if she had a criminal record.'

71

Her voice wavered. 'And I think it was a good decision, overall.' She looked to Mr Guille again, who was unresponsive.

'It *was*,' she insisted. 'She saw a social worker, started going to that youth programme; Leap it's called. She took some music lessons, got back into her singing. She enjoyed it. She was getting back on her feet. *I* thought she was.'

'You disagree, Mr Guille?' Michael asked, gently.

He shrugged his shoulders. 'The youth club did seem to be a positive influence. I was glad to see her out and about. She was always shy, so it was good to see her making friends.'

'But?'

He hesitated. 'She didn't trust us after we called the police. She'd had problems before. Depression, low self-esteem, issues with food.'

'Did she ever self-harm?' Michael asked, gently. 'I know we've asked you about the cuts on her arm and you say you hadn't noticed them and there's certainly no evidence of it elsewhere on her body.' He paused, the word hanging in the air between them. He knew they were picturing her right now, as they'd last seen her. 'The marks were fresh. Inflicted shortly before death. They may have been indicative of her state of mind. You'd not known her to hurt herself before?'

Amanda's father shook his head. 'She never did that. Not that we knew about, anyway. But she would have hidden it from us, wouldn't she?' He shook his head again. 'We kept writing things off, we thought it was all part of a phase, that sort of thing, but when we found the drugs, well, we panicked. My wife thought calling your lot was the best plan. Now I wonder if she thought we'd given up on her.'

Mrs Guille spoke softly. 'We agreed, John. We agreed that we needed to do something drastic.' She looked to Michael. 'I love my daughter. *Loved* her. Yes, she had some problems. If I'd had any idea that calling the police that time would lead to something like this, of course I would never have done it. She looked at her husband, eyes brimming with tears. 'We *agreed*.' A whisper now. 'It was the right thing to do.'

Michael nodded. Of course, he said, they were doing their best. And sometimes a sharp shock like that did the trick. It was worth a try. They shouldn't even think about blaming themselves, there was never one reason something like this happened. It was never that simple. He paused.

'As her parents, you knew her better than anyone. So I'm afraid I have to ask: do you think Amanda could have taken her own life?' He looked to Mr Guille, who stared at his hands intently.

'It's possible. She was unhappy. I don't know what went wrong.' He slumped back and the sofa seemed to swallow him up.

Michael patted his shoulder on the way out.

He gave them six months.

13

Jenny

Thursday, 13 November

Something had woken her. She sat up, listened. Trees and bushes swaying outside, the patter of rain on the roof. She walked to the window, pulled back the curtains, looked out into the night. Small solar-powered lights shaped like old-fashioned gas lanterns marked the fence at the bottom of the garden, only a few yards from where she stood. Beyond lay open fields and then greenhouses, which years ago had belonged to Sarnia Flora, one of the island's biggest growers. Jenny remembered when her parents worked evenings there, picking freesias and carnations. They would take Jenny with them and she would run amongst the plants, the scent of the hot, dry earth mingling with the delicate perfume of the flowers. The company had gone out of business twenty years ago and the greenhouses had fallen into disrepair, their wooden frames now like the skeletons of some long-extinct beasts, the earth around them littered with broken glass. Beyond, the nearest houses were just visible in the distance, the odd illuminated windows shining like beacons and she was struck by the thought that if anyone was out there, she was framed, a bright target in the darkness. She startled at a hollow thud from behind her and pulled the curtains closed.

There was a blocked-up fireplace in her room and on stormy

nights the wind rattled through the chimney; finding no escape at the bottom, it buffeted about angrily in the flue. This sounded louder than usual and she walked over to the chimney breast, put her ear to the wall. She listened and heard the telltale scratching and chirping of a trapped bird. And something else. From the hallway.

Muffled sobs.

Margaret. Another nightmare.

She could just go back to sleep. She lay back down on the bed, closed her eyes and tried to concentrate on the sound of the wind and the rain outside. If she listened very carefully she could hear the sea in the distance. As a child, when she felt anxious or worried, the sound had soothed her; the gentle swish and sway of the water on calm nights or the violent smashing of the waves during a storm. She listened for it now, but the whisper of the distant sea was no match for the gentle thudding in the chimney or the hushed sobbing in the next room.

Margaret's light was on and her door was ajar. She was propped up on her pillows, sipping from a glass of water. There was an unopened packet of tablets and a Josephine Cox novel on her bedside table. She still slept on 'her' side of the bed. She had wanted to get rid of the double and get a single after Charlie died but Jenny had persuaded her not too, had thought her mum would feel his loss more keenly seeing space for only one person after so many years, but perhaps this was worse. The pillows on the left-hand side were smooth, the duvet unruffled, a constant reminder of his absence.

Jenny sat on the end of the bed.

'Can I get you anything?'

Margaret shook her head.

'You've got work in the morning, you should get back to sleep. I'm fine. It's just these nightmares. I hardly sleep and then when I do . . .' Her voice trailed off.

'What are you dreaming about? Is it Dad?' Jenny rubbed her bare arms against the cold.

'Get into bed.' Margaret pulled back the covers.

'OK. But please, will you take one of these?' Jenny popped a sedative out of the packet and climbed in next to her mother. 'Bit of a turn around, isn't it, me coming to give you a cuddle because you're having nightmares?'

Margaret laughed and wiped at her nose with her sleeve.

'So are you going to tell me about them or can I go back to sleep?'

Margaret sighed. 'You know who I've been thinking about?'

'Who?' Jenny stifled a yawn.

'Elizabeth Mahy.'

'Who?'

'Elizabeth. The friend of mine who died.'

'You've never mentioned her.'

'I have. I must have done. You probably weren't listening. Anyway, it was a long time ago, before you were born, before I met your dad even.'

'I don't remember you talking about any Elizabeth. How did she die?'

Margaret looked at the little white pill in her hand and then swallowed it down with a sip of water.

'She drowned. At the bathing pools. A long time ago.'

Margaret told her story, animated at first, threading it through with a hundred tiny details about her and Elizabeth; the clothes they wore, the places they went to and what had happened – at least, as much as she knew – until slowly, as the sedative took effect, the details became hazier, her voice softer, and finally it trailed off completely and her breathing slowed and deepened. Jenny got out of the bed and tucked her back in. She had not seen her mother sleeping for a very long time. She watched her for a moment and then turned out the light.

The storm had calmed. Jenny slipped back into her bed and closed her eyes. The sea was a quiet roar, like the sound you could hear when you held a conch shell to your ear. And much closer, behind the blocked-up fireplace, she could hear the muffled beating of frantic wings. She listened to it, helpless, until dawn broke and the singing of the birds outside drowned it out.

Pembroke, a wide, sheltered bay at the northern tip of the island, was always crowded during the summer, the long, flat stretch of golden sand interrupted by brightly coloured windbreaks, families gathered around picnic blankets, children paddling in the shallows. Cold November mornings were a different story. It was freezing underfoot, even before she'd got to the sea, the sand chilled by the icy water just under the surface. The flag on the Martello tower, which stood sentinel on a grassy bank at the head of the bay, flew with hardly a flutter, so brisk and unyielding was the breeze. Several turrets of smooth rocks which at low tide formed a natural children's playground of rock pools and hidey holes, were nearly fully submerged, only the round, flat tops visible, poking out like seals trying to keep their heads above water.

Even near the shore the waves were powerful and relentless, whipped up by yesterday's storm and yet to settle. Usually, Jenny would relish the challenge. It was one of the reasons she liked to swim outdoors. You had to focus, be aware of your surroundings – the currents, the weather, the rocks. You were at once immersed in nature and battling against it. Today, however, Jenny was tired, and the sea was winning. She moved slowly through the water, the muscles in her arms complaining each time she pulled a stroke. She should look at the bathing pools for her daily swim. They would surely offer more shelter from the wind. And they had changing rooms. She had forgotten about them until her mum had told her about Elizabeth.

She could not remember hearing about Elizabeth before,

although Margaret insisted she'd told Jenny all about it. Most likely Jenny had not listened. She had always been more interested in Charlie's stories of adventure and mischief than Margaret's cautionary tales.

Margaret and Elizabeth had been great friends as teenagers. Sometimes they would tell their parents they were going to each other's houses and then change into miniskirts and high heels before hitting the bars in town. One Saturday night Grandpa Le Page had stopped Margaret from going out. One of his friends had seen her the previous week in a bar. He had checked her bag, found her outfit, and slapped her round the face. Grandpa Le Page had been a benign, smiling man who never seemed to get out of his armchair. He would do the football pools, sipping at a whisky and ginger ale, or tell Jenny stories about his time in the navy, his visits to the Far East and India, while they made jigsaw puzzles together. She had never heard him raise his voice. He'd even died quietly, sitting in that same armchair, watching his beloved Pompey Chimes.

'He hit you?'

Margaret had nodded. Not for the first time either, she said. He'd had a terrible temper when he was younger and he drank a lot more whisky back then too. That Saturday, when she'd been forced to stay in, nursing a bruised cheek, Elizabeth went out without her. She never came home. She was found the next morning at the bathing pools. Dead. Drowned. In her underwear. The police said she'd been drunk and gone skinny-dipping, suspected there may have been someone with her but no witnesses came forward. Margaret had known Elizabeth had a boyfriend, someone older, but she'd never met him. She was no help at all to the police.

The wind was picking up and the undertow strengthening. Her arms tired, Jenny pushed through it towards the beach, feeling with her feet for the sand concealed beneath the leaden waves, wading the last few feet to the shore, the water slapping at her thighs, an admonishment for her foolhardiness. She walked back to the large, flat rock she had left her things on. Each bluster of wind seemed to strip a layer off of her wet skin, already blue with cold, and she struggled to wrap her towel around her shoulders as the edges caught and billowed away from her. She rubbed at her pale, shaky legs with the rough towel to bring some blood back to the surface. She peeled her costume off, one hand securing the towel around her neck, while she inelegantly pulled her jeans over her damp skin and a T-shirt and sweater over her head. Too cold to fiddle with undies and it was only a few minutes on the bike back to her house.

She stuffed her wet things back in her rucksack and hoisted it over one shoulder, pulled her wet hair back from where it was whipping at her face. That was when she saw him. A man behind the sea wall. Watching her.

He was dressed all in black, a hoody pulled up over his head, and she thought about the man on the motorbike, wondered if it was him. She wouldn't have heard him approach, not while she was in the sea, with the waves crashing around her. She walked towards the wall, gripped with the overwhelming need to know what the fuck was going on, ignoring the screeching in her head telling her to run and hide. There was nowhere to go anyway. The beach offered no shelter. Not from this.

Her head was pounding and she wondered if blood was pumped to it in times of crisis to aid the brain, so you could think more clearly, make life-preserving decisions. It wasn't working. It was her legs that needed help now. They shook as she walked, her thighs stiff from the cold, protesting each step she took towards danger.

She was too far away to make out his features clearly, but there was something familiar about him. About the shape of him, the bend of his neck, the way his shoulders sloped. He was a tall man but looked uncomfortable with his height. She had known a boy like that once. But it couldn't be him. If she was being followed, it was by someone from London, someone who knew what had happened to Madalina. Someone who wanted Jenny to keep her mouth shut. *Bitch*. But there was a sliver of doubt now. A flicker of fear that she'd got it all wrong, that perhaps it wasn't her new past haunting her, but her old one.

As she got closer to the wall, he turned and ran. Not quickly, more at a jogger's pace, but by the time she'd climbed the wooden ladder to the car park he was a spot in the distance, black top, black shorts, bright-white running shoes. She paused. Just an early morning runner, distracted by a lunatic swimming in the sea in winter. She let out the breath that was burning in her lungs. Felt her heart rate slow.

She was paranoid. There was nothing to be afraid of. She sat on the wall until her shaking legs were still.

Brian was waiting for her with a list of things he wanted her to follow up on, now the dust had settled a bit. Talk to the girl's friends, he said, get a few quotes, follow up with where the police were, check if the results of the post-mortem had come through. What else was she working on?

'I thought I might look into other similar cases, concentrate on the suicide angle.'

'Yes, great idea. Focus on young people. Nobody cares about some fat middle-aged bloke topping himself. I mean readership wise, obviously.' His face suddenly lit up. 'Look at mental health funding too. This has been an issue before. We could tie it up with the recent budget cuts.'

'Do you remember any similar cases, Brian? While you've been working here?'

He thought for a moment.

'There's been the odd body washed up. We ran a piece a couple of years ago after there was a spike in the rate. Tends to be men, you know. You women seem to be better at getting on with things.'

'What about drowning, specifically?'

'There have been a few. Not all suicides, obviously. Plenty of accidents. You know that, of course.' He looked vaguely apologetic – and something else, uncomfortable, perhaps. It was unlike Brian to be sensitive to the feelings of others. She thought about acknowledging his sympathy, but decided ignoring it would be easier for both of them. She paused for a moment, before pressing him further.

'I just wondered if there might be something there. Perhaps suicide rates are higher amongst women here than elsewhere. We could compare to the UK statistics. My mum mentioned something interesting, actually. A young girl found at the bathing pools, back in the sixties.' She looked at him questioningly. Brian's face fell.

'Well, I wouldn't remember that, would I? Good grief, how old do you think I am? And what has some story your mum told you got to do with anything? This is a newspaper, not a bloody WI meeting.'

He marched back to his office, shutting the door with a little more force than usual.

She walked down Smith Street. The results of the post-mortem were back. Death by drowning. The toxicity screening showed that Amanda had ingested several Valium in the hours prior to her death. No sign of foul play. There would be an inquest, of course, but the police expected a verdict of death by misadventure. Without a note they were always loath to call it suicide but everything pointed that way. Case closed by the sound of it. Even Brian seemed to have lost some of his earlier enthusiasm for the story, suggesting, as it all seemed open and shut, that she might want to turn her attention to the Save the Islander campaign, the story Elliot was working on. There was a demonstration planned for later in the week and it might need both of them, he said, and told her to catch up on the background. Which would have been a day's work, except Jenny had already read everything there was to know about Save The Islander and Deputy Tostevin, the man who had started it all. So she could afford to spend another half a day doing her own thing, with Brian none the wiser.

Jenny had felt death. When she'd stared, through eyes swimming with tears, at her father's coffin, it had been dull and heavy in its inevitability, its truth real but distant, an ordeal you knew you had to face but had years to prepare for. When her own life had been threatened, it had felt quick and sharp, like the knife at her throat was already in her gut, twisting her insides, and she'd known, if it came down to it, she would do anything to stay alive. But this girl, Amanda . . . If the police were right, she'd felt death and embraced it, overridden the most basic human instinct. Jenny wanted to know why. And if the police were wrong, she wanted to know why a young woman had been found dead on a beach with no clue as to how and why she got there – like Elizabeth Mahy, all those years ago. Either way, Jenny figured there was a story.

The sky was the same colour as the pavement and the air was damp and cold. She kept her head down as she walked through the narrow streets of St Peter Port to Market Street. Cafes nestled under the archways of the fruit and vegetable halls and the main building, a beautiful nineteenth-century structure of brick and granite, was filled with clothes shops and a record store. The closest thing to a market here now was a small branch of the Co–op, selling imported, cling-film-wrapped versions of what went before. She remembered coming here with her dad to choose a crab for Saturday lunch. They would look for the one with the fattest claws, where the sweetest meat would be, and put it in their basket along with a fresh baguette, a slice of *pâté de campagne,* some French ham. She could smell the place: the earthy sweetness of the skinned cow carcasses hanging from the ceiling, dark flesh marbled with yellow fat, the barrels of live lobsters, fresh and briny, the smoked mackerels, their black, iridescent skins set against crushed ice.

Opposite the market stood the Guille-Allès library, a tall, handsome building with steep steps leading up to an entrance arch. The last thirty years of the *News* had been bound and archived at the *Guernsey News*'s office, an expensive project, which had been abandoned halfway through due to a lack of funding. So, while budgets were being balanced, pre-1985 copies were kept here, at the top of the library.

Automatic doors slid open as Jenny approached. She walked through them into a high-ceilinged entrance hall with an intricately patterned tiled floor and a sweeping staircase, which led to the main collections. Self-checkout machines and a small information table had replaced the imposing wooden front desk that Jenny remembered standing on tiptoes to place her books on as a child.

She climbed the stairs, past the adult fiction and children's sections, up another flight and through a door marked 'Archives' which led along a narrow corridor and up a winding staircase on to a small landing. The ceiling here was low and uneven, reflecting the shape of the roof above. Afternoon's fading light glinted through a small window, the only one in the room. An elegant woman in her fifties, with close-cropped, salt-and-pepper hair, sat at a desk peering through a magnifying glass at a glossy sheet of microfiche files.

'Hi, Miriam.'

The woman looked up from her desk and smiled. Long silver earrings shaped like feathers dangled from her ears. 'How are you, Jenny?' She stood and kissed Jenny on both cheeks. 'How's your mum?'

Miriam had lived round the corner from Jenny for years and

had babysat her on the rare occasion Margaret and Charlie had gone out for dinner, years ago. She dropped in for a cup of tea every now and then. Jenny told her they were well and that she must pop in and see them sometime soon.

'What can I help you with today, Jenny?' Jenny gave her the dates of the newspapers she was looking for and waited while Miriam fetched the relevant films from the heavy steel cabinets which lined the walls, then followed her into the reading room. Miriam loaded the first slide in. 'Well, you know what you're doing. Just shout if you want anything printed.' She closed the door, leaving Jenny in a room barely bigger than a closet, a bright screen speckled with grey flecks displaying the lopsided front page of the *Guernsey News,* 13 June 1966. She turned the handles on the front of the machine, one to angle the page correctly, the other to focus. Only a few lines accompanied the headline.

BODY FOUND AT BATHING POOLS

The body of a young woman was discovered early yester-day morning at the bathing pools at La Valette, St Peter Port. Police are unable to release any further details at this point but are appealing for witnesses. Please contact Police Constable Roger Wilson with any information.

She scrolled down but that was all the information about Elizabeth's death in that day's paper. She loaded the next slide.

BODY AT BATHING POOLS LOCAL SCHOOLGIRL

The body of the young woman found at the bathing pools at La Valette, St Peter Port, early yesterday morning, has been identified as that of Elizabeth Maude Mahy, 16, a student at Les Beaucamps Secondary School. She is believed to have

84

spent the evening before her death in St Peter Port, specifically in the bar at The Yacht Hotel. Police are appealing for witnesses who may have seen Miss Mahy on the night of the 11 June, particularly anyone who might be able to identify a gentleman companion she was seen with, to contact Police Constable Roger Wilson.

It was the picture, though, not the words, which caught Jenny's attention. It was a school photograph, black and white, a little grainy. She turned the handle to sharpen the image. Long blonde hair, big, pale eyes, dazzling smile. She was younger, a little rounder in the cheeks perhaps, but the resemblance was striking. Elizabeth Mahy looked just like Amanda Guille.

It was nearly dark when she left, but not late. A miserable drizzle now fell from low-lying cloud and the cobbles of the high street were black and slippery. There was just enough wind to make an umbrella a waste of time. She turned up her coat collar, pulled her hat over her ears and clutched her bag to her side.

Two girls drowned forty-eight years apart who happened to look alike. Hardly a story. Still, she had sat in the archive room for another hour, printing off copies of the *News* following Elizabeth's death so she could read them later. Then she had compared Amanda's picture to Elizabeth's. It wasn't just the hair and the eyes or the smiles. There was something else about them, she thought. A look. A vulnerability. They were both school photographs, which probably explained it. Both smiling in that same, slightly forced way, both on the cusp of adulthood, self-conscious, perhaps, in their uniforms. It was probably nothing. It was *definitely* nothing. A coincidence.

The dull, comforting familiarity of the high street. Only mid-November but already decked out for Christmas, the shop windows sparkled red and gold. Stripped of clothes, the mannequins of Creasey's department store wore outfits of bright wrapping paper, finished off with huge parcel bow hats. Little gold boxes sat next to the diamonds and watches in the window of the upmarket jewellers. Poetic phrases stuck to the window reminded shoppers that true love cost real money. Next door the cut-price option offered 20 per cent off of everything and cash for gold by the ounce, so at least there was something for everyone.

She took a left on Smith Street and walked towards the public records office, or the Greffe as it was known. She wanted to check the death records. Check how many other people had drowned over the last fifty years. If there was nothing interesting in the records she would wait for the official verdict into Amanda Guille's death, get a couple of quotes from her friends and put the story to rest.

She passed the Sunken Gardens. Steps led down to a little patch of grass, a few flowerbeds, a green wooden bench. The same wooden bench where, years earlier, she'd lost her virginity to a Nirvana-obsessed, angst-ridden seventeen-year-old. They'd carved their initials on the back of it with a penknife. No doubt it had been painted over many times, but it was etched on her memory, the whole mortifying experience. The guy worked for a bank now. He was clean-shaven and wore smart suits, carried a briefcase. She knew because she saw him all the time. At the coffee shop, or in M&S, or on the way to his car after work. Ironic really, that this was where she had come to escape her past. Because that was the thing about Guernsey: your past followed you, bumped into you, waved hello. There was no running from it, no hiding. You had to smile at it pleasantly instead.

14

October 1961

*M*ill Street was a bustling part of town. The post office, located halfway up the winding, cobbled hill, brought plenty of shoppers to the grocer and chemist and the bric-a-brac shop and to Island Books, which was nestled between a picture framers and an antique dealers.

The shop front was painted royal blue. Elaborate gold lettering spelled out its name in a rainbow shape, stretching right across the window. The whole thing was an indulgence, his uncle had explained, but he had reached a point in his life where he could afford to do something he loved. A small section at the front was dedicated to bestsellers, but if people wanted paperback fiction they could go to Buttons on the High Street and get a much-wider choice at a cheaper price. Island Books was the place to come for George Métivier's Dictionnaire Franco Normand, *for Victor Hugo's* Les Travailleurs de la Mer, *and for a wealth of work and essays on Guernsey history, some never published; the only copy held in the shop and available for reference only.*

It was amongst these books and papers that he found some of the most fascinating words he'd ever read. There was one book in particular he went back to time and again, a diary written by a German soldier posted in Guernsey during the war and left behind in the rush to leave. A local German speaker had translated it. He lost himself in those words, saw the island through the eyes of one of those great invaders, who seemed to view the place as nothing less than a paradise. This unnamed soldier wrote of the fine weather, the beautiful beaches, the hidden coves, the richness of the farmland and the abundance of fruit and vegetables which grew on it. He seemed also to be something of a historian and several of his entries told of stories he'd heard from locals, legends surrounding landmarks, beaches to avoid at full moon, where to find the Devil on All Hallows' Eve.

The islanders were superstitious, he knew that. Mother used to buy little packets of powder from the woman across the street, reputed to have knowledge of healing, and bury them in the garden once a month, to help cure her 'headaches'. He was certain it was nothing more than Brown and Polson's, but Mother swore it helped. Then there were the witches. All the local children knew you shouldn't walk down Pedvin Street if you could avoid it. Too many witches lived there. If you were unlucky one might give you the evil eye and then you'd get sick or be plagued with misfortune until you paid her to reverse the spell. But those were fairy tales. Strange, that a German soldier would be interested in them. He asked his uncle about it. Uncle Peter, who, most surprisingly, considering he was related to Mother, was an almost entirely inoffensive presence, expressed surprise that he should ask such a question. Didn't he know the Nazis were fascinated with the occult? Hitler himself was said to have called on the advice of mystics during his rise to power in Germany. Some even said the Nazi party had its roots in an ancient pagan sect, that it was more of a religion than a political party.

'In that way, they probably found themselves right at home here.' Uncle Peter smiled.

'How do you mean?'

'Well, if you believe the stories, Guernsey is a better place than most to meet with the Devil. If you are interested in the island's *legends you should read this.' Uncle Peter handed him a large book, its jacket faded green leather, tooled with intricate patterns.* Guernsey Folk Lore *by Sir Edgar MacCulloch.*

'This is one of the original copies, published in 1903. I'd appreciate if you read it only in the shop.'

He nodded, placed the book on the counter, and began to read.

Le Trépied. Of all the places he'd visited since he'd started his reading, this was his favourite. He had been several times. On a clear night, he would lie on the large, flat stone, which formed the roof of the tomb and look out over Perelle Bay and towards Lihou Island. He would close his eyes and imagine the witches at Friday-night sabbats. He would try to conjure the sounds of laughter and dancing and he could almost see them, naked and beautiful and worshipping and he would reach out and fancy he could touch them, feel the lightest brush of soft skin or the gentle flick of long, loose hair as they whirled round and round, until he opened his eyes and the vision was gone.

Tonight, it was raining, so he sat inside, soaking up four thousand years of history from the chamber's walls. He touched the rough, dry stones and thought about who had placed them here; about the gods they were trying to please or the dead they were hoping to honour. There was nothing like this now, he thought. There were churches, of course, and prayers. But not like this. The people who laid these stones had asked, not for redemption, but for survival, for fair weather and good crops, freedom from plague and pestilence. And the ones who came thousands of years later, the witches and the Devil worshippers, they had understood. There was something pure and true here. He took the German soldier's diary out of his pocket. He had read it so many times his uncle had let him take it, amused that he found it so fascinating. It was fascinating. Because after the Druids and the pagans, it was the Nazis who had really appreciated this place. This one, and the dozens of others like it, spread across this tiny island. They had recognised it. Tried to harness it. This deep, elemental connection between the ancient and the new.

But they had failed. And they were all gone now.

Now there was only him.

15

Jenny

Friday, 14 November

'**S**orry I'm late. It's the weather. Traffic's a nightmare so I had to leave the car at Salarie Corner and walk and I'm soaked.' Amanda's friend, Chloe Bishop, took off her coat and sat down. She was a large, plain-faced girl with wide-set eyes and a downward turning mouth. She was wearing the uniform of the Blue Line ferry company: a navy suit and crisp white shirt. She worked on the check-in she explained, and her boss was a right bitch, she couldn't be late.

'Don't worry, this shouldn't take long. Do you want anything? Tea or coffee?' Jenny motioned to the miserable red-haired waitress who walked over and pulled a notepad from her apron pocket.

'I start work at eight, I haven't got time.' Chloe looked at her watch and Jenny ordered one coffee.

'Are you not eating?' The waitress stood, pen poised on notepad. 'Only there's a queue for tables.' She gestured around the room. The place was full. The men at the table next to them wore suits and were talking loudly, looking at a laptop, but everyone else was wearing overalls or heavy-duty work gear with sturdy, battered boots. It was hot, the heating turned up high to combat the draft from the permanently open door and the smell of grease and coffee was tinged with the paint fumes and engine oil which evaporated from the wet clothes of the builders and fisherman who filled the place. Jenny scanned the menu and ordered a bacon butty. She was rewarded with a brief but brilliant smile, a stack of paper napkins, and a ketchup bottle shaped like a tomato.

She turned to Chloe. 'I was just wondering if you could tell me a little bit about Amanda. What sort of person she was, what she liked to do, and why she might have been near the water last Saturday evening?'

Chloe rolled her eyes and told her she'd already talked to the police and she didn't know anything about it.

'Did she have a boyfriend? Someone she might have been with?'

'No. A lot of boys asked her out and that, but she was shy. Didn't think she was pretty, see? Even though everyone was always tellin' her.' Jenny detected a hint of bitterness in this last remark and looked up from her notes.

'I weren't jealous or nothin', if that's what you're thinking. Yeah, it was annoying, her getting all the attention. But I wouldn't have swapped places with her. She was sad all the time. An' I don't want you printing none of this. I'm not a gossip.'

'Of course not. I'm just trying to find out what Amanda was like. I don't have to mention your name at all if you don't want me to.' She paused. 'Did Amanda have any hobbies?'

Chloe shook her head. 'Not really.'

'How did she spend her free time?'

'Honestly,' Chloe, said, 'she'd got really boring recently. We went out most Saturday nights but Amanda didn't stay out late 'cause she sang in the church choir on Sundays. S'pose that's a hobby.'

'Which church?'

'St Andrews. She liked singing. She weren't good enough to be a professional or nothin' but she had lessons as well.'

'At the church?'

'At her house, I think. I'm going to have to go.' She made no move to leave.

'Just a couple more things. Last Saturday. You were all at the fireworks – Amanda didn't meet you?'

'No. We all met at a friend's first, to have a few drinks. Amanda was off the booze.'

'Why?' Jenny interjected.

Chloe sighed again, as if the whole conversation was painful. 'She'd been depressed. Like I said, she was sad all the time. She thought maybe the booze was making it worse. Read it in one of them leaflets from the youth club. Anyway, she was s'posed to meet us at Vale Castle later. We were planning on going into town afterwards but I wasn't surprised when she didn't turn up. That's why I didn't call her mum or nothin'. Like I said, she didn't like to stay out late on Saturdays and sometimes she'd get down and just didn't come out at all. She wouldn't have told her mum her plans neither, they didn't get on.' She looked up at Jenny. 'You know her mum called the police on her? Found cannabis in her bag. I know for a fact she was only looking after it for a mate.' She went red, perhaps worried she had said too much. 'Amanda had barely spoke to her since then anyway, so she wouldn't have worried when she didn't come home.

'We were on our way to town when I saw all of the police cars, heard people saying there was a body. I had no idea it was Amanda until her dad phoned me the next day to ask if she'd stayed with me. Said she hadn't come home. It was only then that I thought about the body. That it might be her, you know.' She bit her lower lip. There was clearly something she wanted to say. Or something she didn't want to say but felt that she should. In Jenny's experience, you just had to get them to keep talking.

'Just one more question: there were cuts on Amanda's arm. They look almost like some kind of symbol.' She pulled a sketch out of her bag and showed Chloe.

Chloe looked at it, shook her head. 'Amanda never cut herself.'

'Looks like some kind of marking. It doesn't mean anything to you?'

'Nope. No idea.'

'This must be hard for you. Have you spoken to anyone else? Thought about getting some counselling? It can really help. I could put you in touch with someone, if you're struggling.'

'I wasn't a good friend to her, was I?' The tears started flowing. 'If I'd called to ask her where she was, or checked with her mum, we might have found her before she done this. I could have stopped her.'

Jenny handed her the napkins. 'I'm sure you were the best friend you could be. It doesn't sound like she made things easy for you. And you're helping even now. Perhaps you can think of something, *anything*, which might help us to figure out how she came to be in the water last Saturday?'

'I told you, she had issues. She never thought she was good enough at school, or pretty enough, or thin enough. Her mum was always hard on her. Always pushing her to study and that. She was dead disappointed when Amanda didn't stay on to do A levels. Said the course we was doing was a drop-out course. And then I went and dropped out, didn't I? That probably didn't help. They had a row about her friends. 'Bout me, I s'pose. Then, after her mum called the police, Amanda got even worse. She was really messed-up. The last few weeks she'd been quiet. More than usual, I mean. Come to think of it, I'm not even sure she was still singing. She mentioned something about it making her feel uncomfortable. She got like that sometimes. Funny around people. I knew somethin' was up. But I did nothin' to help her. I have to go now. I need a ciggie before work.' She stood, pulling her hood up over her head and wiping her nose on her sleeve. She left without a goodbye.

The waitress placed a plate unceremoniously in front of Jenny.

'Enjoy,' she said, and then dropped the bill next to it before hurrying off to clear tables for the ever-growing queue of waiting customers at the door.

Jenny looked around. She was the only person eating alone. She wondered who the police would talk to if her body were found washed-up on the beach. There was her mum, obviously, and Sarah, her oldest friend. But she had made no real effort to get back in touch with the rest of them. After what happened, they'd hardly been friends by the time they'd all left for university anyway. At best they'd tolerated her and some had stopped speaking to her altogether. Jenny had become introverted, protected herself by pulling away from people. Perhaps that's what Amanda had done. Only Jenny had always had Sarah, who had stuck by her, believed her side of the story without question, forced her to come out, to hold her head up high, to face people. Would Amanda be alive, Jenny wondered, if she'd had a friend like Sarah?

She watched the rain through the window. She hadn't planned on staying in Guernsey this long. She had a life in London. Good friends. Only the longer she was away, the slighter those connections became. How long before she was just another Guern whose time in the big city was no more than a rite of passage, just a small step taken on a well-worn pathway that seemed to lead them all back here. Water spilled from the gutters above, falling down on to the panes in thousands of tiny rivers. People hurried by with bright umbrellas, cars drove past, engines humming, tyres spraying water in their wake, the shapes and colours rippling through the wet glass, edges blurred.

She might have sat there all day, but her phone buzzed, reminding her she had a meeting with Elliot to go over the Save the Islander demonstration taking place the next day, which Brian was now insisting she cover as he'd decided the Amanda story 'had no legs'. Which was odd, she thought. Teen suicide would normally be right up his street.

16

June 1966

*T*he light. He lay in bed looking at the beams of spring sunshine penetrating the gaps in the thin curtains and coming to rest on his bedroom ceiling and thought: the light is different today. Brighter. Whiter. Purer. As he washed, the smell of the coal tar caused his eyes to water, his nostrils to flare and his airways to open so that the next breath he took was deep and primordial, filling his lungs as if for the very first time. As he slipped his shirt over his taut, muscular body, the sweep of the starched cotton against his nakedness sent a thousand tiny bolts of electricity through him, each one like the touch of the finest needle on his skin.

Small things. They would have been imperceptible to most. But they were signs.

He should have been prepared, then, for when he got there. The concrete-edged bathing pools, with their elaborate diving boards, were all too familiar to him. As a child he had come here for swimming lessons with the school, earning red and white ribbons for conquering widths and lengths. As young teenagers, groups of boys gathered at the diving boards and performed for the girls who sat sunning themselves below. He would sit and watch, fascinated at these displays, but never partaking in them himself. As time passed, as those children who had taunted him moved on, lost track – too busy, knee-deep in cow shit or fucking their girlfriends to keep tabs on their favourite Jerry-baby – he realised it served no good purpose to be thought of as a loner.

He worked on his social skills. Made friends. It was so easy. All people wanted was a smile, a few questions, a compliment every now and then. Even a couple of jokes, which were more difficult to get right, he found, so he left the humour to others, making sure that he laughed at the right time and for just long enough. They came here, to the bathing pools. They played water polo. He was good at it. Everyone wanted him on their team. They had races, just for fun, but he always won. On occasion he would climb the sturdy metal diving frame, to the highest board. He would take only moments to gather himself, to raise his arms skywards, before plummeting, sagittal, into the water, emerging to the sounds of applause. They should be good memories. To him, though, they were banal. Pedestrian. Mundane. And so were the pools.

Until today.

And it all started with the light. Exquisite, pure and pale, for the sun had not yet fully risen. It shone over the castle and on to a silver sea, each wave and ripple illuminated, crushed glass scattered on a mantle of blue.

The pools were in shadow, the water calm and blue-black. And there she was, at the edge of the ladies' pool, a soft, pale interruption on the hard black rock. He faltered at first, as if afraid that his approach might wake her, though he knew, of course, that the dead could not be disturbed. Still, he trod carefully, alert to his surroundings, listening to the sea and the gulls and the protesting whine of an overburdened engine as, out of sight, a lone car struggled up the Val de Terres. He looked around. Satisfied that it was too early for passers-by and willing to take the risk that it was not, he knelt at her side.

Her eyes were blackened with kohl and mascara; black tears spilled across pale cheeks. Her lips, blue beneath the red of her lipstick, were smeared and bruise-like. Her nails were neat and crimson. And everything else was white. Death had drained her of colour. Her hair and skin and underwear were white, white, white against the dark wet stone. It almost hurt to look at her. He wanted nothing more than to envelop her, to place his body over hers, to absorb her strength and beauty. Instead, he calmed himself. He gripped his knees with his hands and pressed his lips together, so as not to spoil her, not even with his own breath.

Outside calm, inside turmoil. What does it mean? His eyes moved rapidly. Her hair. Her face. Her breasts. Her hips. Her thighs. Her knees. Her ankles. Her toes. What does it mean? He looked over and over her silent, motionless form for what felt like hours until his eyes were aching and dry and then, all at once, he realised. It was what he had been waiting for.

She was a sign.

She was his purpose.

He closed his eyes, breathing deeply as he did so, opening his mind and his heart and his soul to her. When he opened them again, he saw her as if for the first time. He took in every part of her again, this time appreciating what was before them. Her hair. Her face. Her breasts. Her hips. Her thighs. Her knees. Her ankles. Her toes. When he'd had his fill of looking, he placed his face next to hers and breathed in her scent: sea salt and cheap perfume, and behind that, the yeasty sweetness of a fallen fruit. Already it was getting warm. The flies, which had scattered in his presence, returned, lulled by his prolonged stillness. They landed on her face, attracted by the moisture present in her eyes and nose and lips. A few of them tried their luck on him, lured by his warmth, confused by his proximity to their intended destination. He batted them away. Time to move. One last, deep, breath as he got to his feet. One last chance to remember.

It seemed as if the sun rose as he did, pouring over him and drenching her damp white body in warmth and light, splashing her hair and eyes and skin with colour, an artist with a palette of yellow and gold. The warmth added to the feeling of well-being and strength he had imbibed from her and he stretched, flexing his arms and his legs. He rubbed his knees, sore from resting on the hard ground and brushed off his jacket and trousers. They were coming. He had business to attend to. He tried to disguise the spring in his step as he walked away from her.

At the end of a predictably busy day, he drove to Moulin Huet. He hoped to be alone but the lengthening hours of daylight ensured this was not the case. An elderly couple gave a friendly 'good evening' as they walked past. Their bright-eyed border collie sniffed at his ankles and gave a low growl. Dogs usually liked him. He wondered if it could smell death on his shoes.

He sat on his rock. Sat and watched the setting sun. The very same sun that had risen that morning, that had brushed the earth with the lightest golden touch now lay red and bloated, too heavy for the darkening sky. He watched it bleed into the ocean, until the last of it had been consumed and he felt the warmth of the day, settling into his bones, strengthening his body and mind. He had spent years wondering, searching inside himself, trying to find a way to fulfil this aching desire to do something, anything, to make a difference. He closed his eyes. Smiled. Finally, he had a plan.

17

Jenny

Friday, 14 November

The rain eased off around lunchtime but there was a cold wind. The perfect opportunity to test out her theory that the bathing pools would be more sheltered than the open sea. She walked through town and on to the seafront. A few boats swayed and creaked in the Albert marina. Small yachts and catamarans, fishing boats, mostly local, the odd French flag. Not many tourists made the trip across the Channel at this time of year. Further out there were a few floating gin palaces, Sunseekers, Fairlines and the like, which tended to be the tax exiles' vessels of choice. Boats with big engines, whose owners preferred to lounge around on the deck while sipping cocktails and wouldn't know what a jib or a mainsail looked like, let alone what to do with them. It seemed strange, to move over here, to this backwater, to go to all that effort to save money and then to blow it on an overpriced boat which only got taken out a couple of times a year. Probably small change to them. And it meant they could join the Yacht Club, which was the only place for a snob worth their salt to be seen over here.

She carried on out of town, past the bus terminus and Castle Cornet, to the bottom of the Val de Terres, a steep, winding road leading up to Fort George. Here, she turned left, following the seafront to the bathing pools.

There were three pools, one each for ladies, gentlemen and children, plus a small, shallow, horseshoe-shaped pool used for paddling or as a warm-up spot before committing to the deeper, colder water further out. The pools were man-made, huge concrete troughs edged with the ever-present granite the island provided, but at the same time they were part of the sea; it was both within and without them, filling them and draining them as the tide ebbed and flowed. Jenny had never swum here. She knew they were once popular. She had seen black-and-white photographs of school children in their old-fashioned bathing costumes, lined up at the edge, eagerly awaiting swimming galas, but nowadays, when it was no longer frowned upon to be seen in a swimsuit on a public beach, there seemed little use for the place. It was archaic, a relic of a bygone age, a quieter, more genteel time. It was beautiful.

Several cars were parked on the road alongside the pools, facing out to sea, pensioners inside, sipping tea from Styrofoam cups, taking in the view. Across the inky water, under low-lying cloud, Castle Cornet was grey and foreboding, looking more like the fortification it once was than the quaint museum it had become. Behind them, the cliffs rose sharply, ochre rocks, slick with rain, jutting out from beneath dense foliage, providing a natural shield from the wind.

Three women in bright green swimming caps were doing lengths in the ladies' pool. Jenny changed quickly and stood at the side of the pool, but only for a moment. You couldn't give yourself time to consider the cold, had to train yourself to think only of what needed to be done to get into the water. Keep moving forward, never hesitate. Waves broke against the pool walls, but, within, the water was calm. She dived in. Ice-cold, painful at first, then numbing. Her limbs shocked and frozen, it took every effort to move them. Slowly, she found a rhythm. It was easier to swim here than in the open sea, the calm water less demanding. It was easier to think too. About dead girls. Elizabeth, lying on the pool's concrete edge. Amanda, on a bed of stones. And Madalina. Where was she? Epping Forest, most likely. In a shallow grave.

Jenny put her face into the water. Closed her eyes. Swam in the dark, remembering.

London, two years ago. An unpleasantly hot summer, untempered heat absorbed by roads and pavements and then thrown back up in hazy, iridescent waves floating above the sticky Tarmac. No breeze. No whisper of sea spray in the air to cool hot cheeks with its fresh, salty touch.

The net curtains blew pathetically in the tiny breeze created by the clip-on fan she had attached to her desk. She pushed them aside in the vain hope of encouraging fresh air into her stale room. A van was parked outside, a red pick-up, driver's-side door wide open, Radio 5 Live blasting out from inside. Two men sat next to it, on top of a pile of bricks, shirts off, handkerchiefs tied around their heads, sipping coke from a two-litre bottle and arguing in lilting Caribbean accents about whether or not Arsenal had over-paid for their newest striker. Somewhere in the distance a police siren wailed.

A bluebottle flew through the open window and started rhyth-mically throwing itself against the pane of glass. She couldn't kill it. She couldn't open the window wider to let it out either. Large bolts on either side of the frame prevented it from opening any more than a crack. The fly buzzed and throbbed around her. Sweat pricked her top lip. She had to get out. She should go to the library, although she was unlikely to make it past Venetia's coffee shop. She put her laptop in her messenger bag (finally, a useful Christmas present from her mum) and left the house.

Across the street, a slim, dark-haired woman stood in front of the neighbour's door, fiddling with some keys. There were small holes in the hem at the bottom of her T-shirt and her jeans were skin-tight and faded to almost white. There was something nervous about her movements. There had been a spate of break-ins over the last few weeks, some in broad daylight and although this slight lady seemed an unlikely burglar, you could never be too sure.

'Are you OK there?'

The woman turned. Her skin was the colour of skimmed milk and had the same thin, transparent quality. She had bruise-like marks under each of her green eyes, a sharp nose and her lips, pressed tightly together, were two hard, pale lines of pink. For a moment Jenny thought she was going to ignore her, but the woman looked down at the keys and then at the door and seemed to decide she needed help after all.

'I cannot open the door.' Thick, hard accent.

'Are you a friend of the family?' Jenny took the keys from her. One of them looked particularly shiny and had dimples imprinted on the blade. She tried it in the deadbolt and heard a satisfying click as the cylinder turned. Her question unanswered, she held on to the keys. The woman pointed to a grubby tote bag on the step next to her, packed full with rags and sprays, polish and a feather duster.

'I am the cleaner.' She held her hand out. Jenny's face flushed as she handed the keys over. The woman disappeared into the house, closing the door behind her.

Two hours later, Jenny returned home in time to see the woman leave. She was struggling to fit an overstuffed black sack into the dustbin at the front of the house. She was sweating, a thin film of moisture clinging to her pallid face, dark patches under her arms. Jenny held the dustbin while the woman pushed the sack into it before jamming the lid back on and wafting the sickly sweet smell of decay into their faces.

'Thank you.' She nodded and picked up her bag. Her slim wrists were bruised on the inside. She saw Jenny looking but said nothing.

'Where are you from?' Jenny asked.

'Romania.'

'I'm Jenny.' She held out her hand. 'I live opposite.'

The woman nodded again. 'Madalina.' she said. She left Jenny's hand unshaken and walked towards the Chatsworth Road.

A week after their first meeting, Jenny decided to go for a walk in Victoria Park, catching Madalina on the way out. Jenny smiled and gave a small wave to her and received that same curt nod in return. The week after, she helped her with the bins again. Madalina had a deep purple bruise on the side of her face.

'What happened to your face?'

'I fall over.'

'Really?'

'What is you want?'

'Nothing. You look like you might need some help. There are places you can go. If you need help, I mean. I can get you a number.'

Madalina was hostile. 'You always here. Don't you have job?'

'I work from home, mostly.'

'Doing what?'

'I'm a journalist.'

'For newspaper?' She seemed interested and Jenny was struck with the feeling that this woman had a story to tell. 'I've been thinking about doing a piece on foreign domestic workers, actually,' she said, without thinking it through. She hesitated as she tried to come up with what an article like that might cover. 'What it's like cleaning other people's houses, the things you see, the wages, the hours, living conditions. Maybe you'd be interested in being interviewed,' she handed over her card. Madalina looked at it momentarily and then back at Jenny.

'I have already a long day,' she said. 'I go home.' She dropped the card in the bin, picked up her things and left.

Jenny took a deep breath and tucked her head into the murky green water which filled her ears and washed the sting of tears from her eyes. She swam down. A layer of sand and seaweed covered the concrete floor of the pool and she sculled around so she was almost sitting on the bottom. She looked up to the surface. It was barely lighter than the deep. She stayed there too long hoping that, fully submerged, the memory and the pain would be somehow diluted, until her chest was sore and she could no longer hold the breath burning in her lungs. Seawater crept in through her nose as her body, desperate for air, tried to override her efforts to keep her airways shut, and she arrived at the surface, coughing and gasping, salt water scalding the back of her throat.

She pulled herself out of the pool, her flesh white from the cold. Her hands were stiff, the skin on her fingers heavy and swollen and she struggled to walk to the changing rooms, the towel wrapped around her shivering shoulders. She heard chattering as she dried and the three women from the pool entered. They were all in their seventies, perhaps older. One approached Jenny, pulling off her swimming cap to reveal long, white hair knotted on top of her head.

'You're new,' she commented, drying herself off. 'Don't see many young people here these days.' She stripped off her costume and began dressing. She saw Jenny avert her eyes and laughed. 'No shame at my age, dear! I've been swimming and changing here for fifty years, I'm not about to get shy now.'

'No, of course not,' Jenny laughed. 'Do you meet here regularly?'

'Every day. Either first thing in the morning or lunchtime. There are less of us each year, unfortunately, one of the downsides of the average member's age being somewhere around seventy-five.' She chuckled. 'You should have a look at our website. The Guernsey Outdoor Swimming Club. We have a few young-sters turning up in the summer. Just us oldies at this time of year, though. And you, of course.' She unknotted her hair. It was thick and wiry and fell almost to her waist. She brushed and plaited it expertly, twisted it into a bun and perched a pair of silver-rimmed glasses on to her nose.

'It was nice to meet you.' She extended her hand.

'You too. I'm Jenny.'

'I know who you are, dear. I saw your picture in the *News*. I never forget a face. I'm Sylvia.' Her handshake was firm. 'Perhaps we'll see you again then? Remember, we're here every day.'

By the time Jenny had walked back to the office, her head was freezing and she had a damp patch down the back of her shirt. If she did decide to go for another lunchtime swim, she resolved to take a leaf out of the swimming club's book and wear a swim-ming cap.

'Here's a list of the people I thought we should talk to before we cover the demonstration.' Elliot dropped a sheet of paper on her desk. 'How have you managed to get soaking wet since I saw you this morning? Is it raining?' He glanced out of the window.

'No. I went for a swim.'

'Where do you swim around here?'

'The sea. I swim every day, actually. I'm trying to, anyway.' She wondered if he'd be impressed, if he liked outdoorsy women. Probably not, she thought. She could see him with one of those clever but poised types, a young lawyer, perhaps, in a short, smart dress, with glossy hair, a briefcase in one well-manicured hand, Elliot's hand in the other. Jenny blushed. Again. She had to stop this. It was getting ridiculous. He was shaking his head at her.

'What?'

'Nothing!' He held his hands up. 'Love a November swim. I'd be out there myself but, you know,' he pointed to his foot, 'I have a verruca.'

She tried not to laugh as he walked off with an exaggerated limp.

Her phone rang. The registry team at the Greffe had printed out the records she was waiting for, a list of people who had drowned over the last fifty years. It was waiting for her to collect. It would be a relief, Jenny thought, to pick up the list, and then close the Amanda story off. She needed to concentrate on the Save the Islander story to actually produce some publishable copy before Brian noticed she'd been wasting her time chasing ghosts.

She knocked quietly as per Sarah's texted instructions. The door opened almost immediately and Sarah held her finger to her lips. They tiptoed into the kitchen and Sarah shut the door soundlessly.

'I'm pretty sure they're all asleep. I hope so. I've had a bitch of a day. Have you eaten? I've got fish fingers and potato waffles?' She held out a baking tray with, presumably, the remains of the kids' tea on it. Jenny shook her head.

'Where's Simon?'

'It's Friday. Band practice. They've got a gig next week. You should come.' She ate a handful of leftovers. 'Anyway. You look agitated. What's going on?'

'I can't come and see my friend unless something's going on?' Jenny sank into a leather sofa and picked up a cushion, badly embroidered with a lopsided bird standing outside a beach house. Needlepoint was Sarah's latest creative fad. She'd previously been obsessed with knitting, scrap-booking, quilting, and, very briefly, pottery, abandoned after only a couple sessions following a traumatic incident with a potter's wheel she refused to elaborate on.

'Nice . . . seagull?'

'Ha! I'm getting better.' Sarah beamed. 'Simon thought the last one was a dodo. Do you want a drink?'

'Coffee?'

Sarah lived in a proper house, with an open-plan kitchen and living room, a garden and rooms for all the kids plus a guest bedroom. It was bright and modern and decorated with prints of London place names spelled out in quirky fonts and Scandinavian-style etchings of deer and forests. It was nice – but so grown-up. Although, everything looked grown-up when you lived with your mum. Sarah was rummaging in the cupboards, completely at home amongst the trappings of domesticity.

'No coffee. Only tea.' She looked at the box. 'And it's decaf. Fuck it. Let's have a glass of wine.'

She brought over two tumblers filled to nearly overflowing, then picked up the baby monitor from the coffee table and pressed it to her ear for a moment.

'Snoring.' She sighed contentedly, took a swig of wine and put her feet up on the coffee table. 'Come on then. Talk to Aunty Sarah. Tell me all about it.'

Jenny rolled her eyes. 'You're not funny, you know. But you've asked, so I'll tell you. Or rather, it's easier if I show you.'

Jenny reached into her bag. She laid a picture of Amanda Guille and the one of Elizabeth Mahy she had printed from the archives next to each other. 'Here. Take a look at these. Tell me if you think I'm losing the plot.'

'What am I supposed to be looking at?'

'The way they look. Wouldn't you say they look alike?'

'Sure. They look alike. Who is this?' Sarah pointed at the picture of Elizabeth.

'Elizabeth Mahy. She drowned. Just like Amanda Guille. Only fifty years ago.'

Sarah looked at her, eyebrows raised.

'It's not just these two. There are more.'

'More what?'

'I went to the Greffe and requested a list of all the people who have drowned in the last fifty years. I thought there might be an angle for the piece on suicide I was working on. I picked up the list today. It turns out there have been plenty of bodies recovered from the sea over the last fifty years,'

'Jenny,' Sarah interrupted, 'is this healthy? I mean, dwelling on all this?'

'This is nothing to do with my dad, Sarah. It's about Amanda Guille.'

Sarah nodded, but the concerned expression remained.

'As I was saying, plenty of bodies recovered over the last fifty years. Fisherman, like my dad, a few people who shouldn't have been out on the water in the first place and hit bad weather or rocks – all reported missing and their bodies eventually found. And of course there have been suicides. Cars driven off the cliffs, people jumping off Pleinmont Point.'

'Makes sense.' Sarah nodded. 'There's a lot of water around here. I'm sure a fair few people have drowned.' She said it gently.

'How many people do you think, excluding the boating accidents and the obvious suicides?'

'I really have no idea, Jenny. Twenty?'

'Eight. All originally suspected suicides, but all recorded as open verdicts by the Magistrates' Court. Which essentially means nobody really knows what happened. It's the verdict Amanda's death is likely to get too.

'Two were men, middle-aged. I made a few of calls, found out about their backgrounds. One was recently divorced and his wife was threatening to take his kids away, one had a history of mental health problems. The suicide rate is highest amongst men aged forty-five to fifty-nine, that's true for the mainland and Guernsey. Nearly three times higher than it is for women in that age bracket.

In fact, statistically, the least-likely demographic to take their own lives are women aged ten to twenty-nine. Surprising, then, that the other six unexplained drownings, presumed suicides, were all women. Young women. So I went back to the archives, found the *News* reports on their deaths and printed out their pictures. Then I sat at my desk and stared at them for a couple of hours and, when I couldn't stare at them any more, I came here.'

Sarah sat forward.

'Here they are.' Jenny laid the pictures out in a row, starting with Elizabeth Mahy, ending with Amanda Guille. She pointed at each one in turn.

'Elizabeth Mahy, sixteen years old, drowned, 1966. Mary Brehaut, eighteen years old, drowned, 1974. Janet Gaudion, aged eighteen, drowned 1985. Melissa Marchant, aged twenty, drowned 1994, Hayley Bougourd, eighteen years old, drowned, 2002. And Amanda Guille. Eighteen. Drowned. Six days ago.'

The girls stared up at them from the blurred photographs. Fair hair, blue eyes, wide smiles. All young. All attractive. All dead.

Sarah looked at them but said nothing.

'Well?'

Sarah cleared her throat. 'Does seem like a lot of dead girls.'

'It is a lot of dead girls. And it's a very small island.'

18

Michael

Something didn't sit right. Come to think of it, *he* wasn't sitting right. He rubbed the back of his neck and arched his back. His chair had been 'ergonomically designed' according to a faded label stuck on the back of the headrest, but judging by its worn and torn exterior that was at some point in the early nineties. He should request a new one, although he'd probably need some medical reason to justify it. The chair wasn't even the worst thing about his office. That prize went to the desk, a highly polished monstrosity with mean black metal legs, one of which he constantly caught his hip on as he left the room. There was no money any more. Not for a new chair or desk. Not even for a decent police investigation.

Bloody budget cuts. With all the wealth flowing around this island he should be sitting in a twenty-first century police station right now. The island's schools should be head and shoulders above the mainland schools. Their hospital should be state of the art. But someone, somewhere, had monumentally fucked up and the only people benefitting from all the tax-avoidance millions the island attracted seemed to be the ones working in the bloody banks. Not that he was a regressive; there were plenty of those about, moaning that the finance industry had ruined everything

111

and that they'd all been better off in the fifties when they relied on tomatoes and flowers and milk for their livelihoods instead of trust funds and captive insurance policies. That was a load of bloody rubbish, but something was going wrong somewhere. He thought momentarily and not for the first time, about going into politics. Surely he could do a better job than some of those numpties in the States? Only he had no desire to deal with all that pettyminded toing and froing. All the arguing over tiny issues all the time. Maybe when he finally retired and had nothing better to do.

He got up and looked out of his window. It was a much calmer day than yesterday. The eye of the storm, if he wasn't mistaken. They were predicting hurricane force winds for next week. His office overlooked St Julian's Avenue, a wide tree-lined road and one of the main routes into St Peter Port. Between the police station and the road there was an attractive green space, planted with exotic-looking ferns and spikey, red-leaved bushes. It would all be very pleasant if not for the public toilets right in the middle of them. As he knew from personal experience, they were perfectly positioned for the pissheads heading out of town on a Friday and Saturday night, many of whom made it as far as the building but then took some twisted pleasure in urinating, or worse, against the wall or over the gravel pathway. On Monday mornings the smell was enough to make you retch. Still, at least he had a window.

He picked up Amanda's file again. Drugs, alcohol, borderline eating disorder, according to her dad. It was all self-harm really. Like those cuts on her arm. He'd read plenty about it in his time, part of the training they did to help them recognise vulnerable youngsters, those at risk of abuse from others – or themselves. They'd learnt about kids who took scissors to their arms and legs, hiding scabs behind long sleeves and trousers. Awful. He shook his head. Did people used to do these things? He didn't think so, but then parents didn't used to pay so much attention to their kids. His mother, for example. She'd loved him, cared for him, but there'd been no talk about feelings. She'd always been too busy to give him more than a ruffle of the hair, a kiss on the cheek before bed, a shoo out of the kitchen and into the fields to run wild until teatime. He'd been almost entirely self-sufficient by the time he'd been thirteen. It wasn't necessarily a better way to be. Just different.

He thought of Ellen. Perhaps he'd let her down by not encouraging her to share more with him. But she had been a happy, well-balanced child. Even as a young teenager she had kept them close, confided in them. It wasn't until she'd reached fifteen that she'd started to withdraw. By the time she'd left for Exeter University he'd barely known her. It was normal, he'd thought at the time, all part of her transition to adulthood. But perhaps it wasn't. It was an accident, Devon and Cornwall police had said, after they'd found her. A tragic accident, nothing more. But then they asked him questions, which he hadn't been able to answer. Was she worried about anything, stressed? Did she have a boyfriend? Friends they could talk to? How would he know? He hadn't said that. He'd made some comment about teenage girls always being worried and stressed, that she'd mentioned a couple of people in her calls home and he'd ask his wife if she remembered the names, but that she'd only been at university a couple of months, she was settling in, finding her feet and then he'd run out of words. There were none, he realised then, that would help. They'd nodded, smiled sympathetically. Someone had given him a tissue. He hadn't even realised he'd been crying.

He felt an all-too-familiar tightness in his chest. He had to keep his stress levels in check. He tried to let his memories of Ellen leave of their own accord. If he forced them out they only came back when he was least expecting them. He focused again on Amanda.

It was suicide. Everything was pointing to suicide and

113

everybody on the case was convinced of it. Even her parents seemed to accept it. Young girl, depressed, troubled. It was the obvious conclusion to draw. It was the easiest and the cheapest one too.

He sighed and looked again at the pictures from the scene. Those cuts on her arm, three long vertical lines, a shorter, horizontal one underneath. It looked like some kind of tribal mark, the kind of thing you might paint on your face if you were the Indian in a game of cowboys and Indians. Not that you were allowed to play that any more. Too violent for today's kids – and they weren't even Indians, nowadays. Indigenous Americans or something. He sighed again. There was nothing here. Nothing to investigate. The girl took too many pills, for whatever reason, and drowned on purpose or accidently. It made little difference; the end result was the same, after all.

But something didn't sit right. He needed a fresh perspective.

Which was why he'd agreed to meet with Jennifer Dorey.

She was an interesting one – sharp as a tack. He'd read some of her articles. Well-written, well-researched. The real deal. Presumably she was back home because of her dad, Charlie. Old school, he had been. Fished all his life. Knew the waters around here like the back of his hand. And then tripped and fell off his boat, apparently. He'd raised a couple of questions about that at the time, but in the end he'd had to accept it was an accident. They lived on a bloody island, for goodness' sake; with all of the beauty and pleasure that brought, you had to accept there was a price to pay occasionally.

He passed Marquis's desk on the way out.

'Nose to the grindstone, eh, Marquis?' The young constable jumped and his pale face blushed a deep red. He made a move to close his computer screen but Michael was too quick for him.

'Jennifer Dorey, eh? Well there's a coincidence. What are you emailing her about then?' By now Marquis was an angry puce colour.

'It's just, well, she's my second cousin, sir, and she was asking me about the case, Amanda Guille's case, that is, and – and I haven't said anything, sir. I was going to check with you first.'

'Of course you were, Marquis. I'm actually on my way to see her right now, but feel free to send her an update from your point of view. Stick to the guidelines, obviously, don't go giving away all of our secrets, now will you?'

She probably knows more than you do anyway, he thought. He didn't say it though. No point disheartening the troops.

He'd arranged to meet Jenny at Bordeaux, and arrived with fifteen minutes to spare. Which was perfect, because he wanted to check a couple of things before he spoke to her. He parked up and walked down to the shoreline, which was swathed in slick brown ribbons of vraic, the islanders' name for the local seaweed. It covered the wet, leaden sand in thick banks, lighter-coloured branches reaching up out of the piles, like emaciated arms searching for daylight. In the summer, the smell was overpowering, rotting and stale, and the flies were legion. Now, in November, the smell was bearable, almost pleasant, a sea-earth hybrid of salt and vegetation with only the odd sleepy bluebottle taking a break from the tip down the road to hover around a dead fish, scales shimmering between the seaweeds' fronds.

Michael stood on a patch of wet-cement-like sand, which suckered around his boots, its glassy surface littered with curling sandworm trails. He surveyed the boats being tossed about in the swell. White cabins, bright hulls, red or blue. Never green – at least not dark green, not if you had any sense anyway. Green was unlucky, the colour of the land, not the sea. Superstitious lot, fishermen. Michael remembered a fishing trip with a mate, a part-time fisherman (the rest of the time he worked in insurance, only way to pay the bills). They'd been out half an hour and Michael had thought he'd heard a bell. *A bell?* His mate had gone deathly pale. He hadn't heard any bell, he'd said. Probably nothing, Michael had said, probably tinnitus, I'm getting old. But his mate had turned back. A bell, he'd muttered, means death at sea. Sheila had been in a right mood that night. Michael had promised her fresh sea bass for tea.

The Blue Line Express ferry to the mainland was just visible in the distance. He wouldn't like to be out there on that. Give him thirty minutes being bashed about on a plane over three hours on the vomit-comet any day. Jethou and Herm were shadowy hills on the horizon, Sark invisible, hidden by an ubiquitous, low-lying sea fog. He stood there until the flood stream lapped at his feet, reminding him he had a job to do.

He paced up and down the beach, from the spot where Amanda's body was found down to the shore and back again, scattering nervous sandpipers as he went, and then over to where several small fishing boats were moored, tied to rings bolted into rocks. He tugged on a rope, seeing if he could pull one in singlehanded. It was cold and oily to the touch, the fibres rough and uncomfortable in his grip. The boat, *Little Boy Blue*, came towards him, slowly, but it was hard work. Surely too heavy for a slender eighteen year old? He stood for several minutes, contemplating, and then shook his head and walked back to the car, leaving the sand churned over with his footprints.

19

Jenny

Most of the beaches on the island had a kiosk; a small building with a large, open window in the front from where you could buy an ice cream or a cup of tea, a fishing net, a first-aid kit, a bucket and spade. Some of the larger ones at the busier beaches were proper cafes you could walk into and sit down, order a crab sandwich and a glass of rosé from a laminated menu. The one at Bordeaux was just a stone hut with a couple of wooden benches outside, the chalked writing on the board outside faded, the toilets at the back padlocked for the season.

DCI Gilbert was sitting on a bench, his hands wrapped around a paper cup, steam billowing up into his face as he blew on it. He rose to his feet when he saw her.

'How are you, Jenny?' He shook her hand, firmly.

'Well, thank you, DCI Gilbert.'

'Michael. Please. Let me get you a drink. And a bit of cake, maybe?'

He fetched another coffee and two slices of buttered gâche, a rich, sweet bread made with dried fruit and candied peel. His hands were no steadier than the first time they'd met and crumbs sprinkled over his chin as he bit into the thick slice.

'So, I hear you've been doing some research, Jenny. For a piece you're working on, eh?'

'Yes.'

'Found anything interesting?'

'Just the usual. Mostly gossip, I'm sure. We're concentrating on the suicide angle, really. Tying it in with mental health provision on the island. That sort of thing.'

'Hmm.' He sipped his coffee. 'One of my favourite spots, this. At least it was. Can't really say that now, eh? Used to bring my daughter here when she was little. We'd look for those little pieces of sea glass, all smooth from knocking around in the sea. She called them jewels. Thought they were going to make her rich.'

'How old is she?'

'She died.'

'I'm so sorry.'

He shrugged. 'Wasn't your fault.' He took a picture from his wallet and handed it to Jenny. A short-haired, elfin-looking girl standing on the beach next to a tall, red-haired woman, arms around each other, thumbs up at the camera.

'That was just before she left for university, a few months before she died.'

'She was beautiful. And this is your wife?'

'It was. Sheila. Divorced for, goodness, must be thirteen years now. She remarried and moved to Jersey. Left me for a *crapaud*, as if things weren't bad enough!' He used the derogatory term, meaning toad, which Guernsey people often used when referring to their neighbours in Jersey, but there was no bitterness in his laugh. 'So, there you go. Nice, sad story for you, eh? Surprised you don't know it already, all the questions you've been asking. I suppose you have some for me too?' He tucked the photo back into his wallet and looked at her.

Perhaps she shouldn't have written him off on first impressions. Dead girls probably weren't his favourite subject.

She asked him about the investigation, whether or not Amanda's family was satisfied with the results of the post-mortem and where was the police inquiry going now? He answered as she expected: official sound bites, no suspicious circumstances he said, the case would no doubt be closed very soon. He repeated nearly verbatim the official statement they had printed a few days ago. She wasn't going to get anything here. Not without showing him what she'd been up to and she wasn't sure she wanted to do that. Not yet. Not until she had something concrete, something more than a few dead girls who looked alike. He was still talking, about the tide.

'That was the only thing that raised a bit of a flag with me.'

'I'm sorry?'

'Well, as I'm sure you noticed, Jenny, it was low tide when Amanda's body was discovered, yet she was at least halfway up the beach.'

'Is this something that's being investigated?'

'No, it's not. General opinion is she could have been dead for anything up to a few hours before she was found. So her body could have been washed up and discovered a couple of hours later, after the tide had receded. Certainly can't find anyone that walked past there in the hours immediately before she was found and, even if we did, it was dark, the body would have been near the water and it's likely it wouldn't have been seen. It's perfectly possible the body had been there for a couple of hours.'

'But she was soaking wet. Saturated.'

'She was.'

'Why are you telling me this?'

'Well, I'm not. Not officially. Just, like I said, it's been playing on my mind. You seem the curious type. Thought you might be interested.' She hadn't been expecting this. That he might want to work with her. It seemed too sophisticated a technique somehow, for the Guernsey police. It happened all the time on the mainland. The police tipped the press, the press tipped the police, journalists met coppers in bars and coffee shops. But here? She adjusted her opinion of DCI Gilbert for the second time that afternoon.

'How do you see this working, exactly?'

'All I'm saying, Jenny, is this investigation is going to be over. Soon. Dead bodies on the beach are bad for the island. We're under a hell of a lot of pressure from the States to close the case. As far as most people are concerned, it's a straightforward drowning. Amanda had been in trouble a few times over the last couple of years, as you know, and she'd had some issues with depression. I don't have the resources to pursue this any further. Not with what I have. Which is three parts speculation to one part gut instinct. And, between you and me, my instincts are often met with irritation. I'm considered something of a pedant.' He seemed untroubled by this, and took another sip of his coffee.

'So, what happens now?'

'What happen now with the case is: the Magistrates' Court will conduct an inquest, which will most likely return a misadventure verdict, maybe even an open verdict. They won't call it suicide without a note. That will be that.' He paused. 'However, seems to me you're rather intent on sticking your nose in. Thought we might be able to make some use of each other.' He gave her a smile, as if he knew that he'd thrown her. A permanent furrow in his brow meant that, even smiling, he seemed to be wearing half a frown. Deep lines radiated from the corners of his eyes. This was a tired man, someone who should have given up years ago by the sounds of things, and yet here he was, encouraging her to look into something the rest of the force had written off, sharing his suspicions with her, inviting her to get involved. There was nothing else for it. She reached down into her bag and pulled out her file on the dead girls and handed it to him. He raised an eyebrow.

'My research.'

He opened the file and slowly turned the pages.

She left him sitting there reading and walked to the grassy verge at the edge of the beach. She sat and finished her coffee. Waves broke gently on the shoreline and a flock of seagulls wheeled around a fishing boat returning with its catch. Rats with wings, Charlie always called them, on account of the fact that they rifled through rubbish bags, or stood, watching, beady-eyed, as you sat on the sea wall eating your fish and chips. They were bold enough to swoop down and grab at your food, cawing in delight as they carried off a fat, greasy chip in their clutching claws. She'd always thought she hated them, but it was one of the things she had missed in London; the sight of a gull launching itself off the sea wall, its ugly, heavy body transformed in flight to a pair of simple, linear curves, elegant brushstrokes on the horizon, its strange, discordant cries filling the air.

She walked slowly back up the beach, to the spot where Amanda had been found. She stared at the bed of stones and imagined she could see an imprint, like the hollow left in a soft mattress after a long sleep. Stupid. These weren't even the same stones Amanda had lain on. The tide would have dragged those out to sea, washed them clean, replaced them with new ones. She heard pebbles clattering as Michael made his way over to her. His face was pale, his expression determined, and there was something else there too, stress perhaps, or worry.

'I'll be needing a copy.' He handed the file back to her. 'Probably best to keep this between us for now. If you've really found a connection between these cases . . .' His voice trailed off and he shook his head. 'I don't even know what to say. I'll be in touch.' Jenny watched him walk back to his car, and it struck her then. He hadn't look worried. He'd looked terrified.

The demonstration was in full swing. Which was not saying much. Forty or so people gathered outside Sports Direct at the old market, some with placards with the Save The Islander logo emblazoned across it, a smiling donkey, teeth bared, kicking up his back hooves. Guernsey people were known as donkeys, because of their stubborn nature. Presumably Deputy Tostevin was hoping to harness some of that stubbornness during this campaign. Elliot was in his element, interviewing an elderly man who was leaning heavily on his walking stick (hip replacement, he'd winked at her as he'd said it, she was trying to work out the intended implication). His name was Clive, ex-army, he'd told them proudly, been all over the world, seen it all; absolutely, positively, *not* a racist he'd said. In fact, he very much liked to visit multi-cultural places, but it just wasn't right for Guernsey. Not at all, he said. And you can quote me on that. Jenny was finding it hard to concentrate, leaving most of the questioning to Elliot.

'But I think what Deputy Tostevin is proposing is not a curb on immigration as such, just a change in the laws surrounding Right to Work documentation. Making it more difficult for non-locals to find work here?' Elliot obviously sensed he was on to a winner with Clive and was going to get some gold star quotes. Jenny was impressed with the way he worked. People liked Elliot, they opened up to him.

'Well, that's how we'll get rid of them, isn't it? If they can't work here they'll go somewhere else, somewhere more suited to, you know, different religions and such?'

Elliot thanked him so much for his time and watched him as he disappeared into the rapidly dwindling crowd.

'It's a fucking mess, isn't it?' Elliot had turned to her.

'What?'

'This whole thing. I wanted to do a proper piece on it, you know. All the shit Tostevin's been spouting against the facts and figures. Brian wouldn't let me. Said *this* is the story.' He gestured to the people milling about in front of them. 'Said it was about how people *feel,* not whether or not there was any truth in it.'

'Is that what you were arguing about?'

'That and the five or six other stories he's blocked because they don't seem to fit in with his world view. Which is reactionary, by the way.'

She nodded, checked her phone for messages.

'What's the matter with you? I know you wanted this story. Thought you'd be trying to wrestle it off me, what with the Amanda Guille thing fizzling out.'

'It hasn't fizzled out. I'm still working on it.'

'Oh?'

She contemplated sharing what she'd discovered with him. Telling him about her meeting with DCI Gilbert. He might be useful. He was a good reporter for a start. And she liked him. He was looking at her expectantly, one eyebrow raised. She should trust him. She should let him in.

'Just tying up some loose ends. Look, there's Tosser-tevin.' She pointed to the deputy who was talking to another elderly man, this one waving a leaflet in his face.

Deputy Tostevin was slick. Not in manners, although he did have a way about him, an easy charm, which could be described as smooth, but in appearance. His tanned skin, wrinkled and leathery, glistened, and his thick white hair, long enough to tickle his collar at the back and combed forward over a high forehead, was sticky, unmoving in the sharp blusters which blew through the square. He smelled faintly of almonds and Jenny wondered if he used some kind of nut-based oil on his face or his hair or both. When he smiled, as he did now, his wide, pale mouth stretched from ear to ear.

Not a disappointing turnout at all, he replied to Elliot's question about attendance. In fact, he said, this was very encouraging considering it was the first one and had been organised at relatively short notice. A December rally was being planned already, he said; they should be sure to be there then, when people would no doubt come out in their hundreds.

'More rallies?' Elliot asked. 'What are you hoping to achieve with them? Surely the best way to get what you want is through debate in the States?'

'It's an issue people feel strongly about. Protecting our jobs, our housing, our unique cultural identity. If the States appreciate how strongly islanders feel about it, we're more likely to achieve our aims.'

Elliot continued to question the deputy about his policies, his views on the housing and job markets. All threatened by lax laws and misguided do-gooders, apparently. Jenny scribbled some notes. Elliot wrapped up the interview. Deputy Tostevin turned to Jenny.

'Terrible business, finding that poor girl on the beach.'

She nodded.

'We should count ourselves lucky, you know. Things like that happen so rarely here. And I truly believe it's because of our community.'

'In what sense?' Jenny asked.

'In the sense that, until very recently, everyone knew each other. I don't mean literally. Obviously, one can't be on first-name terms with sixty thousand people.' He laughed. 'What I mean is, everyone was *familiar* with each other. And that's what kept us safe for so long. Our connection to one another, through friends and family and – I know you young people struggle with this – but through our shared culture, too. Shared values. When we lose sight of those things, Jenny, cracks start to appear on the surface. Job losses, depression, petty crime and then . . .' He raised his hands, shrugged his shoulders, 'well, who knows? I don't want to find out. That's why I'm doing this. I want to protect what we have. Because it's so precious. Don't you agree?' He didn't wait for a response, just smiled and nodded, went to talk to some of the straggling protesters.

'What do you think?' Elliot asked.

'I think he's terrifying.'

'You want to write this up? Or too busy tying up your loose ends?'

She handed him the notes. 'Do you mind?'

'No problem. But if you want me to keep covering for you with Brian, you might have to let me in on whatever it is I'm covering you for.' He looked at her with the faintest hint of a smile, but she sensed he was serious.

'Give me until the end of next week. If there's anything to tell you by then, I will. OK?'

'OK. It's a deal.' He held out his hand. She took it. His grip was firm, the palm of his hand warm and dry and she wondered, just for a second, what it would feel like on her cheek.

20

Jenny

Monday, 17 November

She heard the church of Saint-André-de-la-Pommeraye before she saw it – a bleak, slow clanging of the bells, a funeral toll. A fitting day for one – a grey Monday, mid-morning already, and the sun yet to appear, obscured by swathes of pale yellow cloud, which wrapped the sky like bandages. She rounded the corner and drove down into the lush valley at the heart of St Andrews parish. The road was narrow and steep, lined with tall beech trees, stripped almost naked of their leaves by the previous weeks' high winds. It was green here though, the hedgerows and the gardens watered by tributaries, which flowed down grassy slopes from the Talbot Valley to the west of the parish.

In the car park, two older ladies, both dressed in smart, buttoned-up coats, stood chatting quietly, one murmuring that it was a lovely service, the other nodding in agreement, adding that it was a shame you miss your own really. They smiled at Jenny as she walked past them on to the gravel path which led to the front of the church.

The doors were open, and the vicar, a large, soft-featured man, was gathering up stray service sheets from the back row.

He looked up at the sound of her footsteps and smiled gently. 'I'm afraid you've missed the service.' He had a deep,

126

commanding voice, which no doubt did an excellent job of under-pinning a poorly sung hymn. She explained she was here to see David De Putron.

'Ah, here for the choir, are you? Wonderful, wonderful, we're a little melodically challenged at the moment, we could do with some young blood!' He led her to the back of the church.

'David!' he boomed. 'Young lady here to see you.' He excused himself with another smile and left her standing in the empty church. She sat on a pew and picked up one of the service sheets. A black-and-white picture of a young man in Royal Navy uni-form, she guessed during the Second World War.

In Loving Memory of Len Le Poidevin – he loved his family and the sea.

So simple. She'd agonized for hours over what to put on Char-lie's service sheet and had eventually gone with a quote from Ebenezer Le Page which hardly anyone had recognised. She felt a sudden wave of annoyance and regret and placed the sheet back where she found it.

'Jennifer?' A soft, mellifluous voice, belonging to a distinguished-looking man. Jenny thought she could just about see the resem-blance between him and his great-great-grandfather, whose portrait she had stared at countless times while sitting, bored rigid, during school assemblies at the Ladies' College. De Putron was the name of one of the school's four houses, the teams girls were assigned to in their first year. The other three houses were named after equally prestigious Guernsey families. Jenny couldn't remember how the De Putrons had risen to island fame and fortune. Something to do with the military she thought. And then, of course, a couple of hundred years of good breeding and fine schooling on the main-land and then back to the island to lead and govern and lend their names to various roads and a park and a particularly nice manor house.

David De Putron certainly looked the part. He was elegantly

dressed in a white shirt, silver waistcoat, and navy woollen trousers. Undoubtedly handsome in his youth, he had a long, straight nose and a strong jaw, softened now by gentle folds of age-loosened skin. He was holding a bundle of sheet music, bright blue veins forming a twisted relief on the back of his pale hands. He led her through the vestry to a small room with a piano and began to put the music away in a folder.

'I know them all off by heart, of course, but you never know when somebody else will need them. I believe you wanted to talk about Amanda?' He frowned. 'Terrible business, but I'm not sure I should be talking to you. Do the family know you're writing about her?' There was something of the theatre about him, she thought, his eyebrows raised questioningly, his expression exaggerated, words enunciated as if he was projecting to the gods, not wanting any of the cheap tickets to miss out on the performance.

She skirted around the issue. She just wanted to find out what kind of person Amanda was; she was really writing about mental health, depression, the effects of drugs and alcohol, the dangers of the sea. Did Amanda strike him as the type who might have risked her life in this way, taken her own even?

David De Putron looked perplexed. 'Well that's exactly what happened, isn't it? She was a lovely girl, really quite beautiful, and she had a very nice voice. Such a shame . . . Her poor parents.'

'Do you have a lot of younger choir members?'

'A few. Mostly our members are older, very few men unfortunately, but we have three young ladies. Well, two now, I'm sorry to say.'

'So was Amanda a regular churchgoer, before she joined the choir?'

'Well, no, she wasn't, actually. I have to confess, I rather browbeat her into joining. I was teaching her piano, through a youth programme I volunteer at, and she mentioned she wanted to sing. I offered to give her lessons if she joined the choir.'

'So you knew her well, then?'

'Only as well as a teacher knows a pupil. She was serious about her singing, came to choir regularly, always practised before her lessons. She had a pretty voice, talked about songwriting.' He sighed. 'It seems everyone wants to be a pop star these days. So little enthusiasm for classical music.' He spread his hands, a gesture of helplessness. 'I really don't know what else to tell you.'

'Amanda's friend mentioned she'd stopped taking singing lessons in the weeks before she died. Did anything happen that might have upset her do you think?'

He didn't answer immediately, looking pensive for a moment instead.

'I rather got the impression she had some problems. Not that I had any issues with her, I'm not saying that, not at all, but she seemed like a bit of a lost soul to me. Confused about life. Just my impression, you understand. Nothing concrete to go on as such.' He paused. 'When might the article be published?'

'I'm not sure. I have some more research to do. The police can't say for sure if it was a suicide or an accident so I'm looking into both angles, similar incidents, other deaths by drowning.'

'Oh. I see.'

She gathered her things and stepped towards him. He was a tall man and she had to look up to meet his eye. His face was pale and, close up, deeply lined. He was old enough, she thought, to remember.

'I've looked back to the sixties, actually. 1966. A girl drowned at the bathing pools. You would have been very young then, I'm sure.' She smiled.

Did he flinch? She thought he did. The tiniest jerk of his head, a flicker of the eye. He recovered, quickly, looked thoughtful, wrinkled his brow. He did remember it, he said. Vague details. It was just before he left the island to study.

'Music?'

'Law. Family tradition. But I must be a bit of a black sheep. I didn't really take to it. Music's always been my thing. Music and teaching. Well . . . If that's all, Jennifer, I should be getting on.' He gave her hand a gentle squeeze, the sort that men of a certain age reserve for women and placed his other hand on the small of her back, guiding her towards the exit. He gave her a small shove over the threshold and closed the door before she could say goodbye.

The bell tower cast a long shadow on the gravel pathway. She followed it around the perimeter of the church and emerged into the graveyard. There was a neat, mounded rectangle of freshly dug earth at the end of the newest row of gravestones, furthest from the church. She walked over to it.

The earth would need to settle before a stone was erected, so for now a small wooden cross marked Len Le Poidevin's final place of rest.

He loved his family and the sea.

And now he was so far from both.

She turned to walk to the car, startled by a figure standing at the corner of the church, near the top of the path she had just walked down. It was David De Putron. He had put on a long black coat against the late afternoon chill. She could not tell if he was looking at her or over the gravestones, towards the setting sun. She raised her hand in a half-hearted wave. He did not respond. Her phone rang and she fumbled in her bag for it.

'Hi, Brian.'

'What the fuck are you doing?' He spoke slowly, quietly, but there was fury in his words.

'I'm in St Andrews. I'm on the way back to the office now.'

'I know where you are. I asked what you were doing.'

'Following a couple of leads, Brian. Finishing up on the Amanda story.'

'There *is* no Amanda story. We've discussed this. Now stop

fucking around and get some real work done. I'm losing my patience with you.' He hung up.

Jenny dropped the phone back into her bag. What the hell was his problem? And how did he know where she was? She looked back up at the church. But David De Putron was gone.

21

May 1974

Liberation day. Red, white and blue bunting criss-crossed the sea-front, triangular flags fluttering in a brisk breeze. There was a chance of showers according to the forecast but nobody had let that put them off. On the pier, beneath a white tent, men in navy sweaters were playing Crown and Anchor. They hunched over the green canvas board, placing bets and throwing the dice over and over again, shouts of triumph and groans of defeat carrying over to where he stood.

A cry of 'Worro, Len!' as a man in a British Navy uniform clapped his hand over the shoulder of an identically dressed brother-in-arms. Every year they dusted off their uniforms and strutted around like ageing peacocks, preening each other's fading feathers, showing the masses they had answered the call of duty all those years ago. A few measly years in the armed forces and then back to their farming and their fishing and their fucking, carnival clowns in meaningless, moth-eaten costumes. He smiled at them. Gave a respectful nod. Thank you for your service.

The parade was about to start, crowds moving to one side or the other along the seafront, behind the barricades. Families in their Sunday best stood eagerly awaiting the beginning of the celebrations. Some of the children ate candyfloss, the spun sugar crystallising into sticky pink threads as it made contact with their warm lips and cheeks. Some of them waved flags, smiling gaily with their Union Jack or St George's Cross on a stick, arms linked, chattering and laughing.

Look at them all. It should be uplifting, he knew that. A people bound by such a singular history, coming together to celebrate and to remember. But all he could see were little people with little lives. Giving gratitude. Giving thanks. To a dead man and his long-defunct government, who twenty-nine years ago deemed it fit to free the islands they'd so casually allowed to be occupied. Nobody seemed to remember that bit, the fact that Churchill had left them undefended in the first place. That he hadn't felt them worth fighting for. That he'd sat there, drinking his whisky, smoking his cigars and allowed the Germans to take them, their 'Dear Channel Islands'. So dear that they were the only part of British soil to feel the weight of the jackboot, year after year, to have their land plundered, their women defiled. The Occupation wasn't the Nazis' fault. Britain deserved to have her islands taken. They were jewels in the British crown, waiting to be stolen.

The brass band started marching. 'Sarnia Cherie'. Always. He hummed along, smiled with the crowd. Soon there were thousands of voices.

'Sarnia Cherie, gem of the sea,
Land of my childhood, my heart longs for thee,
My voice calls thee ever, forget thee I'll never,
Island of beauty, Sarnia Cherie!'

He joined in with the cheering and waving as the anthem reached its climax.

The parade continued in earnest. He stood on the steps along-side Boots the Chemist, where he had a good view over the rest of the crowd. The Boy Scouts marched next, followed by various ex-servicemen, and then women dressed in 1940s fashions, hair rolled back from their foreheads, lips painted red, singing, 'Bless 'em all, bless 'em all, the long and the short and the tall . . .'

It was just then that he saw her.

Mary.

A flash of bright purple. She always wore bright colours. Her hair was long, straight, white blonde. It hung like curtains so you could never see all of her face at once, just enough to know that she was beautiful and he wanted nothing more than to see her clean, truly clean and pure, stripped of her clothing and scrubbed of her make-up and glistening in the sunlight. Just thinking about it he felt that kernel of elation, that feeling of intense joy inside he had felt so precious few times before. She was laughing now. Not at him, but it seemed that way, and the feeling faded. She was talking to her boyfriend. He wore his hair in the same fashion as hers but had added a long moustache and beard. He was part of the alternative crowd, beatniks and hippies who talked about changing the system but lounged around smoking marijuana and listening to loud music. They fucked, he supposed. Everyone did. He couldn't understand how she, so pure, so delicate, could let any man possess her, let alone a lanky, greasy boy.

He closed his eyes and saw Mother. He'd not been more than nine or ten when he'd first looked through the keyhole. He'd thought she was being beaten at first, that the man, naked and on top of her, was hurting her. He'd stood there, a helpless boy, wondering what he should do. But then he had caught that look on her face. Seen her hands wrapped tightly around that thick, hairy neck, pulling the man closer and closer to her, lifting her body, pressing against his, making those noises, those ugly, animal noises which had woken him from sleep. He felt physically ill at the thought of it.

When he opened his eyes again, Mary was gone.

*

Evening approached. The family crowd dispersed, replaced by a younger, rowdier demographic. Pub-crawlers. Revellers. They would drink until they were sick, some of them. It was said alcohol affected different people in different ways. Happy drunks. Nasty drunks. Violent drunks. He didn't believe that. Nastiness and violence were always there, lurking beneath the surface. Alcohol set the truth free. He never touched it.

He was driving home when he spied her again. She was sitting on a bench at the bus stop. She looked like she'd been crying. He was ready. He'd been ready for weeks. He slowed and rolled down the window.

'Are you OK? It's Mary, isn't it?'

'Yes.' She leant forward and squinted at him. 'Oh. Hello.' She rubbed at her eyes. 'I'm fine. 'Sno problem. 'Sjust Derick. We had a fight. He can be a bit of an arsehole.' She slurred and couldn't sit up straight.

'Can I offer you a lift home? It's getting late and there won't be a bus for ages.'

'You're sweet.' She seemed to be thinking about it. Then shrugged. 'Sure. Why not?' She got into the car. She smiled and turned towards him, fixed him with those beautiful blue eyes before closing them and resting her head back. 'I don't really have anywhere to go though. I'm sort of homeless.'

He smiled back. 'I'm sure we can think of somewhere.'

It was almost too easy. Almost. She was drunk. She had nowhere to go. He took her to Portelet, a secluded bay on the south coast, surrounded by tall trees and lush vegetation. It was dark and deserted, the only light coming from the stars and the rhythmical flashing of Les Hanois lighthouse. She laughed as he led her down to the beach. She hadn't expected this, she said.

It was too cold really. There was sharp chill in the air. Summer would have been better. She faltered a little, as she took off her clothes. 'It's cold . . .' She shivered as she said it, but he could be very persuasive. He took off his jacket and shirt. 'Come on, you're not scared, are you?' he teased. 'Not scared, just fucking freezing!' She screeched a little then and he shushed her – people were sleeping, he said, they didn't want to get into trouble, did they? No, she whispered, she'd had enough trouble to last a lifetime, thank you very much.

Naked, her breasts and hips were heavier than he thought they would be and he wondered if he should feel disappointed, but he forced himself to concentrate on her slim waist and her skin. Her skin was perfect. White, like moonlight. He thought how wonderful they must look together, two beautiful people, happy and free, and how important this was, that he saved her. From the filth and the alcohol and the little people and the loathsome, repellent men, whose hands would never touch her again. She ran to the water. He followed. Their bodies clothed in darkness, their footsteps silent on the soft sand, their splashing obscured by the breaking of the waves, he pulled her towards him. Stroked her arms, from her wrists, over smooth skin, soft hairs tickling his fingers, to her elbows, which were bony and rough, and then up to her shoulders. She shook. Laughed. He pushed her under. She was smiling as her head dipped beneath the water, her hair fanning out on the surface, spun gold, like in a fairy tale, rippling and flowing, a life of its own. She didn't struggle, not at first. It took her a moment, he supposed, to understand. And then he felt her, bucking and thrashing, her screams silent, carried away with the tide. Gently, but firmly, he held on. And then she was still. So, so still. He held her limp body against his in the water. Absorbed the heat as it left her. Stayed there for as long as he could, until he was sure he had taken as much of her warmth as he possibly could. Only when his shivering became uncontrollable did he make the move towards the shore.

Out of the water, she was heavy. He knew she would be. He remembered the sheep, lugging its dead weight on to his shoulders, *throwing it into the wheelbarrow. He remembered that heaviness against the lightness of the feeling he held inside. That was nothing compared to this. He stared at her, wet and glistening, not quite able to believe that the scene he had imagined so many times before was a reality. He had to finish. If he didn't move now he might stay here for ever.*

He dressed her again. It was difficult. Her limbs were heavy and hard to manipulate and the fabric stuck to her damp skin. He tried to be gentle, as if she were sleeping and he didn't want to wake her, but by the time he was finished he was sweating. He carried her back into the sea for a good soaking. It was a shame, to weigh her down with garments but a naked body would raise suspicion. He laid her carefully back on the damp sand, treading carefully as he arranged her as naturally as he could. She looked beautiful. But there was something missing. He had thought very carefully about how he could make her death truly his. He had made preparations. His trousers were sticking where he had pulled them on to his wet skin and he had to fumble around in his pocket. First the leaves – just a few, not enough to be noticed, certainly not by the Guernsey police. He scattered them over her. Then the knife. He lifted her top, exposed her belly, flat, but soft and pliable. He marked her with the lightest of touches. It was perfect. She'd be written off. A troubled teenager. A lost soul. Nothing to live for.

22

Jenny

Tuesday, 18 November

Brian had spoken to her only briefly when she'd got back to the office last night. He'd been calm, businesslike, and suggested she talk to the news editor, pick up a few stories that needed covering. Charlie had always said that the best way to get Jenny to do something was to tell her to do the opposite. Headstrong, he'd always called her. That might be, but Brian's insistence that she abandon this story was starting to look like more than just professional incompetence. Something was very wrong. Something to do with Amanda. She couldn't escape the fact, however, that apart from a few strange cuts on Amanda's arm and the ravings of a possibly disturbed teenager, there was nothing suspicious about her death. Nothing that any sane person would listen to anyway. She needed more. To link the other girls' deaths with Amanda's, to show that, at best, all these young women had been failed somehow. And at worst? At worst was a fucking nightmare. Either way, she was going to start at the beginning. With Elizabeth Mahy and the police officer who had worked her case, fifty years ago.

Roger Wilson had come a long way since then. He had risen through the ranks of the Guernsey police from a cadet to chief officer, retired for several years now, but still a special advisor to the force. He served on several charitable boards, was a member of the Rotary Club and was a keen sailor and fisherman according to a bio Jenny had found on the website of the local lifestyle magazine, *Guernsey View*. They had photographed him standing in front of his house, which she was now desperately trying to locate.

Torteval was the smallest and most rural of Guernsey's ten parishes. The name came from the Guernsey French for 'twisting valley' and it was obvious why. She drove at a snail's pace through the narrow Ruette Tranquilles, the fifteen-mile-per-hour speed limit entirely unnecessary as it was impossible to go any faster through the single track lanes with their steep, grassy banks and hedgerows on either side. Road signs were non-existent and she had long given up trying to locate where she was on the Perry's Guide map she kept in her glove compartment for the frequent occasions the satnav failed on this bloody island. She was now following the tried-and-tested method of taking alternate left and right, right and left turns until she eventually found what she was looking for; it always happened at some point, each route leading back to a main road from where you could start again until you'd covered the whole network of lanes in any given area. It was just a matter of how long it would take to find the right one.

After fifteen minutes, tall hedges gave way to a low wall. A wooden sign attached to gateposts topped with stone eagles announced she had arrived at her destination. 'Beauregarde'. Even from the road you could see the sea as you looked past the house. A livid blue, nestled between the trees, it glistened even on this sunless November morning. She turned into the wide, gravelled driveway and parked in front of an imposing stone house.

Roger Wilson had sounded friendly when she spoke to him that morning, asking if she could stop by and get his take on the Amanda Guille case. Slightly perplexed, but friendly nonetheless. She felt nervous as she approached the front door. She was going to start with Amanda and then refer back to Elizabeth Mahy's case. Depending how that went she would decide whether or not to run the rest of it past him, try to get a couple of decent quotes about the historic cases.

The wooden door had blackened iron hinges and a heavy circular knocker made of the same material. She struggled to lift it before noticing the modern doorbell fitted into the doorframe. She pressed and a cheerful tune rang out from inside the house. She waited. Nothing. She checked the time. Eleven thirty. She'd said she would be here around twelve. Perhaps he was out. The gravel driveway narrowed to a path leading around the side of the house presumably to the back garden. The view from there would be spectacular. And anyway, the house was vast; she should try the back door.

The back lawn was untended. Clover and thistles grew amongst the grass, which rolled down a gentle slope towards open fields, which seemed to meet the sea in the distance. A small barn stood in the neighbouring field, the wide doors fastened shut with a plank of wood.

'You could skip down to Rocquaine from here, couldn't you?' Jenny startled and turned. A tall man with a shock of white hair and thick white eyebrows perched over intelligent eyes stood next to her. He held a basket of logs under one arm and extended the other towards her.

'I'm sorry, I made you jump. Roger Wilson. You must be Jenny?'

'Yes. I didn't mean to snoop around. There was no answer at the front so I was going to try the back door but I stopped to admire the view.'

'Of course. I was just getting ready for this storm the weatherman's been going on about. No central heating in the old place, so I need to get the fire stacked up. Don't want to be running out for logs in the middle of the night. Come on in and we'll have some tea. It's going to pour down any minute.'

The kitchen was warm and bright. A fire burnt in the stone hearth and the table was covered in a checked yellow-and-white oilcloth, a jug of white daisies placed in the centre. Roger Wilson pulled out a chair for Jenny and placed the kettle on the hob before excusing himself to wash and change quickly. 'Make yourself at home, I'll only be five minutes.'

She wandered over to the sideboard to study a neat row of photographs. A young couple outside the church on their wedding day: him, handsome in bell-bottom trousers, her, short and slim, long hair, elegant in a lace gown. Next, the same man, deeply tanned and muscular, one foot on the prow of a rowing boat, white sand next to an impossibly blue sea. Greece, maybe? In the next picture he was in a policeman's uniform, smart, smiling, holding some sort of certificate. Then the woman again, close up and middle-aged, sitting on a bench, looking out to sea. Guernsey this time, Vazon Bay. Finally, the man in uniform, older, the white hair shorter and neater than it had been this morning, thumbs up, next to a set of golf clubs.

A huge map of Guernsey hung on the wall next to the sideboard, with numerous points circled in pink, yellow or green, a legend at the side.

'Tea?'

She turned, walked back to the table. 'Sorry, I'm being nosey.'

He had changed into a checked shirt and chinos and smoothed his hair.

'You're a reporter, aren't you? I expect you need to be nosey to get the job done. And I'm exactly the same. Or I was, anyway. Not so much now. You get to a point where you feel like there's nothing left to learn about people. Or at least, nothing left that you want to know. Although I gather from our conversation this morning that you are not at that point just yet.'

'I'm not in the habit of commenting on active police

investigations you know, but I have to admit your call was intriguing. From what I understand Amanda Guille's death was a tragic accident, so I'm wondering what it is you want to ask me about?'

'Actually, it wasn't really Amanda I wanted to ask you about. At least, I'd be interested in your thoughts about the case, but I really wanted to talk to you about another girl who drowned back in 1966. Elizabeth Mahy.' She hesitated. 'Your name was given in the *News* as the person to contact with any information about her death.'

'It was.' He nodded. 'Although, if you don't mind my saying, you're a little slow off the mark. Why the sudden interest in a girl who died nearly fifty years ago?'

'I've been doing some research into death by drowning on the island. Focusing on those deaths deemed accidental or suicide or perhaps where an open verdict was recorded. I started with Amanda and it led me to Elizabeth and a few others over the years too. It struck me that there were some similarities between a handful of these cases. You were on the force during all of the investigations except the present one.' She pulled out her notes. 'It's probably easier if you look at this and ask me questions afterwards.'

'I remember it like it was yesterday.'

He had read everything carefully, laid the pictures of the six women out next to each other, looked at each in turn, asked a few questions and then returned everything to the folder. Everything apart from the newspaper report about Elizabeth.

'It was just awful. I was so young and I'd never seen a dead body before. I had nightmares for weeks afterwards. Not that I told anybody at the time. It was all stiff upper lip back then.' He shook his head.

'I'm not sure what you want me to say, Jenny. I was a very junior officer at the time. It was my bad luck really that I was first on the scene. They made me the point person for potential witnesses, anyone who had information. You'd need to speak to the more senior officers who worked the case to get anything of use, and I know for a fact they're both dead.'

'But you were there. You must have had a sense of how the case was managed. Do you think Elizabeth's death was thoroughly investigated? There's no doubt in your mind it was an accident? There were reports she had a boyfriend, that she may have been with someone when she drowned. How was this person ruled out of the inquiry?'

Roger smiled. 'You're obviously a very bright young woman, Jennifer, and I can see how you think you're on to something, but I assure you, Elizabeth's death was properly investigated. We can't know anything for sure, but there was nothing to make us think this was anything other than a tragic accident. It was the same for all of these cases.'

He told her what he remembered, that they had suspected someone went to the bathing pools with Elizabeth that night. They'd spoken to a barman at the Yacht Hotel, who had remembered seeing her with a man. They'd not managed to get a decent description – the barman, unsurprisingly, remembering more details about Elizabeth and her skimpy outfit than the man she was with. Regardless, there was nothing that pointed towards foul play. They appealed for witnesses, of course, but none had been forthcoming. They knew, from the barman, that Elizabeth had had several drinks that evening. She was drunk, she went swimming, she drowned. What reason was there to suspect anything else?

Jenny had asked several people about Roger Wilson. Everybody who knew him was of the same opinion. He had been a good policeman. Well-liked and missed following his retirement ten years ago. But surely even a good policeman might be unwilling to see something that might reflect badly on him. What would it say about him if, during his forty years on the police force, he had missed something of this magnitude?

'I know what you're thinking.' He put the report back into the folder and slid it over to Jenny. 'You're thinking I wouldn't want to admit it even if I did think there was something to all of this.'

'Perhaps.'

'And perhaps you are right. But I was a good detective and, despite what you might think, I was not the only one. We might have spent some of our time investigating stolen bicycles and sabotaged greenhouses, but there's a darker side to this island, Jenny. I've led plenty of investigations into complex cases. Drug smuggling, domestic abuse, paedophilia . . . I've seen some serious stuff. Not as much as someone in my position in a big city might see, but enough. If something needed investigating, either me or one of my colleagues would have investigated it.'

'Of course.' She sighed. 'I'm sorry. I didn't mean to imply that you wouldn't have. It's just, with the time between the deaths, it would be perfectly understandable if a connection had been missed.'

'Have you taken this to the police?'

'I have. Michael Gilbert has all of my research.'

'Ah. DCI Gilbert. A very good detective. Very . . .' He paused for a moment. 'Thorough. He's very thorough. If there's anything to investigate, I'm sure he'll get to the bottom of it.'

He shook her hand as she left. So lovely to meet her, he said. He told her to keep in touch and to ask if she needed anything. He had a lot of contacts in the police force, he'd make a few enquiries himself, would likely be called in if there was anything to look into, he'd keep her in the loop.

'You'll not be printing any of this, of course? I presume even the *Guernsey News* requires some form of corroborative evidence before they run with something like this?' Jenny had the distinct impression that he was offering advice rather than asking a question. He held her car door open for her.

'Certainly not right now, no. I need to take it to my editor for a start. See if he thinks I'm stark raving mad.'

'Oh I don't think you're mad, Jenny. Takes a certain kind of person to see things others might miss. You need a bit of gumption, a bit of imagination. You obviously have both. Maybe a little too much of the latter, eh? We'll speak again, Jenny.' He stood in the gateway and waved as she drove out.

Jenny glanced at the folder she'd thrown on the passenger seat. Roger Wilson was sure the investigation into Elizabeth's death had been thorough. She believed that he believed that. But there were five more dead girls' pictures in there. Five more investigations that might have missed something. She was going to find out what. Because Jenny was done with running from the past, however ugly and frightening it might be. Someone had to fight for these girls. Someone had to tell their stories.

23

Michael

He wasn't sure what he'd been expecting. He'd known she'd been looking into things, of course he had. She was a reporter, she had to report something, and she'd been seen by a PC at the White Rock, talking to Amanda's friend. It was one of the things that made the island so special, everyone knowing each other's business. Having an illicit affair? No romantic dinner dates for you, that's for sure. You'd be discovered in a heartbeat. Teenager sneaking out at night? Good luck with that. A neighbour or a teacher or another parent from school was bound to spot you sooner or later and report back home. Same went for underage drinking. Try getting into a bar with a fake ID when the doorman is friends with your dad and knows for a fact that you're not eighteen yet. Love it or hate it, Guernsey was a very, very small place. It was impossible to do anything 'off the grid'. Made the policework pretty easy, to be honest. Or so he'd always thought.

He'd managed to find all of their files, which was nothing short of a miracle. They had relied on a simple card indexing system well into the early nineties, and the digitalization process had been haphazard, to say the least, so he'd been expecting a struggle. It turned out Marquis was actually half capable when it came to computers and he'd helped to locate the earlier records without asking any questions. Some would say a lack of curiosity in a detective constable was a worrying trait but, as far as Michael was concerned, reticence was a highly underrated quality. Perhaps Marquis was a thinker. Perhaps he would make something of himself after all. Perhaps he was just bloody useless, but it was nice to give people the benefit of the doubt.

He went through the records one by one. The earlier ones were less comprehensive, but he had something on all of them; brief backgrounds, photographs, witness statements. They didn't make for very interesting reading. But there was something in that. The fact that the files were thin, the investigations into the deaths cursory.

There were similarities, plenty of them. They all looked alike, for a start. They were all, apart from Elizabeth Mahy, found drowned on the beach, fully dressed. They all came from troubled backgrounds or had gone off the rails in one way or another. There was Hayley Bougourd. The family was known to the police. Hayley had had a couple of warnings for underage drinking and making a nuisance of herself with a gang of kids up at Le Guet. Melissa Marchant was the only one with an actual police record – for shoplifting from Woolworths as a teenager. Janet Gaudion's parents described her as 'difficult'. She had dropped out of school at fifteen. Depression probably wasn't diagnosed so easily in the eighties, but from the file it seemed nowadays that was what she'd be labelled with. And Mary Brehaut, back in 1974. Her parents had kicked her out a few months before she died because of her 'inappropriate' relationship with a lad they disapproved of. She'd been close to homeless, sleeping on friends' floors, drinking a lot.

He knew how these things worked. It was a sad but true fact that none of these deaths would have caused the force too much consternation. They would all have been considered wayward teens, perhaps too stupid, perhaps too depressed to look after themselves. There had been no need to look any further than the seemingly obvious – suicide, a careless accident. Nobody, it seemed, had paid very much attention to these girls, alive or dead.

Not even the police. Which meant something might have been missed.

Only Elizabeth Mahy didn't really fit. He had not been able to find out much about the investigation into her death. Some of the older files had obviously got lost in the ether (or more likely in the shredder when the lackey inputting the stuff got bored and thought no one was looking) but he had some background information on her. She was from a good family by all accounts. She'd never been in trouble. She looked right, though. Young, blonde, pretty.

He wondered if these cases would have been treated differently if the girls had had different stories. What would have happened if Ellen's body had washed up on the beach? She was a good student, theirs was a good family, would her death have been cause for more concern? He knew he wouldn't have rested until he was certain he knew what had happened to her. He would have spoken to every friend, every teacher, every bloody person she'd ever known or talked to or looked at; he would have questioned them all. He would have turned her room upside down looking for evidence she was unhappy or in trouble. He would have combed the beach and dredged the sea looking for any clue that might help to discover the reason behind her fate. Did anyone do that for these girls? Or did they just accept that the police and the coroner and the magistrates had done their jobs?

He realised his fists were clenched and his knuckles white with tension He spread his hands on the desk, relaxed his shoulders, let out the breath that was caught in his chest. Mostly people did the best they could. He knew that. Not everyone had it in them to ask questions and push for answers. Some people just accepted their fate, tipped their hat to authority, and that was that. And sometimes there was simply nothing that could be done.

Like with Ellen. The only thing he'd been able to do when she'd died was identify the body. No window to cry against back then, no separate room. They'd taken him right up to the table.

He'd just stood there as a slightly built man in a lab coat pulled back a sheet in a stark, cold room and nodded. Yes, that was her. His baby girl. Her face white as the strip lights above, her lips grey as the steel she lay upon, her mangled body already in a shroud. What he wouldn't have done, right then, to breathe his life into her, to take her place on that steel table, to have her nod, yes, that's him, and then walk away, to continue her life. A young girl with everything to live for, in the place of a middle-aged man who had already had his chance.

He reviewed Amanda's file last. At the back, someone had stuck some notes that he hadn't seen before. An interview with a Matthew Roussel. One of her friends perhaps, although he couldn't remember seeing his name before. He skimmed over them. Something about a Guy Fawkes. Ah, that was it, the kid who was in, upset about a guy he'd found up at Pleinmont. Jenny had mentioned him. Said she thought he might be a bit disturbed. Michael read the notes more carefully. When he finished, he sat quietly for a moment. Then he opened each of the dead girls' files, rifling through until he had pulled out all of the post-mortem photographs. He picked up the first one and brought it up to his nose, twisting it this way and that, screwing up his eyes. He put it to one side. The next received the same treatment. The third he studied for longer, squinting at one spot until his head hurt. He placed it in front of him. He continued, discarding some pictures, placing others in a row and each time he added one, panic built, rising from his gut, slippery and cold. By the time he finished he felt actual tears welling, the result predominantly of eyestrain, but also of sheer bloody anger and frustration and he squeezed the top of his nose to quell them. He couldn't be certain. Not until he'd had them magnified. But if he was right, what then? There was no precedent for this here – or, he'd hazard a guess, anywhere. Not over this time frame. Not without anyone noticing.

He hoped to God that he was wrong.

24

October 1985

*H*e paused, put the scissors down, listened. Downstairs, his wife talked on the telephone. She was making plans already, for a party to celebrate his birthday. It was months from the actual date but she knew there was a chance she would be dead by then and she wanted to organise it before it was too late.

Cancer. She'd taken the news meekly, as she took everything life threw at her, including him. They'd given her a year to live three months ago and she'd taken only a few days, closeted in her room alone, before emerging, centred, settled, ready to engage with her new reality. He was not sure if this was a sign of strength or weakness. He suspected the latter, although she had shown a certain resilience over the years. She cooked and cleaned and adorned his arm at work functions, knowing when to talk and when to be silent. She listened, which was of the utmost importance, never questioning his house rules. Only once had she ventured into the attic, to clean and tidy, to please him, she said. He had not even needed to hurt her to make her understand his displeasure. He simply held her throat with one hand, cupped the other under her chin and tilted her head upwards, so her eyes met his. He squeezed, just a little, not enough to leave a mark, and told her firmly, in a low, measured voice, 'Don't do that again.' She had thick black lashes which caught her tears and held *them fast until he let her go. She looked down and they fell, leaving round, wet spots on the carpet. She did not repeat the mistake. She was an old-fashioned girl. She respected him. He had chosen well.*

For his part, he provided for her and paid her compliments and fucked her regularly, allowing himself to succumb to the weakness within for the sake of a functioning marriage. And every now and then, as he went through the motions of day-to-day life, as a husband, a partner to this woman for whom he felt nothing more than familiarity, he forgot. She would ask him if he fancied a stroll and he would say yes, and they would walk together. He would laugh along with her when she told a story about a neighbour who had lost his cat and then found it asleep under the bed, or a friend who'd run his boat aground after one too many pints at lunchtime. She would take his hand and he would squeeze it a little tighter as they walked over uneven ground, down farm tracks or over the cliffs, and he would forget that he was pretending.

So he would miss her. He did not love her, not like he had loved the others, but he had grown used to her presence, comfortable in her company, and he fancied she added a much-needed layer of softness to his outward persona, a fine cashmere scarf draped over the shoulders of a stiff leather coat.

She continued talking, in her sing-song way, no doubt checking the hotel reservation, confirming numbers, menus. It was to be held at the newly built hotel at Rousse, formerly a rugged, windswept headland with no facilities to speak of – a small kiosk and a fisherman's pier. Now a ninety-bedroom monstrosity dominated the whole area, the developers seemingly bribing the planning department and the population into submission with the promise of an all-you-can-eat buffet, which his guests would gorge themselves on at his expense.

He picked up the scissors again and continued to snip, snip, snip. The trousers were perfect. He'd taken them from a charity bin at work, stonewash jeans, the same brand that Janet wore. The top, however, was too big. He was being cautious, so he had stolen it. It was more difficult than he'd anticipated. He sweated in the shop, made too much conversation, his nerves forcing him to overcompensate and he rushed, failing to check the size before he tucked it under his jacket. It was cheap polyester but the most perfect cornflower blue and silky to the touch. She had worn one just like it a few months ago, and when she had walked past him it had brushed against his arm and it had felt just like this one did. He let it slip and slide under his fingers, creating a layer of static, which gently crackled when he rested it on his bare legs.

When he'd finished adjusting it he pulled it carefully over the straw girl, making sure not to catch it on the rough edges around the wrists, then he tied each cuff with embroidery thread, blue, like the blouse, and stood back to survey his work.

The hair, while styled correctly, was too brassy. It should be a pale, white-blonde, but this was the closest he could find and he did not want to draw attention to himself by asking for another, not even in Southampton, where he'd found the costume shop while wandering the city with a few hours to spare before his flight home. He had tried his best with the face. He was not an artist but he had drawn her wide eyes and full mouth as best he could. The colours bled into the hessian, blurring his strongly drawn lines. She looked relaxed, sleepy even. The outfit was good. It was just what she would wear on a Saturday evening, out with her friends. Before he stripped her and cleaned her and washed away the shit and filth. His breathing quickened and he felt himself harden at the thought of her, wet and naked. No. Stop. Control. He slowed his breathing and took the needle he had placed between his teeth, pushed it into the flesh of his thigh until the pain obliterated all other sensations.

When he was focused once more, he tidied away the scraps of fabric and straw and moved her to the corner of the room. He would place her somewhere appropriate when the time came. The Druids had done it this way, with an effigy of wood and straw. It was the perfect way to mark the sacrifice.

He rubbed at the spot of blood on his chinos. He would have to put them to soak.

Downstairs, his wife was making tea. Her movements were slow and measured, partly the effects of her illness, but she had always been this way. Thoughtful. Purposeful. She smiled when she saw him, asked him if he wanted a cup. No, thank you, he said, he was going to do some work in the garden. She crinkled her nose, her way of admonishing him. He suspected she thought it endearing. 'You shouldn't work so hard, darling. The garden looks beautiful, sit and have some tea with me?' she asked. 'It looks beautiful,' he said, 'because I spend so much time in it.' He touched her nose – she liked it when he did that – and left her sitting with a book.

In truth, he spent very little time on the garden. He mowed the lawn, pulled the weeds, but the majority of the land he owned was pasture. He paid a neighbouring farmer to cut the grass a few times a year. The real reason he spent so much time in the garden was the bunker.

It was another one of many signs he had had over the years that there was a guiding force in his life, ensuring that all that should be, was. On the day he'd exchanged contracts, he had wandered through the house, swinging the keys back and forth, enjoying the feeling of possession. Once he had walked through every room, he had walked around the perimeter of the building and then out into the garden and to the fields beyond. He had found it in the first one. He hadn't known what it was at first: a bare patch in an otherwise overgrown field, rotting wood. He had lifted a piece and it had fallen apart in his hands. He had moved another, blackened and sweet-smelling. It, too, crumbled at his touch. And then he had seen. The wood covered not earth, but air. A hole in the ground, steps down. Buried treasure.

He was careful not to make too much noise as he carried her down to the front door. He propped her against it while he retraced his steps, sweeping the stray pieces of straw into a dustpan and refolding the ladder up behind the hinged trapdoor in the ceiling. He shut the front door quietly and checked for passers-by before he placed her gently in the boot of his car. He would like to have had her in the passenger seat, to create a more accurate representation of how it would be, but it was not worth the risk.

The roads were quiet. It was a calm night, the only movement from the odd breath of wind unsettling the piles of dried leaves gathered at the edges of the pavement. He had been unsure, initially, if he should place her before or after the actual event but had settled on before, feeling that he should be able to enjoy the saving itself fully and completely, that it should be the true zenith of his preparations. Next, he'd given careful consideration as to where she should be placed. There were many options, but he'd finally settled on Rousse. It was the new hotel that decided him. It created an imbalance, which he felt he could help to redress. He drove down Port Grat, past the Houmet Tavern before turning on to a single-track road out on to the peninsula.

The hotel was on the left, its sickly yellow walls thankfully obscured by the darkness, although the row of flags flying from poles at least twenty-foot high were illuminated in the moonlight; the Union Jack, the Tricolore and the brand new Guernsey flag – a St George's Cross with the addition of a golden cross in the middle to represent William of Normandy, who brought together his Duchy, including the islands, with England when he conquered her nearly one thousand years ago.

The flags were there to, 'represent the countries which had contributed to the rich and mixed heritage of Guernsey', according to a quote printed in the News when the display was unveiled weeks earlier. They'd forgotten one, though. Ironic, considering a few hundred yards further along the narrow coastal lane was a Loophole tower, which the Nazis had altered to serve as a lookout and gun battery during the occupation. One of hundreds of similar sites across the island. It wasn't just the buildings they'd left behind, either. How many more were there like him? How many other living, breathing contributions had the Nazis made during their years here? Quite an oversight, he thought, not to have included a fourth flagpole.

The concrete road surface gave way to a gravel-and-sand parking area. It was deserted. He took her from the boot of the car and walked with her leaning over his left shoulder, her legs anchored under his arm. He relied on the moonlight to guide him until he knew he was close to the right place. Then he took out his Maglite and shone it on the rocks. The torch was a new acquisition and he was impressed with the power of the beam compared to the size of the unit, which was small enough to fit in his pocket.

He climbed over crumbling sand banks until he found what he was looking for. A cluster of rocks, one puckered, a depression the size of a fist in the middle of its flat surface. Le Pied du Boeuf. It was here that the Devil, chased by a saint, was said to have left the island, leaping for Alderney, leaving his hoofprint in the rocks. He settled her next to it, looking out to sea. He could not leave Janet here. He would have liked to. But a drowned girl must be found near the water. So this was the best he could do. A proxy of straw. A poor substitute, he knew, but it served as both a portent and a celebration of what was to come. He sat with her until the dawn quickened on the horizon. Before he left, he took his knife and sliced the mark into her thigh, Or, at least, into the denim which clothed her leg. It was clumsy, a far cry from perfect. But the occasion had been marked.

Janet Gaudion and his wife died within a month of each other. One, in as glorious a fashion as it was possible to imagine, on a crisp, starlit night scented with brine and sweet marram grass, the other in an overheated hospital room, heavy with the smell of ammonia and shit.

He cancelled his birthday party. Everybody understood. A party, so soon after a funeral, would have been quite inappropriate.

155

25

Jenny

Wednesday, 19 November

Hayley Bougourd's mother lived on the Mare de Carteret estate, one of the nicer ones on the island. Row upon row of cream, box-like houses with red roofs arranged in a cul-de-sac, each with a small garden in front and the same behind. They'd be called council estates in the UK, but here, with no council, they were referred to as States' houses. Most of the lawns were covered in scrubby, patchy grass, and some of them were adorned with overly large trampolines or broken children's bicycles. Every now and then she passed a well-kept garden, the grass healthy and green, a small pond with garden gnomes in attendance, or a neat border of winter pansies. But, for the most part, the estate had a depressing, uncared-for appearance. She drove around twice before she found a parking space between a rusty Yamaha motorbike and a grimy, dented Ford Fiesta with a *'Guernsey Donkey and Proud'* decal stuck on its dirty back windscreen.

Hayley had drowned twelve years ago. Jenny remembered it and Hayley's friends would be just a little older than her. Jenny had asked Sarah to check with friends and family, to see if anyone remembered anything and would be happy to talk about it. Guaranteed Sarah would deliver. She was one of those people who knew everyone, through school or work or toddler groups. Plus she had twelve cousins, all of whom still lived on the island. Her whole family met up regularly for chaotic Sunday lunches and Christmas celebrations and weddings – the opposite of Jenny's family, with Margaret an only child and Charlie's sister never having had children.

Hayley's mother lived at number twenty-five, one of the houses with the better front gardens. There were no flowers or shrubs, but the lawn was tidy and there was a faded doormat on the top step with WELCOME emblazoned across it in bright letters. She rang the bell and, almost simultaneously, a dog started barking. There was a yell, a thudding of footsteps, some kind of scuffle, and the door opened. A woman, whippet-thin, her bobbed hair dyed an unnatural shade of red, stood holding the collar of a boxer, which probably weighed twice as much as she did. The dog barked again and strained to be released, its front legs raised off the floor, but the woman held fast. Jenny took a step back.

'He won't hurt you, love, he's soft as shit. I just don't want him running into the road.'

He was wagging his tail now, tongue lolling out of his mouth, and Jenny relaxed. 'I'm looking for Mrs Le Cheminant?'

'Yes, that's me.' She looked Jenny up and down and pushed the door a little. 'What do you want?'

'I was hoping to talk to you about your daughter.'

'Look, I've told you people before: she's left home, I'm not responsible for what she does any more. If there's some kind of problem with her rent or something, you need to speak to her.' She began closing the door. Jenny stepped forward, setting the dog off again, so she had to shout over him, 'No, Mrs Le Cheminant, I'm sorry, I wanted to talk to you about *Hayley*.' The door of the next house opened and a young woman balancing a red-faced toddler on her hip shouted across at them, 'Jackie, can you please shut that dog up? It's Ryan's nap time!' She slammed her door shut and Jenny looked pleadingly at Jackie, who seemed frozen on the doorstep.

'Can I come in?'

*

'Nobody's asked about Hayley for so long.'

They were sitting in a small living room on an old sofa, uphol-stered in red velvet fabric. Jenny could feel the springs through the thin cushions. The carpet was threadbare, the swirled cream and brown pattern completely worn away in places. Dust motes hung in the air, whirling around as Jackie wafted the smoke from her own cigarette out of her face. Jenny stifled a cough and sipped at her orange squash, which seemed to be three-parts squash to one-part water. She had explained to Jackie that she was looking into suicide rates on the island, asked if Jackie would mind telling her about Hayley. She could tell Jackie was torn, suspicious of Jenny but desperately wanting to talk about her daughter.

'Nobody was interested when she died, you know. Nobody wanted to know what happened to her then. Not the police, not even you lot. Suicide, they said, even though there was no note, nothing. But they all took one look at her, at us, and didn't think we were worth bothering about.'

'*I'm* interested. Please, tell me about her.'

Jackie lit another cigarette. The skin on her hands was dry and flaky, her knuckles red and chapped, but her nails were long and looked professionally shaped. She picked off flakes of pearly pink polish and flicked them on the floor.

'She was really pretty. That's what people always said about her. She was so pretty. She was clever as well, though. Worked really hard until she got in with that Goth crowd, started drink-ing and doing God knows what else.'

The dog was sitting at her feet and she played with his ears, pulling them gently and stroking his head. He whimpered with contentment until a motorbike roared past and he was up, bark-ing at the front door again.

'For fuck's sake, Frank, siddown!' She dragged him out to the kitchen and shut the door.

'Fucking dog. Kids went on and on about getting one but they never trained him and now they're all at school or left and I'm stuck with the fucking thing.' She shook her head. 'Anyway, what good is it, raking all this up again? Hayley's gone. I tried my best. Tried to stop her messing up like I did. I was sixteen when I had her. Still a kid. Never married her dad, he was just some boy from school. He didn't even come to her funeral. My other three I had later, with my husband. My youngest, my Jax, is the same age Hayley was when she died. Getting himself into trouble as well, that one is.'

'It's a difficult age.'

'You're telling me, love.'

'So could you tell me about her? About Hayley? It might help other girls like her. To know her story.'

Jackie finished her cigarette, grinding the stub into a cut-glass ashtray resting on the arm of the sofa. She brushed at her leggings, picking off a few stray dog hairs and dropping them on to the carpet.

Hayley was a good girl, Jackie said. She passed her eleven plus and was the first one in the family to go to the grammar school. She did well. Stayed on to do A levels. Jackie couldn't help much with her schoolwork, but she encouraged her. They all did. They were proud. She wanted to be a designer or go into advertising. She hadn't decided. But then things started to change. Small things at first. The music she listened too, the clothes she wore. Soon everything was black, her make-up, her hair, her nails, her mood.

There was a boy. There always was, wasn't there? Jackie said. He wore all black too. And they started hanging around at Le Guet, there was a crowd of them who met at the little abandoned building at the edge of the woods. They would all drink and make trouble. The police were involved a couple of times, nothing too serious, noise complaints and making a nuisance, that sort of thing. She hadn't worried too much at first, kids messed around and got into scrapes, it was all part of growing up, wasn't it? It hadn't been that long since Jackie was a kid herself, she remembered what it was like. But it got worse. Jackie was worried that Hayley was taking drugs. She stopped studying, was out all night, nobody knew where. But what could she do, Jackie asked? Hayley was nearly eighteen at this point, almost an adult, and she wouldn't listen.

A social worker had put them in touch with a charity that helped young people going off the rails, like a youth club with counsellors – Jackie couldn't remember the name of it. They offered music lessons and art therapy.

'What sort of music lessons?' Jenny interrupted.

'She was learning to play the piano. We all took the piss a bit, to be honest. Just teasing, like, asking her she was going to run away and join an orchestra, stuff like that. She laughed, it didn't upset her or nothing. Anyway, we didn't have one here, so she used the one at the centre.'

'Who taught her?'

'I can't remember. You want lessons or something?' Jackie seemed annoyed at being interrupted. She took another cigarette.

'No, sorry, please, go on.'

'I did meet him once. He was an older bloke, bit posh. He was ever so nice to her, though. He would let Jax come along to her lessons when I was working. Until she got into one of her moods and stopped taking him.'

'Why was that?'

'Oh I don't know. Teenage stuff I suppose, didn't want Jax cramping her style. We had a right old row about it as it happens, 'cause I had to find someone to watch him while she was out, but she was adamant he couldn't go with her any more. That was just a couple of weeks before she died. I'd completely forgotten about that. All seems so stupid now.' She shook her head. 'Anyway, apart from that, she was in a good way, right before it happened. She started talking about studying again. I really thought she was getting better. And then one night, she didn't come home. The next day her body was found. Washed up at Rocquaine. The police thought she probably jumped at Pleinmont. She'd taken pills, sedatives. There was no suicide note though. But they all seemed pretty sure that she killed herself. The police, the social workers, they all just wrote her off.'

'Here.' Jackie left her chair and got down on all fours, her cigarette balanced at the corner of her mouth and opened a cabinet underneath the television. She pulled out a Christmas-card box, a picture of a robin in the snow on the battered lid, and took out a small pile of photos. She looked at them one by one, and then handed them to Jenny.

'I only kept the good ones. I sorted them all out and threw the bad ones away, the ones that were out of focus or badly lit, you know. I don't know why I did that. Must have been too upset to think properly.' Her voice was thick now. She pointed to the photo Jenny was holding. Hayley with a boy. Both of them golden-haired and blue-eyed. A younger brother. 'That one's my favourite. Her and Jax. She was really good with him. Took him out with her, even when she was acting up at home. He liked her better than me, I reckon.' She smiled and wiped her eyes. 'I'd frame it . . . if I could bear looking at her every day.'

Jenny walked back to her car. There was a small boy, perhaps four years old, sitting on a bike, leaning against the wall across from where she had parked. He had short, clippered hair and wore a pair of faded dungarees, dirty green rubber shoes on his feet. She smiled at him but he just stared back, his eyes knowing, as if they were many years older than his face. She could see him in the rear-view mirror, watching her, as she drove away.

Her head ached. Amanda and Hayley both went to some sort of youth programme and took piano lessons. David De Putron said he volunteered at a youth group and had taught Amanda. Had he taught Hayley too? Because, surely, that would be one hell of a coincidence? She would run it by Michael. But first she needed space to think and some fresh air to clear her head. She found herself on the coast road, heading south, past the friendly yellow beaches of Cobo and Vazon with their chip shops and ice-cream kiosks, now closed for the season but still bright and welcoming. As she drove on, the road narrowed and twisted into Perelle. Here the landscape was harsher, flat sand replaced with sharp black rocks, the sea wall crumbling in parts. Landward, wide, empty fields of brittle grass were dotted with the odd greenhouse or fisherman's cottage. There was a beauty in the bleakness here, an honesty, as if the island was showing its true self, unsweetened, unadorned – *this is what I really am*.

The road ended at the Imperial Hotel. She parked opposite. She had often come here with Charlie. It was one of their favourite Sunday-morning walking spots, a place they escaped to while Margaret was at home fussing over a roast dinner or 'giving the house a good once-over'.

Autumn was fast becoming winter. The few trees that lined the road seaward were bare of leaves, black and skeletal against a stark, white sky. Opposite, the entrance to a German bunker formed a black hole in the foliage covering the cliffs. It was a small one, a U-shaped tunnel, the exit a few hundred yards further up the hill. As a child she had loved running in, the light behind her disappearing as she turned the corner into a pitch-black corridor, only her hands on the cold rock to guide her until she turned again and her dad was standing there, a dark shape framed in the exit, waiting to catch her as she dashed back into the fresh air.

Now it was all she could do to force herself to the entrance. She placed a hand on the wall, physically fixing herself to the outside. Beer cans and cigarette butts littered the steps down and the air was thick with the smell of urine. Presumably it hadn't been like this twenty years ago, although knowing Charlie Dorey, it could have been. He wasn't one to let a bit of piss and rubbish spoil the fun. She peered at the blackness inside. It was viscous, tangible somehow and trying to pull her in. Her whole body recoiled from the darkness and from the narrow, enclosed space. She could feel the walls closing in on her, the wet, slippery stone under her desperate, clawing fingers.

She shivered. The memory left her skin cold and her mouth dry. She left the bunker behind her and walked up the road towards Pezeries Point.

She came to the Fairy Ring. *La Table des Pions,* the stone next to it said, but nobody called it that. A circular trench dug out of the earth formed the seating and the grassy area in the middle was the table. What the stones were for and where the fairy idea came from was anyone's guess, but according to local legends this place was a riot of witches dancing with the Devil when he chose to make an appearance. No sign of them at the moment. Just a couple of dog walkers hurrying back to the car park before the weather turned.

Charlie and Jenny would sit at the edges and make daisy and buttercup chains and throw them in for good luck. Charlie had always said the witches would find out if anyone disturbed their favourite spot and put a curse on them. Sometimes he would dare her to go in and she would, but only for a second, and she would say sorry, in her head, to the witches. She said it now, as she stepped through the stones and into the middle of the circle.

There was a blackened area towards the centre. She crouched next to it, stroked the scorched, brittle grass. Something had definitely burnt here. She walked around the edges, looking into the trench, crouching down to examine the odd pebble, a sweet wrapper. She was about to give up when she saw it, threaded through some scrappy grass. She pulled it out. A long, pale-yellow hair. She ran it through her fingers, felt it squeak against her skin. Not a real one. From a wig.

Someone else had stepped in here in the days before Amanda died. Someone who had left a straw woman lying on the grass, a straw woman with blonde hair and blue eyes and cuts in its arm.

She wrapped the hair around a pen and put it in a pocket at the front of her bag. She stepped out of the circle. An icy mist was descending, not exactly rain but freezing and damp, just the right consistency to find its way under the coat collar and chill the bones. She walked, head down, along the path to the headland. Springy grass and bracken soon gave way to sticky red soil and jagged rocks, small at first and then larger and larger, as the cliffs rose out of the earth. She scrambled up and over, as far as she could go, right to the edge, where the only way onwards was down. She looked out over the channel – eighty miles of churning, steely sea between here and the mainland. From where Jenny was standing, it could have been a thousand.

Waves thrashed the rocks below. She was not afraid of falling; quite the opposite. She was sure she would enjoy it. Not the ending, she didn't want to die, but the fall itself. She liked to think about what it might feel like, the cold air rushing through her hair and around her body, the speed, taking her breath away. There was something thrilling about wanting to jump, but knowing she never would, something empowering about exercising control. She wondered if there were people who couldn't do that, people who couldn't stop themselves, who walked all the way to the edge and then kept on going. Not because they were hopeless or desperate, but because of the thrill of the fall.

26

April 1994

*S*he was nervous. Her hands shook as she sipped from the bottle he had given her. As she swallowed he felt a stab of anxiety. *She might notice. He had used a whole packet, unsure of how much he could persuade her to drink. He had chosen the sweetest, sickliest energy drink he could find in the hope that the sugar and artificial flavourings would mask the taste of the pills, but even after he had shaken and shaken the bottle there was a chalky, bitter taste to it. Perhaps he was only detecting it because he knew what was in it. He had not wanted to try too much, for obvious reasons. He was on edge anyway. This was a new method for him and it made him uncomfortable, having to rely on anything other than himself to achieve his aims. There was no other way though. He had been unable to cultivate a relationship this time. He had not even tried, deeming it too risky. Instead, he had watched from afar; her visits to the social worker, the youth club. He'd even nodded at her once, given her what he hoped was a fatherly smile and a jovial 'Hope you lot aren't up to no good!' as he passed her and her friends smoking and laughing outside the toilets at the North Beach car park. He knew there might only be one opportunity, and when it arose, he would have to be ready. The bottle had been in his glove compartment for weeks.*

He'd seen her that afternoon, outside the police station. She'd been in some sort of trouble. Her mother had been screaming at her in the street that she could make her own way home. He saw her beautiful face, hardened with anger and rage, slowly soften. He saw the tears welling in her wide-set eyes and rolling down her cheeks, leaving tracks of mascara in their wake, saw her lips moving. 'Don't leave me . . .' Her plea fell on deaf ears.

She wondered aimlessly around town. He followed, keeping at a safe distance. He tried to look relaxed, nodding and smiling at acquaintances as he passed them by. As late afternoon turned to evening, she fell in with a crowd of friends gathered in front of the row of telephone boxes at the end of the High Street. She and another girl sat on a bench in the shadow of the town church. He kept walking, taking the few steps down to the sea front. He had a moment of indecision. He could keep going and risk losing her, or he could find a place to watch and risk . . . what? What could he possibly be suspected of? He was doing nothing more than taking a walk through pretty St Peter Port on a fine spring evening. He climbed the steep steps up into the Cosy Corner, a dingy pub housed in the last building on the High Street. The tiny gap between the tavern's roof and the outstretched gargoyle on the church wall next to it gave rise to the much-beloved claim that Guernsey had the closest pub to a church in the whole of the British Isles. He would pour no scorn on that claim now, as from the window next to his seat he could just about see the tops of the heads of Melissa and her friend below.

He ordered a tonic water with a slice of lemon and, as it was suppertime, a plate of fish and chips. They stayed out there, smoking cigarettes, their voices getting louder as the light faded. He was just thinking he would have to move when she pulled away from the group, shaking her head. He couldn't hear what she was saying, but it looked like she was leaving. She walked directly under the window he was sitting at and crossed the road, heading towards the Crown Pier. She was going home. He would meet her there.

He parked at the side of the road, just before the entrance to the

Delancey Housing Estate. These were the worst States' houses on the island. They were vulgar. Dirty and poor. He'd read a report once, probably commissioned by the States at great expense, which concluded that real poverty did not exist on Guernsey. Perhaps it didn't, not absolutely. After all, satellite dishes adorned most of the houses, cars, which appeared to be in good working order, were parked at the side of the street, and no doubt the residents had food on their tables each night. Teenagers leant against the wall at the corner wearing tracksuits, white running shoes and baseball caps, smoking Bensons and drinking bottles of Brody.

He checked the rear-view again and wondered if he'd misjudged. Perhaps she hadn't been heading home after all. Perhaps she'd stopped off on the way or decided to stay over at a friend's. It was already after nine. He could not wait here all night. He should go home. But then this would all have been a waste of his time, and time was a dwindling, precious commodity. He would stay. It was the right thing to do.

He hated this. The indecision. He clenched his teeth together until his jaw hurt. His face felt hot and he could hear the beating of his own heart as if his ear were pressed to his chest. It fluttered. Once, twice, three times. Palpitations – a weakening of the body to match the weakening of his mind. He wound down the window and gulped down the cool air.

It was just then that he saw her. She was alone and swaying slightly. She must have stopped for a few drinks at the Red Lion on the way home. Perfect. He closed his eyes. All would be well.

Two a.m. It was done. He lay naked on his bed. He could smell her and the sea on his skin. He would not wash. Not until the morning. He felt cold and he pulled the bed sheets around him. Usually, afterwards, sleep took him quickly. Tonight, there was a buzzing. Like a tiny wasp was trapped inside his head. This was not the first time he had noticed it. He knew it. Knew its name and purpose. It was called Doubt. And it was here to torment him. He tried to kill it, to flatten it with his thoughts. He closed his eyes, went all the way back to the beginning. To Elizabeth. Remembered that morning; her, resplendent in the golden sunlight. And those that had followed, he thought of them. Tried to soothe his tired, aching brain with the memories of their deaths; the sweet smell of their skin, the feel of it, cool and wet against his own, the elation he felt at the knowledge that he, and he alone, had saved them.

The buzzing.

He opened his eyes again. Could he see it? On the ceiling? A tiny shadow, flitting round and round the lampshade.

He got up and switched the light on. Nothing. The sound of a motorbike revving in the distance. He pulled on his robe. He climbed the ladder to the attic. Although he had lived alone for years now, he could not shake off his habit of retreating away from the rest of the house when working. He needed to be separate from everything that anyone else had touched or seen. He had thought about moving everything out to the bunker, but he liked to keep that just as he found it, a monument of sorts, to his and the island's heritage. And, besides, there was always the chance, despite his best efforts to secure it, that a tourist or an amateur historian would stumble on it and get in somehow. It was better to have his work here. Where he could protect it.

He sat at the desk. Flicked through his research. Reassured himself. She was a clear-cut suicide risk. Alcoholic father, possibly abusive; ill-educated mother who struggled to cope. She'd been getting into trouble for years. And then there was the drinking, the downward spiral. It made sense, after today, that she would load up on alcohol and Valium and walk into the water, leaving her short, troubled life behind her. He rearranged the desk. This was idiotic. It was unbecoming. He'd done this so many times. He was careful, cautious. He knew how it worked. Nobody would question this, he was sure of it.

He went back to bed. He slept like the dead.

27

Jenny

Wednesday, 19 November

They stood outside the entrance to the Fermain Tavern, or 'The Tav' as it was affectionately known, while Sarah texted the sitter for the second time since they'd left her house fifteen minutes ago. A deep, thudding bass permeated the air and the crowd whooped and cheered from inside as the tune picked up. Jenny had spent many a night here as a teenager. It was the best place on the island to rock out with a pint of Breda. At least it used to be and, judging from the noise coming from within, it was as popular as ever.

'So this is Simon's band.' Jenny looked at the poster on the door, a sepia-tinted photograph of four men, one of whom was Sarah's husband, Simon, sitting on the edge of a tractor-trailer filled with musical instruments – guitars, a drum kit, violins, a harp, a flute – sticking out of the top of the pile. Across the bottom it read, *'Live Tonight! Tom Le Jardin and The Wrecks.'*

'Yep, Simon plays bass. And that's Tom, the guy I was telling you about.' She pointed to the man at the front of the photograph. 'He knew Hayley Bougourd. Went to school with her. Which is fantastic, because, let's face it, you wouldn't have come out just for the fun of it, now would you?'

'I would have! It's just a bonus this guy knew Hayley. Thanks for asking around. He'll talk to me, you think?'

'Sure. He's a nice guy. Friendly. Good-looking. Single.' She did not meet Jenny's eye.

'Are you and my mum in some kind of club?'

'I don't know what you're talking about. Do you want to borrow my lip gloss?'

It was crowded inside. Packed. There was hardly room to stand. And it was dark. Much too dark. Jenny took a step backwards, towards the open door behind her, tried to give her eyes time to adjust, but already there were more people coming in and the momentum of the crowd carried her towards the bar. Bodies pushed and shoved against her and the air was warm and heavy with other people's breath. When she reached it, she held on to the countertop of the bar with one hand. She pressed her other hand tightly to her side, squeezing her thumb and index finger together, simultaneously releasing a long, slow breath. She had a safe place for when she was stressed. The therapist had apparently locked it in her brain, somewhere, and the thumb-squeeze was the key to opening it. She had a sneaking suspicion it was bullshit, but the act of doing anything at all to combat the fear seemed to help. She tried to visualize her room as it was when she was a child, her bed, the smell of newly washed bedclothes, the sounds of the birds in the garden and of her dad mowing the lawn. Safe. Calm. Safe. Breathe.

'Do you want a drink?' Sarah shouted into her ear, shutting the door to the room in her memory and bringing her back to reality.

'I'm going to the loo,' she shouted back. Her voice reverberated around them, the sound waves bouncing off those of the music, vibrating and distorting.

'What?' Sarah cupped a hand around her ear.

'Toilet!' She pointed towards the door to the ladies, a few feet from where they were standing.

Sarah nodded. 'I'll get you a beer!' She mouthed the words slowly and gave her a thumbs up.

Cooler air washed over her as soon as she opened the bath-room door and she breathed in deeply, filling her lungs with the smell of bleach and urine and artificial pot-pourri air fresh-ener, dispensed, unprompted, every few minutes by a small white machine stuck to the wall. The music was muffled in here, only a little, but enough for her to calm her racing thoughts. She stood at a sink, the white porcelain stained yellow, the plughole rusting, and splashed cold water over her face, letting the droplets run down her neck. She'd been in plenty of dingy bars over the last few years with no problem. She was already anxious, that was the reason. Pushing herself too hard. And for what? The *News* didn't want the story. This was all on her. She could stop whenever she wanted to. Maybe she should. She would talk to this friend of Hayley's then she'd go home, take a bath, read a book, try to relax.

She patted her skin dry with a paper towel, trying not to smudge what little make-up she was wearing. Next to her, three girls crowded around a phone, discussing the right way to respond to a text message one of them had received. One of them wore a tight Care Bears' T-shirt, her large breasts straining against the bright pink fabric. They all wore skinny-jeans and had private-school accents, the air of the returned university student about them. One of them caught Jenny looking, asked her if she was all right. Jenny nodded and forced a smile but didn't move, and then they were all looking at her and she realised they wanted her to leave so she did, although she wasn't really ready to. She'd needed a couple more minutes to clear her head.

She pushed her way back to the bar, where Sarah was waving a ten-pound note at the barman, trying to get served. Jenny tapped her on the shoulder and pointed to the door to the beer garden, which was on the far side of the stage. Sarah nodded and Jenny started to make her way through the crowd. The band had stopped playing and fill-in music blared from the speakers. Stage lights flashed, bathing the room in colour, first blue, then green, then red. People jostled around her, heading back towards the bar: the brush of a damp T-shirt, a bare arm, the sharp tang of fresh sweat and spilled beer, faces washed in red. One or two were familiar and she nodded, forced a smile as she pushed past. One step, two steps, she was making progress. A group with their backs to her, heads tipping back as they swigged from bottles, blocked her way. She reached out, tapped the shoulder of a man. A man in a black hooded top. He turned.

It was him. It was Jamie. He looked different, broader, his once-lanky teenage body now filled out and older, obviously. But she'd never forget that smile, twisted and sardonic. Her cheeks burnt and her eyes watered as blood pumped furiously to her head, flooding her brain, slowing her thoughts so they became thick and foggy, like in a dream. He showed no signs of recognition but stepped aside with a little mock bow and held his arm out, making way for her. She walked past, forcing each step, her legs heavy, head down, pressing forward, heading for the door, but the further she got from the stage the darker it became and soon she could see only shapes, black against red, and it felt like she was swimming through thick tar and it was filling her eyes and her nose and the music throbbed and hummed and flowed through her ears and filled her head, and for a moment she fancied she could actually taste the noise; it flooded her mouth with metal and salt, thick like blood but cold, ice cold, like seawater.

She'd been sixteen. It had been the first time she'd lied to her parents, at least about anything important. She'd said she was going to Sarah's house. Sarah said she was going to Elaine's, and so on and so forth so that none of them were where they were supposed to be and nobody's parents had the faintest clue what they were up to. Which was nothing very much, really. A few beers, some cigarettes – and one of the boys had some pot.

They met at a house near Fauxquets Valley, Jamie's house.

Jenny didn't know him very well, but he was tall and good-looking and all the girls fancied him. Not Jenny, though. He made her uneasy, although she often wondered if that was hindsight, if she remembered it differently after the fact. Jamie had suggested they walk through the valley to look for the headless horseman. She'd laughed and said everyone knew the horseman only came out in the winter. Then they'd all laughed except him and he'd looked at her strangely, asked her what the fuck did she know?

They'd walked through the valley on a rough path of dust and shale, shaded by trees, drinking beer and making stupid ghost noises. It was a hot summer's evening, a rumble of thunder in the distance but the sky clear and blue through the canopy of leaves above them. She'd been happy and relaxed, smoked a couple of cigarettes, chatted along with everyone else.

They'd turned off the path, through a metal farm gate secured with a loop of rope. They'd walked through long, dry grass until they were on high ground, looking down over more fields as far as the sea. Storm clouds gathered out over the water, a safe distance away. Someone had brought a blanket, someone else a portable stereo. Soon they were listening to Gomez and drinking warm beer and waiting for the sun to set over Albecq.

Jenny had remembered there was a bunker in the fields somewhere. She'd asked Sarah if she wanted to look for it, but Sarah was stoned, or pretending to be, lying on the blanket waving her fingers in front of her face and giggling. So Jenny walked alone.

At least, she'd thought she did.

It was a little further than she'd thought. She'd crossed two wide fields, the sun warm on her back, dry grass tickling her bare ankles and grasshoppers scattering with each step she took, before she found what she was looking for. It had been fenced off and covered with 'keep out' signs. She could see the entrance, a hole in the ground, a little wider than a well opening. It ran vertically down about fifteen feet where it connected to a narrow tunnel, which led off into a deep chamber. Last time she'd been there she and her dad had climbed down the rusty iron ladder attached to the side and explored the dank space with a torch, but from what she could see through the fence, the ladder had been removed. She remembered thinking she would have to tell Charlie. He would moan about health and safety ruining all the fun. She'd turned. Jamie was standing there, a few yards away.

'What you looking at?' He'd ambled over. Those relaxed, sloping shoulders, a practised nonchalance in the way he moved.

'It's a bunker. You used to be able to climb into it.'

'Let's have a look then.'

He'd climbed over the fence easily, crouched down, looked right into it. She shouldn't have followed. The sun was setting. And she'd known there was something not right about him. But it was *her* bunker. She'd set out to find it. It annoyed her that he should be the one in there. She'd climbed over the fence. Crouched down a few feet away from him. Looked down into the blackness.

His hands on her. One on her breast, one on the back of her head and he'd pulled her towards him, pressed his lips against hers so hard it hurt, and she had tasted the beer on his breath and felt his tongue in her mouth and she'd tried to pull her head away but he'd forced her towards him so she'd done the only thing she could think of to get away. She'd bitten down on his tongue. He'd yelled, pushed her back, held his hand to his mouth, pulled it away, bloodstained. And then he'd laughed. *Bitch,* he'd said. *Fucking bitch.*

It had happened so quickly she'd had no time to scream. A shove, a rush of air, and then suddenly she was face down in a pile of leaves and rubbish, which softened the impact, but her nose felt broken and maybe her wrist. She'd cried. Looked up, saw him standing there, a dark shape above her.

And then he'd left her. At the bottom of a pit, with no way out. She'd shouted. Then she'd waited. He would come back, she'd thought. Or one of her friends would come looking for her. By the time she'd realised no one was coming and she'd started to scream there was nobody there and the rain had started.

She'd moved inside the tunnel. The ceiling was not high enough for her to stand. The failing light outside meant she could see only four or five feet in front of her and then it was pitch black. She'd stayed calm. Someone would come. Her friends would ask Jamie where she was. He would tell them. But some part of her had known that he wouldn't. Her parents wouldn't worry – she was supposed to be at Sarah's house. But she'd kept calm. She'd gone back into the entrance. Looked up at the twilight. Felt around for a foothold. Run her hands over the walls but felt only slick, cold concrete. She'd found the holes where the ladder once was but there was nothing substantial enough to get a hold of and eventually, soaking wet and exhausted, she'd crawled back into the tunnel.

She'd huddled there, in the dark, her head throbbing and she'd shivered against the cold and the wet. That was when it started.

Flashes. Flickering shapes.

As they came closer, she'd seen that they were faces. Ghoulish, twisted faces, each one more frightening than the one before. They'd floated passed her. She'd closed her eyes but that only made it worse. They were brighter, closer, scarier in her head than they were outside. She'd known it was some kind of trick of the mind and she'd folded herself into a ball, wrapped her arms around her aching head, creating her own cocoon, inhaling her own breath. She'd felt safer like that. She'd relaxed, just a little, felt almost sleepy after a while.

Until she'd heard the noise.

From behind. From the chamber. A scratching and scraping, like something was trying to burrow and claw its way out. It got louder and louder and then the shrieking started. High-pitched and relentless, like no creature on earth she'd ever heard, and she'd screamed until she hadn't been sure if the noise was coming from her or whatever was behind her and she'd thrown herself out of the tunnel and scraped and clawed at the walls until her nails were broken and bloody and her hands were shredded and she'd screamed and screamed for what felt like hours until she'd heard shouting from up above, not just any shouting, someone calling her name. 'I'm down here,' she'd sobbed. 'I'm down here!' And it was her dad who'd replied, who had brought the rope and a couple of mates to help drag her out.

Sarah had raised the alarm. She'd sobered up when they'd got back to Jamie's house, asked the others where Jenny was. Called everyone who had been out with them. Nobody knew. Not even Jamie. Not until Charlie had driven over there, to ask him exactly where they'd been, which roads they'd walked to the fields and back, and Jamie had mentioned, casually, that he'd last seen her looking for a bunker.

There'd been talk about prosecuting him afterwards, assault, or reckless endangerment. But he'd denied everything, even told the others that she'd thrown herself at him and then gone off in a huff when he'd turned her down, that he didn't know how she'd ended up down there. Some of her friends had believed him, or at least questioned her to the point that she'd felt they did. The police had believed her, but his dad was an advocate, a senior solicitor in the Guernsey courts, and he'd fixed it all somehow. They'd sent him away for a while. Nobody was sure if it was a school or a hospital. She'd heard he'd come back. Like the rest of them. They'd all come back in the end.

As for what happened in the bunker, it was the concussion they'd told her. She'd hallucinated because of the concussion. And the noise was probably rats. Rats, burrowing and scratching and shrieking. But she'd never been able to shake off the feeling there had been something else down there, something trapped and desperately trying to get out; a malevolent presence, a sleeping evil woken by her stupidity. From that day on she could not bear to be alone in the dark.

'Fuck, are you OK?'

Sarah's voice cut through the fog in her brain.

'I'm fine. I just . . . I'm fine. I got a bit dizzy, I had to lie down.' She pulled herself off of the floor, brushed damp grit off of her jeans and the sleeves of her jacket.

'On the concrete? Are you sick? Should I call your mum?'

'No!' She shook her head and tried to stay focused. 'It was so hot in there.' She paused. 'I saw someone.'

Sarah looked confused. 'Who?'

She sat on a wooden bench, dropped her head into her hands, rubbed her forehead. She looked up at Sarah. 'It doesn't matter.'

The beer garden was less of a garden and more of a small car park, walled off, the remains of a few half-dead clematis hanging limply from a wooden trellis. There were picnic tables, each with an ashtray and a couple of beer mats scattered over them. Jenny picked one up, played with the edges where the smooth, printed top layer was peeling away from the foamy white interior.

'Shit, Jen, I should get you home. You can talk to Tom another time.'

It was only then that Jenny noticed there was someone else with them, a figure in shadow, leaning against the wall. He stepped forward and extended a muscular arm. He was heavily tattooed, blue-black ink covering his skin from where his T-shirt ended and finishing neatly at his wrist, accentuating the paleness of his slender hand.

'Tom.' He nodded towards Sarah. 'I think Sarah might be right. Maybe we should do this another time?'

'I'm fine.' Jenny insisted. 'We can talk now.'

'Sure thing.' He sat down, seemingly unfazed by the evening's events. 'I've got twenty minutes before we're back on.'

Sarah looked unhappy. 'I'm going to get you a hot drink.' She went back into the pub.

Jenny was shivering. She was wet from lying on the floor and a freezing drizzle enveloped her. Tom sat in his T-shirt and cut-off cargo trousers like it was the middle of summer, studying her intently.

'Sarah said you knew Hayley Bougourd?' Her teeth chattered as she spoke and his face fell.

'Hang on a minute.' He disappeared back inside. She wondered if she might have to call it a night after all. She trembled, and for a moment thought she might cry. She rubbed her face and her arms. *Pull yourself together, Jennifer.* The sound of the door swinging to and fro and then a heavy, quilted coat was draped over her shoulders from behind.

'Thank you.' She pulled the coat tightly around herself.

'Don't want you dying on me.' Smiling but there was concern there too. 'Sarah's trying to sort out a cuppa. Not sure she'll have much luck, but she's got that determined look on her face so you never know.'

Jenny smiled. 'She's a force to be reckoned with. So, you knew Hayley?'

Yes, he said. She'd been in the same year as him at the grammar school. All the guys fancied her. She was gorgeous and had a reputation as being a bit wild. He was hazy on the details. She had a boyfriend, couldn't remember his name.

'I spent a lot of my time back then stoned, so I'm probably not the most reliable witness.' He grinned. 'Are you feeling better?'

'Yes. Thanks.'

'Maybe we should talk about this somewhere warmer. Over a drink.' His tone was offhand but his eyes were interested. She hesitated, lost for words. She wondered whether this reticence, the barriers she constructed around herself, were all part of the anxiety that plagued her, or if it was learnt behaviour, a reaction to the fact that she had, over the last few years, had a tendency to run into complete bastards who seemed more interested in trying to kill her than buying her a drink. The door opened and Sarah appeared with a steaming cup of tea

'They must have twenty different types of vodka in that bar, but do you think anyone can find a teabag in less than fifteen minutes? It's a bloody shambles. You drink that and I'll bring the car round.' She left them alone again.

'So?'

'There's nothing else you can tell me about Hayley?'

'If I give you all the info now there'll be no reason for you to come out with me.' He grinned.

'If you tell me something interesting, I'll think about it.' She smiled, relieved she'd got out of it without having to say an outright no.

He sighed. 'Well, now I really wish there was, but there's nothing interesting to tell. We were all shaken up by it, obviously. The police spoke to us after she died, all the crew that hung out together, asked us if she'd ever talked about killing herself and stuff like that. I think we were all too worried about them finding our little stashes of pot to really focus on what happened. We were just stupid kids.'

'And had she talked about killing herself?'

'Not as far as I know – and certainly not to me. She'd stopped coming to Le Guet anyway, that was where we all hung out, in the watchtower up there. Maybe she was depressed or whatever. Definitely nobody had seen her for a few weeks before she died. The last time I remember seeing her was when we found the scarecrow.'

'The what?'

He laughed. 'It was so stupid. One night, we found this scarecrow. It was dressed as a woman, standing at the edge of the woods. I know Hayley was there that night because I remember her screaming, shit-scared, before we figured out what it was. She was even more freaked out than the rest of us because she'd thought it was wearing one of her dresses. Wasn't actually hers, obviously, but it was the same as one she had, black with moons and stars on it. I know because we took it off the scarecrow and told Hayley she should take it if she liked it so much, but that just set her off again. We all laughed at her but, honestly, I shat myself too. Not what you want to see when you're off your face, a fucking creepy straw woman grimacing at us all. A bunch of us grabbed it and chucked it into the sea.' He stopped smiling. 'From the look on your face I'm starting to think we might be going out for that drink after all.'

'You have to tell me what's wrong.' Sarah stopped the car outside Jenny's house and turned off the engine. 'Seriously, I'm locking the doors and not letting you out until you tell me.'

Jenny raised her eyebrows at her and turned to stare out of the window.

'I mean it, Jenny.'

So Jenny told her. About the emails and the fact that someone was following her – maybe. Or maybe she was imagining it, but not the emails; they were real, she had them all saved, no one could say she was imagining those.

'But who's sending them? And why are they following you?'

Jenny shook her head. 'I don't know. I thought I did. I was sure it was to do with the woman I told you about, the story I was working on in London. When the people she worked for found out I was helping her, they warned me off. Told me they'd be watching me. But now I'm not so sure.' She paused. 'I just saw Jamie Collenette.'

Sarah closed her eyes. 'I'm sorry. I should have warned you. He's often at band night. I didn't think. I see him around a lot. I suppose I forget. That sounds callous. I don't mean I forget what happened to you, but I forget it was him. He seems so innocuous now, works for his dad, hangs out at the pub with his mates.'

'What does he do for his dad? He's not a lawyer, is he?'

'God, no. He didn't even make it to uni. After what happened his parents sent him to finish his A levels at some boarding school, to get him out of the way I suppose. He went completely off the rails, came back without any qualifications. He does admin stuff, I think, answers the phones.'

'Might explain why he'd be pissed off with me.'

'That was all his doing, Jenny, you know it and so does he. Do you really think he'd be threatening you? After all these years?' Her tone suggested she was doubtful.

'Probably not. I'm just paranoid. Because of everything else that's going on.' She told Sarah about the dead girls and the fact that a DCI thought that Amanda's death might be suspicious and had encouraged her to look into the others. She told her about what Tom had said about the scarecrow appearing before Hayley died, about how she was convinced, now, that they were dealing with a serial killer. She said those words out loud for the first time. *Serial killer.*

Sarah listened. When Jenny had finished, Sarah put a hand on her shoulder.

'This is too much, Jenny.'

'What do you mean?'

'I mean it's too much for one person to deal with. I don't know if someone is following you or not, but someone is threatening you, that's for sure. And as for the serial killer stuff? Jesus, Jenny.'

'You don't believe me?'

'It's not that I don't believe you, it's that it shouldn't be on you to prove or disprove something that the police should be working on. What the fuck are they doing while you're obsessing over dead girls?'

'I get the impression it's complicated.'

'You're damned right it is.' Sarah sighed. 'First thing tomorrow you need to go and see my mum. Don't look at me like that. You know you do. I'll tell her you're coming in – she'll make time for you. And, after that, you need to sort things out with this DCI Gilbert. He should be worrying about all of this. Not you.'

Jenny nodded. 'Can I get out now?' Sarah opened the doors. Jenny didn't hear the car start up again until she was inside the house.

Margaret knew something was wrong as soon as she saw her.

'You're so pale, what's happened?'

'I'm just tired, Mum. And I need a shower.'

'Well, of course you're tired,' Margaret said. 'You're hardly ever here and have you just finished work? It's nearly eleven o'clock, don't let . . .' Jenny shut the bathroom door and turned the shower on. She stripped off her clothes and stood under the water, letting it run over her face and her hair, turning the temperature up hotter and hotter until she could barely stand it.

She emerged, skin red and steaming, and wrapped herself in a towel. She peered through the condensation on the mirror. The circles under her eyes were almost purple, her lips were dry, her skin pale. She felt the small bump in her nose from where she'd broken it all those years ago.

She'd come back here for the quiet life. She accepted that now for the first time. It wasn't because her dad had died, or because her mum was cracking up. It was because, despite what had happened to her as a teenager, she had always felt safe here. You could walk home alone at night, knowing that the worst thing that could befall you was an unlit country lane and a ditch. At least, that's what she'd always thought.

Now, it seemed, there was something to be afraid of. Something far worse than the fear and anxiety she had brought home with her from London. The more she thought about it, the more she was convinced. The danger she faced now was real and imminent and home-grown.

28

September 2002

*H*e was hidden by the trees. Thick pines, their needles a soft carpet, swallowing his footsteps. It wouldn't take much for them to find him, but nobody was looking. Besides, he was doing nothing wrong. Unlike them. He could smell the marijuana, sharp and sickly sweet, could hear them coughing and laughing as the smoke hit the back of their throats. It was not dark yet, so he could not move close enough to see. Another half hour or so and they would turn on their camping lights and he would sit, right at the edge of the woods, and he would watch them. He would watch her.

Le Guet. The Watch. The tower itself was Napoleonic, but there had been a lookout point here for centuries, on this wooded hill, overlooking miles of flat, sheltered bay. This was an ancient place. A sacred place. The Black Witch of Cobo had held court here for many years, casting spells on those who angered or offended her, transforming their clean clothes to vermin-infested rags, souring the milk of their cattle, paralysing their horses so the vraic could not be gathered from the beaches and their crops went unfertilised. He smiled at the thought. No doubt this witch was no more than a disciple, like he was, using her wits and ingenuity to trick the peasants who invoked her wrath.

He heard her laugh. He wished he could see her. He had found *her dress, the one she wore more than anything else, in a little shop on Mill Street, right next to where the bookshop used to be. It sold candles and lava lamps and rings with skulls and spiders on them. It had only been luck he'd gone in there. He'd seen a book about black magic and thought it looked interesting, but it was not. Written for teenagers and full of rubbish about the phases of the moon and love potions. As he'd turned to leave though, he'd noticed the rack of clothes on the back wall, and right at the front, her dress. Black, with stars printed on it, each one with a tiny mirror sewn into the middle, so that it glinted in the sunlight. It was beautiful. So he bought it. Said it was for a niece, although the shop assistant didn't ask, barely looked up from her magazine as she served him.*

Nightfall. A twinkling through the trees as they lit their lamps. They were listening to music and did not hear the snapping of a twig as he moved towards them, too quickly. He was eager to see her. He stood, one arm wrapped around a slim tree trunk to anchor him there, at the edge of the woods. He raised his free hand to his face, and as she came into view he whispered into his open palm, whispered the words he would say to her, imagined the pain and the fear and, in that final moment, the ecstasy as he unleashed her soul, for truth and beauty, for blood and soil. He wept and his tears soaked into the earth, and he would put the figure there, he decided, right where his tears fell. And she would see it and she would know that he had chosen her.

29

Jenny

Thursday, 20 November

Jenny had known Sarah's mum, Rosemary, or Dr Bradfield as she was known professionally, for longer than she had known Sarah. She'd been Jenny's doctor for years, had guided her through all of her medical milestones; vaccinations, check-ups, an embarrassing request for the morning-after pill. When the panic attacks had started, she had helped her with those too. In her calm, no-nonsense way, she had saved Jenny from otherwise inevitable madness. At least, that's how Jenny felt. So she was prepared to listen. To take on board what Rosemary told her.

'You're re-traumatised.' Rosemary relaxed back into her leather chair. She had the same colouring as Sarah, olive skin and dark hair, cut short and combed to the side, and she had the same dancing eyes, although now they were narrowed and serious, studying her patient. Across the desk Jenny sat in the same stiff, wooden chair she had sat in as a child, only back then her feet had swung inches from the floor and her mum had been there to hold her hand.

'What does that mean?'

'You suffered a traumatic event as a teenager. A few months later, you had your first panic attack.' She glanced down at her notes. 'You told me then that you weren't sleeping, that you had developed a fear of the dark and a sense of paranoia, that you were being watched or followed.'

'But that was years ago.' Jenny interrupted. 'I went through the treatment, I got better. Last night was the first time I've had a panic attack in eleven years. And until recently I was OK in the dark. Not comfortable, but not terrified either.'

'You look tired, Jenny. Are you sleeping? Any paranoia?'

Jenny bit her lip and looked at the floor.

'Jenny.' Rosemary's voice was gentle but firm. 'Two years ago you were the victim of a violent assault. I don't know the details, only what your mum told me when it happened, which wasn't much. But from what I can gather it was enough for you to come home for a while. Six months later your father passed away suddenly and now you're living here, back in the place where you suffered the trauma that caused your original issues. I know it was years ago, but you're seeing the same people, visiting the same places. You're being forced to remember. And your brain is reacting to those memories. As crazy as it sounds, even the *memory* of the way you felt back then could have triggered this panic attack.'

'So I'm panicking about the fact that I might panic? You're right. It does sound crazy. *I* sound crazy.'

She was nothing of the sort, Rosemary said. There was a reason it was called post-traumatic stress. It was because it happened after the event – sometimes days, sometimes months, sometimes years after. Sometimes, as in Jenny's case, the stress could be dealt with and then triggered again. Treatment was an ongoing process. It was nothing to be ashamed of. She wasn't crazy. She was unwell. She would get better.

'Are you doing plenty of exercise? You swim, don't you? Your mum mentioned it once, said she was worried about you going out in all weathers.'

Jenny nodded.

'Well, carry on. You can tell your mum doctor's orders.' She smiled. 'And maybe try something more relaxing. Sarah's just signed up for a jewellery-making course at night school. Don't roll your eyes! It might keep you out of mischief. And here.' Rosemary turned to her computer screen and typed in a few notes. The printer churned out a prescription.

'We'll get you an appointment with mental health services but there's a wait, a month or two perhaps. In the meantime, take this. Just in case. It's for a very mild sedative.' Jenny grimaced. 'You don't have to take them,' Rosemary said, 'sometimes just having them to hand can help.'

Jenny thanked her and promised to try to take it easy. She walked back out to the waiting room, checked her phone for messages. There was one from Michael, asking her to come over to his house, not the station, as soon as she could. She stared at the message and then at the prescription in her other hand. It was for the same medication her mother was taking. As if moving back in with her wasn't sad enough, they had matching prescriptions now too. She screwed it up and put it in the bin. She didn't need pills. She needed to face up to what had started this whole nightmare up again. She needed to deal with what happened in London.

September 2012

She had been glued to her computer screen for hours, trying to put the finishing touches on a piece about a campaign to have a local pub granted Community Value status. Developers were threatening to buy it and turn it into a luxury apartment block. It was a favour for a friend, a worthy enough story, but unlikely to pique the interest of the nationals. She was hoping to call in a couple of favours at the *Guardian* – there was a slim chance they'd go for it, but it was more likely going to end up on her blog.

She snapped her laptop shut, reached again for the piece of

paper on the top of the pile of reports and research she kept pushed to the corner of her desk. It was an address, Madalina's address. Gripped by an overwhelming need to do something, she put it in her pocket, grabbed her jacket and bag and headed for the Tube.

She had tried to talk to Madalina several times after the day she'd seen her with the bruise but Madalina had not even acknowledged her presence, hurrying past her, head down. She had looked thinner and more haggard each week and then, suddenly, she had stopped coming. Jenny had asked her neighbour about her, under the pretence that she was looking for a cleaner. She was sick, the well-dressed woman who answered the door had said. Do you know what's wrong with her? Jenny had asked. No, the woman said, she didn't even know her surname, as it happened; all she had was a number. She had given it to Jenny and then she'd disappeared back into her house, as if it was perfectly normal to have no information whatsoever about a woman who had the keys to your well-appointed Victorian terrace. Jenny had tried the number, a landline, a few times, but it went through to an answering machine and something stopped her from leaving a message. So she had had it traced and found an address: 42 Fairfield Road. She hadn't been interfering, she told herself. Madalina was in trouble, she was sure of it. And so often trouble meant a good story.

Fairfield Road was in a rundown part of town between Stoke Newington and West Ham, yet to benefit from the regeneration of the area that the Olympic Park was supposed to have brought. Jenny walked from the station through the Stratford Centre, a covered shopping mall, where she bought a bunch of flowers, out on to Broadway, before joining Romford Road. She passed a tall redbrick block with a hoarding on the side advertising 'Refurbished Offices TO LET', a strip of shops – a nail salon, a *Chickens 'R' Us*, a grocer's with produce arranged outside on stacked plastic crates covered in grass matting. She turned off the main road on to Fairfield Road. Number 42 was halfway down.

She had thought about how to do this. She was aware that if Madalina was being abused by a husband or boyfriend, that her showing up could make things worse. If anyone other than Madalina answered the door, Jenny would say Madalina cleaned for her, she wanted to bring her some flowers and check when she'd be back at work. It might not be what most employers would do, but Jenny figured it was believable and easy enough for Madalina to explain away if she had to.

The house was dilapidated. Paint peeling from the window frames, an old, stained mattress resting on scrubby grass in the tiny front garden. Jenny hesitated. Then she knocked.

Movement inside, a gentle thudding, a door slamming, but nobody answered. She waited a couple of minutes and then knocked again. She stepped back, looked up to the top-floor windows. Filthy net curtains twitched. A man's voice called out. 'Who is it?' Heavily accented English. 'I'm a friend of Madalina's,' Jenny said. 'Just coming to see how she is.' The door opened. A stocky man in a leather jacket and highly polished shoes. He would be handsome, Jenny thought, if he smiled, but his face was set in a frown, his eyes cold.

'Who are you?' he asked.

Behind him, at the back of the hallway, she glimpsed a woman. Not Madalina. Another woman, thin and pale. The man turned and shouted something in a foreign language. The woman disappeared behind a door.

'What do you want?' He looked her up and down.

'I just . . .' Her resolve faltered as he stared at her, unblinking. 'Madalina cleans for me. She said she was sick. I suppose she must be better?'

'She's fine,' the man said. 'She's out.' He slammed the door shut. Jenny stood there for a moment, wondering if she should knock again, trying to think of another question to ask, some way to get into the house. But the way he'd looked at her . . . She walked away, still holding the flowers. She looked back up at the top window. The curtain was pulled aside and Madalina was looking out at her, her face stricken with fear.

A week later there was a knock at Jenny's door. It was late, past ten. The others were out and Jenny hesitated before answering.

'Madalina . . . ?' The question mark hung in the air between them. The woman looked behind her and pushed past Jenny into the hallway.

'I need money.'

'What for?'

'I need one thousand pounds. For my life.'

* * *

Jenny led her into the kitchen, poured them both glasses of cheap wine. Madalina grimaced as she sipped it.

'My family make wine. It is good. Not like this.' She put the glass down and wiped her mouth with the back of her hand. 'So, you help me?'

'I don't have a thousand pounds, Madalina.'

'You must get. You borrow. It is your fault. You come to house, you make them worried. I need to get away *now*.'

'Get away from who? From the man I met? What are you so afraid of?'

'Get me the money. Then I tell you story. When I'm gone you sell it to the newspaper, they pay you. Simple.' She gazed at Jenny, her eyes like pebbles, dull and lifeless.

'I'm sorry if I caused you trouble. I didn't mean to. I was trying to help.'

'Well, you did. Big trouble for me and now you pay.'

Jenny shook her head. 'You won't even tell me what it's for.'

'I tell you, you will help me?' It was barely more than a whisper.

'If you tell me, at least I can try.'

Madalina told her story.

*

Her family owned a small vineyard in Urlați, she said. She was the youngest of three. Her elder siblings worked for the family business, she was finishing school. But things were not going well. They were struggling. Her father had an idea. They would try to attract tourists for wine tasting and meals, perhaps provide rooms. It was decided she would come to England. Many people had come to England after the borders opened. She would work and send money home to help her family, and she would learn English so she could help with the business when she returned.

She had an uncle. He was not really an uncle. He was someone her mother knew. He said he knew people who could help. They ran a cleaning agency. Hard work, he said, but good money. They would give her a job. They would pay for her journey and she could pay it back when she had earned some money. They would find her a nice room. He showed them all pictures on his phone of a redbrick house on a street with trees and a room with yellow walls. She could stay there. There were other girls there. She would make friends. She would work and she would learn and then she would come home.

A man met her at Luton airport. He smiled at her and was kind. He was warm and friendly and smartly dressed in a leather jacket and shiny shoes. He was a friend of her uncle, he said. He carried her bag. He had a nice car. He drove her through streets with trees and rows of redbrick houses. They did not stop there. They kept driving. When they did stop, finally, she was almost asleep. Her flight had been early and she had not eaten all day, she was tired and weak. The man opened the car door and shook her. There was no time for sleeping, he said. They had paid her uncle one thousand pounds for her and she needed to start paying it back. She was confused. She knew nothing of a thousand pounds, only her flight, which she would pay back out of her first month's wages, it had been arranged. Stupid fucking bitch, he had said. Always such stupid fucking bitches.

There was no bedroom with yellow walls. There were no bedrooms at all, just mattresses on floors, two in each room, filthy and bare. The walls were unpainted, stained with damp and mildew. In one room a woman in leather trousers and a black bra was bent over, painting her toe nails bright red. In another, a woman with peroxide blonde hair lay half sleeping, in a dirty, shapeless T-shirt. The man pointed at the mattress next to her. That is yours, he said. She would pay for her bed, her clothes and her food every month. Anything left over would go towards paying her debt. When the debt was paid, she could go.

'They give you choice.' Madalina almost smiled. 'You can work for agency, cleaning, or you can work for shop, fucking. It is very clever, I think. If you work for shop, you have money. You pay more of your debt. You are free in a year. If you work for agency, you do not earn enough. I am working twelve hours a day, every day, for more than six months – and still they say I owe one thousand pounds. Everyone starts in agency. Everyone finishes in shop.'

They met several times over the following weeks. The last time, Madalina had seemed the most desperate.

'When will you get money?' It was the first thing she said as she walked through the door, rubbing her thin arms against the autumn chill.

'I'm working on it. There's a big newspaper interested in the story and they're willing to put me on staff while I investigate/I may be able to claim some expenses, but it's going to take some time. How are you going to explain the money anyway, when you do get it?'

'I will worry about it, not you. They only want money, I think. Look at me.' She was gaunt, her skin sallow, the circles under her eyes almost black. 'I am not good for them anyway. They need fresh girls.'

'You should stay here. We can go to the police together, right now.' Jenny had known it was useless.

'I tell you already. I go to police, my family will be hurt, maybe killed. I have to do this way. I'm sorry.'

'You have nothing to be sorry about.'

'I will come here again. Sunday. And then you will have money?'

'I'm doing my best, Madalina.'

Madalina squeezed Jenny's hand, her fingers rough and calloused. 'Thank you for helping me.'

She did not come back that Sunday.

Jenny never saw her again.

She pulled up outside Michael's house, a neat white bungalow at the end of Pont Vaillant Lane in a nondescript corner of the Vale. The Vale was considered less desirable than the Southern Parishes. Jenny had found that out on her first day at the Ladies' College. She'd won a scholarship there and her parents hadn't even been able to afford the uniform, with its duffle coat, wax jacket and hockey stick for winter, blazer and lacrosse kit for summer. They'd had to take out a loan, three hundred pounds, to pay for it all. When she'd arrived, she'd been cornered, along with the other scholarship girls, by the girls who had come straight up from Melrose, the prep school. They were asked where they lived, what their fathers did, where they holidayed, whether or not they were members of the Pony Club or the Yacht Club, did they ski? All of the prep school girls lived in the upper parishes: St Martins, St Saviours, Torteval, the pretty parishes with the big houses and the sea views. When Jenny said she lived in the Vale, one of them said, knowingly, that her dad owned an estate agency, and you could get good value for money there.

She'd been embarrassed at the time, wished she'd lived anywhere but the Vale. Stupid, the things you worried about as a kid. She loved it here now. It was flat and sandy and windswept, from L'Ancresse and Pembroke in the far North, through L'Islet, with its surf shop and downmarket supermarket, the Vale Church and Rousse. Beautiful Rousse. Hours spent jumping off the fishermen's pier into the water, clear as glass, so deep and so, so cold, fish tickling your feet as you swam to the rocky bay, gasping for breath, salt in your ears and your eyes and your hair.

She saw Michael standing in the front window, no doubt wondering why she was sitting there daydreaming. She got out of the car, wished all she had to worry about was whether or not the tide was high enough to jump from the pier.

Stone ornaments stood on the well-maintained front lawn, most of them animals – a cat with a kitten, a bloodhound looking mournfully towards the house, an otter posed on a log, an old man with a round nose wearing a sou'wester. They were all surrounded by carefully placed pieces of sea glass, waves of blue and green rippling around each figure. There was something sad about the scene, she thought. The figures looked trapped. Or, not trapped so much as marooned, the water around them unmoving. Frozen in time.

A slice of polished tree trunk etched with the word 'Karaikal' hung to one side of the front door. It was a strange Guernsey affectation, naming houses like pets. She wondered who or what Karaikal was. The house next door, another bungalow ('Four Winds') was unkempt, the paintwork stained and the gutters full of leaves. There were three cars in the driveway, one with the engine running. A man emerged from the front door before turning back and shouting something in a foreign language. He pulled the door shut. His head was shaven, the muscles in his neck sinewy. Jenny knocked loudly on Michael's door. The man nodded at her and smiled a 'good morning', before getting in the car, revving the engine and spinning the wheels as he turned right on to the Longue Rue and sped off towards town.

The door opened. Michael clearly hadn't slept. He had heavy bags under his eyes and a day's worth of stubble on his face. His breath smelt of stale alcohol and his lips were stained red. They stood on the doorstep. A young woman emerged from the house next door, dressed in a navy pinafore and white apron, her mousey hair pulled back into a tight bun. She gave a smile and a wave. Michael returned the greeting.

'Come in.' He stepped aside to let Jenny in. She hesitated before she followed him through a narrow hallway.

'What's the story next door?' She asked.

'Multi-occupancy housing. Polish, I think. It's a three-bed place and there are at least nine people in there so far as I can work out. Young lady there works at one of the hotels. One of the lads is a cook. They're no trouble. They only sleep there – the rest of the time they're working.'

The walls of his hallway were mostly bare. A simple crucifix hung next to an old-fashioned entry mirror with shelves underneath and hooks at the side holding a set of keys and a small torch on a wrist strap. The kitchen, for the most part, was neat and sparse. White walls, no pictures, clear surfaces, a chrome kettle and toaster, a mug tree with three white mugs hanging from it, a bread bin. No clutter, no mess. And then, in the middle of the room, was the table. Every inch of it was covered in papers and photographs, scribbled notes, open files, crisp wrappers, a banana skin, three half-drunk mugs of what appeared to be black coffee, a wine glass, and an empty bottle of red wine.

He moved the bottle, placed the mugs and the glass in the sink and filled the kettle. He seemed even bigger in this small kitchen, the kettle diminutive in his large hands. He turned to her.

'Thanks for coming at such short notice.'

Jenny gestured to the table. 'What have you found? Am I right? Or am I going mad? Because I really don't know any more.'

'I don't think you're going mad. I wish you were.' He glanced at her. 'No offence.'

'So you think the deaths are connected?'

He didn't answer immediately, but moved the food wrappings

and police reports to one side and just left some pictures on the table, pictures of dead girls. Not whole, dead girls, parts of them: an arm here, a leg there, a close-up of a shoulder. He lined them up, checking the back of each one before he placed them in order. Then he pulled out a chair for her.

'Sit down, Jenny.' She sat. He pointed at each picture. Amanda Guille, Hayley Bougourd, Melissa Marchant, Janet Gaudion, Mary Brehaut.

'Elizabeth?'

'There are none in the file. Seems they went missing at some point over the last fifty years.'

She picked up Hayley's. Her right arm, covered in tattoos – Celtic symbols, Chinese letters, and on her wrist – what was it on her wrist? She pointed to it, left her finger hovering over it. Michael rifled through some papers and placed one on top of the picture of Hayley.

'I had it blown up. Look.' A close up showed the marks clearly. Three long, vertical scratches and a shorter, horizontal one underneath.

'And here, on Janet Gaudion.' It was there, on the top of her right thigh.

'Melissa. And Mary.' Michael placed the magnified images side by side.

Jenny looked at each in turn and then to Michael.

'He's marked them.'

Michael nodded.

'Jesus Christ, Michael, this is proof! Someone killed these girls and left a bloody calling card and nobody noticed. And it's not just the marks.' She told him about her meeting with Tom Le Jardin.

'The kid who found the guy a couple of weeks ago, no one took him seriously.' Michael said. 'It was only luck his notes ended up in the file. Taken on its own, this guy or scarecrow, whatever it was he found, could have been written off as a coincidence.

But taken with what this Tom Le Jardin said?' He paused, scraped at his stubble. 'This is methodical, planned. Ritualistic, even. And it's been going on for decades.'

Jenny picked up the picture of Amanda, studied the marks on her cheek again, and was again struck by the feeling that the mark was familiar to her, that it existed somewhere in her memory, that it was there, waiting for her to grab hold of it. She searched through another pile of photographs, these ones all taken at the scenes where the bodies were found. *Crime scenes,* she thought. She looked at each girl in black and white, all of them lying on the sand.

'He hasn't hurt them.'

'Hmm?' Michael rubbed at his eyes.

'I mean, he hasn't beaten them, or raped them.'

'What do you mean?'

'It's just . . . it doesn't feel violent, the way they were all found. When you look at them all like that, they look almost peaceful.'

'Like they're sleeping. I thought the same thing. But it's murder. We're looking for a violent individual. Never mind he doesn't want to spoil his victims' pretty faces.'

'So what do we do now? Where do we start?' She put the pictures back on the table. 'Did you look into David De Putron? He gave Amanda piano lessons at the youth club, he may have taught Hayley too, that's significant, isn't it? Perhaps he knew all of these girls somehow? And there's something off about him. I'm sure he had Brian call me, to warn me off.'

'I started doing a bit of digging after you spoke to Hayley's mother, and I'll certainly do some more. But, Jenny, you have to remember that everyone knows everybody else here, one way or another. I even looked up piano teachers in the yellow pages. There are only twelve listed. The fact that one man may have given two of the girls lessons is not surprising.'

He hesitated. 'I need to be honest with you about something.'

'I think I know what you're going to say, but it's OK, really.

Unless it's going to affect what's going on right now.' She pointed to the wine bottle and raised an eyebrow.

That wasn't it, Michael said. He'd been drinking, yes, but it didn't happen very often, at least not any more. He rubbed his eyes again, pulling his hand down over his chin, scraping the coarse hairs backwards and forwards. She felt an almost over-whelming desire to put her hand out, pat his shoulder, to tell him it was all going to be OK. She took another sip of her tea instead and looked at him expectantly.

'I used to drink a lot, as it happens,' he said. 'Started off as part of the job, few pints after work, but it soon became more than that. I needed the alcohol to function. It wasn't just me, mind you, there were plenty of us turning up hung-over on a regular basis, it was part of the culture. Not that I'm trying to make light of it, but I did a better job than most, even when I was half drunk. It never affected my work. Not until Ellen died.' He shook his head, as if trying to convince himself, and then looked at her. 'After that, it was a different story.' He paused.

'I turned up drunk a couple of times. A couple of times I didn't turn up at all. The force was understanding. I took a leave of absence, but that made everything worse. Without work to distract me, I hit rock bottom. Nearly died, as it happened. Forced me to take a long, hard look at things. And that was when I found God.'

Jenny tried not to look uncomfortable. He went on.

'I cleaned up my act, stopped drinking, worked harder. I'd always been a good copper. With a clear head and a sense of purpose, I reckon I was probably one of the best. Started to see things more clearly, saw some of my colleagues for what they really were. Lazy, entitled jobsworths, some of them, thought they were better than everyone else because they wore a uniform. Thought they could get away with anything. Only I couldn't let them. Not any more.'

'What happened?'

'Not long after I'd turned things around, started to get on with my life, a young lad was brought into the cells. Drunk, throwing up, mouthing off. Said something one of my colleagues took offence too and got a good kicking for it. The family lodged a complaint. There was an investigation by Internal Affairs. They took statements. Four coppers saw what happened. Three told one story. I told the truth. Some of them have never forgiven me for it.'

They sat in silence, Jenny unsure for once what response was required. He seemed to pick up on her uncertainty. He stared at her, and for the first time she noticed his eyes were not the brown she'd assumed and which would match his swarthy, island complexion, but a dark, unsettling blue.

'I have very few friends on the police force, Jenny. I'm telling you this so you understand. They're not going to like this. I'm going to accuse the force of being blind to a serial killer when there was evidence right under our noses. We're going to have to be careful.'

'How *could* this have been missed, Michael?'

He shook his head. They moved around a lot on the force these days, he said, from department to department. Over the course of a career an officer might work Fraud, Traffic, Criminal investigation. He'd been on the force nearly forty years and he'd not come across these cases before. He remembered them, of course, you always remembered the bodies, but he'd not worked on any of them. She had to realise, he said, that none of these cases were considered crimes. The files were all slim, nothing to them really. He'd spoken to the officers who'd worked Hayley's case already, and he was sorry to say it wasn't given the attention it should have been, whether through oversight or laziness, well, that he wouldn't like to say.

'As for what we do now, I'm going to have to concentrate on Amanda. It's the only open case and I need to review it, in light of all this.' He shook his head. 'And I'm going to have to take this to the chief. Today. You need to leave this to me now. This is a murder investigation, multiple victims; I can't have you involved, not like this anyway. I can't stop you reporting on it, obviously, conducting your own investigations, as it were. Only . . . tread carefully, Jenny. We don't know what we're dealing with here.'

She nodded. 'I understand. But this is a story now. A really big story. I'm taking it to Brian. See what he makes of it.'

'Give me some time. I need to give everyone at the station a chance to get on top of things, to prepare a response. I might not be their favourite copper, but I'm still a copper, and this,' he gestured to Jenny and the paperwork, 'this is only going to work if we keep each other on board.'

'End of today?'

He nodded. 'I'd better get on with it then.'

'You might want to take a shower before you go in. Freshen up a bit?' She pointed to the wine. 'I thought the church saved you from alcohol?'

'The church saved me from a lot of things, but you can't appreciate faith unless you know what it is to doubt, Jennifer. Every now and then, I doubt. And when I doubt, I drink.'

He gave her a pat on the shoulder as she left. 'I'll call you with an update as soon as I can.' The door clicked shut behind him.

It was mid-morning but the sky was sombre, the sun obscured by thick slashes of slate-grey cloud, heavy with rain. The street was empty. The forecast had been for good weather but islanders knew better than to trust a weather forecast. Centuries of fishing and farming had bestowed them with a sixth sense. They could feel it in the air and see it in the movement of the trees and the sea. Even Jenny.

30

Michael

He looked at the mess on the table, picked a mug out of the sink, rinsed it, and made a cup of instant coffee. He drank it while it was too hot, scalding his tongue and the back of his throat in his haste to finish. Then he showered, quickly but efficiently, and stood in front of the bathroom mirror.

He was old fashioned when it came to shaving. His razor, for example. He'd had it for twenty years. A present from Sheila. Anniversary or birthday, he couldn't recall now, and he probably hadn't appreciated it at the time because it was nothing fancy. But it had become, over the years, a constant in his life.

He applied the shaving foam liberally. Scented with lemon and menthol, it helped to clear his head and felt cool on his tired skin. He liked shaving. Other men complained about it, found it a hassle. Not him. Holding the razor's bone handle, slowly, steadily, pulling the blade over his cheeks and his jaw, paying careful attention to the areas where his skin had loosened under his chin and was more likely to catch if he rushed. It was one of the rare moments in his day when he was completely focused on the task in hand but also completely relaxed.

Most days, anyway. Today, he was tired, his arm unsteady, his hand trembling more than usual. He couldn't keep his thoughts from the mess of paperwork on his kitchen table, from the files and the notes and the pictures, from the marks on the dead girls' bodies, from what they meant. There was no doubt about it in his mind, none at all. He winced as he nicked himself. He pulled some tissue off the toilet roll and pressed it hard against his chin until it stuck fast.

He went to his room. He'd done nothing to it since Sheila left. He dressed in a crumpled white shirt, pulling a navy V-neck over the top, thus rendering the creases a non-issue, and a pair of corduroy trousers. He combed his hair and looked at his reflection in the mirror on the wardrobe. He looked old. He was past the minimum retirement age for a copper, could have taken his pension already. Why hadn't he? Stubbornness? Determination? Fear? He wasn't sure he knew. Whatever the reason, this case would change everything. For him. For the force. A serial killer on the loose. In Guernsey. After today, nothing would be the same again.

He sat at the foot of his bed, closed his eyes, clasped his hands together. It took practice to pray effectively. It looked easy, but it wasn't. You had to block out the noise, your own and other peoples'. It was easier in church, with the support of the congregation and with the reverend to guide you. At home, he found himself distracted too easily, found his mind wandering, his silent words interrupted by the roar of a motorbike or the barking of a dog. It was especially important today, though, to be quiet and centred, to ask for guidance and strength, to pray for the girls and their families. To pray for Jenny, for the island. To ask for forgiveness. For himself, always, and for the police force, for letting those girls down. And for him – whoever was doing this. He prayed for forgiveness for him and asked that they might find the sick bastard. Because justice started here, in this world. With Michael.

On the way out of the house, he checked his chin in the hallway mirror. Blood had seeped through the toilet paper and dried, forming a tissue skin. He peeled it away, carefully, reopening the wound as he did so. He grimaced at the mirror as he surveyed the damage. It was a bad cut. It would bleed for hours.

*

He arrived at the station at lunchtime. Years back, everyone would have been in the mess hall. Canteen you'd call it now, a big room with a small kitchen behind a serving hatch where a couple of cheerful ladies would serve up hot food, school-dinner style. Nothing fancy. Sausage and mash or fish and chips or, his favourite, a bowl of steaming bean jar, a delicious, meaty, bean casserole, with bread and butter to mop up the thick juices. They'd all take their allotted hour, loosen belts, kick back and relax over a hot meal. There would be card games; euchre or cribbage, football pools being argued over, plenty of chat and banter. Until the chief officer or the deputy chief officer came in. Then you'd stand up as they walked by, only sitting down when they told you to.

Not any more. These days, hardly anyone glanced up as he entered the office, despite him outranking the lot of them. The few who did gave him a nod and a muttered 'sir'. Everyone else remained glued to their screens, sandwich in one hand, the other resting on a mouse or holding an iPhone, the act of eating barely interrupting the flow of report writing or various other onerous administrative tasks which were now all part of a day's work. He missed the typing pool. For many reasons, not least that the well-trained, well-dressed young ladies in it used to handle all these mundane jobs so efficiently, freeing up the coppers to keep the streets safe. It wasn't a sexist thing. He was all for female officers. Crikey, he'd take an all-male typing pool if it meant his paperwork would be reduced.

DC Marquis was at his desk eating a pallid, soggy-looking wrap and washing it down with swigs of a bright pink drink claiming to be some sort of vitamin-enriched water.

'Do you have a minute, Marquis?'

'Yes, sir.' He jumped to his feet. 'What can I do for you, sir?'

'Come with me.'

'Certainly, sir.' He wiped his mouth with the back of his hand,

and then his hands on his trousers, leaving a faint trace of mayon-
naise on the shiny fabric. 'Where are we going, sir?'

'We're going to talk to the chief.'

Marquis' eyes widened and his face turned a now-familiar
shade of red. Michael gave him a reassuring pat on the back. 'It's
nothing to worry about, Stephen. I just might need you to back
me up on a couple of things. Follow me.'

Prior to the appointment of Chief Officer Hammond, all the chiefs
of the Guernsey police had been Guernsey born and bred. That
was not to say, by any means, that they had all been good. The last
one, Chief Officer Le Noury, had been an affable buffoon. They
couldn't retire him quick enough. But before him there was Chief
Officer Wilson. Good old Roger. Michael had liked him as much
as the next person until the incident with that boy, assaulted in
police custody. Chief Wilson had told him his unwillingness to
'see things from the other officers' perspective' was bringing the
force into disrepute. Never mind the officers who'd beaten up a
young lad. No mention made of those bastards. According to
Roger Wilson it was Michael who had let them all down, broken
some sort of code. He was still knocking about – special advisor
or some such.

Now, Chief Officer Hammond, he was English. No matter he
came with excellent qualifications and years of experience and
had actually made some positive changes to the force's somewhat
outdated working practices, he was an outsider and, therefore,
according to general opinion, at least amongst the ranks, not to
be trusted. But it struck Michael right now, as he sat opposite the
somewhat beleaguered chief, that in this case, having a mainlander
at the helm might be a positive advantage. No prior involvement
with any of the cases. No baggage. No history.

They had been sitting in his office for several minutes, Hammond turning the pages of the file he had given him slowly and

without comment. Marquis was fidgeting in his seat and rubbing at the stains on his trousers. Michael sat still and straight, reading the various certificates and diplomas framed on the walls, taking in an old photograph on the desk of two little girls, twins if he wasn't mistaken, in matching school uniforms and a newer picture of the same girls, much older, in caps and gowns, scrolls held aloft. He stared at their smiles. Always pained him a little, graduation photographs. You could almost see the hopes and dreams in their eyes.

Hammond closed the file and looked up through rimless glasses. He had a heavy, well-cultivated moustache, which he stroked with his left hand while his right tapped the desk rhythmically. He looked to Michael. *Tap, tap.* Then to Marquis. *Tap, tap.* Then to the file. *Tap, tap.* And, finally, back to Michael. He placed both of his hands on the desk in front of him. Michael took a deep breath. He could see it coming. He was going to get laughed out of the station.

'This all looks plausible to you?'

Michael nodded.

'And you, DC Marquis, you're a relation of Jennifer Dorey's, I understand? A lot of this seems to have stemmed from her research.'

'Not a close relative, sir, a second cousin.' Michael raised his eyebrows at him. 'But she's very thorough, sir, very professional in my experience.'

'You can see where my findings have tallied with hers.' Michael added.

Hammond nodded. He removed his glasses and rubbed his eyes.

'You'd better get a team together, Gilbert. Pull everything we have on the closed cases and see if there's anything left in the evidence room. We'll need to reprocess it according to today's procedures. As of now we're only officially treating Amanda's death as suspicious. We'll look into the others on the quiet. Let's try to contain the panic.' He glanced down at the file again. Michael nodded and rose to his feet, motioning for Marquis, who appeared glued to his seat, to follow.

'We had a special term for this kind of thing in the Met, Gilbert.' Michael turned back to the Chief.

'Yes, sir?'

'We'd call this a clusterfuck, Gilbert. I hope you're the kind of copper who can deal with one.'

'Yes, sir.'

Michael pulled the door shut behind them as he left.

All in all, it had gone better than he hoped.

He stood, Marquis at his side, and explained the situation to the rest of the force. Slowly, as they realised what he was saying, they stopped eating their sandwiches and swigging their cokes and listened, open-mouthed. It was a wonderful feeling, having them listen, the usual looks of derision or disinterest wiped from their faces by the words he was saying. Amanda's death was to be treated as suspicious. And they needed to get their arses in gear and investigate it. Properly, this time. He assigned a new team to interview everyone again, another team to review the evidence. This time enquiries would not be routine. This time it was a murder investigation. As he spoke, unseen by the rest of the room, Chief Hammond opened his office door and stood, leaning in the door frame. He nodded to Michael and listened. Michael continued. There were a number of other deaths which might be linked to Amanda Guille's, he said. A small team, headed up by him and DC Marquis, would be looking into those. If and when a connection was made between the deaths, the investigation would be adjusted accordingly. Several looks of incredulity passed around the room. Fallaize raised his hand. Annoying little shit, Fallaize was. Wore too much product in his hair and was always flashing a new watch or pair of cufflinks. He must come from money because his police salary certainly wasn't paying for it all.

'Yes, Sergeant Fallaize?'

'What are we talking about here? Are we talking multiple murders? Because if so, where are the other bodies? We've hardly been tripping over them, have we? *Sir.*' He emphasized the 'sir', as if it were a bad joke that Michael should be senior to him, which no doubt the arrogant little bastard thought it was. There were a couple of nervous sniggers from the back of the room, which rapidly dissipated as Chief Hammond walked over and stood next to Michael.

'Watch your tone, Fallaize.' The offending officer flushed red. Everybody else sat up a little straighter.

'Please continue, DCI Gilbert.'

'We're looking at several historical cases, young women who drowned ten, twenty, up to fifty years ago. There have been similarities noted in these women's backgrounds and in the way that they died.' He rolled back on his feet a little and looked to Hammond. 'Anything you'd like to add, sir?'

'Thank you, Gilbert.' He addressed the room.

'If you've not been assigned a specific task relating to this investigation, you're to get on with your routine work. The last thing we want is to induce panic. DCI Gilbert will be the only point of contact to the press on this. The *Guernsey News* is already ahead of the curve and it won't be long until the nationals are on the scent. I've just been on the phone to Hampshire Constabulary. They are sending over a team as soon as possible to conduct an independent review. This is routine in cases where no significant progress has been made over this sort of time frame. Clearly, we're on the back foot here. We haven't been investigating a possible murder. Now we are and it's time to play catch-up. Let's make sure our house is in order before they arrive, show them we're on top of this.' He walked back to his office and shut the door.

For a millisecond there was complete silence. Then a low murmur began to swell amongst the ranks.

'*Fuck me.*'

'*Is this for real?*'

'*Sounds like it. Fuck.*'

Michael surveyed the room for a moment and then returned to his office, leaving the door open. He sat back in his chair. It would be wrong to enjoy the moment. There should be no pleasure taken from a situation arising from the murder of a young woman. Young women. But it was good to see the smiles wiped off of some of those bastards' faces.

Marquis appeared in the doorway, hesitated, and then knocked, timidly.

'It's open, Marquis. No need to knock.'

'Wondering what I should start with, sir?'

'You can start with this bloody machine. I can't get Google running for some reason.' He moved his chair out so that the younger officer could wave his hands over the keyboard and mutter some magic charm, which miraculously reinstated Internet Explorer.

'Thank you, Marquis.'

'No problem, sir.'

Worth his weight in gold that boy was.

Michael positioned his hands awkwardly over the keyboard. Despite having to now write up his own reports he had never mastered the art of touch typing and looked on his younger colleagues with a mixture of wonder and envy as their hands flew over the keys, producing three paragraphs in the time it would take him to write one. Fortunately today he only needed to write a couple of words. He pressed the keys slowly and deliberately, L E A P G u e r n s e y, clicked the search button and found the website. Bold letters were emblazoned across a hazy background of smiling young people punching the air on a gloriously blue-skied day.

Learn, Empower, Achieve – change your Path!

It took him a second to work it out. He sighed. Bloody stupid acronyms. They were everywhere these days and most of them didn't even make sense. This one was a case in point. LEAP. 'I ask you,' he sighed to himself. Stupid name aside, he had to admit it looked like a worthwhile organisation. Trying to get kids off the streets and involved in art and drama, giving them a space to hang out. It probably didn't work. Kids with the sorts of problems this place was trying to help always ran with the wrong crowd. It was shaking the crowd that was difficult. Didn't matter how many nice activities you provided, most kids would rather be out getting into trouble with their mates. You had to try, he supposed. You couldn't just give up. Where would you be then? Hopeless, that's where. He'd been there and back again. He wouldn't wish it on anyone else.

The police didn't refer kids directly to this place but he knew social services did. Amanda had attended. According to Jenny's notes, Hayley's mother couldn't remember the name of the group she went to but he was pretty certain it would be this one. Come to think of it, he was waiting for her Social Services file to be sent through. There should have been a copy in her police file already but it was either never requested (which, he thought, would be a shocking oversight, even for a small force like theirs) or it had gone missing. Either way, he wasn't going to hang around waiting for it. This place was a direct link between at least two of the victims. He needed to pay them a visit.

The youth club occupied a bright and airy space in St Martins, right behind the community centre. The walls were painted in bright reds and blues, one was covered in graffiti but the artistic sort, not just random scribbles and squirts. The polished wooden floor smelt of beeswax with a hint of lavender. There was a coffee bar at the back, plenty of shabby but comfy-looking sofas to relax on. He could quite easily have put his feet up and enjoyed a coffee here. There were no kids, though. The presence of a ragtag bunch of borderline juvenile delinquents would probably affect the atmosphere.

He walked over to the bar and shouted through to the kitchen.

'Hullo! Anyone around?'

'We're closed! Open at four.' A man emerged from a side room, wearing a stained apron and wiping his hands with a dirty cloth. He had smudges of something, possibly mud, possibly chocolate, all over his face. He was youngish, mid-thirties, with curly brown hair which fell to his shoulders and made Michael think of a cocker spaniel.

'Oh. How can I help you, man?'

Michael noted the board shorts and boating shoes.

'I was wanting to talk to somebody about Amanda Guille. I believe she came here in the year or so leading up to her death?'

'Yeah, man, that was terrible. The police already talked to me and Cathy – that's my wife – we run the place.'

Michael consulted his notepad. 'You must be Nicholas?'

'Yeah, man, call me Nick.' He shook Michael's hand. 'You're from the police?'

'I am indeed. DCI Gilbert. I just wanted to run through a couple of things with you.'

'No worries, man. Let me get cleaned up and I'll grab us a coffee.' He removed his apron and went behind the counter where he washed his hands and took out some mugs. Michael wandered over to the room Nick had emerged from. It was a workshop. One of the tables was covered in lumps of wet clay.

'We're doing sculpting this afternoon. It's usually very popular. I was just getting prepared,' Nick called over.

They sat on one of the sofas and Michael asked Nick to run through how the club worked, what activities they did, who attended and how often, was it only kids who'd been referred or could anyone come along?

Nick was passionate about his work. He spoke with enthusiasm and made liberal use of his hands as he described what they did, waving them around, gesturing, slapping the table. They were mostly arts based, he explained. There were plenty of sports groups around, but not so much opportunity to get stuck into creative stuff. And there were so many studies that showed art could be a form of therapy, it couldn't be refuted. A lot of the club members had trouble expressing themselves; they had issues with depression or anger or came from violent backgrounds where self-expression was not encouraged. LEAP was a place where they had an opportunity to try new ways of communicating, through painting or music or sculpture.

'It all sounds very good, Nick, but does it really work?' Michael asked. 'I mean, I know the studies tell us it does, but have you seen it stop these kids from reoffending? Amanda, for example. When she came to you she'd been in trouble with the police, was depressed; did you notice an improvement in her? Were you surprised to hear she might have killed herself?'

'Yeah, man. It definitely helps. Sure, there are kids that don't want to know and you can't help them if they haven't recognised they need help. They have to be open to the idea. Amanda was. I told this to the first guy who asked. She seemed happier, came a couple of times a week. She seemed good. So sad she didn't stick with it, man. Some of these kids just need to hang in there, you know? It's never as bad as it seems.'

Only sometimes, Michael thought, it really is.

He smiled at Nick. He liked positive people. Appreciated them. The world would be a better place if it were full of Nicks, always looking on the bright side and trying to make things better. We should try to learn from people like this, he thought. He wondered if he should suggest some art therapy to the rest of the force.

There were a few anger and resentment issues at the station that might benefit from a spot of pottery.

'I wonder, how far do your records go back, Nick? I see you've been in operation for over twenty years. Could you check on a couple of names for me, tell me if they ever attended the club?'

Sure, Nick said, he'd go and check. He came back a few minutes later with an unsettled look on his face and two yellowed index cards in his hands.

'Hayley Bougourd and Melissa Marchant.' He held out the cards. 'They both came here.' He was quiet for a moment. 'They're both dead, aren't they? Listen, dude, what's going on here? Because I've only worked here for, like, four years. If there's anything funny going on, you'll need to speak to my predecessor, or someone on the board.'

'Actually, that would be very helpful. A list of staff, past and present and board members is just what I need. Is that something you can get me, Nick?'

He could try he said. The administration wasn't done from here; it was computerized and his wife managed that side of it. He could get it sent through. Michael gave him his email address. Nick still looked worried.

'These kids are troubled before they get here, you know? You can't hold us to blame if shit goes wrong. We're the ones trying to help. Some of them always slip through the net, man.' He ran his hand through his hair, chewed on his lip.

Someone has definitely slipped through the net, thought Michael. Was it someone who met three of his victims here?

'Just one more thing: David De Putron, he teaches piano lessons through the centre, I understand?'

'That's right. We all call him Mr De Putron – he doesn't go in for first names. He comes Tuesday and Thursday evenings.'

'And how long has he volunteered here for?'

'I'm not sure. Years. Before my time. I'd have to check with Cathy.'

'Thank you. That would be great.' He shook Nick's hand. 'Sailor, are you?' He nodded at Nick's shoes.

'All my life. Cathy and I just bought a boat, actually. Nothing swish, but sleeps two. We'll be out on it all summer, I hope.' He didn't look very happy about the idea.

'Chin up, Nick. You have nothing to worry about. Just routine enquiries. You've been very helpful.'

Nick nodded. 'I'd better get on with this.' He pointed to the workshop. 'Or it will all dry out.' He walked slowly to the table and picked up a piece of clay, started kneading it, then stared at it like he couldn't remember how it got to be in his hands.

'Keep up the good work, eh?' Michael gave a wave as he left. Poor guy. He looked like a frightened puppy. But he'd bounce back. He'd be wagging his tail again in no time.

31

Jenny

She had heard nothing from Michael. But it was nearly the end of the day and they had an agreement. She knocked on Brian's door.

'Come.' He stared at his computer screen for several seconds before he turned to her with a cold smile.

'Jennifer. Have a seat.' She sat and placed her report on the desk.

He skimmed through the pages, a look of mild interest quickly replaced by one of confusion and then what she could only guess was panic.

'A serial killer?' His face was ashen. 'This is what you've been working on? A fucking serial killer?' There was a quiet fury in his voice.

'I've only just pulled everything together.'

He turned the pages, back and forth. 'What do you expect me to do with this?'

'I was thinking we could do some more research, get a quote from the police and then print it?' She tried to keep the disdain she felt out of her voice. He clearly didn't know what to do with a *real* story.

'We can't print this! This is a nightmare. A fucking nightmare. I told you to leave this well alone!'

'I don't understand. Everything in there is on the record.

There's no speculation. It's all fact: six dead women, a possible serial killer – and maybe some police incompetence thrown in. Whatever else it may be, it's a great story, Brian. I'm working with a DCI. He's on board.'

'Fuck.' He shuffled through the papers again, his hands shaking. He took a deep breath. Put the file down. Attempted a smile.

'You're a good reporter, Jenny. I know that. It's why I hired you. It's just this . . .' He waved his hand over her report. 'I need to think about it. About what we do with it. How we present it. I need to make some calls. Speak to Legal, that sort of thing. I should have had some warning. You should have warned me this was coming.'

'Sorry to have caught you off guard, Brian. Really, I am. Other than my police sources you're the first person I've taken this to.'

Brian's face relaxed slightly but his smooth forehead remained unusually creased.

'You should go home, Jennifer. Get some rest. You look tired. We'll talk first thing tomorrow.'

She went back to her desk. Behind the glass walls of his office, Brian continued to stare at her report. He appeared lost in thought. She scrolled through her emails furiously, not reading the content. Was he really that much of a fucking amateur? Lost when some actual news hit his desk? Or was he genuinely pissed off that she'd left him out of the loop? Or was there something more to it than that? He seemed rattled. Upset. Frightened?

A new email arrived in her inbox.

Dear Jennifer, things being taken seriously here. I am up to my eyes in it. I will be in touch in the morning. Regards, Michael.

She rubbed her face with her hands. She should go home. Start with a fresh head in the morning. She was just about to shut down her computer when an email from Stephen Marquis caught her eye, the one that had arrived a couple of weeks ago. He'd wanted to meet for a coffee and talk about some graffiti at Moulin Huet. She'd skimmed through it then but had been distracted and she'd not looked at the attached photos. She opened them and peered at the rocks, daubed with green paint. It looked like pretty standard graffiti to her. Idiots. Spoiling such a beautiful spot. And one of hers and Charlie's favourite places. It was then, thinking about her dad at Moulin Huet, that a memory, which had previously been just out of focus, flitting at the edge of her consciousness, came fully into view.

The mark on the dead girls. She knew where she'd seen it before.

Friday, 21 November

The sun was only just up. Weak, wintery rays barely penetrated the heavy black clouds gathered above them. More strong winds had hit the island during the night, carpeting the narrow lane they walked along with leaves and twigs, which snapped and crunched underfoot. Trees lined the road on both sides, naked branches extending across it and meeting in the middle. Like ribs, Jenny thought. She felt like they were walking through the ribcage of some giant, flesh-stripped animal. They passed stone signposts etched with exotic-sounding place names: Icart, Jerbourg, Le Gouffre. Places to sit and have cream tea or to set up an easel and fancy yourself as Renoir for a couple of hours in the summer. Now they would be desolate.

The lane narrowed further, becoming a sandy pathway. A sign pointed the way: Moulin Huet. They picked their way up and then down roughly hewn steps, past gorse bushes emitting their faint coconut fragrance and on to the cliff path proper. In front of them, it was as if the sea had thrown the sky up out of its depths, for they were both the colour of gunmetal, both wild and tumultuous, white horses coursing through black water and streaking black clouds. The Pea Stacks, a rugged row of rocks poked tooth-like out of the water, standing defiant as the waves lashed them, crashing and foaming, angry at the stone invaders in their midst. Here, Jenny and Elliot were fully exposed to the strength of the wind. Force six, Jenny reckoned, and forecast to get stronger as the day went on.

Elliot stamped his feet against the cold.

'You picked a good morning for a hike.' He had to speak loudly, to be heard over the noise of the wind.

'I thought you wanted in on this story?'

'I do! Is this serial killer you told me about hiding in one of those caves, do you think?' He pointed to the crevices carved out of the bottom of the cliffs.

'It's not funny, Elliot.'

'Sorry. Call it gallows humour. But nothing you told me seemed connected to here. None of the bodies were found here. So why are we?'

'Let's call it a hunch.'

'Really? You call me at the crack of dawn, drag me to the end of the island in a hurricane, and now you're telling me we're working on a hunch?' He looked amused.

'You were away from the island for too long, Elliot. This is a brisk breeze, not a hurricane.' She grinned and strode ahead.

They walked along barren cliffs, looking out over the churning sea. The bottom of Jenny's coat flapped violently about her knees and Elliot's thick, choppy hair blew in every direction. He seemed to be struggling to see as he held it back out of his eyes and gingerly walked down the uneven steps, which led directly to the bay. Jenny followed, sure-footed, but she held on to the iron railing hammered into the steps and the cliff face, steadying herself. She could feel water on her face from here, still yards from the beach itself, the force of the waves and the wind carrying the sea spray to land. Hard to imagine the turquoise millpond it could be on a calm, summer's day, when boats would gently bob in the bay and children would swim across it. Even then, beneath the calm surface, way, way down, it was always like this really. Mighty. Unforgiving. It could take you. Turn on you when you were least expecting it.

It had been early morning when she'd got the call. Too early to be anything good, even before she'd heard Margaret's voice, breathy and wavering. Charlie had been missing all night, she'd said. He'd taken the boat out the previous evening, had been due back for a late dinner. The weather had been fine, there was a chance that he'd run into engine trouble and was just drifting. There was a chance the radio had failed too. It was too soon to think the worst, but Jenny was booked on to the last flight home within minutes of hanging up.

By the time she had landed at Guernsey airport the lifeboat had found his boat, drifting. The engine and the radio were fine, but there was no sign of Charlie Dorey. It would be another week before they found him.

In that week, when he'd been neither alive nor dead, when the faint hope of seeing him again was almost but not entirely over-whelmed by the rational thought that, in all likelihood, he was lost to them for ever, Jenny had revisited some of the places they had spent time together.

She had come here. To Moulin Huet, where they had so often climbed the slippery black rocks on to the smooth, wet sand and waded out to the rock pools, catching caboos and putting them in a large black bucket. Charlie had been a fisherman his whole life, but she was better at catching the tiny fish, their mottled silver brown bodies almost impossible to spot amongst the rocks and the seaweed until they darted out into open water and into her waiting hands.

She felt an overwhelming longing to be back there now, ankle deep in a warm rock pool, her dad's shadow playing on the water's sunlit surface.

'Wish I'd packed a picnic.' Elliot had to yell now to be heard over the storm. They found the graffiti. Someone had spray-painted the rocks leading down to the sand. It would be gone by spring-time. The storms and the sea would slowly strip away the paint, returning the rocks to their unsullied state. She wasn't interested in paint-spattered rocks. What interested her was higher up.

Elliot yelped and cursed as he narrowly avoided falling back-wards on to a sharp-edged rock, instead landing on a damp patch of sand. Jenny picked her way across the pebbles and helped him up.

'We need to get up there.' She pointed to the cliffs above.

'Of course we do.' He brushed the sand off of the back of his coat and rubbed his hands together. 'Come on then, what are you waiting for?' He set off ahead of her. She scrambled behind him, over large, smooth rocks first, until they were on the cliff-face proper. Here the surface was jagged, the footholds smaller, the drop steeper.

'It's up here,' she called out, and pointed to a plateau above them. Elliot got to it first and held out his hand to her, pulling her up and towards him, too quickly, so she stumbled forward.

He put his arm around her to stop her falling. 'Easy! You'll get us both killed.' He pulled her in towards him, let his arm linger around her waist just a moment too long and she found herself breathing in his scent, fresh and clean, soap and damp fabric, the coffee they had drunk in the car on the way here. One arm still around her waist, he brushed his hand across her forehead, sweeping her hair out of her eyes, and she wanted him to kiss her, to crush his lips against hers; she wanted to taste the coffee on his breath and have him hold her steady against the driving wind. All she needed to do was lean in. But she couldn't. That barrier she had built around herself, stopping anyone from getting too close, was in the way. She took a step back. Saw his hand trail back to his side.

'I remember that climb being a lot easier when I was a kid.' She turned her attention to the rocks, hoping that her cheeks were not as red as they felt and that he would think her hands were shaking from the force of the wind. He looked as if he was going to say something but then changed his mind. He took a step towards her. Shrugged.

'I'm sure you never did it in this weather as a kid. What are we looking for anyway?'

She soon found it. The rock was nearly completely covered with moss and lichen but still obvious, its pale colour out of place amongst the slabs of indigo blue and steel-grey. She scraped at the lichen until she revealed the print. It was the only story that had ever truly frightened her.

'Look at this, Jenny,' Charlie had put down the bucket full of winkles and limpets they had collected for Saturday tea. She'd caught up, out of breath, her skinny, seven-year-old legs struggling to keep up as they clambered over the rocks and up the cliffs. He had been rubbing the surface of a large, white rock with the sleeve of his jumper.

'What is it, Daddy?' She'd peered at the rock. It was smooth and pale with thin streaks of silver running through it. It had been cool to the touch, unlike the surrounding granite, which absorbed the heat and became warm and uncomfortable to sit on by the end of the day.

'There.' He had wiped away the dirt and moss to expose a

series of black slashes in the white rock. 'That there,' he pointed at the marks, 'is the Devil's claw mark.'

'From a story, Daddy?' She had reached up and put her hand in his.

'Well, yes. But people believed it was true for a long time. They said it was the mark the Devil made when he landed on the island, hundreds of years ago. He'd been in France, see, trying to trick the young Duke of Normandy. He lured the duke into a rowing boat and bought him here to Guernsey. But he stumbled, trying to get over the cliffs, and that mark there, that's where he clawed at the rocks as he flew over, carrying the duke in his arms.'

She had looked at the mark doubtfully but held his hand a little tighter. It did look like a claw mark. But more like a tiger might make, she thought.

'In Granny's Bible the Devil has hooves, not claws.'

The Bible's nonsense, Charlie had said. Just a big book of fairy tales, and not very good ones at that. He'd given her a sideways glance and a smile.

'Don't tell your mother I said that,' he'd said. 'Or your Granny. I'll have half the Methodists in St Sampsons after me.'

Jenny had wondered, often, if there were things her dad should not be telling her. It was exciting, though. Nobody else's dad said things like hers did.

'Where did he go then?' She'd asked as they walked back to the car.

'Who?'

'The Devil. Where did he go after he climbed over the rocks with the duke?'

'Ah. Well, he dropped the duke from a great height but the duke was a strong man and survived the fall. He settled in Guernsey, married a Guernsey girl, and had a happy life so the story goes.'

'But the Devil, Daddy. Where did he go?'

Charlie had given her a sideways look, opened his eyes wide. 'Who knows, Jenny,' he'd said, 'maybe he's still here.' He must have caught the look on her face, seen the flash of fear, because he had laughed then, told her not to worry, he was only joking. It was just a silly story, he said, and when they'd got home he'd taken a heavy book from the shelf and turned the pages, so thin they were like tissue paper, until he'd found the right chapter. There were hundreds like it, he said. Just stories. She could read them if she liked.

That night Jenny had woken up sweating and screaming, red eyes all around her, watching her, lurking in the shadows and under the bed. Charlie said it must have been a bad limpet. But he'd taken the book from beside her bed and put it away. And he hadn't told her any more stories for a long time.

She took some pictures of the rock and then, unable to resist, placed her hand over the claw mark. Even now, all these years later, she felt a chill, a cold ripple in her stomach.

She pulled her coat tighter around herself and turned back to face the sea. So angry. So beautiful. Whoever had killed those girls knew this place. He had stood here with the wind whipping around his face, tasted the sea spray, touched the rock, felt this strength in nature, its might and its beauty. He *knew* this place. Like she did.

'It could be just a coincidence.'

The car gently rocked in the wind and the trees creaked overhead. Several wet leaves plastered the windscreen, creating an earthy, stained-glass window, tingeing the light with autumnal yellows and browns. Elliot had insisted they run the engine so he could warm his hands in front of the air vents. She had her laptop open and was studying a picture of the mark on Amanda's arm, comparing it to the picture of the mark on the rock, too intent on the task in hand to feel any trace of the earlier awkwardness between them.

'I don't think so.'

'Care to elaborate? And don't tell me it's just a hunch, because I'm not following you around this island in a hurricane on a hunch.'

'I'm not asking you to follow me round the island. And it's not just a hunch. Look at them together. He's drawn all of the vertical strokes exactly the same way as they are on the rock. The outer strokes are longest, the middle stroke is shorter and the horizontal line is at exactly the right angle and in nearly the same position, left of centre. It's not a coincidence. It's the Devil's Claw.'

'You know it's not actually the mark of the Devil, don't you? It's a mineral deposit in the rock.'

'I'm well aware of that, thank you, Elliot. But I grew up hearing about this stuff. My dad used to read me bedtime stories from his Marie De Garis, for God's sake.'

'From his what?'

'*Folklore of Guernsey* by Maris de Garis. That and MacCulloch's *Guernsey Folk Lore*. Most-read books in my house as a kid.'

'Really? No *Swallows and Amazons*? No Roald Dahl?'

'Those too. But mostly folklore and horror stories.' She caught Elliot's look. 'Dad adapted them. So they were kid friendly. Mostly.'

'Jesus. No wonder you're so . . .' He stopped himself.

'So what?'

'Interesting. I was going to say interesting.'

Jenny started the car. 'Let's go to my place.'

'What for?'

'To figure out what the fuck is going on here.'

32

November 2014

*H*e had never intended to be so daring. It was the boat. It tempted him, sitting there in the moonlight, tied to the mooring ring with a simple fisherman's bend, and all of a sudden he thought, wouldn't it be beautiful to leave her in front of the castle, so that she would be soft and beautiful when they found her, so they could see her now, as he saw her, rather than in the morning, stiff and cold and empty? It seemed worth the effort. He was strong and she was frail and light. Even with the weight of the water in her clothes and hair, she was easy to move. He put her in first, then untied the boat. It was not yet fully beached, so it was no effort to pull the bow back into the water. He smiled. Nature aided him. Soon the tide would be low. He would have struggled to drag the boat single-handed down the beach. He was strong, but only human.

It was a short row and the water was calm. He was a confident sailor. It was a gift this island blessed its people. Hard to grow up here with anything other than sea legs, although some managed it. He knew of islanders who had never sailed a boat. They were land-locked, reliant on others to manage their journeys to and from the island. They were, in his opinion, even worse than those few tiny, scared people who had never left this rock, or who had ventured only as far as Jersey, which was different but the same, wrapped in its own thick, cloying blanket of safety and inertia.

He pulled the oars back and forth deftly. They barely made a splash as they broke the surface, and he relished the burn in his muscles and he felt that he could do this forever, on and on into the night . . . He would never let her go. She was his last and he wanted to keep her close, because after this, what? What was there to live for? Sweat trickled down his brow and into his eyes, joining the tears of sorrow and regret.

He rowed. Rhythmically. And his thoughts went back to the beginning. To Elizabeth. To that morning, many years ago, when everything had fallen into place. He refused to believe it was merely good fortune that he had the opportunity to get there first, to enjoy those precious minutes when he had knelt, alone, beside her pale, lifeless body. He had not taken her life, but her beauty in death had given life to him.

So sad, that it was over. Because it was over. He could not continue his work indefinitely. Over the next few years, if he lived that long, his strength would dissipate, his body would stiffen, and he would finish up like the rest of them, old and crippled and nobody, nobody would know what he had been. The knowledge pained him like nothing else he had ever experienced.

He rowed. His arms began to ache and he slowed. He looked up to the stars and then over the water to the lights twinkling on the Norman coast and all of a sudden a feeling of tremendous wellbeing washed over him. It had all been leading here. He was not the first to row to these shores in this way, with a great task to be completed. More than a thousand years ago, the Devil himself had brought the Duke of Normandy to this island in a rowing boat. The claw mark on the rock, on *his* rock, had been made on that fateful night and now here he was, following the path that had been so carefully lain for him. It all made sense. It was meant to be this way.

He looked at Amanda. Her head rolled gently from side to side in harmony with the motion of the waves. He rounded the headland and the castle came into view. It was glowing, ablaze from within. The beach was deserted, the tide ebbing, and he jumped out into the water and pulled the boat to the shore, behind a line of rocks. There was a little light from the power station, enough to allow him to see his way. He carried her up, away from the sea. He stopped before he reached the dry sand, laying her instead on a bed of damp pebbles. He had made the mark on her cheek. He did not want it to be missed this time. He fancied he heard movement, the shifting of sand and stone to his right. He retreated, the way he'd come, scattering the leaves in his wake, his footprints swallowed by the viscous sand.

As he rowed back out, the fireworks began. He could hear, very faintly, the cheers of the crowd from the castle. Further along the coast, there were more; the crack, crack, crack of gunpowder, bright bursts of red and blue and gold, on and on until the air was laden with sulphur. And if they had looked, any of them, if they had glanced out, they would have seen him. The boatman, resplendent under a canopy of false stars.

He was moving out. As a precaution. Not entirely – just his workshop. He was shifting it from the attic to the bunker, removing all traces of his work from his home. He supposed he should burn it all. Pile it all up in the back garden and set it alight. But he couldn't. It was precious. It should be preserved. They should know what he had done for them. Just . . . not yet.

He took one box at a time. He did not want to pull a muscle doing something so mundane. He trudged through the drizzle. The grass was overgrown and the wet fronds tangled around his boots as he walked. He hummed as he worked. It was soothing, helped to quiet the buzzing in his head that lately had increased from an irritant to something more pervasive, almost maddening. As he hummed, he went over and over each girl in his head. He had left no traces, he was sure of that. At least, if he had, they had never been found and now would never be. The passage of time was his friend. Except, perhaps, when it came to Amanda. He had handled her with only the lightest of touches, apart from when she had struggled. He'd held firm and fast and she hadn't scratched him: they would not find his flesh under her nails, nor had she pulled his hair, so they would not find it clutched in her hands; and even if they did, they could hardly DNA test the whole island. A wave of panic. He needed to focus. He shook rainwater out of his eyes and took a deep breath.

He'd had the entrance covered by a round grille of heavy iron, now rusted a deep brown, secured with a padlock. Steep steps took him down to a tunnel and then through to a concrete chamber. There was one other exit, through a similar grille on the far side of the hedge, which separated his two fields.

He carried the box carefully down the steps and through the tunnel, stooping under the low ceiling, not quite head height, at least not for him, emerging, after twenty feet or so, into the chamber. He used his torch to find the gas lamp, one of the many treasures he had found down here and lovingly restored.

After he had found this place it had taken him weeks just to clean out the leaves and rotting debris that had gathered in the stairwells and accumulated in the tunnels. He had had the grilles installed, ostensibly as a safety measure, but as the only holder of the keys they also served to keep the place his and his alone. Festung, the historical society who maintained the island's Nazi fortifications, knew about it. He had allowed them to document and photograph it because he wanted to know everything he could about it. it was a storage bunker, most likely. A large one, of interest to enthusiasts but probably not to the public according to the loud-mouthed pseudo-historian they'd sent over to look at it, along with a bored member of the Culture and Leisure department. They'd have all been more interested, no doubt, in what he moved before they arrived. Helmets and satchels, boots and socks, storage tins, presumably once full of food, the lamp and his prized possession, a Walther P38. Just the one. He suspected it had been left behind accidentally, not stored there. It pleased him to think it had belonged to somebody. Perhaps not just somebody, because it would have made perfect sense, he thought, as he had held the gun for the first time, for this to have been his father's. It was unlikely, he knew it, but not impossible. That was all that mattered. That it might have been.

He reached up for the small wooden box now, took out the pistol. It was polished and in full working order. He fingered it, stroking the barrel, the grip, the trigger. He held it to his temple, felt the cold metal against his hot head. It was soothing. Nothing mattered any more.

And yet . . . And yet . . . It felt wrong, to just give up. Because, this time, he thought, they might actually figure it out. It was nothing to be ashamed of. He'd done so well, to get this far. But if they were going to get him, he should make it something beautiful. He deserved that, at least. A beautiful ending.

He put the lid on the box and placed it back on the shelf. He tucked the pistol into his pocket.

33

Michael

Friday, 21 November

His email pinged – the list of staff members and volunteers from the youth club and a list of trustees and board members. He opened the first file and scanned the document. David De Putron's was the only name he recognised. He would have to bring him in. Connections to two of the girls and he was old enough, from what Michael could remember. He knew him. Not well, just to say hello to. Michael knew a lot of people to say hello to. So in all likelihood, he knew whoever had done this. They were presumably in the same age bracket as he was. It didn't bear thinking about. He supposed he would have to, though. He would have to adjust the way he thought.

There were a few names on the second list he recognised. A couple of deputies. Brian Ozanne. Interesting. He was always keen to boost his philanthropic image. And Roger Wilson. Hard to find something he wasn't involved in. Michael tried to shake off the resentment he felt towards the man. Wilson had been a good chief of police in many respects. Still, Roger had been on the force for all but Amanda's death and had been chief when Hayley Bougourd died. Michael would have needed to speak to him regardless of the fact he was on a list of people involved with the youth club that three of the victims had attended. He added him to his Persons of Interest list. A list which now totalled two.

'Is this really necessary?'

David De Putron was stressed. He was trying to hide it behind outrage and hauteur, but Michael knew stress when he saw it. If David could just tell him about his association with LEAP, Michael said, they could be done and dusted with this in no time at all. He looked at David, encouragingly.

David sighed. He'd been volunteering at LEAP for fifteen years, he said. Yes, he'd come into contact with both Amanda and Hayley. Not that he'd remembered Hayley, not until Michael had just asked him about it. He shifted in his seat. There were other people who had been involved with the programme as long as he had, he said. The caretaker, for example, he'd been there for donkey's years. And what was this all about, anyway, he asked? He waved his hands over the pictures Michael had shown him. Was Michael trying to imply these girls' deaths were connected? Because how could they be? He had a little sweat on his brow now, Michael noticed, despite the fact that it was cool in his draughty office.

'As I explained, Mr De Putron. You're not under arrest. You're free to go at any time. There's no need to get upset.

'Stephen, could you fetch Mr De Putron a coffee? One of the nice ones, from that new machine.' He turned to David. 'We've just got a Nespresso,' he said. 'So much better than the stuff the old vending machine tries to pass for coffee.'

David rolled his eyes but loosened his arms, which had been crossed tightly across his chest. People like David De Putron liked to feel important, Michael thought. And Michael wanted David to feel relaxed, at ease. Talkative. Marquis arrived with the coffee and set it down on the desk. He sat next to Michael and opened his notebook. Michael gave him a sideways glance, a slight shake of the head, and Marquis closed the book, placed it on his knee.

'So,' Michael said, 'you're right, Mr De Putron, you're not the only person who's come into contact with both Amanda and Hayley. Both girls had been through social services, both attended the same youth club. We're going to be looking into all those potential connections. But just for now,' Michael smiled at him, 'we'd like to know about your dealings with them. You say you didn't remember Hayley Bougourd until I just mentioned her. I find that a little hard to believe. I mean, believe me, I know what the old memory gets like as you get older.' He tapped his own head. 'Mine's like a sieve these days. But dead students? I would have thought they'd stick out a bit, eh? Can't have had that many students who have died now, can you?'

'Of course not,' David blustered. 'I remembered her as soon as you mentioned her. Nice girl. Another quiet one, bit like Amanda, and of course deeply troubled. Most of the children who came through the centre were.'

'Her mum says you were nice to Hayley.' Michael glanced down at the notes Jenny had given him. 'Said the piano lessons were really helping.'

'Yes. I *was* nice to her.' David spoke slowly, as if he was talking to a pupil who was struggling to pick up the most basic musical technique. 'I was giving up my own time to help her. Not just her, *all* the children I taught at the centre. Children who didn't have the advantages I had. And now I'm beginning to regret the whole thing.' He shook his head in exasperation. 'Will that be all?'

'Almost there, Mr De Putron. Elizabeth Mahy. Heard of her?'

'No. I've already told you, I haven't heard of any of the others.'

'Only we've spoken to Jennifer Dorey – I believe she interviewed you for a piece she's working on – and she seemed to think you *had* heard of Elizabeth. She seemed to think you were a little upset, even, when she asked you about her.'

David closed his eyes, shook his head slowly from side to side. 'I remembered a girl drowning at the bathing pools. I didn't know her name or who she was or anything about her at all. Once again, I was trying to help this journalist by giving freely of my time, expecting nothing in return and now, well, I don't even know what's going on right now. Am I being accused of something?'

'I've already told you, Mr De Putron. You can leave whenever you like.'

'Well then, I think I might just do that.' He stood, nodded at Michael and Marquis, and swept out of the room.

'Bit of a cold fish.' Marquis said, as they watched David thread his way through the office and out of the station. 'Surprised he didn't mention the fact that he was paying our salaries.'

'What's that, Marquis?'

'He's just the type, sir. You know, the ones who remind you they're taxpayers and we all work for them if you give them a parking ticket. Entitled, I think they call it, sir.'

It seemed to Michael that Marquis was prone to the odd moment of incredible insightfulness. Just the odd moment, mind you, but nonetheless, there were the makings of a good detective in there somewhere.

'Yes. Very well put, Son. I think you've just about got the measure of him.'

'Do you think he's a murderer though, sir?'

Michael thought for a minute.

'Do you know, I was convinced this would be a waste of time, but he's hiding something. He's definitely hiding something. Follow up with him, will you? Give him a day, let him relax a bit and then ask him for alibis and a list of all his students. Let's rattle his cage a bit. See what falls out.'

'Sir?' Fallaize poked his head around the door.

Michael looked back down at his notes. 'I'm busy, Fallaize, what is it?' Any excuse to put the little shite in his place.

'Sir, I think you need to speak to Mrs Bretel.'

Michael looked up and saw there was a woman standing next

to Fallaize. She was young, late thirties he guessed, and would have been beautiful but for a large red birthmark which covered half of her face. A port wine stain they used to be called. Not that he was going to mention it. He stood to greet her and tried very hard not to look at the birthmark, but to look into her eyes, which were opaque and green, like sea glass. She had strong features, a long, straight nose and defined cheekbones, but her face was drawn, almost pinched she was so thin. A small stud twinkled in her nose and several more lined each ear lobe. As he got closer to her, he could see she looked tired, or perhaps she'd been crying, and she clutched something in her hands, a piece of paper, or was it a photograph?

'Mrs Bretel, how can I help you?' Fallaize was hanging around at the door for some reason, and Michael noticed that several other officers had stopped work and were standing in groups, looking over at them.

'It's my Lisa.' Mrs Bretel handed the photograph to Michael. 'She hasn't been home since Tuesday and she's not answering her phone.'

Michael felt the bottom of his stomach fall away before he even looked at the picture. It only needed a glance for his worst fears to be confirmed. A pretty girl, laughing at the camera, big blue eyes, soft, blonde hair falling in curls over her narrow shoulders. He just about managed to pull up a chair for Mrs Bretel before his legs gave way and he sank, heavily, into his own.

34

*I*t was so loud now that it was hard to concentrate on anything else. He'd tried everything. He'd run a bath, submerging himself fully, hoping that the water would run into his ears and wash it away. He'd turned the radio up so loud that the floor had vibrated beneath him. He'd plugged his ears with cotton wool, held a pillow over his head, pressing harder and harder until he couldn't breathe.

He knew it was no use. The noise was on the inside.

He had to be careful when in public lest he sound like the lunatic he feared he was becoming. But at home there was nothing and no one to stop him. So he hummed, as loudly as he could. And in adding to the noise he somehow found it reduced. He was humming along now. In his head, the sound was akin to something between the whine of an air-conditioning unit and the thrum of an engine. It was pitched at middle C. Yes, the predominant note was definitely middle C, sung over and over again by a choir of robots with mechanical voices. He laughed out loud at the image and nearly spilled the peaches he was spooning out of a tin and into a shallow blue-and-white striped bowl. His spirits were buoyed momentarily by the fact that he could find humour in such a difficult situation.

He placed the bowl on to a small wooden tray next to a glass of apple juice. Something sweet ought to do the trick, he'd decided. And there was something so fitting about peaches. A ripe peach, velvet skin, soft flesh dripping with nectar. He added a drizzle of thick yellow cream, which curdled in the juice and pooled in the pink hollows left by the stones. He glanced out of the window. Raining again. He covered the tray with a clean tea towel and carried it to the back door where he set it down on the floor while he slipped his bare feet into his wellington boots. He opened the door and picked up the tray. She would eat the peaches. He was sure of it.

He stopped humming as he left the house. So the noise became louder. And for the first time he thought he could hear more than just a monotonous buzz. He held the tea towel firmly against the tray to stop it from escaping in the wind. He trudged through the wet grass. He listened very carefully. There were no words as such, more a rhythm. But he understood it.

What have you done? it droned.

What have you done? Louder and louder the nearer he got until he reached the steps and it was a roar, like a wall of water washing over him and through him and if he hadn't been holding the tray he would have thrown his head into his hands and cried.

35

Jenny

Friday, 21 November

Jenny showed Elliot through to the kitchen. Margaret's bedroom door opened and she emerged into the corridor, pulling her dressing gown around her.

'What time is it, love?'

'It's ten thirty. Were you sleeping?'

Margaret nodded. She'd woken up in the early hours and not been able to get back to sleep, had finally given in and taken one of those horrible pills, she said, it had knocked her right out. The sound of crockery clattering in the kitchen made her start.

'Who's there?'

'It's just Elliot.' Margaret looked confused. 'The guy I work with,' Jenny added.

'Did he stay over?' Margaret whispered, surprised, and, Jenny thought, not entirely displeased at the notion.

'No he did not! It's nothing like that, Mum. We've been out to Moulin Huet. Working. We're cold and wet and we're having a cuppa before we head back to the office.' She paused and allowed Margaret to process. 'It's nothing to worry about.'

'I'm not worried, Jenny, but for goodness' sake, could you not have given me some warning? The house is a tip!'

'I'm sure the place is perfect, Mum. We'll just be in the study anyway. You're a tip, though. Some clothes wouldn't go amiss.' Margaret put her hands to her hair and hurried over to the bathroom.

Jenny went to the living room. It was spotless, the deep pile of the cream carpet swept into swathes of light and dark by yesterday's vacuum, cushions arranged neatly on the leather sofas (polished twice weekly) and the surfaces, dusted more times in a day than Jenny could count, gleaming. Presumably the mess Margaret referred to was the neatly folded newspaper and a pair of reading glasses left on the armchair. Behind the sofa a bookcase of polished walnut displayed all of Charlie's books, untouched since he'd died. She slid the glass door to one side and ran her finger along the spines. They were all so familiar. A Dickens' collection, bound in green leather with gold lettering, a battered copy of *Animal Farm*, Penguin Classics, orange and cream spines all in a row; Hemmingway, Steinbeck, Hardy. And then the poetry. Philip Larkin, John Betjeman, Ted Hughes. *Crow.* He had loved that one. She pulled out the slim volume, flicked through the pages. She had pored over it in her teenage years, trying to make sense of the bleak, beautiful words.

She'd never considered Charlie's love of reading as anything other than completely ordinary. It was always just part of him. Now she wondered how many other fisherman who left school at fifteen had a copy of the *Complete Works of Shakespeare* on their bookshelves. She found the book she wanted on the bottom shelf, next to Granny's Bible. She smiled. Just like him to put it there. A collection of pagan myths and stories of the Devil's work right next to God's word. She slid it out, stroked the cold, dimpled leather. Even the pages, edged in gold, were smooth to the touch.

In the kitchen, Margaret had taken over making the tea and was slicing up a loaf of gâche, asking Elliot about his family.

'My mother died last year and I'm sorry to say I never knew my father, Mrs Dorey. It's one of the reasons I moved back to Guernsey, actually. To find him.'

'I'm so sorry, Elliot. I had no idea.' Margaret glared over at Jenny, who widened her eyes back at her. She'd had no idea either, at least, she'd heard something, office gossip, that he'd moved back after a family upset, but hadn't paid much attention to it. 'I hope I haven't upset you asking.' Margaret put a hand on his elbow.

'Not at all, Mrs Dorey.'

'Please, call me Margaret. Get the butter out of the fridge, will you, Jenny, the Sark one.'

Jenny placed the book on the table and retrieved the butter. Wrapped in thick, waxy paper it was a pungent yellow, as close to cheese as butter could get, but delicious spread thickly on toasted gâche. Margaret gave them both a slice and told them she'd bring the tea through when it had brewed.

Jenny took Elliot through to the study.

'Wow. You have your own incident room.'

One of the walls of the small room was covered in pictures and post-it notes, smiling photographs of each of the dead girls and clippings from the *Guernsey News*. Jenny cleared a space on the desk, also covered in paper and scribbled notes and placed the book she had been holding on it.

'This is Edgar MacCulloch's *Guernsey Folk Lore*.' She opened it. Stuck inside the front cover, a rectangular certificate, foxed and yellowed with age read in gold lettering, *'Island Books'* and written underneath in an elaborate hand, '5s', a signature, presumably the bookseller's, and a date, *August* 1949.

'Is this worth something?' Elliot asked.

'A couple of hundred pounds, maybe. It's out of print. I'm not sure where Dad got it. That receipt is too old to have been his.'

Mum came in with the tea and placed the cups on coasters on

the desk, tutting at the mess and the dust. She looked up at the pictures on the wall, walked over and carefully removed the one of Elizabeth.

'I know I'm not supposed to get involved in this – Jenny worries about my nerves, Elliot – but do you really think that Elizabeth may have been murdered? And that the same person who killed her killed all of these other girls too?'

'We don't know, Mum. Looks that way.'

Margaret stuck the picture back up. 'I've got some photos somewhere. I must have, in the loft. I should get them down. I've been meaning to clear out up there for ages.' She left the room smiling, her spirits seemingly lifted at the idea of sitting up in the dusty crawlspace under the roof for a few hours.

Jenny flicked through the pages of the heavy book until she found what she was looking for. She pointed to the open page.

'"The Devil's Claw",' Elliot read out loud. 'This is the story about the mark on the rocks?'

Jenny nodded. 'I think whoever is doing this has a knowledge of folklore,' she said. 'There's the mark he's putting on them, the scarecrows, the places he's leaving them.' She turned the book over and opened it from the back, looking at the index. 'Look at this, Le Table Des Pions, Le Guet – they're both mentioned in here. Maybe he even knows this book.'

'You need to speak to Horace.' Elliot said. He wandered over to the pile of back copies of the *News* Jenny had printed off from the library archives and started flicking through them.

'Who?'

'Horace Gallienne from La Société Guernesaise. I interviewed him when he did those Haunted Guernsey walks. He knows all about this stuff. I warn you, though, he's a complete nut job.'

Jenny sighed. 'I'm starting to think it's the sane people who are the exception around here.'

*

Horace Gallienne lived in a large Edwardian house on Les Abreveurs Lane in St Sampsons. She parked at the side of the narrow road, in front of the rectangular stone trough it was named after. In days gone by the island's *abreveurs* had watered cattle herds as they were moved through the lanes to fresh pasture. Water bubbled into this one from an underground spring below, breaking the surface with gentle ripples, flowing over the moss-covered sides and on to a cobbled, shallow basin where it drained back into the earth. When she was little, Charlie would have given her a penny to throw in, told her to make a wish.

She let herself into the front garden through a low wooden gate. On the hedge next to it a wooden crate stood on one side, displaying its contents to the street. A handwritten sign attached read, *POTS 50P EGGS £1*. Clear plastic bags of earth-caked potatoes filled one side of the box. A crumpled one-pound note poked out of a rusty cash tin, which was screwed to the crate and secured with a broken padlock. A hedge veg stall. They were dotted all over the island, selling flowers or fruit and vegetables, even pots of jam or chutney, jars of pickles. Whatever was growing in the garden or the greenhouse and couldn't be eaten by the family would be sold to neighbours and passers-by, who were trusted to leave payment in the tin, aptly known as an honesty box.

A fat orange hen emerged, head shuddering and muttering a low, nervous warble as it ran from the bushes at the side of the house and over the doorstep. Jenny knocked on the front door. Moments later, a scraping from above and then a hoarse, rasping voice.

'Yes?'

She stepped back, looked upwards. A man leaned out over the sill of a small window under the eaves. He had a green scarf wrapped around his neck and wore large, thick-rimmed glasses. She was sorry to disturb him, she called up, but she was wondering if she might ask him some questions about local history and folklore?

The window slid shut, and a few minutes later the front door opened.

'Sorry about that' he said, 'I'm right in the middle of something and I don't want to come downstairs every time someone wants to know if I've got any more eggs. The chickens are done laying for the season. I meant to change the sign.' He was a heavy-set man in his late sixties and his rotund frame filled the doorway. His large feet were bare, bright pink and soaking wet.

'Am I disturbing you?'

'Hmm? No, no. Well, I mean, yes, you are. But it's not a problem. Please, come in.' He smiled at her, the corners of his rheumy eyes wrinkling behind his glasses. 'You'll have to forgive me, I have a terrible cold.'

There was an underlying smell of must in the house, but it was masked with the faint, floral scent of plug-in air freshener and, Jenny thought, something else, something medicinal. Camphor perhaps, or tea tree oil. She followed him through a carpeted hallway to a sitting room, where the reason for the musty smell became apparent. Piles and piles of books were stacked against the walls, over the coffee table and beside the faded, floral sofas.

'Sorry about the mess. I'm having a sort out. I started about five years ago and this is as far as I've got.' He smiled. His face wrinkled and his brow shone with perspiration. 'We could sit in my study, I suppose. It's almost as bad, to be honest, but at least there's a desk in there.'

She followed him up a narrow flight of stairs with creaking bannisters, to the first-floor landing where he opened a wooden door, which looked like it belonged to a built-in closet. Inside, more steps twisted upwards. She hesitated. He noticed.

'Ha!' He coughed and pulled a handkerchief from his pocket. 'It's all a bit *Jane Eyre,* isn't it! I promise you, there's no mad wife up there, just books mostly. Follow me!' His footsteps were heavy as he climbed the steep stairs to the attic. 'Hard going on the knees these days, all these stairs. That's why I'm sorting out. Thinking of moving. Here we are.' He held the door open for her.

It was surprisingly bright in the study, despite the low ceilings. The window he had called down from let in plenty of light and there was one on the opposite side of the room too, with a view out on to fields and greenhouses. There was a small door with a bolt across it in the corner of the room, the top edge sloping, like something out of *Alice in Wonderland,* Jenny thought. There were books everywhere up here and papers too, piles and piles of them on the thin carpet. No smell of must though, because another, pungent aroma filled the air. It was coming from a plastic washing-up bowl steaming under the desk.

Horace saw her looking. 'It's a natural cold remedy. Chinese. Hot mustard powder and eucalyptus. Draws the blood from the head to the feet and clears the airways. I suppose it stinks? Afraid I can't smell a thing.' He blew his nose as if to illustrate his point and then opened the window again, the old sash pulleys squeaking in protest. The desk was directly below it and the papers littering it lifted in the breeze. The opposite wall was fitted with shelves displaying framed prints and what looked to be Second World War objects; a helmet from the occupation and a gas mask, although not like any Jenny had seen before. The other two walls of the room were covered in black-and-white etchings, arranged unevenly and hanging at various skewed angles. Jenny was looking directly at a picture of a woman with a twisted, ugly face, covered in thick hair and boils, laughing and pointing at a painfully thin cow, its shoulder blades protruding, while a milkmaid pulled at its withered udders. Next to it, a picture of a burning pyre, three women, one obviously heavily pregnant cowering in front of it while an official-looking man read to a gathered crowd from a book.

'They're a bit macabre. That's why I keep them up here.' He pointed to the picture of the three women. 'You know this story?'

Jenny shook her head. 'I don't think so.'

'A mother and two daughters burned at Tower Hill, just above Fountain Street. According to records made at the time, this young lady,' he pointed to the pregnant woman, 'Perotine Massey, gave birth in the flames. The baby was rescued but the bailiff ordered it be cast back into the fire. We did a re-enactment a few years ago for the Guernsey Historical Society, four hundred and fifty years after the event. It was terribly moving.'

'People thought they were witches?'

He shook his head. 'Protestants. Out of fashion at the time, sadly. This one's a witch.' He pointed at the women in the other picture. 'Disgustingly ugly or terrifyingly beautiful depending on which particular piece of folklore you choose to believe. It was very common, of course, in rural communities, to blame women, usually older, isolated ladies, for failing crops or sick cattle.' He turned to her. 'Now, what can I help you with? You're from the *News*, aren't you? I've spoken to you lot before about history and traditions. For a piece you're working on, is it?'

Yes, she said. She was interested in a few particular sites around the island. Pleinmont, Le Guet, Moulin Huet. Were they significant, she asked, as far as local folklore was concerned? Well, Horace said, it depends.

'On what?'

'On whether or not you want to meet with the Devil.'

He walked over to a picture, pointed at it: a huge, horned goat, standing on two cloven feet, surrounded by beautiful, naked women.

'That's the Devil at Le Guet. One of the many orgies he allegedly held with the loose women of the island there. The Fairy Ring at Pleinmont, of course, well-known meeting place for the Devil, witches and the like. And Moulin Huet – now that's an interesting one, not a spot he was said to regularly frequent, but there's a rock there with a peculiar marking on it.'

'I know that story.'

'You do? Excellent. It's a good one, isn't? There are plenty more like it too. There's a rock at Rousse with an imprint in it, like a hoof mark. Le Pied du Boeuf, it's called. Supposed to be where Satan leapt from after a confrontation with a mob of angry peasants. That's what you're writing about, is it? The Devil?'

Jenny hesitated. 'The places, really. Their associations. But this is helpful. Thank you.' She scribbled some notes.

'Here, have a seat.' He cleared some of the papers on the desk to one side. She recognised the patois written on the yellowed pages in a faded, scrawling hand, but could not understand it. Her Guernsey French was limited to the word for the snails she would find in the garden, little *collymouchons,* and her granny's *'cor demmie la!'* whenever anything out of the ordinary happened.

'Spells,' he said, standing beside her. He picked up one of the old pages. 'Or rather, antidotes to spells. This one's to counteract curses that kill livestock. It says one should cut the heart from an animal whose death has been caused and then place it on a plate and pierce it with nine thorns while saying the incantation.' He pointed to some lines written in verse. 'The heart is then to be put in a bag and hung in the chimney, before the whole process is repeated, each day, for nine days. No thorn must pierce the same place twice. Then one must burn the heart and the curse will be lifted. Not only that, but the witch who cast the spell shall be revealed in the flames and beg for mercy and forgiveness. Started as a hobby, all this witchcraft stuff, but I have to say I find it quite fascinating. I'm writing a book about it, *Cursed Isle.* Not what you're here for, I know, but perhaps you could make a little mention of it in your article, eh? You scratch my back, and I'll find some pictures for you, how about that?' His laugh quickly turned into a cough. 'This damn cold,' he spluttered, before he got down on his knees and started sorting through the papers stacked underneath the shelves, pulling some out and laying them on the floor. The soles of his feet were soft and pink from sitting in the bowl of water, the flesh on his heels loose and wrinkled, and Jenny felt nauseous looking at them.

In the quiet that followed, Jenny heard a rustling and scratching. Not from Horace as he threw papers into various piles, but from the roof immediately above them, or perhaps behind the walls. Horace heard it too.

'Damn rats,' he said. 'That's another reason I'm moving. Caught one as big as a cat recently. There's a nest. I've had pest control out more times than I can count, but they keep coming back.'

'Do you have another room behind there?' Jenny pointed to the door in the wall.

'Hmm?' Horace looked up. 'Oh, that. No, leads to some storage space, right under the roof rafters. Only people who've been in there in the last thirty years are Rentokil.' He laughed his hacking laugh again. 'Here.' He beckoned her over.

She knelt on the carpet next to him. A large black dog sitting in a country lane and a pretty young woman, *The Devil tempts a seamstress, Talbots,* written underneath. A shadowy bridge; *Pont du Diable, St Sampson.* And the last one, a photograph, a plate from a book – a white rock slashed with black. *The Devil's Claw. Moulin Huet.*

Dead animals and pierced hearts and Devil worship and rats . . . The low attic ceiling suddenly felt lower and stifling and the heavy, cloying smell of mustard and eucalyptus burdened the air. She stood up and turned to Horace, to thank him and say goodbye. Looked again at the shelves, at the strange objects displayed on them.

Horace stood up next to her, rubbing his knees. 'Another hobby of mine. I volunteer with Festung – have you heard of them?' Jenny shook her head. 'Wonderful group. We help to preserve and document the Nazi fortifications on the island. Lest we forget and all that. Most of what we've found goes to the Occupation Museum, but I've collected a few trinkets.' He picked up the strangely shaped mask, two conical tubes attached to what looked like breathing apparatus and a canvas strap.

'Bet you've never seen one of these before have you?'

Jenny shook her head. She'd seen a gas mask, she said, at the Occupation Museum, but not that shape. What was is for?

'Horses!' He sounded delighted. 'Would you believe they had gas masks for their horses? In the depths of all that cruelty and violence. It was strategic, obviously, but it's quite something, don't you think? That they thought to save the horses.'

It was, Jenny agreed. Quite something.

'And this, this is very special.' He held out his hand. A bullet rolled around on his open palm. 'Looks like an ordinary bullet, doesn't it? But look.' He pulled the tip off and showed her. Inside, a tightly rolled piece of paper. Horace tipped it out on to his hand. 'A message. In code. A common way of passing notes around, apparently, but no less interesting for it, eh?' His eyes shone. 'You should write an article about this, you know. So much still to be discovered. We've never fully got to grips with it. The Occupation, I mean. Even now, all these years later, there's so much shame associated with it, it's like a dark cloud hanging over us all. Time we embraced it, I say. Time we remembered, before it's too late.'

Jenny agreed. It was fascinating, she said. And he'd been so helpful, she couldn't thank him enough.

'I'm serious.' He looked at her intently, pale blue eyes wet with cold and something else, not tears, surely? 'There'll be nobody left soon. You young people aren't interested in history, in dead languages or folk stories. My generation heard stories from our parents. Yours maybe from your grandparents, but beyond you, there's nobody. Perhaps you could write about that. When you're finished dancing with the Devil.'

She struggled not to visibly gulp down the fresh, clean air as she left the house. She stopped at the hedge, light-headed, and realised she had not eaten lunch and it was mid-afternoon already. She picked up a bag of potatoes for Margaret, dropping the fifty pence into the tin and then, seeing a tarnished penny in her purse, walked over to the abreuvoir and tossed it in. She didn't make a wish. She didn't know what to wish for. And anyway, even as a kid, she'd known that a wish made on a water trough would not come true.

She sat at her desk in her incident room, as Elliot had insisted on calling it. She'd come straight home from Horace's house, wanting peace and quiet and time to try to figure out what was going on. It wasn't working out so well. A thudding and scraping from above and Margaret singing, her voice high-pitched and wavering as she shifted boxes, sorting out the loft, disturbed what little concentration Jenny could muster. She couldn't shake off the smell of Horace's foot soak, nor the strange, desperate look he'd had in his eyes as she'd left his house. She decided to take a leaf out of Margaret's book and have a clear out.

She made one pile of papers for recycling, another for interviews, placing the notes she had made at Horace's that afternoon on the top. Then she turned her attention to the *News* articles Elliot had been reading. He'd actually left them neater than he'd found them, but she tried putting them in some sort of order and then wondered if they weren't for the recycling pile as there was nothing in them that had shed any light on anything. She wasn't sure why she had printed them off at all. She took a few pages from an edition printed in the days following Elizabeth Mahy's death and flicked through them. She smiled at the picture of a farmer in old-fashioned flat cap, displaying his prize-winning tomatoes, noted the difference in the way the articles were written back then, more formal English, much better grammar. Saw a small column at the bottom of page three. *Drowned Girl's Parents Plead for Witnesses*, and the reporter's name, Brian Ozanne. The same Brian Ozanne, she was sure, who was now editor-in-chief of the *Guernsey News* and who had claimed, indignantly, to be too young to remember Elizabeth Mahy's death. Could he really have forgotten something like that? Surely not. So why hadn't he told her about it, or at least acknowledged that it had happened? She picked up her things. He'd be at work. As she got to the front door, she saw a shadow approaching behind the glass and opened it.

Elliot looked angry and exhausted, his hair a tousled mess, his top three shirt buttons undone. She had no time to say anything before he yelled at her.

'Why aren't you answering your fucking phone?' There was a hint of the rage she had seen before on his face. She took a step backwards.

'What's wrong with you?'

'I've been trying to reach you for an hour.' He seemed to make an effort to relax, taking a deep breath. Softer now. 'I was worried.'

She reached into her bag, pulled her phone out. She had five missed calls from Elliot and three from Michael. 'Shit. I put it on silent when I went to Horace's. What's happened?'

'A girl's gone missing. Lisa Bretel. She's seventeen and her mum hasn't seen her for three days. Guess what she looks like?'

Jenny's shoulders slumped. 'Blue eyes. Fair skin. Long blonde hair.' He nodded.

'DCI Gilbert has called a press conference. We need to be there.' He held out his hand. She took it, followed him to his car, which was parked on the street with the engine running. A missing girl, not a dead one. That was something at least. She might be alive. Hidden somewhere, held captive. Jenny's mind raced through all the places Lisa could be, settling on the image of a girl, alone and terrified, locked in a tiny black space with the scratching and rustling of rats all around her.

36

Michael

The main hall of the Vale Douzaine room was being prepared for the press conference. Under normal circumstances the room was used by the douzeniers, elected officials who dealt with some of their parish's administrative duties – the granting of building permits and dog licences, the overseeing of rubbish removal, the upkeep of cemeteries. The space was also hired out for parties and functions. It was perfect for the press conference the police were about to hold. It was more of a town hall meeting, he supposed, as they had decided to open it to the public, at least those who might have heard the bulletin they had released to the radio and local TV channels an hour ago. Because they needed as many people to know about this as quickly as possible if they were to have any chance of finding Lisa Bretel alive.

Michael paced the floor as officers set up chairs and microphones on the small stage. There had obviously been a children's party here recently. Streamers had been trodden into the scuffed, wooden floor, the colour bleeding out of the frayed edges of the soft paper. The smell of salty, processed food and sour milk drifted into the room from the small kitchen at the back and the high ceiling harboured an escaped helium balloon – a wilting princess with a dazzling smile in a blue dress, its spiralled ribbon tie dangling below, just out of reach. Above the door a large stained-glass window depicted a dove holding an olive branch, the background a garish mishmash of shapes shoved against each other. They flashed as cars passed outside, casting brightly coloured shadows on the dull walls, headlights on already. Not yet five p.m. and it had been dark for nearly an hour.

Michael was floundering. He was trying his best to look like he knew what he was doing, but he was out of his depth and he knew it. They'd never dealt with a missing person before. At least, not like this. They'd had the odd wino disappear for a couple of days, only to be found staggering down the high street clutching a can of Special Brew. Once a man had absconded while on bail. It had taken them a week to find him, holed up at a mate's house. Sometimes families of vulnerable people called in when loved ones went astray, but they always found them quickly, usually within hours; a quick search of friends' and families' property, a glance around the usual haunts, job done. It was such a small place and there were very few places to hide. A wave of heat washed over him. Few places to hide. But to keep someone, against his or her will? That was a different story. Sheds, barns, attics, boathouses, boats. Dear God, what if she wasn't even on the island any more? She could be on Sark or Alderney or in France by now; they might search Guernsey for days and be wasting their time. They had no idea where to start. He rubbed at his chin, felt the scratching of stubble. Had he shaved this morning? He couldn't remember. This morning seemed like a lifetime ago. He should smarten himself up. It wouldn't do for him to look like he was falling apart at the seams. He had to look like he was on top of everything or else people would panic. He sighed. In less than an hour he was going to stand up in front of a room full of people and tell them that, in all likelihood, a serial killer had kidnapped a teenage girl. Panic was inevitable.

But she was alive. He was sure of it. None of the other girls had gone missing for this long before they died. And it had been less than two weeks since they'd found Amanda. It didn't fit.

Something had changed. That was their only hope. Whoever was doing this had abandoned his tried and tested previous methods. He would no doubt be nervous. Maybe he felt as out of his depth as Michael did. The thought that they were both winging it was oddly comforting.

The lights hurt his eyes but at least made it difficult to see the faces of the crowd. He wasn't sure he could say what he needed to if he had to make eye contact with people. There were perhaps one hundred gathered in the hall. Jenny and one of her colleagues sat at the front, along with reporters from BBC Radio Guernsey and Channel News. Next to them, a camera on a tripod was aimed directly at him, red light flashing. The cameraman raised a thumb and nodded over to Michael. Michael took a step closer to the microphone and cleared his throat. The chatter died down. He could feel sweat beading on his forehead but did not reach up to wipe it away. He did not usually suffer from stage fright, but there was a tremor in his voice as he started his appeal.

'Thank you all for coming out at such short notice.' He paused. 'A young woman, Lisa Bretel, has gone missing. We have reasons to fear for her safety.' He clicked on a laptop set up next to him, which projected on to a screen behind. The photograph of Lisa Bretel he had seen for the first time that morning flashed up. Soft blonde curls, a pale face with the same pinched features as her mother, pretty, but careworn, startling blue eyes. Michael cleared his throat again. Scanned the faces in front of him, blurred by the light and a trickle of sweat, which had found its way into his right eye.

'Furthermore, we have reason to believe that Lisa may be being held against her will.' A ripple of disbelief, a few gasps. 'We need to speak with anyone who had any contact with her in the days before she disappeared. The last time her mother saw her was this Tuesday, the eighteenth November at around six p.m., when Lisa was on her way out to visit friends. She never showed up to meet them and she hasn't been seen since.' He raised his hand to shush everyone. 'We are also again appealing for witnesses in the case of the death of Amanda Guille who, as you know, was found drowned at Bordeaux nearly two weeks ago. Anyone who saw or spoke to Amanda in the days and weeks before she died, any details she shared with you about her life, how she was feeling, who she was seeing, we need to know. Finally, we are appealing for any information people might have on a number of historic cases. Full details will be published in the *Guernsey News* tomorrow, on the police website, and are available at the station. For now, if you could all listen carefully to the following.'

He listed the historic cases. Read out the names of five, long-dead women. There was complete silence for a second, and then the weight of what he had said seemed to sink in. The room erupted into shouts of incredulity, people talking over one another, questions fired from all directions. He did his best. They were a tough crowd – as they should be. He was under no illusions. This was on them – they'd fucked up. Now they had to deal with it.

By the time the questions finally dried up, his throat was sore from talking and his head ached with the stress of trying to answer people coherently. His underarms were damp and prickly with sweat, which had soaked all the way through to his jacket. He kept his arms pressed firmly to his side as he closed the meeting.

'I'm sure you can all appreciate that we have a lot to be getting on with. A team of detectives from Hampshire will be joining us tomorrow. This is routine when forces like ours have to deal with cases of this nature. We are sure that their presence will help us bring these very serious investigations to swift conclusions. In the meantime, if I can ask you all to remain calm? And I appeal to all of you here, and the people watching at home, to think about whether or not you have any information that could assist us with our investigations. If you can think of *anything*, anything at all which might be of use, please call us. If not, I would ask you to let us get on with our jobs.' There were heckles from the back of the room,

'Pity you couldn't have done that a bit earlier!'

'Too bloody right! How could you have missed this?'

'Who's next? None of us are safe!'

Michael stepped off the stage, and pushed through the crowd, nodding and reassuring people, avoiding the flashes of cameras as best he could. He made his way out into the corridor and to the bathroom, where he locked the door behind him and sat on the closed lid of the toilet. A small window, set high in the wall was propped open and he could hear people outside, the shock in their voices audible, even if their words were not. He shivered in the chill of the cold, tiled room. People thought being a copper made you impervious to fear and panic, as if putting on a uniform and holding a badge could somehow nullify basic human emotions. Some of his colleagues even acted that way, cold and businesslike, in the face of trauma and tragedy. It was bullshit, of course. They were all scared. Not of injury or death – at least, not always, but of failure.

Saturday, 22 November

He arrived at the station at just gone six a.m. He'd slept properly for the first time in days, could only imagine that the previous day's press conference had drained every last drop of energy out of his body and his brain had had no choice but to follow suit and shut down for a few hours. He'd woken well before the crack of dawn, but he felt refreshed, ready to face whatever the day threw at him. Including that morning's copy of the *Guernsey News*, which arrived just as he returned from nipping out to get his breakfast and a coffee from Wally's next door. Brian Ozanne had agreed to run Lisa Bretel's picture on the front page for a week, or until she was found, whichever came first. She stared out at him, the word MISSING and the Crimestoppers' number printed underneath. He turned the pages as he ate a toasted Guernsey biscuit with butter and jam. Jenny's coverage had been fair, he thought. Not kind, that was never going to be the case, but fair. It was all he could ask for. He checked his watch. Nearly nine. Nearly time for the next big challenge of the day: his 'sit down' with Roger Wilson.

Roger had sounded pleased when Michael had phoned him the previous day, asking him to come in. Typical, Michael thought. Roger falling over himself to be involved. You'd think he'd feel embarrassed. After all, he bore as much responsibility for this mess as anyone. More, even. Chief of police and this madness going on under his nose? Michael chided himself. He must be fair. None of them had picked up on this. It wasn't Roger's fault any more than it was his. He looked up when he heard Fallaize's simpering tone, welcoming the chief back.

Roger had not been into the station for a couple of months and he took his time making his way to Michael's office, stopping and talking to people on the way. A friendly word here, a pat on the back there. He was laughing softly over some joke he'd shared with Fallaize as he walked through Michael's open door.

'How are you, Gilbert?' He smiled and sat down without being asked. He was dressed smartly, a gingham shirt tucked into navy cords, which hung loosely at his waist. He'd lost weight, Michael thought. He shook his head at Michael's offer of coffee and furrowed his brow, his expression now one of focused concern.

'God no, thank you. I don't think I slept a wink last night as it is. I just can't believe this, I really can't.' He shook his head. 'That journalist came to me, you know, last week, asking about all these girls, I thought it was funny. I really thought she was just some hack who had found something that didn't exist. I mean, it's unbelievable, isn't it?'

Michael nodded. 'It's horrendous, Roger. There's no way around it. We've monumentally fucked up.'

Roger did not disagree.

'We're going to need you to sit down with one of the DCs and go through everything, all the historic cases.'

Roger nodded. 'I thought as much. Anything I can do to help. I've cleared my diary for the day.'

The golf course would no doubt miss him, Michael thought.

'There's not a lot to go on, Roger. The files are all pretty thin.' He left it hanging there, not quite an accusation, but a challenge nonetheless.

Roger nodded, slowly. 'Well, the investigations were very straightforward, Michael. As you know. Obviously, if we'd had the information you have right now, the files would have been much thicker.' He closed his eyes, put his hand to his head, kneading his brow.

'Are you OK?'

He glared at Michael. 'Well, of course I'm not OK, Gilbert. And nor should you be. Because of our failings, my own personally and this force's as a whole, six young women's deaths were written off. And now, somewhere on this godforsaken island, another young girl's life is at risk. How are we going to explain this without looking like complete amateurs? And the families of these girls, we've let them down so badly. *I've* let them down. It's a nightmare. So if you've finished pissing around, let's get to work, shall we?'

There it was. Everybody liked Roger Wilson. Except Michael. It wasn't just because Roger had treated him unfairly all those years ago, had made Michael a pariah for sticking up for the truth, for trying to protect a young lad from police brutality. It was because of this. The arrogance. The condescension. The barely disguised contempt Roger had for him.

'You're right, chief. We should get to work. Let's start with where you were and what you were doing on the following dates.' He slid a list across the desk. Roger glanced down at it without picking it up.

'You want alibis? *I'm* a suspect now? For God's sake, man, do your job! There's a girl missing!'

'This *is* my job. It's routine, I grant you. But as well as having to have this information for the internal investigation which is undoubtedly going to follow this fifty-year fuck-up, you're also on the list of board members for LEAP, the youth club three of the girls were known to attend. It's just about the only lead we have right now and we have to follow it. Sorry, chief. Let's start with the list of dates and then move on to getting your input on the files. I'll get you that coffee.'

He left Roger sitting there, could practically see the steam coming out of his ears as he glowered at the paper in front of him. Michael tried very hard not to feel satisfied, but the glimmer of a smile played on the edge of his lips. He even managed to nod at Fallaize as he walked through the office to the coffee machine.

37

Jenny

She put the phone down. Michael was in a meeting. Obviously. The guy was not going to be having a break for a while. She'd told Stephen Marquis about the mark on the rock at Moulin Huet and her suspicions about Brian, that he might know more than he was letting on about Elizabeth Mahy's death. Stephen had promised to pass on the information. He'd sounded distracted, though, and she couldn't help worrying that he was just a little bit incompetent. It was unfair, really. She couldn't shake off her memory of the time he'd wet himself in the paddling pool one summer twenty years ago when all the cousins had got together for some family celebration, a ruby wedding anniversary maybe. He'd actually been very helpful to her over the last couple of years, always willing to share a good tip. And Michael seemed to rate him. It was always difficult, adjusting to people you'd known as kids being grown up and having serious jobs, Jenny thought.

Saturdays were usually quiet at the *News* but there were more people in than usual today due to the fact they were going to print a Sunday edition entirely dedicated to the search for Lisa Bretel. Even Brian was in his office. Another police car rolled past the window. She'd lost count of how many she'd seen today. All police leave had been cancelled, even the parish constables, who were civilian volunteers, had been called up to help. They were knocking on doors and handing out flyers with Lisa's picture on. It wouldn't help. They might have already knocked on the killer's door. He might have taken the picture, furrowed his brow, looked suitably concerned and all the while Lisa Bretel might be just out of sight, bound and gagged or drugged or dead. She couldn't sit around waiting for Michael to call back. She walked over to Brian's office.

Brian sat forward in his chair, his chin resting in his hands. His usually tanned skin was pale and a fine layer of stubble peppered his face.

'It's not what you think.'

'I think you know more than you've been telling me. When I asked you about Elizabeth Mahy, you said you had no recollection of her. And yet you were working on the paper at the time she was found dead. You were working on the story. You don't honestly expect me to believe you'd forgotten all about it? And your reaction to my report? You were panicked. Why? What do you know?'

He shook his head. 'I know nothing about these other girls.'

'But Elizabeth?'

'I made a promise.'

'To who?'

He sighed deeply. 'Elizabeth's boyfriend. David De Putron.'

He and David both attended the private boys' school, Elizabeth College. They were in the same year. Not good friends, but David had struggled fitting in. Brian had the impression that David's family life was complicated and Brian was a good listener. Always had been. He let David talk. Learnt secrets. Saved them up.

'I knew what I wanted to do, even then. I took a job at the *News* the summer I finished school. I was only just eighteen.'

A lot of the other boys went off to university, he said, but David started work at a law office to get some work experience before he went to study. He and Brian fell into a habit of getting a beer after work once or twice a week. Their friendship grew.

'We rarely discussed our personal lives. I knew he was seeing somebody, but he was cagey about it. Never brought her out.'

Brian met Elizabeth by accident, he explained. He was out on a work night, somebody's birthday, and they ended up at the yacht. It wasn't somewhere he usually went, it catered to a different crowd, older, non-professional. That was probably why David chose it, Brian said. He didn't think he'd see anyone he knew there. Of course, you could never count on that in Guernsey.

He could see straight away why David hadn't wanted anyone to find out about her. She was very young; short skirt, low-cut top. Not the type of girl you'd take home to meet your upper-class family or your public-school friends. Brian had spoken to them and they'd had a drink together.

'The next morning, David called me in a panic. He said there had been a dreadful accident. He was terrified it would ruin his career, or worse.

'According to David, he and Elizabeth were both drunk and it was her idea to go swimming. David had no idea she was in trouble until it was too late. It was some sort of terrible accident. He begged me not to come forward and I agreed. And when the police investigation backed up what he'd told me, I had no reason to believe I'd done the wrong thing. I was merely helping out a friend.'

'That was kind of you.' Jenny looked up from her notes.

'What do you mean?' His eyes narrowed.

'Well, you and David must have been very good friends. You risked incriminating yourself to protect him?'

'We were. But we didn't see much of each other after it happened. I suppose it put a strain on our friendship. And anyway, he went to university, to study law as planned. He didn't manage to make a career out of it, though. He had some sort of breakdown a few years after he qualified and gave it all up to teach music. I presumed it was the weight of the guilt that did it – the fact that he didn't manage to save her. Maybe there was more to it than that.' He looked at Jenny with red-rimmed eyes. He'd aged ten years in ten minutes.

'I believed him. I believed it was an accident. Even before –' He stopped.

'Before what?' Jenny pressed.

'This doesn't make sense!' He seemed more focused all of a sudden. 'He's just not the type. I *know* he's not. Not to do this. I never considered for a minute that he'd killed her.' He covered his face with his hands. 'Or that he might do it again.'

'This is a terrible idea. We should wait for the police to get here.'

'Lisa Bretel might be in here. We can't wait around for the police. Anyway, they're on their way. If he tries to kill us they'll be here in time to rescue us I'm sure.'

'I can't believe you're being flippant about this.' Elliot shook his head.

They had parked outside David De Putron's manor house on Fort Road, a long, straight road, which connected the town of St Peter Port to the village of St Martins. They had rung the entry bell three times but there had been no reply on the intercom.

'Come on.' Jenny grabbed hold of the gate and started to climb over.

'You've lost your mind!' Elliot shook his head, but followed her over nonetheless.

Their feet crunched loudly on the gravel path leading to the house, which widened to a large circular area with a stone fountain in the middle of it, a cherub holding his hand outstretched, water playing through his fingertips. The front door had another intercom system next to it and Jenny pressed the button again. After a moment or two, David De Putron's voice, crackled with static, replied.

'Who is it?'

'It's Jenny Dorey from the *Guernsey News*. I have a few questions for you.'

'Questions? About what?'

'About Elizabeth Mahy.'

A pause.

'I don't want to speak to you people. Stop harassing me.'

'No problem, Mr De Putron. We'll just wait until the police get here.'

* * *

'I knew this would happen. I always knew it would come back to haunt me. I suppose it's only right that it has. I should never have left her there. I should have called the police, explained it was a terrible accident, that there was nothing I could have done.'

'Why didn't you?' Jenny asked. 'If you were blameless, why not just come forward?'

She sat in a formal sitting room in one of the most beautiful houses she had ever been in. Elegant wooden chairs with cushions covered in silk were arranged around an old-fashioned card table. Under a bay window was a baby grand piano with the lid propped open, strings gleaming inside. Under another window was a large, mahogany desk. Huge oil paintings hung from wood-panelled walls. David sat across from her while Elliot was pacing the room, looking nervous.

'It was an accident, I swear it, but I panicked. I didn't think anyone would believe me.' His face crumpled. He pulled a handkerchief out of his jacket pocket and blew his nose. Between deep, gulping breaths, he told his story.

They'd met in a bar, he said, only weeks before she died. She was the first girl who had ever shown any interest in him. It was because she was young. He'd known that. She'd said she was sixteen but he'd thought she might be younger. It was one of the reasons he didn't bring her out to meet his friends. That, and the fact that they would have looked down on her. She wasn't the type he was used to. His only experience with girls had been at the dances his school had held with the Ladies' College, formal, supervised occasions. He was awkward, tall and clumsy. Took a while to grow into himself, that's what his mother always said.

But Elizabeth had made a beeline for him. She'd been sitting alone at the bar in a mini dress, her blonde hair piled on top of her head, heavy make-up around her eyes. Like Dusty Springfield, he'd thought, when he saw her. She'd been so forward, asking him to buy her a drink. They'd got talking. She'd been impressed he was going to university, that he had a job and money to spend. He hadn't cared.

'Even now, I'm ashamed to admit it. I was nineteen and still a virgin and I thought she'd be easy.' His cheeks burnt red. 'It's shameful, I know it is. But I was so young myself.' He blew his nose again, and then continued.

They'd been seeing each other for a few weeks. He'd grown to genuinely like her. It had been nice, being with someone who didn't take life too seriously. She hadn't wanted to leave the island, didn't worry about her future, just wanted a steady job and a nice house. She'd known he was leaving for university at the end of the summer. She'd known it wasn't a serious relationship. That night, he said, she was the one who had suggested going to the bathing pools. She'd had too much to drink. So had he. Dutch courage, he said. He looked up at Jenny.

'I don't know how it happened. We were swimming and laughing. She was teasing me and she swam away, told me to try and catch her. When it went quiet, I thought it was all part of it. I thought she'd gone underwater so I wouldn't find her. I didn't want to shout for her because we shouldn't have been there at all. After a few minutes I got out of the pool and walked around the edge – and it was then that I saw her. Floating. I dived in, hauled her out, but I knew she was already dead.

'I ran all the way home. Here. As soon as I arrived I vomited all over the driveway, from the exertion or the fear, I'm not sure which. I had no idea what to do. Brian was my closest friend. I asked him.'

'Brian said you asked him not to say anything.'

'No.' David shook his head. 'I just wanted to talk to a friend. I was going to go to the police. Once I'd calmed down, I knew it was the right thing to do. It was Brian who persuaded me not to. Told me I should keep quiet. He made so much sense. Of course the police would question why I'd run from the scene. And then there was the matter of my skinny-dipping with a drunk, possibly under-age, girl. Any way you looked at it, it didn't look good for me. That's what Brian said. And maybe he was right.' There was a bitter edge to his voice now.

'What happened, between the two of you?'

'I suppose, with everything that had happened, it was difficult for us to remain friends.' His lips tightened. 'He kept my secret. Protected me for years. I'd appreciate if he wasn't dragged into this.'

A woman appeared in the doorway. She was in her late fifties, tall and handsome, features too masculine to be considered conventionally attractive, but she had beautiful deep blue eyes and her silver hair, cut into a sharp bob, had the sort of shine that could only be achieved through regular trips to the salon. Her face glowed with just the right amount of bronzer or illuminator or whatever it was women put on their faces to make themselves look glossy and perfect. Jenny had never got further than a stick of concealer when it came to cosmetics and skin care, but she guessed this was a woman whose face cream cost a week's wages.

'I'm so sorry to interrupt, I didn't know David had guests.'

David seemed to tense up more, if that were even possible.

'This is my sister, Diane. Excuse me. I won't be a moment.' He left the room, guiding the woman out with him by the elbow.

'This is bullshit.' Elliot stood in front of Jenny.

'You don't believe him?'

'No way. He's lying through his teeth.'

Jenny sighed. 'You're right. Stay here. Tell him I've gone to the toilet or something if he comes back.'

'Jenny!' He somehow managed to shout and whisper at the same time. She turned back. 'If you want to help, see what you can find over there.' She pointed to the desk. Then she crept out into the hallway.

She stopped and listened. The ceiling creaked above. Footsteps. Pacing. She stood at the bottom of the staircase, steadying herself on the highly polished balustrade. Two voices, low murmurs. She could not make out any of the words. Soft carpet underfoot muffled her footsteps as she made her way up the stairs and on to a bright, well-lit landing. The voices came from a door on the right, set ajar. She walked, painstakingly slowly, angling herself so she was concealed by the open door but could just about see into the room. David's sister had her back to the door and was blocking Jenny's view of the room.

'. . . shouldn't have let them in, you fool!'

'Calm down. It's under control.'

David came into view as he walked in front of his sister and Jenny instinctively took a step backwards. The floorboard behind her creaked, not loudly, but it might have been enough. She ran along the corridor to the next door, which was open, and into the room, flattening herself against the wall. She was in a bedroom, decorated in the same elegant style as the room downstairs, with yellow satin bedclothes and heavy curtains draped at the window. The voices had stopped and she heard footsteps and then the sound of a door shutting before they resumed talking, but the words were muffled now and she couldn't make them out. She tried to relax, crept carefully out into the hallway and looked into the next room, and the one after that. All bedrooms or bathrooms, all empty. She heard raised voices and then something smash behind the closed door where David and his sister were, their argument apparently getting heated. She ran down the stairs on tiptoes, reached the sitting room just as she heard the door upstairs open. Elliot looked up as she came in and waved a paper at her. She nodded her head towards the door, indicating that David was coming back and Elliot looked indecisive for a second, before folding the paper and slipping it into his back pocket.

When David entered the room, Jenny was sitting where he'd left her and Elliot was gazing intently at a picture of a ship being tossed around in a storm.

'I'd like you both to leave now, please. Nothing I've told you is to be printed. If you have a problem with that, you should talk to Brian Ozanne.' His eyes were narrow and his lips were tightly set.

The severe weather warning issued earlier that day had achieved its desired effect. There were very few cars on the road. Elliot had the paper he had taken from David's desk unfolded on his lap.

'Fleur de Lis holdings, the company that owns the *Guernsey News*.'

'What about it?' Jenny asked.

'This is a page from the latest board meeting, showing a list of shareholders. Top of the list with a 51 per cent stake in the company is a Diane De Putron.'

'David De Putron's sister owns the *Guernsey News*?'

'Would explain a lot, wouldn't it? Like why David suggested we talk to Brian about not printing what he told us.'

'It would,' Jenny agreed, her expression grim.

She dropped Elliot outside his flat at the top of Mount Durand, turning down his offer of a drink and something to eat, despite being hungry and thirsty, because she needed to sort everything out. She was missing something. She needed to talk to Michael.

38

Saturday, 22 November

*H*e *trudged across the garden, through the gate in the hedge. Such a long day. Endless questions – that journalist. He should have done something about her at the outset. He should have made sure she kept her mouth shut. There were ways to keep people quiet. He'd done it before, so many times. A threat here, a bribe there. People were weak and scared, only too willing to take the easy option. He thought of the dull-eyed, bleating sheep from years ago, impervious to their surroundings, immune to the sorrow and suffering of others. Not her, though. He'd sensed it when he first met her and had been proved right.*

He'd followed her. Watched her. She understood the island. Not like he did, but she had an inkling, he thought, of the forces which flowed through it, of the strength held in every rock, every blade of grass, in the winds and the rain and the very soil that lay beneath their feet. He had seen her, at Pleinmont, pacing the sacred circle. At Bordeaux, she had bent down, run her hands over the stones. And Moulin Huet. He had been there too. He had not dared follow her then. It was too exposed out on the cliffs; there was nowhere to hide. But he knew what she had been looking for. He presumed that she had found it. He was impressed at her drive and tenacity. But she was becoming tiresome. And dangerous.

He shook himself. He couldn't remember the last time he'd felt this tired. He had no patience, then, for any more nonsense from little Lisa. No more trying to tempt her with delicacies. She would eat now whether she wanted to or not. He took the steps carefully. He had not been taking care of himself and he felt weak. His joints ached. He could not remember the last time he'd taken the host of vitamins and minerals he bought monthly, in a seemingly futile attempt to resist the relentless march of time. Even his hair had started to thin, but he thought that was more to do with his state of mind than anything else. He had woken that morning, not for the first time, with a clump of it grasped in his fingers and had had to comb it carefully, to cover the patch of scalp now exposed above his right ear.

She was still in the chair. Of course she was, she could hardly get off it. He'd bound her wrists behind her back with rope and then fed it under the seat and wrapped it around her ankles. Her head was bowed so he couldn't see her face, but he presumed, as she was silent, that her mouth was still sealed shut with one of his clean white handkerchiefs. At least, it had been clean when he'd first tied it, three – or was it four? – days ago? He was losing track. He put the Tupperware box full of sandwiches he'd brought with him on the floor next to her. He wondered if she was sleeping. Perhaps she was dead? It would be a relief, he thought, and he realised that he must do it soon. It was going to drive him insane, the stress of her, and the journalist, and the detective – and the godawful noise following him everywhere. It was no wonder he was tearing his own hair out. He laughed. Saw her flinch. He put his hand under her chin. Lifted her head so she was looking at him.

It was hard not to show his disgust. Her right eye, where he'd hit her with the pistol (he'd had no choice, she was screaming and would not listen to reason) was so swollen that only a slit of white was visible, glinting in the midst of an angry purple bruise. The other eye was bloodshot, presumably from lack of sleep or crying.

The handkerchief was filthy, crusted with mucus and saliva and, at the corners, blood where her skin had split. He had tied it too tightly.

A wave of remorse. What had he done to her? Beautiful girl. She was ruined. That had not been his intention. What had been his intention? He hadn't thought it through, had he? He had taken her with no plan. He had been forced to injure her, to spoil her, and then he couldn't simply save her, not like he had with the others, because they would have known. They would have seen the cuts and the bruises and they would have known.

They would have known anyway, fool.

He stayed very still, his hand on her chin, his eyes fixed on hers. He was unsure if the voice in his head was his own or if it was some sort of mutation of the noise he had carried with him for so long. Whichever it was, it spoke the truth. One body every decade. It had worked so well . . . He had been out of his mind, taking this girl. Out of his mind. He laughed again. Tears coursed down her cheeks, clearing a path through the layer of grime that had settled on her soft, pale skin. He wiped it and she closed her eyes as he did so, made a gagging, gurgling noise as he traced the salty path down, widening the track of clean skin. 'That's better,' he murmured, 'nice and clean.'

It came to him, then. Everything happened for a reason. Her death could not go unnoticed. However he did it, they would know it was no accident; they would hunt him down – they were hunting him already and it was only a matter of time before they found him. He would not wait, like a fox in a hole, for the hounds to flush him out. This was his chance to do it properly. Strength poured back into his aching bones. He straightened himself, placed his hand on top of her head. 'You will eat,' he told her. 'You will eat and you will drink, and then we are going to get you nice and clean and everything is going to be just fine. Just fine.' He turned. He needed supplies. Hot water and soap, fresh clothes, something clean and white. He felt almost light-headed with relief. Finally, after all these years of working in the shadows, he could step out, into the light.

39

Michael

He had to admit, the incident room looked very professional; a bank of six telephones on one desk, each one ringing off the hook, several flat-screen computers, a huge whiteboard, and a couple of the guys from the tech department were attempting to get HOLMES up and running. Now there was an acronym that actually worked. Home Office Large Major Enquiry System. It was a brilliant piece of kit, pulling together details from thousands of cases, allowing them to search and process information at a phenomenal speed. Problem was, having secured funding for the hardware several years previously, budget cuts had meant nobody was properly trained to run the bloody thing, so they were waiting for the expert from Hampshire to arrive. He'd been delayed, along with the independent senior officer and lord knows who else they were sending to breathe down his neck, by a thick layer of fog at the airport, which had backed up all of the weekend's flights. It was a nightmare getting to and from this island in winter. Between bad weather getting in the way of air traffic, and planes suffering technical faults, and a virtually non-existent ferry schedule, people could be trapped here for days. With no national newspapers, only local mail and a dodgy, low-speed internet connection, they could feel, on occassion, completely cut off. Well, Michael didn't have time to wait around for the fog to clear. Until backup arrived, he was just going to have to get on with things the old-fashioned way.

He sat at a desk and lined up the now all-too-familiar files once more, scanning them for anything that could hint at this bloody lunatic's motives. He tried to block out the background noise: the telephones and the chatter and the toing and froing as officers followed up on potential leads called in by a panicked public. He focused on the pictures. On the marks. It was horrifying, looking at it now. So obvious. How could it have been missed? It was the time frame that made it difficult, the fact that no one officer worked on more than one of the cases. Actually, that was a little odd but not unthinkable. Until recently there was no way of connecting details except by trawling through paper files and card indexes. The press wouldn't see it like that, though. They were going to have a field day. He could see it now. *BUMBLING ISLAND COPS ALLOW SERIAL KILLER TO RUN RIOT FOR FIFTY YEARS: DCI MICHAEL GILBERT HELD RESPONSIBLE.* He rubbed the top of his nose and massaged his eyebrows and temple.

'Sir?' Marquis stood in the doorway, a coffee in one hand, a paper bag in the other, and a guilty look on his face.

'What is it, Marquis?'

'I brought you a coffee and a sandwich, sir. It's nearly seven and you haven't eaten anything all day.'

'What are you, my bloody wife, Marquis? God help me, forget I said that.'

'He's right, you need to eat something.' Jenny poked her head around the door.

'How did you get past the front desk?' Michael asked.

'I came through the back.' She nodded towards Marquis. So that was why he was looking guilty.

'You can't be in here, Jenny.' He got up from the desk. 'And you can't be at David De Putron's house, either. We've had a complaint from his sister and she's a right bloody cow, that one. Excuse the turn of phrase – nothing wrong with cows. Or women. She just got up my nose.' He reddened.

'You've arrested him, though? You got the information I sent through? He admitted he was there when Elizabeth died. Surely that's enough to keep him here while you search his property – or properties, more like. His family is loaded. Did you know they own the *Guernsey News?* I work for them, for fuck's sake!'

'Jenny, believe me, I hear you. We've brought him in for questioning. But he has an alibi for the entire week surrounding Hayley Bougourd's death. We've checked it out and it's solid. He was one of the chaperones for a group of kids at the Young Choristers' competition in Chichester. And if what he says about Elizabeth Mahy is true, we've been barking up the wrong tree with that one. Plus our timeline is out by ten years, which means we need to update our profile of the killer to include younger men. Or at least my age and older.' He ran his hand through his hair and pulled at his chin. 'We just keep hitting dead ends! I don't know what to tell you. I don't know what to tell anyone. A fuck-up on this scale, Jenny . . .' He shook his head. 'I'm telling you, there's no benchmark for this. But we need to keep calm.' He seemed to be talking to himself now, pacing as he did so. 'I agree. There's something funny going on with these De Putrons. And, Marquis, you're right, I need to eat. I feel a bit light-headed. We can talk while I refuel. Not here, though. Follow me.'

He took her to one of the relaxation areas they had at the station. A couple of battered sofas and a low coffee table covered in dog-eared copies of *GQ* and *Top Gear* magazine.

'It's odd that it's Diane, the sister, who heads up this company, don't you think?' Jenny asked. 'I mean, he looks much older than her, and he's a man. I would have thought an old Guernsey family like the De Putrons would have handed things over to the oldest son.'

Michael nodded. 'It is strange. But he's admitted he has no interest in business. Dropped out of law school and I get the impression he's a bit of a black sheep.'

'He said so himself,' Jenny agreed. She tugged at the back of her hair. Michael had noticed her do it often, usually with a distracted look on her face, like she was remembering something, and he realised now it was a sign that she was stressed.

'This is getting us nowhere.' Jenny sat forward, shaking her hair loose. 'David has an alibi; Elizabeth's death was an accident; he's not the killer – and we're no closer to finding who is or who has Lisa Bretel, because can we even presume it's the same person?' She leant her head back against the chair. She looked very pale, Michael thought, her skin almost translucent.

'When was the last time *you* ate, Jenny?' He tore one of his sandwiches in half. 'I have a feeling Marquis made these with his own fair hands.' He looked distastefully at the pale, plastic-looking slice of ham poking out like a loose tongue from between the slices of thin bread. 'But it's better than starvation.' He handed it to Jenny, who took it and ate automatically, her mind somewhere far away.

'The book,' she said, after a couple of minutes. '*Guernsey Folklore*. Did you get the pages I sent over?'

'I did.' Michael sat up, pleased to be able to talk about a lead that might actually take them somewhere. 'You're right, the mark is very similar to those found on the girls. I've got Marquis looking into it. It's not a popular story, this Devil's Claw. I asked around, nobody here had heard of it. And that book's been out of print for years. There's a copy at the Priaux library, but there are no records of who's taken it out, at least not going back that far, so that's a dead end, but we're going to look into Island Books. Until it closed down we reckon it would have been the only place to get books about island folklore and history. Maybe someone who worked there remembers something. Maybe someone knows what happened to the stock. It's a long shot but worth a try.'

'None of this is going to help Lisa Bretel.' Jenny stared over his shoulder, out of the window that looked out on to a cobbled courtyard at the front of the station. Police cars had been driving in and out all day and would continue to do so all night as every available officer searched the island for the missing teenager.

'I don't know what to tell you, Jenny. Every resource we have is on the case. The team from Hampshire will be here soon and we'll see what they have to say – maybe they'll have some bright ideas.' He spread his hands out, helpless. 'We're doing everything we can, short of raiding every single house on the island. Our best bet is to keep working on trying to find out who did this so we know where to look.'

'That girl, Michael. She must be so scared. We *have* to save her.' Her eyes shone with tears. He thought of Ellen, of how, if things had been different, he might be comforting her over some dilemma, a boyfriend perhaps, or a work crisis, offering advice, giving her a hug. He reached over, touched Jenny gently on the top of her arm. He felt a lump in his own throat. She was not his daughter. It was not his place.

'Go home, Jenny.' His voice caught as he said it. 'Get some sleep. This isn't your responsibility.'

The way she looked at him though, as she left. He'd swear that she thought it was.

It was past seven p.m. but it could be midday there were so many people working. Nobody could accuse them of not doing their best, Michael thought. Their best wasn't good enough, that was the problem. Marquis was at his desk, head bent over some paperwork. The chief was in his office, on the phone. He'd been on it all day. Even the superintendent was in. Didn't see him about often. No doubt he was counting the cost of the whole bloody thing, passing his concerns on to the chief who would then be tasked with putting the pressure on Michael to get the whole thing sewn up quick sharp with minimum use of resources. It was enough to give him a headache just thinking about it all.

'How are you getting on, Marquis?'

The lad looked up from his desk. Always looked like a bloody rabbit in the headlights.

'I'm trying to verify one of Roger Wilson's alibis, sir. Conference in Bournemouth. It was a long time ago and I'm struggling to find travel records that tally with the ones he sent through, but they look genuine. He said he hoped that would suffice for now as he's struggling to remember where he was on the other nights in question over the previous forty years.' Marquis looked up from his notes. 'I think he was being a bit sarcastic, to be honest.'

'Yes. Thank you for that, Marquis. What have you got for me on the bookshop?'

'I'm still working on it, sir, but I have some information.' He flipped the pages of his notebook.

'Island Books was sold some time in the eighties, following the death of the owner.' He looked up, 'Actually, it was where that tattooist, White Spider, is now. You'd never know it used to be a book store; the walls are all painted black and silver and there are no shelves or anything.' He caught Michael's raised eyebrow and looked back down to his notes.

'Apparently it was the only decent bookshop on the island for many years and used to be very popular, but after Buttons opened, and then the Lexicon, it couldn't compete. It mostly stocked local interest, history and maps and was a good place to go for Christmas presents.' He glanced up again.

'You found all this in the records, did you, Marquis?'

'Yes, sir. Well, not exactly *in* the records, but Daphne, that's the lady who works at the Greffe, she gave me a lot of information. She remembered there was a bit of a scandal with the man who owned the shop because his sister was a Jerry-bag.' He paused. 'Those were her words, sir, not mine.'

'Hmph. All very interesting, I'm sure, but did your friend Daphne have anything other than gossip and recollection for us, Marquis? Like records, for example? Names?'

'I'm going back to collect them tomorrow, sir. They were all microfiched so she had to request them.'

'Right. Well. Good work, Marquis.' He left him flicking through thirty-year-old travel records and went back to his desk.

It was always the way round here. There was never any problem getting information. Too much information, that was the bloody problem. People had such long memories. Talking about Jerry-bags nearly seventy years after the Germans left! He remembered his mother talking about them. During the war, she said, you could spot one because she'd be wearing nylons. The rest of them had to make do with a carefully drawn seam down the back of a bare calf, but the Jerry-bags, they had real nylons. As if those women risked their reputations for a pair of tights. All of their husbands and boyfriends were off fighting the war and they found themselves alone and a German soldier offered to buy them dinner, to keep them company. It was human nature. Probably didn't hurt that the Germans were tall and blonde, bit of a change from the average Guernsey lad.

He looked at the photos on his desk again. He imagined what they must have looked like in person, imagined them all standing there in front of him, begging him to help them. He closed his eyes. Tried not to despair at the image.

'Marquis!'

'Yes, sir?'

'Fetch me another coffee, will you? And if there are any more of those delicious sandwiches floating around, I'll have one of those too.'

Michael sat. He was thorough. People said that about him and he knew they were being snarky, implying he was pedantic and slow. But there was a lot to be said for thoroughness. He couldn't undo the mistakes of the past, but there was a girl out there who needed saving. Something in these files could lead him to her. The least he could do was find it.

40

Jenny

The roads were scattered with small branches and litter from overturned rubbish bins, which were easily navigated, but just past Oatlands Village a tree had come down, blocking the way. She followed the signposted diversion through tiny, poorly lit lanes. She would have to reverse if anything came from the opposite direction. Normally at this time of day it would be busy, but tonight she had a clear run, emerging out on to the seafront without incident. Waves lashed the sea wall, leaving pebbles and vraic in their wake. It was only a matter of time before this was closed too. She drove slowly, trying to avoid the larger stones. Michael was right. None of this was her responsibility. She should be thinking about her own life, not chasing around trying to figure out what happened to other people's. She gripped the steering wheel and swerved to avoid a deep pool of water at the side of the road where the sea had breached the wall. Another weather warning on the radio.

> *. . . and the latest advice from the environment department is to stay in this evening unless your journey is absolutely essential. It's hairy on the roads already, and there's always the chance of falling trees, so stay safe, people!*

She turned it off. She couldn't stop. Not until they'd found Lisa Bretel. It wasn't too late. Not for her.

October 2012

The nights had drawn in and it was already dusk as she entered Victoria Park. She would need to run quickly to reach the well-lit streets at the other side of the park before dark. A generous layer of leaves and twigs covered the path, glistening and slippery from the earlier rain. The air smelt at once fresh and old, the scent of wet grass mingling with the sweet staleness of decomposing foliage. She put in her earphones, shuffled her playlist.

She ran, breathing deeply. It had been nearly four weeks since she had seen Madalina. The police had looked into her disappearance. They'd been to the house, discovered the rooms were being sub-let in contravention of the tenancy agreement, but that was an issue for the landlord, not them, they said. All the women were here legally. They were working for a cleaning company and Madalina had been homesick so she'd gone home. They had no reason to investigate any further.

She'd done everything wrong. She'd put Madalina in danger to get a story. She should have just done a human-interest piece, flogged it to a tabloid, earned a few hundred quid. Wouldn't have helped Madalina much, but she'd probably still be around to be pissed off about it. It didn't work like that, though. She'd followed a good lead, secured a staff job while she investigated. It would have been a huge story with a big payout. Better for her, better for Madalina. Except it hadn't been. Because Madalina had disappeared. She might be dead. And it was Jenny's fault.

And so it went, round and round until she thought she would scream. She picked up her pace and tried to concentrate on the music. It was almost dark now; she needed to reach the streetlights. She left the park and ran full pelt along the canal to the Olympic Stadium and on to Stratford, reaching Romford Road just as dusk faded to black. Here it was busy with returning commuters, heads down, engrossed in iPhones, and shoppers, laden with carrier bags.

She slowed to a walk, pulled out her earphones and tucked them into her top. She pulled up her hood against the fat drops of rain, which fell gently at first, but, by the time she turned off on to the street, were bouncing frantically off her waterproof.

She stopped on the corner of Fairfield Road, stood under the bus shelter that seemed to have been designed to ensure maximum discomfort while waiting for a bus, and watched, as she had done nearly every evening for the last two weeks. Because she was determined. If the police weren't going to investigate, she would. She had to tell Madalina's story. If something terrible had happened to her, Jenny would find out about it. On her previous visits she had watched from the shadows as three women left the house at around eight p.m. Each time she had followed them, walking ten minutes or so to a dilapidated building next to a chicken takeaway. They had knocked at the door, waited a matter of moments, and then walked in. Tonight she was determined to talk to them.

Just before eight, the front door of number 42 opened. The women walked out, their voices low in muttered conversation. Previously they had stopped to light cigarettes before starting their journey, but this time they kept walking, heads bowed against the rain, pulling their thin, shiny jackets around themselves. They headed round the corner, and then left and right, through the rat-run of streets that led back towards Romford Road. Jenny followed at a distance.

The rain was now so heavy it was hard to see where she was going. Instead, she listened for the clack-clack of the heels up ahead. They walked, further than they had before, through deserted streets and Jenny felt the first quickening in her stomach, a tightening in her chest, a heaviness in her heartbeat. She felt for the torch in her pocket. Just knowing it was there eased the panic. The footsteps up ahead slowed. Was one of the women looking back at her? Did they know they were being followed? She should stop them, see if they would talk to her. Did they turn right or left up ahead? She pulled back her hood.

She was on a street she did not recognise. There was an area of wasteland on one side and an abandoned car sat next to a skip full of angular shapes, casting long shadows across the broken, weed-strewn concrete. On the other side was a low, rectangular build-ing, fallen into disrepair; boarded-up windows, a faded Help The Aged sign over the door visible in the glare from the street light overhead. Jenny hesitated. The women were nowhere to be seen. She stopped, blood pounding in her ears. There was a movement in the shadows and she spun on her heels, just in time to see a fox emerge from behind the skip. It trotted past her, sleek and strong, its rust-red coat shining with health. She exhaled. So stupid! She was going to go mad if she carried on like this, following people through the streets of Newham like a fucking lunatic, some kind of vigilante crusader. She reached for her phone to try to figure out where she was. It was then that she saw. The car across the street – it was not abandoned at all. There was somebody in it, a man in a black hood. And he was looking right at her.

Smiling.

A hand over her mouth and nose, the harsh smell of tobacco and cheap soap. She tried to breathe but there was no air, just the taste of his skin, and she clawed and kicked but suddenly every-thing was black and all she could feel was the cold pressure of a blade at her throat. They tightened the blindfold, the fabric cut-ting into the side of her face and pressing her eyelids tightly shut. A hoarse whisper.

'*Silence.*'

The grip around her nose and mouth loosened enough for her to take a gasp of breath and then she was propelled forward.

'What do you want?' she whispered. The hand tightened

around her face again, the blade pressed so firmly she felt sure it would puncture her skin.

'*Silence!*'

She heard the car door open and then a searing pain at the back of her head.

Silence.

Everything black, the smell of warm earth and rubber, a pressure across her eyes and over the top of her nose. The blindfold! Don't panic. She mustn't panic. She must think. Her legs ached. Not just sore, but bound. Tightly. Throbbing. There was a weight on her right thigh, the thrum of an engine. She was in a car. She was lying on the floor in a car. She was lying on the floor in a car, blindfolded, with her hands tied behind her back. She was fucked.

'*Don't. Fucking. Move.*'

Voices. Muffled. Nothing made sense. *Listen harder.* Three voices. Two in the front, one in the back.

The weight on her thigh was his foot. His foot on her leg. Simon and Garfunkel's 'Bleeker Street' on the car stereo. Laughter. Coughing. A deep, hacking cough. Someone lit a cigarette. A rush of air. An open window. She listened.

Where the fuck were they going? What the fuck were they going to do to her?

The facts. She needed to focus on the facts. There were three of them. One of her. Don't cry.

Don't let the fuckers see you cry.

The car stopped. Doors opened and closed. Rough hands pulled her to her feet and dragged her out. Soft ground. Cool air. Hard, cold blade at her throat.

Someone gripped the top of her arm and pushed her forward. They walked. Twigs underfoot. Dog barking. Cars in the distance. They stopped. Barked orders. Foreign language. *Romanian?* Footsteps.

Something hit her legs and she fell forwards, face on the ground, wet leaves in her mouth, the taste of iron and bile in her throat. He was close to her.

'You like to write stories. It is good, to write stories. I have a little girl. She likes to write stories too.'

He pulled her head up by her hair, held her hair back from her face, held it tightly.

'You are all the same, you little girls, I think. Little girls with your little stories.'

'Please . . .'

A pause.

'I'm not going to kill you, Jenny. I want to. You are causing me big problems. But you would be a bigger problem dead. Too many people to miss you, I think. Too much trouble for me. For now.'

The blade was cold against her cheek. He scraped the point down to the corner of her mouth and let it rest. Then it touched her ear.

'Know this. I am watching you. Always. I see you again near my girls, I will kill you. You write again about my girls, I will kill you. You look again for your little friend, I will kill you. I change my mind, I feel like it, maybe I will kill you too.' He pulled her hair back, twisting it tighter.

'Pretty, Jenny. Very pretty.'

The swish of a blade, a burning at the back of her neck, her head falling forwards to hit the cold, wet ground.

'You know, my little girl, she likes stories about princes and princesses and fairy godmothers. You should write one of these stories, Jenny. They usually have happy endings.' He paused for what felt like minutes. Then warm breath in her ear. A whisper.

'I will follow your work, Jenny. I will look out for your fairy tale.'

And he was gone.

A cool breeze floated in through the open window, ruffling the curtains and allowing a shaft of autumn sunlight to fall on her face. She squinted against the brightness. A familiar rustle of papers, the turn of a page, a shake to ensure the surface was smooth and easy to read. She opened her eyes fully.

'Dad?'

'Morning, love.' He was sitting in her desk chair, turned to face the bed. His full beard was greyer than she remembered, but the hair on his head was thick and black. He wore, as always, a navy Guernsey and navy twill trousers. All he needed was his hat and he'd be ready to go out on the boat.

'What are you doing here, Dad? And how did you get in?' She felt a rush of panic. Was the front door unlocked? Could anyone just walk in off the street? She sat up.

'Your flatmate let me in. Maja. Lovely young lady, she is. Can't make a decent cup of tea, mind you.' He folded his paper neatly into four and placed it on the desk. 'Speaking of tea, will I get you one?'

'Why are you here, Dad? It's lovely to see you but you didn't need to come.'

'That's not the way I heard it, love.'

'Heard from who?'

'Let me get you that cup of tea. I'll get myself a decent one while I'm at it. And then we'll talk, all right, love?' He was a tall, strong man and it was easy to forget he was nearing seventy. There was no sign of age in the way he held himself or in his confident gait as he left the room. She heard the sound of voices from the kitchen. It must have been Maja. She must have phoned her parents. Fuck.

She went to the bathroom and splashed water on her face, ran her fingers through her unwashed hair. She tried pulling it back into a ponytail although she knew it wouldn't go. He had cut it just too short. She let it flop down again over the dressing on the back of her neck. She gargled with some Listerine, pinched her cheeks to bring some life into her ghost-like complexion, then smoothed some concealer under each eye for good measure. Her mum would have seen through it in no time, but there was a chance her dad could be persuaded she was OK.

Charlie came back into the room and placed one mug carefully on the desk. He handed the other to her. 'Maja tells me you've hardly been out of your room in days.' Jenny started to protest but he shook his head.

'No. Listen to me, Jen. I was willing to believe you when you said you were OK, even though I could hear it in your voice. As soon as I picked up that phone I knew you were anything but OK, but I said to myself, she knows what she's doing. She's a smart girl. Who am I to argue if she wants to stay? And, God knows, I've encouraged you. I know I have. Filled your head with ideas, telling you to get off the bloody rock, to put that brain of yours to good use, to do something more exciting than get a job in a bloody bank, but look where it's got you, love! You were reckless, Jenny, you could have been killed!'

'Dad, I *am* OK. I was scared, I'll admit that. And I was stupid. But I promise you, I've learnt my lesson.'

'But these men, the ones you were investigating, the police haven't found them. They threatened you. Maja's filled me in. There's a lot more to all of this then you let on. What's to say they won't come after you again? And next time maybe they won't stop at hacking your hair off! Come home, love.' He was pleading now. 'Even just for a couple of weeks. Have a rest, let you mother feed you up a bit. Don't give me that look. You need looking after. You'll never admit it, but you do.' He seemed self-conscious all of a sudden. He cleared his throat and picked up his newspaper.

'It's a nice day. Bit chilly, but the sun's out. Why don't you get dressed and we'll go and get a spot of lunch? Saw a nice-looking pub down the road – I can get a Doom Bar, a decent pint for a change. Not like that piss they serve at home.'

*

283

She went home and stayed until Christmas but she had been back in Hackney for the New Year. She had to admit that the rest had done her good and she was almost feeling herself again.

Almost. The feeling of the knife at her throat, of his hands in her hair. It came back to her. Often. When she looked in the mirror each morning. When she went out with friends. When she laughed. And every time she looked over her shoulder.

Jenny hung her coat on the hook in the corridor, next to Margaret's. There were three more hooks, all unused. They had always been full when Charlie had been alive. Grief suddenly washed over her, soft waves, less violent than the piercing, physically debilitating pangs she had felt in the days and weeks after his death, but no less painful now, almost two years later. People talked about missing someone so much it hurt – and it did. She had got used to the pain, had tucked it away so that she could think about Charlie, talk about him, without breaking down. It was the emptiness she couldn't get used to. The fact his absence was almost tangible: a clean doormat, once peppered with sand and seaweed, a neglected bucket, lying on its side in the back garden, a space on the wall where a coat should be.

'Jenny? What are you standing there for? I saved you some dinner.' Margaret stood in the bathroom doorway, steam billowing around her. 'I've finished up in the loft, cleaned it, sorted it, and I've found some brilliant stuff up there. Let me get dried and I'll show you.'

They sat in the kitchen, Margaret showing Jenny old school photos and report cards. 'We should keep them down here, make an album or something, don't you think?' Margaret asked. 'Let's sort out the good ones.'

Jenny carefully wiped some dust off of a brown cardboard

sleeve edged with gold before opening it to reveal a picture of Charlie at about five years old, in a flat cap and blazer, shorts and knee socks. She removed the photograph from its frame. The back was yellow and damp-stained, the paper soft with age. In the corner someone had written, *Vauvert* '52. His first day of school, Jenny thought. She put it to one side. Took a bundle of pictures from the pile. Margaret, this time: a teenager. Jenny smiled. 'Check out your miniskirt, Mum.' She held up the photo.

'I had great legs, didn't I? So do you. You should try putting on a skirt every now and then. Get out of those jeans for a change.'

Jenny ignored her and looked at the next picture. 'That's Elizabeth?' She pointed at the girl next to Margaret. Margaret nodded. 'Who's that?' Jenny pointed to a small boy standing next to them.

'That was Elizabeth's brother. I forget his name. Billy? No, Bobby, that was it. Bobby. Followed us round everywhere. So different back then. Look at him, he can't have been more than six or seven and he would always be turning up on his bike all by himself. I didn't mind. I quite liked it, not having any brothers and sisters, and I was always a bit envious of Elizabeth having someone to mother. What is it? Where are you going?'

'I have to do something, Mum, I won't be long.' Jenny walked to the hallway and pulled on her coat.

'You've just got in, you can't go out in this!'

Jenny stood in the open doorway, the wind blowing leaves and twigs into the house.

'I'm just going round the corner, I'll only be a few minutes.' Margaret looked distressed. 'Put the kettle on, Mum. I'll be back before you've made the tea.'

It was a five-minute drive to Amanda Guille's house. Jenny saw the blue flicker of light from a television glinting through the drawn curtains. It was late, but there was never a good time for a journalist to doorstep a grieving family so she knocked. She hadn't thought about how she was going to ask what she needed to know without causing them more distress, or if they'd even have any answers. The door opened and Amanda's mother stood there, hollow-eyed, at her side a small boy wearing faded Spider-man pyjamas, trailing a little grey donkey on the floor behind him. He looked up at her and she saw fear flicker across his face. She was another stranger bearing bad news. Jenny couldn't do it. This family had known enough horror. If there was more to come, it could wait until the morning.

'I'm sorry to disturb you.' She stepped back. 'I must have the wrong house.' Amanda's mother looked nervous.

'Whose house are you looking for?' she asked.

'Who is it, love?' Amanda's father appeared behind his wife.

Jenny turned and walked back to the car.

Amanda had stopped her singing lessons with David De Putron. Something had upset her. Hayley had refused to bring her little brother Jax to her piano lessons. Elizabeth's brother had followed her everywhere. Jenny felt sick. Had Elizabeth noticed something was amiss? Had she challenged David? Was that how she ended up dead? The others too? Jenny had nothing to go on. Just a hunch. She had to ask more questions. Starting with Brian. She had a feeling that he already knew what she suspected: David De Putron had never been interested in teenage girls.

Sunday morning. The presses were rolling. She got a coffee from the machine and watched one of the delivery guys, a skinny man in his twenties, still in his coat, whistling along to his iPod as he stacked and bundled the papers. He saw her looking and pulled out one of his earphones, pointed to the front page.

'What's going on with this, then? My sister used to be friends with her at primary school. I remember her when she was nine or ten, coming round for tea.' He shook his head. 'It's terrible. Things like this shouldn't be happening here.'

Jenny nodded. 'It *is* terrible. The police are doing the best they can, I know that.' She didn't know what else to say. Elliot came in, sweating despite the cold, the bottom of his jeans soaking wet.

'What happened to you?'

'Had to negotiate four or five different diversions to get here. Got stuck in a ditch trying to get out of the way of a van in the Green Lanes, had to push the car out. The exhaust is practically hanging off now, I only just made it here.'

He sat at his desk, beckoning Jenny over and took a file out of his rucksack.

'What have you found?' Jenny nodded at the papers.

'Company registration documents, showing that Diane De Putron's family is the majority shareholder of the *Guernsey News*. She owns several hotels and restaurants and I've also got a list of businesses she's sold or wound up over the years. Everything is in Diane's name. Doesn't look like David got anything.'

'Where did you get all this?'

Elliot raised his eyebrows at her.

'Sorry. Don't tell me.'

'So. What do you think is going on?' Elliot asked.

'I think Brian is in with the De Putrons. Either they're threatening him or bribing him, I don't know for sure, but he's working for them, and not just as editor of their newspaper.'

'Maybe we'd better ask him to explain.' Elliot pointed to the door where Brian stood, immaculate as always, in a tan belted mackintosh which he was unbuttoning, shaking off the damp which had settled on the collar before he hung it on the coat rack. He looked over at them. He might have dressed well, but he could not disguise the shadows under his eyes.

'What are you doing here so early?' His voice was hoarse.

Jenny motioned to Elliot to stay where he was, gathered the papers and joined Brian at the door to his office.

* * *

'He has alibis. The police are satisfied with them. And I've spoken to him. He told me himself. I believe him. There's no way he killed those girls.'

'You were worried enough to ask him about it, though, weren't you? You've been covering for him, keeping his secrets for years and you panicked, didn't you? What do you know, Brian? If the police raid his house, what are they going to find?'

'How the hell should I know? Apart from the call he made a few days ago, asking me to stop you from harassing him, I haven't spoken to him in years!'

'I have a theory.'

'Please share it. Enlighten me, why don't you?' He folded his arms, leant back in his chair.

'I think you were convinced of David's innocence because you knew full well that women and girls were of no interest to him.'

'What's that supposed to mean?'

'You said, last time we spoke, that David "wasn't the type". I thought you meant you couldn't believe he was capable of murder, because you knew him, because you were good friends once. But there's more to it than that, isn't there, Brian?'

He shook his head. 'I don't know what you're talking about.'

'Yes you do. I think David De Putron has used his position as a music teacher and a respected member of the community to groom children. Seven and eight year olds, Brian. Little boys like Amanda Guille's brother and Hayley Bougourd's and Elizabeth Mahy's. Maybe many, many more. And I think you knew about it.'

Brian's hand slammed down on the desk.

'I did not!' His voice cracked as he shouted. Jenny saw Elliot get up from the desk and approach the office door. She shook her head at him.

Brian spoke, still angry. 'There is no – and never has been – evidence that David actually abused kids. If there had, I would have done something about it. I'm not a fucking monster.'

'But you knew something. You suspected. You got mixed up with his family. How?'

Brian rubbed his face, rested his head in his hands and stared out of the window. Then he reached into his desk and pulled out a packet of cigarettes.

'I need a smoke.' He walked out of his office and headed towards the exit. She followed.

He crossed the road, Jenny a few paces behind, and stood on the slipway leading on to Belle Grève Bay. The tide had receded and the sun, still rising, threw a milky yellow light on to the rock-strewn sand.

He waved the packet at Jenny, who shook her head.

'What, your body a temple or something?' He lit up and blew the smoke over his shoulder, away from Jenny. 'My wife, Helen, begged me to quit. Her dying wish. Fucking pain. Feel guilty every time I have one now, which is stupid. It's not like she knows about it.' He laughed, humourlessly. Jenny said nothing. They stood there in silence, until Brian shook his head and turned towards the sea.

'I confronted David, the morning after Elizabeth Mahy's body was found. Like I told you before, I knew he was with her that night, I wanted to give him a chance to turn himself in. He begged and pleaded and cried like a baby. Said it was all an accident, told me the story I told you. I said I'd give him until the end of the day and he agreed he would go to the police. I was a junior reporter then, just starting out. I went back to his house that evening, to make sure he'd done the right thing, but David wasn't there. I spoke to his mother. She told me exactly the same story. That it had been an accident. But the police might not see it like that. There was no point ruining David's future, she said. She offered me money and a job for life at the paper. Told me I'd be the youngest editor in chief the *Guernsey News* had ever had. And I was.' He sat on the edge of the sea wall.

'I should never have done it. But once I had, there was no going back. As time went on I was less and less convinced by David's version of events. I'd never seen him with a girl before Elizabeth, and there were very few afterwards. I snooped around. Heard rumours. Eventually I broke into his house, when he was away at university. Found photos he'd taken of boys. They weren't pornographic.' He looked at Jenny, fixed her with his cold stare. 'There was nothing sexual about them. They were just pictures of little boys, out playing in the park, taken from a distance, nobody was being hurt. But obviously it was wrong. The man is sick, I know that. I took them to his mother, threatened to blow the lid on the whole thing; Elizabeth's death, the photos, everything.'

'So why didn't you?' Jenny struggled to keep her voice even as nausea rose from the pit of her stomach. It took every ounce of self-control she possessed not to scream and shout that, yes, he *was* a fucking monster, that was exactly what he was, because who could keep something like this a secret?

'She promised to get him treatment. He dropped out of university, went to some sort of hospital. They paid me more money and the company was passed on to his sister after his mother died. A punishment, I suppose.' He dropped his cigarette butt and watched as it fizzled out in a puddle of seawater caught between the cracks of the cobbled slipway.

'Listen, I was knee deep in shit and there was no way out. I'd covered up his involvement in Elizabeth's death, kept quiet about the photographs, taken bribes, made sure none of Diane's pet projects received negative coverage.'

'What pet projects?'

'Save the Islander is the latest. She's an old friend of Tostevin's, so she discourages any coverage of the immigration debate. I've found ways to be OK with it. I've given most of what they gave me to charity. And, like I said, I don't think he hurt anyone.'

'You can't know that. How could you keep quiet, knowing that children were at risk?' She made no attempt to hide the contempt in her voice.

He shrugged. 'He told me he just liked looking at them. And no one has ever come forward to say any different.' He paused. 'I did wonder about Elizabeth Mahy, about whether she found something out and he killed her. And when you came to me with the research into the other girls' deaths I did panic, thought it could have been him. But it's not. Which means it's someone else. Maybe you should be spending your time trying to figure out who because it doesn't look like the police are getting anywhere.' He left her standing, shivering on the slipway and walked down on to the beach, dodging between rocks and on to the sand until he reached the sea. He stopped at the edge of the water and lit another cigarette.

Jenny wished that he'd kept on walking.

41

Michael

He'd spent half the day dealing with this David De Putron mess. Brian Ozanne was in a cell awaiting questioning and he was going to be there a long bloody time because, frankly, Michael had more important things to worry about than that despicable excuse for a man. As for David De Putron himself, he was nowhere to be found. Must have scarpered as soon as they'd released him the night before. Michael had a couple of officers searching the house and talking to the sister. She was a piece of work, he thought, acting like they were inconveniencing her, as if they had no business being there. She knew, though. He could see it in her eyes. Michael had been in two minds as to whether or not to arrest her too but had decided not to on the basis that he couldn't spare the resources.

On any other day, this would have been the biggest thing to happen in the station for years: a member of an illustrious Guernsey family, at the very best a sick man who had failed to come forward when a young girl had drowned, at worst, a paedophile, maybe even a murderer. Jenny had floated the idea that he might have killed Elizabeth, if she'd found out his secret, challenged him to protect her brother. It was a possibility. But nobody was really talking about it, due to the fact that they were also dealing with a serial killer and a kidnapping and four officers from

Hampshire constabulary had finally arrived and were breathing down everyone's necks. Rightly so. Four days Lisa Bretel had been missing. They all knew that time was running out.

He went back to his files. Before Jenny's call that morning, he'd thought he was getting somewhere. He'd read and reread everything, knew the cases back to front and inside out and was sorting through all of the information in his head, arranging and rearranging the pieces until something made sense. Now the noise, the phones ringing, the chatter, the constant toing and froing of officers in and out of the room, was ruining his concentration. He'd handed over copies of everything to the lads from the UK. Maybe a fresh pair of eyes would do the trick. But he was nearly there, he knew he was.

The mark. Some kind of Devil's footprint. The straw figures. The locations. They were looking for someone interested in the occult. Someone who knew the island's history and legends. He thought about the evidence. No fingerprints, no hair, no fibres, no footprints – nothing. Drowning was a nightmare, professionally speaking. Everything was being reprocessed but he held little hope they'd find anything new. He glanced down the list in Mary's file. They'd collected samples of sand, surrounding pebbles, and some oak leaves.

A shift. That's what it felt like. People talked about cogs turning, but for Michael, whenever he'd had these moments of clarity, it felt more like a movement forwards, like his brain had clicked up a gear. Why were there oak leaves on the beach? Yes, there were trees around Bordeaux, but not many. And no oak trees so far as he could recall. He flicked back and forth through the files, as he'd done hundreds of times in the last two weeks. He rechecked each evidence list, then rechecked the photographs taken at each scene, but this time he looked for something new. And he found it. Not on all of them. But there were a couple in the far corner of the crime-scene photograph of Janet Gaudion, right next to her collarbone. One tangled in Hayley Bougourd's hair, removed and noted at the post-mortem and Amanda . . . He didn't even need the evidence list. He squeezed his eyes shut and forced his memories of that night back to the forefront of his mind, checked with himself that he was indeed remembering, not imagining. They had blown over his feet. He remembered the sound of them rustling against his shoes. Oak leaves. On the beach.

'Sir?' Marquis stood over the desk, mug in one hand, a file tucked under his arm. 'I bought you a coffee.'

Michael looked up from the computer screen and saw that it was nearly dark outside. There were fewer people in the incident room now and it was considerably quieter.

'What time is it?' He glanced at the clock at the top of the screen. 'Five o'clock!' He took the coffee and swigged it back. He had no need of the caffeine; he felt more awake than he had done in years, but he was dehydrated and it wouldn't do to keel over now.

'What do you know about oak leaves, Marquis?'

'Not much, sir. I mean, I know what they look like and that they come from oak trees.' He shifted nervously from one foot to the other.

'It's not a trick question, Marquis. Until a couple of hours ago, that was all I knew too. But thanks to this wonderful machine,' he pointed to his computer screen, 'I now know an awful lot more.

'For example, did you know that oak leaves have been used symbolically throughout the ages, by pagans, Celts and, more interestingly, by the Nazis?' He was aware he sounded slightly crazed and his eyes were stinging and probably red and he had not taken a break all day – and by the way Marquis was looking at him there was a chance that he wasn't actually managing to string together his sentences as effectively as he might have liked.

294

'I didn't know that, sir, no.'

Michael rose from behind the desk and began to pace the room.

'And do you know what else interested Nazis, Marquis?' He didn't wait for an answer. 'The occult. Paganism. Black magic. Dark forces. And tell me something else.' He placed each of the dead girls' photos in a row, 'what do these girls all look like?'

'Well, sir,' he swallowed hard, 'we've considered the fact that they all look similar in that they are all blonde, blue-eyed . . .' Realisation seemed to dawn on him.

'Exactly!' Michael took a triumphant bite of his sandwich. 'They all look like something straight off a bloody Aryan-nation poster.' He paced again. 'It struck me before, but I couldn't put my finger on it. The lack of violence prior to death, the marks, the ritual – there's something almost reverential about it. He doesn't hate these girls. He's not punishing them. He's fixated on them somehow. Worships them, maybe. I don't know.' He shook his head. 'I want lists made up now: anyone who fits the age range, who has any affiliation to any right-wing groups, anyone who's ever said or done anything that could be construed as racist, fascist, neo-Nazi . . . What's the matter? You look like you've seen a ghost!'

Marquis stood, pale and trembling, holding the folder that had been tucked under his arm.

'It's this, sir. The information you asked me to get about Island Books, it's just come through. I thought it was a strange coincidence but with the Nazi connection . . . Although, I'm not saying that just because of the Nazi father thing. It wouldn't be right to think that, would it . . . ?' His voice trailed off.

'What is it, Marquis?'

'Island Books, sir. I was telling you, there was a bit of a scandal around the family, what with the sister of the owner rumoured to be a Jerry-bag and her son apparently the result of an affair she had with a Nazi officer.' He swallowed.

'Spit it out, Marquis, for God's sake!'

'The owner was a Peter Wilson, sir. After he died, the shop, the books – they all went to his nephew, Roger.'

'With all due respect, sir, the evidence is circumstantial because that's all we have to go on.' He nodded. 'Yes, yes, he has an alibi, for at least one of the murders, a conference that we're rechecking as I speak.' He let out a deep breath. Nodded again. 'Yes. Yes. OK.' He slammed the phone down so hard that the handset bounced back off the desk and on to the floor. 'Bloody idiot!'

He'd look everything over, Hammond had said. As soon as he'd finished with internal affairs. And Michael needed to get a hold of himself. He should go home, take a shower, get some rest. Rest, my arse, Michael thought. He paced the room, trying to figure out what to do.

Marquis was proving once again to be something of a trooper and was working with the HOLMES technician, searching for the mark of the Devil and oak leaves and for any other Aryan-looking murder victims who might have popped up recently, to see if they could connect anything to Roger Wilson. Because Michael's current theory was that the retired chief of police and all-round good-deed-doing-model-bloody-citizen was a crazed Nazi occultist serial killer. He rubbed furiously at the stubble shadowing his chin.

He needed to get out of the office. Take a walk. Get some proper food. He felt light-headed. He'd worked twelve hours straight on a piece of bread and jam and an egg sandwich. He picked up the newspaper. Lisa Bretel stared back at him. He was struck with the need to run all this by Jenny, see if she thought it sounded plausible. Off the record, obviously. He called her work number. It rang several times before Mark, the news editor, picked up. Jennifer had left, he said, around an hour ago. Michael was surprised.

'She's gone home?'

Mark laughed. 'She's not gone home. It's crazy here and she's gone to talk to Roger Wilson. He called earlier, wanted to speak to her about something to do with the cases he worked on.

'How long ago did she leave?' Michael's ear burnt with the pressure of the handset clutched against it.

'About an hour ago, a little more maybe. Is everything OK?'

Michael hung up the phone and stood quite still. Phones were ringing. Hard drives were humming and whirring. Blood was pounding in his ears.

Dear God, don't let this be happening. Don't you *let* this happen, God. Not on my watch. Not again.

'Marquis!'

'Yes, sir?' He looked up from the screen.

'Stop fucking around with that machine and come with me! And you!' He pointed to another officer who had been eating chips out of a plastic tray. 'And you too!' he shouted at Fallaize, who had just walked into the room. 'Quickly!' he yelled. His colleagues followed him out of the station, half jogging to keep up.

'What the hell is going on? Where are we going?' Fallaize shouted.

Michael stopped. Turned. 'We're going to stop a murderer. So, for once in your life, shut your fucking mouth, get in that car and follow me!'

42

Jenny

She pulled into the driveway and turned off the engine. She yawned and rubbed her watering eyes. Sleep felt more and more like something that only happened to other people.

It was a clear evening, black sky unsullied by cloud. It was only a few yards from the car to the front door, and although most of the house was in darkness, a warm glow from a dormer window in the roof was enough to get her there without the need for her torch.

Despite the light from upstairs, something about the house felt empty and she was unsurprised when the ring of the doorbell went unanswered. She checked her phone. No messages. Strange. He'd insisted he needed to speak with her. He struck her as the sort of man who would take criticism badly and she presumed he wanted to tell his side of the story, to explain how he could have missed the fact that there was a serial killer at work, undetected, while he was leading the police force. She tried the doorbell again. Waited another minute. Perhaps, if he was at the top of the house, he couldn't hear her. She opened the door.

It was darker inside than out and she used the glow of her phone screen to find the light switch. She stood in a narrow corridor, two closed doors to the left and a staircase to the right. The air smelt damp and stale. Cream Artex covered the ceiling and the walls with a complicated pattern of swirls and dimples, which had bubbled and lifted in patches, leaving flakes of plaster on the floor. It was a beautiful floor, an intricate mosaic of brown and orange tiles arranged in stars and squares, but it too was in disrepair. Many of the tiles were chipped or absent altogether, the black spaces where they once were like the gaps left by missing teeth. How different and disconnected this corridor felt to the homely kitchen she had visited last time. As if it belonged to a different house, a different person.

She was aware she should call out. *Hello? Roger?* But the words stuck in her throat, and instead of trying to get them out she found herself keeping them in, swallowing them back down and treading lightly across the tiled floor.

She opened the first door. A sitting room, the faded floral wallpaper peeling at the corners and the heavy velvet curtains covered in dust. In the next room, a beautiful grand piano stood in the alcove of the bay window, the light reflecting off of its highly polished surface. Stacked next to the piano were boxes. She walked over to them. They were unsealed and she carefully lifted a flap. The unmistakable musty vanilla smell of old books. She picked up the top one. It had a heavy, faded green cover. *Black's Guide to the Channel Islands.* The one underneath, a slim pamphlet, the paper soft with age, *Cartulaire de Guernesey,* 1924. She flicked through the pages, bent down to pick up the loose paper which fell from between them. The title of the book, the price, a space for the date to be filled in. A receipt. From Island Books. She tried to still her shaking hands enough to take some decent pictures before she left the room, pulling the door shut with a gentle click, which, in the silence of the corridor, reverberated like a clap of thunder.

Roger was connected to Island Books somehow. A coincidence, surely, another consequence of this place being so small. It wasn't as if having an interest in local history and folklore made him a killer. Anyway, he had an alibi for one of the murders, Michael had told her. A police conference. Nothing could be more watertight than that. Why, then, did she feel like the only sensible thing to do was run out of the front door, back to her car, and then drive away as fast as she could? To call Michael, to let the police do their jobs, to leave the story, because following it now would be reckless and what else did she need anyway? There were hundreds of books in that room. If she looked she knew she would find the MacCulloch in there. And he was the right age. And in the perfect position to make sure the cases were never connected, to limit the investigations, to hurry them along. To fabricate an alibi? She listened. Not a breath of noise.

She looked at the front door. Took a step towards it. *Lisa Bretel could be somewhere in this house.* She turned and took the stairs.

The landing was carpeted in the same faded red as the stairway and opened out on one side into a seating area in front of a bay window. She looked out on to the gravel driveway to her car, the red security light blinking from the dashboard every few seconds to show her it was safe and secure.

She shouldn't be here. She was breaking the law. *I was worried about him. We'd arranged to meet. I thought perhaps he'd fallen ill upstairs.*

The first room she looked in was a study with an old desk, clear of paperwork and with empty drawers, an old-fashioned dial telephone and a swivel chair. The next was stuffed with furniture, a polished wardrobe, tall lamps with their shades askew and a bed covered with piles of women's clothing. She picked up a couple of pieces. Outdated. Not a young woman's wardrobe. There were books too, Jackie Collins, some historical romances, cookery books. His wife's things. A bathroom was notable only in that it was as shabby as the rest of the house and in stark contrast to the fourth room, the master suite, which was fresh and modern and neat, with a cream carpet and fitted wardrobes filled with neatly hung rows of jackets and trousers and shirts. A glass of water stood on the nightstand, next to a lamp and a book, a popular airport thriller. She sat on the end of the bed. Calmed her breathing. Tried to think rationally. What had she been expecting? Some kind of psychopath's lair, walls covered with pictures of dead women, diaries filled with the scrawlings of a madman? It would have made a great story. But other than the fact that Roger Wilson seemed inconsistent in his approach to home décor, there was nothing to see here. In fact, all she had was wild speculation and the books. She hadn't even looked through them properly. Perhaps the rest of them were bestsellers and self-help books. Perhaps she just happened to pick up the two that had come from Island Books.

It was only when she switched off the landing lights before going back downstairs that she noticed the glow coming from around the edges of a hatch in the ceiling. She found the hook leaning against the bathroom wall and pulled down the trapdoor to the loft. It opened easily, the weight of the ladder folded into it pushing down as she pulled. She straightened it and climbed up.

Empty. Nothing up here. A desk and a chair in an empty room. And on the carpet, a scattering of straw.

She sat at the kitchen table, unsure if she was relieved or disappointed, wondering whether it would have been better to have discovered some concrete proof that Roger was a killer rather than be left with this feeling of unease and uncertainty. She shouldn't have come here to his house. It had been reckless. She was being reckless again. She lingered over the sideboard before leaving. All those pictures: a policeman and a husband; a charitable man. Not a killer.

The map of Guernsey on the wall caught her eye. Points all over circled in coloured pen. A logo in the top left corner. *Festung Guernsey.* Horace Gallienne had mentioned Festung, the people who maintained the Nazi fortifications. What did Roger have to do with them? She looked closer. All of the circles – they were bunkers. And one of them was right near here. It was labelled *Beauregarde, Les Sages Lane.* Not just nearby. On this property. It was marked in green. Two circles with a hatched line running between them. She checked the legend. Two entrances and a chamber.

She opened the kitchen door and let her eyes adjust. She could make out the tall shapes of the trees at the edge of the property and, in the distance, the sea, lucent under the crescent moon. Between here and there lay a vast swathe of black and shadow she knew to be fields and hedgerows – and somewhere amongst them, a Nazi bunker.

Just like the one that filled her nightmares.

Now was not the time to go looking for it. Not because it didn't need finding. Because she was alone and she was very, very scared. *Not as scared as Lisa Bretel.* She was out there. Jenny could save her. She took out her torch. Shone it in front of her. Took a deep breath. Calmed her thoughts.

I'm not afraid of the darkness.

Only what it hides.

43

*H*e stood at the hedge and watched the lights flick on and off as she made her way through his home. What was she seeing? An old man lost in a big house? It had always been too big, even when his wife had been alive. She had complained about it, too draughty and damp and what did they need all that space for anyway? But he would never have sold it. It was here, in the field where he now stood, that he had knelt, so many years ago and first received enlightenment. Where he had felt old Joe's hand on his shoulder and understood, if only for a moment, what it meant to feel something akin to friendship.

He had become distracted, trying to prepare everything. He'd lost track of time. He had wanted to greet her. To talk to her. To bring her out here. Because she was different. She wore her vulnerability so lightly, not like the others, the little sparrows with broken wings. She was something else. A seabird. A cormorant. Yes, that was it. Diving beneath the surface, further and further down, trying to solve the puzzle. Too far, little bird. Much, much too far. There were secrets far nearer to the surface. He would help her back up. He would tell her all about them.

He needed to think quickly. Should he run and catch her? Should he shout and lure her out here? He hesitated. Since he had decided to include her his mind had been clear of noise and distraction. But now, the faintest buzzing. Barely perceptible, but it was there. It *was her, she brought it with her. A flash of anger. Don't be rash. Think.*

Light. The back door. There she was. Coming to him.

Clever girl.

44

Jenny

The torch was bright but illuminated only a small area directly in front of her. Everywhere else was black. If she glanced to one side or the other, even for a moment, she knew it would consume her. So she focused. Straight ahead. No bullshit breathing or counting. Just one foot after the other, through sticky, wet grass, clutching at her shoes. The further down the field she walked, the wetter it became, until the grass turned to mud and she trod slowly, carefully, concentrating on how much she could see, not how little, avoiding the shallow slicks of yellow water which lay on the sodden earth.

A hedge. She shone the torch left and then right. A gate. And on the other side of it, just a few steps into the next field, she found it. A metal grille covered the entrance. It was completely dark down there. Blacker than night . . . She shone her torch through the bars of the grille. Steps led directly down. Her pulse quickened and sweat pricked her top lip in spite of the cold night but she ignored the rising panic and placed the torch on the ground by her side, angling it carefully so the light fell directly on her hands and the grille. She tried to lift it. Too heavy. She tried pushing it to the side.

A shadow. Tall and black. And a voice.

'It's terribly heavy, you know. Let me help you.'

*

He had a gun. At least, he told her it was a gun, and she had no reason to doubt him. He pressed it firmly into her back, took her phone from her pocket, threw it into the hedge. Then he pushed her forwards. She stumbled down the first few rough steps. He told her to stop and she heard the clanging of the grille and a click behind them.

'Watch your step, now, we wouldn't want you to take a tumble, would we?

She had no choice but to walk slowly. The steps were steep, little more than a concrete ladder, and she was shaking, unsteady on her feet. At the bottom, ten feet or so from the surface, a solid wall with an arched opening in it, a little lower than head height.

A tunnel.

'It's a little uncomfortable from here, I'm afraid. You have to stoop down. Go on in. Don't worry. I'm right behind you.'

She felt him. Felt the gun between her shoulder blades and, worse, his hand on the small of her back. But she couldn't go on. She stood, frozen. He pushed, harder now. She heard the click of the safety.

'*Do it.*'

She stifled a sob. Bent down. Stumbled in.

Everything black.

She held out her hands on either side, felt hard, wet stone. Eyes streaming. Throat burning. It was choking her, the darkness. She was going to die. Here, in this tunnel.

She heard him, scraping along behind her. The thought of him touching her again was enough to keep her moving forwards. She wiped her face with her hand, wiped away the sweat and the tears and saw there was light up ahead. *Focus.* She moved faster.

She emerged into a dimly lit, rectangular chamber, with low ceilings, just high enough to stand up straight. Directly opposite her was the arched opening of another tunnel, which must lead to another exit, presumably also barred and padlocked.

In the middle of the chamber, laid out on the floor, was Lisa Bretel. Her skin was deathly pale, deep purple and yellow bruises swelling around her eye, her lips split and bloody, her long, softly curled hair fanned out around her head. From the neck down she was wrapped in what looked like a white sheet, the edges grimy where they touched the damp floor. He was still in the tunnel and Jenny knelt at Lisa's side, shook her frantically, felt for a pulse. Her skin was warm and Jenny felt the faintest throb of blood pumping through her veins. She was alive. Barely.

'Lisa, wake up, Lisa, you have to wake up!'

'Stop! Don't touch her.' She stood, swung around. He had the gun trained on her. His hand was shaking.

'Don't touch her! She's clean. She's ready.' He took a deep breath, forced a smile. 'I brought you here to help, Jennifer. Not spoil things.'

'What have you done to her?'

'I've looked after her. She didn't make it easy for me. Screamed and cried. Soiled herself.' He grimaced. 'But we've worked it all out. She came round in the end. Had something to eat and drink, something to help her relax, and then I washed her and dressed her. Doesn't she look beautiful?' Shadows danced across his face and, as he looked down on Lisa, he wore an expression of beatific calm.

'We're all ready.' He walked towards her, placed the lantern on the floor. He was a head taller than Jenny, broader than her; even without the gun she would have been frightened of him. The only advantage she had over him physically was her youth, and his age did not seem to have hindered him so far. She forced herself not to look away, keeping her eyes fixed on his as he held a hand up, pulled a tendril of hair away from her face and tucked it behind her ear. Only when he let his hand linger on her shoulder did she turn away from his touch. He raised the gun, slowly. Placed it against her cheek. Cold. The smell of oil and sweat. He guided her head back towards him, left the gun barrel resting against her face. Then he took her arm and walked her to a chair in the corner of the chamber, pushed her shoulder firmly down so she sat. He stepped back, the gun at his side, but she could still feel it on her cheek, as if the metal had burnt her.

He picked up the lantern, held it aloft, between them, so she was dazzled by it and could no longer see his features and he became just a shadow behind the glare.

'If you move from this chair I will shoot you in the face.' A lump of fear lodged in her throat like a stone. 'Do you under-stand, Jennifer?' She nodded.

'You're a curious girl, aren't you? I wonder what it is that makes you so interested in other people's business. Is it a reflection on your own life, do you think? Is there something missing, Jenny? An empty space inside you need to fill?'

She stayed silent, eyes half closed against the glare. Let him talk. Talking was better than shooting.

'Or perhaps it's not your fault at all. Perhaps it's all in the genes. Because you're just like your father. He didn't know when to keep his nose out of things either.' She twitched and her eyes widened as she strained to see his face.

'Oh, you didn't know? Yes, old Charlie was always getting himself into scrapes. Fancied himself as bit of detective, always had a conspiracy theory to share. It was a source of great amuse-ment to us all in the force. He was such a nice chap – well, you know that, of course, and we all thought it was rather funny, here comes Charlie with another story. Until somebody stopped laughing.'

'What are you saying?' She could not conceal the tremor in her voice.

'I've got you, haven't I?' He smiled. 'It's too easy, really. Always a daddy issue, you see. You. Me. All the little birds. Daddy didn't care or Daddy wasn't there. It always comes back to that.'

'What are you talking about?'

He ignored her.

'What do you know about my father's death?' Boiling tears of anger and frustration rolled down her cheeks.

'Oh, not much really. I've been retired for a while, as you know. But I've kept my fingers in a few pies. I have my friends on the inside who have followed in my footsteps, who are happy to help the right people for the right price . . .'

'What do you know about my dad, you sick fuck?' she screamed at him and he took a step towards her, his finger tensed on the trigger. She turned her head involuntarily, braced for impact but he just stood there, unmoving.

'I want you to write about me.'

'What?' It came out as a whisper. She turned back to look at him.

'I want you to tell everyone why I did what I did.'

'I don't know why you did what you did.'

'I helped people, Jennifer. That's all I've ever done.'

'How? Are you helping Lisa right now? Look at her, Roger.'

'Of course I am. They were nothing, before I took them. They were sad and damaged and ignored and I made them something beautiful.' He seemed to be struggling to get his words out and he held one hand to his ear, rubbing and pulling at it, distracted. 'I want you to tell people. Will you do that, Jennifer?' He knelt beside Lisa, gun at his side and stroked her cheek. 'I gave all the others to the water. I had to. But now, now we can do this properly. We can give her to the flames.'

Jenny tried to keep her voice even. 'Roger, you're not helping her. You're hurting her. Look at what you've done to her. She has a mother who loves her. She has friends, she's at college.'

'You don't know her, Jennifer, not like I do. I've read all about her. The cutting, the drinking, the problems she has at home. I choose carefully, you know. I do my research.'

'Jenny!'

Faint. In the distance. But they both heard it and it seemed to focus him. He stood, turned to Jenny, raised the gun, pointed it back at her head.

'What a shame. We didn't have time for a proper chat. We're going to have to work quickly.' He left the lantern on the floor and walked to the shelves, towards a row of cans. She couldn't risk attacking him. Not while he held a gun. But she needed to buy some time.

She threw herself out of the chair and kicked the lantern with as much force as she could muster, away from Lisa and against a wall where it smashed in a burst of blue flames, and in the final surge of light before it died, she saw the look of horror on his face as he spun back towards her and she felt it a second before she heard it, a searing pain in her shoulder, then a noise like no other she had ever heard, ringing and reverberating off of the concrete walls and she fell to the floor, deaf and blind in the dark.

She opened her eyes. No difference. Pitch-black. Ears ringing. Shoulder throbbing. Arm twitching. The pain was good. It focused her. On staying alive.

She moved her hand tentatively up her arm, felt the damp warmth of the blood well before she reached the point of entry. She tried to sit. Dizzy. She'd passed out. Not for long. At least, it didn't feel like it.

It was Michael's voice she'd heard, calling for her. But he wasn't here. Why wasn't he here? Think. *Think*. He didn't know where the bunker was. Might not even know there was one. Even if he found it, Roger had locked the grille behind them. She screwed her eyes tightly shut, thinking the darkness within might be a comfort, a barrier to the darkness all around her, but it didn't work. She took deep, ineffective breaths, but the oxygen got lost somewhere between her throat and her lungs, and, instead, panic flowed through her veins, up to her heart and her brain and if she let it in she was done for.

'Silly girl, breaking the lamp.' He tutted.

Movement, shifting, clanging, objects falling over. 'Don't worry. There's a torch here somewhere.' Humming. He was humming as he blindly searched the shelves. Monotonous, tuneless. Like the buzzing of a bee.

Think.

They were both in the same boat. Both blind. Her ears were ringing from the shot. His would be worse. She was injured. He was unhinged. Equal match.

'They're coming. You know they are. They're going to find us.' She tried to sound matter of fact, not desperate.

'Who? Your friend DCI Gilbert?' He said it with disdain, enunciating each letter as if it pained him to say them. 'Oh, he's been and gone, he and a couple of little stooges. They couldn't get in. It's locked, you see. Here's the key.' She heard the clang of metal hit the floor somewhere to her right. 'Yes, they sounded terribly panicked. They've gone off to fetch a bolt-cutter and call for backup. It was all very dramatic. Sounds like he's very fond of you, poor old Gilbert. I do hope your daddy issues haven't gone too far, Jennifer.'

'Fuck you!' She spat it towards the sound of his voice.

'Now, now, no need to get upset over that sad excuse for a man. He's always been a thorn in my side, with his bloody conscience and his "no stone unturned" every time a fucking tomato plant disappeared. Always reviewing the evidence, is DCI Gilbert. Such a tedious man. I had high hopes he'd kill himself a while back. And then, of course, there was the heart attack, but he lived through that too. I wouldn't have minded, if he'd been a worthy opponent. Someone like you, Jennifer. Someone with a little chutz-pah, as the Jews would say. I would have enjoyed that.'

A moan from the middle of the room.

'Lisa!' Jenny called out. 'Lisa, stay where you are. They're coming for us, we're going to be OK.'

'Oh, she won't be going anywhere fast, don't you worry. I gave her a very large dose. I'd be surprised if she ever woke, to be honest. I don't want her to suffer. In the flames.'

'They're coming back, Roger. They know it's you. You'll only make it worse for yourself if you kill us. Or if we die here. I'm bleeding badly. It's not too late. You don't have to do this.' She edged on her knees towards the area where she'd heard the keys fall.

'I appreciate your concern, Jennifer, I really do, but having a couple more deaths on my hands would hardly make a difference to my fate.

She tried to keep her breathing regular and her voice calm. She extended her good arm in front of her and painstakingly ran her fingers over the rough floor, side to side, scraping off patches of her freezing skin in the process. She shook, from the cold and the shock and the pain. She needed to be careful, to make sure she didn't jangle the key when she hit it. And she needed to keep him distracted.

'I could write about you, Roger. But I'd need more information. About Amanda and all the others. About what happened to my dad.' She sounded faint, far away, her own words echoing in her ears.

Stay awake, find the key, and then, and then . . .

'Poor little bird. You don't sound very well. I was so hoping to say a proper goodbye. I had such big plans. I fear you've ruined them.' More clanging and shifting. 'Where is the damn thing?' He was frustrated. She needed the key before he found the torch. She shuffled forward and searched again, rough concrete and more rough concrete until, there. Cold metal. She placed her hand over it, muffling the harsh scraping sound it made as she pulled it towards her. A small ring and two keys. Two exits. A way out.

Behind her. There was no way she could drag Lisa out with her, not with her injured shoulder, not quickly enough to dodge a bullet. There was no way she could leave her down here either. He was fussing and muttering and she edged back, towards where she thought Lisa was.

Noise from above, scraping and clanging. And then light, through the first tunnel. She looked behind her, bit her lip, held back a cry as she jarred her shoulder.

'Jenny! Are you down there, Jenny?' Michael, his voice hoarse.

She could see Roger, in silhouette. He turned to her, raised a finger to his lips, pointed the gun towards the tunnel. She continued to move, crawling, towards Lisa. Roger remained fixated on the tunnel, as Michael headed towards a bullet.

'Stop, Michael!' she screamed and simultaneously pushed herself to her feet, grabbing Lisa under the shoulders. Tiny bursts of light flashed and floated in front of her eyes as the pain from her wound caused a wave of nausea and dizziness and she stumbled and lurched and screamed as she dragged Lisa into the tunnel behind them.

There was a yowling, like an injured animal behind her, but she kept moving, kept dragging Lisa, first with two hands, then with one as she clutched at her mangled shoulder, trying to protect it. They scraped through the narrow passageway and she cried in pain as she bumped into the walls over and over again. Finally, she could go no further and she let Lisa drop to the floor, sat next to her, sobbed, completely disorientated. She had no idea how far they'd come. She strained her eyes, looking for the faintest glimmer of light, and it was then that the panic was unleashed, so that her next cry was not one of pain but of fear. She got back to her feet, stumbling, unsure at first which way was forward and which was back. She felt for Lisa's arms and screamed as she touched not human flesh but warm, damp fur, heard the shrieking of a rat as it scurried away. She stretched an arm out again, wondering what other terrors could be hidden in the blackness, until she found a hand. It was cold and lifeless, but she took hold of it, dragged with all her might, walking backwards, checking in front of her every few steps until finally, there, just ahead, steps. She could see them. She took a breath in, the first in what felt like minutes and tasted the fresh air. She cried, 'Michael' and scrambled forwards, leaving Lisa, who was moaning softly. Shouts up ahead and behind, a gunshot, but Jenny didn't stop. She threw herself up the steps and grabbed at the metal bars which lay between her and safety, cried out again, and then Michael's voice, rough and broken, 'We'll cut through it, just hang on!'

'I have the keys.' She pushed them through the grille.

Moments later she was sitting in a field and it was light as day, the glare from headlights and flashing sirens as welcome as the morning sun.

45

Jenny

A murmur of voices. The crackling of the fire. Newspaper rustling. Dad. Watching the news and reading the paper at the same time. It must be teatime. He always caught up on the day's news before tea. He'd have been out on the boat. He'd be tired. He was getting too old for it really, her mum was right. Jenny should talk to him about it. It was time he thought about retiring. He and Mum could take a cruise. They'd talked about it enough. Although you'd think he'd have had enough of boats to last a lifetime. She smiled, still more than half asleep and shifted on the sofa. It was hard to get comfortable. Her shoulder ached. It ached and throbbed. She forced her heavy eyelids fully open and sat up, wiping a trail of saliva from her cheek as she did so. An open paperback, one of Margaret's romances, which had been resting on her chest, fell to the floor.

'Let me get that for you.' Not her dad. Of course not.

'Thank you.' Her throat was dry. 'How long have you been here?'

'Oh, a little while. I was chatting to your mum; she said you've not been sleeping too well at night so I didn't want to wake you.' Michael examined the book before placing it next to her. 'Funny, I'd have had you down as more of a thriller reader.'

'Mum suggested something a bit less dramatic than my usual reading matter. She thought it might help me to relax.' She glanced at her watch. 'Sarah's coming over soon to take me out for a walk.' She snorted a laugh. 'An afternoon nap followed by a little stroll. Clearly I've skipped turning into my mum and gone straight for my granny.' She winced as she jarred her shoulder. 'So what's new? How's Lisa?'

'She's going to be fine. You saved her life. He'd given her so many sleeping pills it's a wonder she was still breathing when you got there. Then there were the cans of petrol as well as all sorts of strange paraphernalia. Candles with weird symbols carved into them, a book of incantations. Seems he was going to try to raise the Devil.' He looked at her. 'Not that you need to worry about any of that.'

'How could he have kept this hidden for so long? He's completely insane. He managed to fool everyone. The whole island fell for it.'

'There are a lot of questions need answering. His alibi, for example. We're not sure how he did that, so we're not sure if all of the logs can be trusted. Or all of the force, for that matter. The team from Hampshire is going to be here for a while. We've never seen anything like it here. Even the boys from the mainland seem overwhelmed. It would help, of course, if we could get him to talk, but that's unlikely to happen.'

'There's no chance he'll recover?'

'Well, nobody knows for sure. But he shot half of his face off and he's no spring chicken. Plus, who's to say anything he told us would make any bloody sense? Honestly, the more we look at this, the more fucked-up it gets, Jenny. The man lived in a fantasy world, thought he was some kind of dark Messiah sent to save us from ourselves. Some of that material we found in his bunker . . .' He stopped short as Margaret entered with tea and biscuits.

'I hope you're not upsetting Jenny with any of this. She's under strict doctor's orders to relax.' She set down the cups and looked at them both. Jenny gave her the most relaxed smile she could muster.

'I'm fine, Mother.'

'Hm. Elliot called again. He's adamant he's coming to see you. I said tomorrow. All right?'

Jenny nodded, remembering him at the hospital while she was groggy, stroking her forehead, telling her he'd kiss her but he was worried about his safety, leaving flowers on the bedside table, deep blue irises. It seemed he knew her well enough not to bring roses. She smiled. Margaret was still fussing.

'Let me get you another pillow. Your neck isn't properly supported on those cushions.'

'You're lucky to have her, you know. She really is a lovely lady.' Michael avoided her eyes as he said it. 'Anyway, as I was saying, we found some pretty disturbing stuff in that bunker. Including the original photographs of Elizabeth Mahy. He was the first officer on the scene. Only a young lad, then. Seems it had an effect on him, seeing her like that and well, you weren't wrong to connect her with the others. I think she might have been his model, what he looked for in his victims.'

'Do you think this is it?'

'What do you mean?' Michael looked confused.

'I mean, he was on the police force for forty years, Michael. Do you think he was involved in other criminal activity, aside from murder and Devil worship?'

'We'll be looking into it. All the cases he worked, everything that went on while he was chief. It's going to take years.'

'What about my dad's case? Will you be reviewing that?'

'Jenny.' He spoke gently. 'Like I said, we'll be looking at everything. *Hundreds* of cases. Your dad's will be one of them. But you need to prepare yourself. Roger Wilson is insane. It's more than likely he was playing mind games with you. Don't let him win.'

Jenny was unconvinced. 'We need to talk about this some more, Michael, I'm not going to let it go.'

'Don't I know it! Right. One more thing. Your friend, Sarah. She told me you'd been getting some threatening emails.' He stared at her, eyebrows arched, a disapproving look on his face. There was no point denying it. And after everything that had happened, the threats hardly seemed worth worrying about.

'What about them?'

'You should have reported them! You need to hand them over to us and we can look into them. I'm not having you worried and stressed about this, trying to sort it out on your own. That's what we're here for, Jenny.'

A knock at the door.

'That will be Sarah now.' Jenny moved slowly from the sofa.

Michael stood and made to help her to her feet.

'There's nothing wrong with my legs,' she huffed but let him hold her good elbow and help her on with her coat.

'We'll talk more next time. Try to get some rest. Do some Christmas shopping. Go to the office party. Do some normal young people stuff.'

She would have bristled at the suggestion had it come from anyone else, but the look on his face was one of genuine care and concern. And he was right. She did need to relax.

They sat on the wall looking out over Pembroke Bay with an ice cream each. It was cold, but the fading afternoon sun warmed her face. Bright streaks of pink and gold adorned the otherwise pale sky. Sailor's delight. A seagull landed next to her and hopped from one foot to another, its tiny yellow eye fixed on her cone. She broke off a piece and tossed it on to the sand, watched the bird dive for it and gulp it down before coming back and waiting for more.

'When are you going back to work?' Sarah asked.

'I'm not sure if I am, yet.'

'What are you talking about? Where else are you going to go? Not exactly spoilt for choice here, are you? Wait, you're not leaving Guernsey, are you?' She sounded incredulous at the idea.

'No. Of course not. Why on earth would I want to leave this little slice of paradise? Best decision I ever made, leaving the mean streets of Hackney for the quiet island life, wasn't it? It's been a real tonic.'

'All right. Fair point. What are you going to do?'

'I was thinking about going freelance again. No reason why I can't write for the nationals from here, not now that we're well and truly on the news map. And it would give me a bit more flexibility to pursue other things.'

'Like what happened to your dad, you mean?'

'Maybe.'

They sat in silence for several minutes, watching the setting sun and gulls wheeling in the twilight. Sarah jumped off the wall and held her hand out for her. 'I've got to get back. My mum's watching the kids and they'll be doing her head in by now. Anyway, you've had enough excitement for one day. Let's get you home.'

'You go ahead. I'm going to take a minute here.'

'Are you sure? Your mum said I wasn't to leave you on your own. And the sun's nearly set.' She looked worried.

'Stop fussing. I have a torch. I won't be long.'

She climbed the ladder down on to the beach, holding on with her good arm, and leant against the wall while she pulled off her socks and shoes. Her shoulder was sore but the burning pain had been replaced with a dull, uncomfortable ache. She'd been lucky. The bullet had missed the bone, which would have been excruciating, and an artery, which would have been fatal. As it was, she would make a complete recovery. Whatever that meant.

She pushed her feet into the wet sand, enjoying the sensation of the coarse, cold grains against her skin. She walked to the shore-line, sending a flurry of sandpipers running in her wake. The sea shone silver, a faint rosy glow just visible on the horizon. She stepped into it, her feet numbing instantly, and dug her toes into the soft, sticky sand. It sucked and smoothed around them, absorbing and embracing. She stared at her feet, planted there, and at the icy water lapping around her ankles. She could move. Back to the city. She could carve her way through the dirt and the noise, through the constant, beating movement of millions of discon-nected people and make a life for herself there. She could do that. If she wanted to.

She shook her feet loose and watched the sand slide back into the imprint she had made. Then she turned and walked barefoot along the shore, towards home.

Acknowledgements

They say it takes a village to raise a child – I would argue the same is true for a novel. It has taken the love, support, help and encouragement of so many people to conceive, bring forth and develop The Devil's Claw from a twinkle in my eye to a real-life book. Here are the thank yous (by no means an exhaustive list).

To David Savil, whose Creative Writing MA at St Mary's University made all this possible. Turns out the brutal feedback was worth it in the end. To my fantastic agent, Sophie Lambert. Sophie championed The Devil's Claw when it was little more than an MA dissertation, and, along with the rest of the team at C+W, Jake Smith-Bosanquet, Alexandra McNicholl and Luke Speed, has taken this book places I never dreamed it would go. To my editor, the fabulous, approachable, hilarious Sam Eades, and the team at Trapeze Books. Your enthusiasm and energy are boundless, I am so lucky to have you all on my side.

In writing this book, I found myself inhabiting worlds I had little personal knowledge of. I am so very grateful to everybody who gave freely of their time to educate me on their various areas of expertise. Special thanks to Michael Watson, who knows all there is to know about policing on Guernsey (having policed it himself for many years), Nick Mann and Nicola Gibbons at the Guernsey Press and Tom Bradshaw, who has answered a hundred random questions on a hundred random subjects over the last couple of years.

To my writing group, Louise Fein, Jennifer Small, Magdalena Duke, Alex Dugarte, Gwen Emmerson, Andy Howden and Chris Bowden. Your feedback was invaluable, the moral support even more so. I miss you all. Thank you also to Joanne Dickinson, who gave me so much encouragement and industry insight, from the moment I pitched the idea of The Devil's Claw, all the way through to pitching to publishers.

It turns out that doing an MA and writing a book while being a stay-at-home mum with three small kids is quite tough. There have been so many occasions when I wanted to give up, when it really felt like I'd bitten off more than I could chew. To Pilar Ferreira, you are beautiful inside and out and so much nicer to my children than I am – I wouldn't have been able to do this without your help. To my in-laws, Heather and Alan Dearman, thank you for all the last-minute babysitting – especially since your grandchildren are a trans-Atlantic flight away. I credit my wonderful friends with providing encouragement, tea, wine, cake, chocolate and cheese whenever called for – a special thank you to Hanna McCarthy, Zeta McDonald, Emma Robinson, on one side of the Atlantic, and Tricia Alcamo, Louise Barclay and Tina Sherwood on the other.

Thank you to mum and dad for the books and the stories and the walks through the woods, fields, beaches, bunkers and caves of Guernsey. I'm not convinced they are all actually haunted, but thank you for telling me that they were. Consider the dark side of my imagination well and truly overdeveloped.

Finally, thank you to Andrew, Lily, Charlie and Lena. It is not easy having a tortured writer as a wife and mother. You have all endured bad moods, frayed tempers and borderline neglect over the last two years. And that was just on the good days. Thank you for not only putting up with me, but supporting me, even when you secretly thought this was a waste of time. I love you all more than anything. Now let me get on with the next book, will you?

Glossary

Bean jar – A casserole made with beans and a pig's trotter.

Crapaud – Toad. A derogatory term for a person from Jersey.

Crown and Anchor – A simple dice game, traditionally played by sailors in the Royal Navy. Still popular in the Channel Islands but can only be played legally on certain occasions.

Deputy – A member of the States of Deliberation, elected every four years by popular vote.

Douzaine – The main administrative body of each parish, usually made up of twelve members known as Douzeniers.

Douzenier – Parish representatives with civil and administrative responsibilities such as supervision of polls during elections, rubbish collections, the granting of building and dog licences.

Euchre – A trick-taking card game, originating in Cornwall. Popular in Guernsey where it is played competitively in leagues.

Gâche – A bread made with dried fruits and candied peel.

Her Majesty's Greffier (commonly referred to as "The Greffe") The office of the clerk of the Royal Court and Registrar General of births, marriages and deaths.

Guernsey Biscuit – A bread roll, usually served toasted.

Jerry-bag – A woman who fraternised with German soldiers during the Nazi Occupation of the Channel Islands.

Loophole tower – Towers built by the British in the late eighteenth century to defend Guernsey from French invasion. Each tower has two floors above ground and 'loopholes' to allow musket fire to cover all approaches.

Ruette Tranquilles – A network of back lanes with a fifteen mile per hour speed limit where cars must give way to pedestrians and cyclists.

The States of Deliberation (commonly referred to as "The States") – Guernsey's government, made up of deputies from each of the island's ten parishes.

States' House – Council house

Vraic – Seaweed found in the Channel Islands. Traditionally gathered and spread on crops as fertiliser.

Guernsey French Translations

Collymouchon – A snail

Cor chapin! – Good gracious!

Cor dammie lar! – An exclamation of surprise or incredulity

P'tite goute – A tipple

N'faut pas faire lè cotin dèvant què lè viau set naï – One must not build the crib until the calf is born

Reading Group Guide
TOPICS FOR DISCUSSION

1. What is the effect of hearing the story from the voice of the killer in those short chapters? How did it make you feel?

2. Guernsey feels like an extra character in the novel. Discuss how the island setting is used in the story.

3. How does the author pull the wool over the reader's eyes in preparation for the twist about the missing girl? Did you see it coming? Or was it a surprise?

4. Discuss the relationship between Michael and Jennifer, and how it changes over the course of the story.

5. Did you suspect who was the killer was? What clues did the author leave?

6. Discuss the role of local legends and folklore.

7. A theme the author explores is how the past affects the present. How does she show this through the characters and the story?

8. The ending is intentionally ambiguous: what does life hold for those characters? What will happen next?

9. Jennifer and Michael join forces to catch the killer. Share your favourite films/TV programmes/books about detective duos.

10. What did you enjoy most or least about *The Devil's Claw?*

Author Q & A
WITH LARA DEARMAN

Why did you decide to have a journalist and a policeman as your main characters?

I've always been addicted to the news and, for a while, harboured an ambition to be a reporter. I somehow ended up working in finance which, while interesting in its own way, didn't quite deliver the same excitement I imagined a career in investigative journalism would. I originally intended for Jenny to be a police officer, but found working within the confines of police procedure a little restrictive. As soon as I changed her career, the character came to life. I also had the opportunity to live vicariously through Jenny, even spending some time shadowing real journalists, which was great. As for DCI Gilbert, I wasn't really expecting him! He was only supposed to have a minor role in the novel, a bit of a bumbling local cop, but he became something so much more than that – he had to have his own story. So I ended up delving into police procedure despite my earlier reservations. I'm so glad that I did. I immensely enjoyed the research involved and was lucky to have the help of a retired Guernsey police officer, whose insight and guidance was invaluable. DCI Michael Gilbert was by far the most rewarding character to write.

How does the setting – Guernsey – shape the story? What is your own relationship with the island?

I'm a Guernsey girl, born and raised on the island, but I don't think I really appreciated how distinctive a place it was until I left. At university, when people found out where I was from they were fascinated and asked so many questions – what was it like growing up on an island, did everyone speak

French, was it the same place as Jersey? Despite being so close to the mainland, the Channel Islands are a bit of a mystery to a lot of people. It seemed only natural to harness the knowledge and insight I have as a 'Guern' in my writing. I've wanted to write a book for years and have notebooks full of plot ideas. Some are for mysteries, some for thrillers, one is a historical romance – the only thing they all have in common is the location. Guernsey was always my starting point, and is every bit as important to the story as Jenny or Michael – its history and culture have shaped the characters and its geography dictates so many of their actions.

As for my own relationship with Guernsey, it was an idyllic place to be a child; buckets and spades on the beach in the summer, exploring abandoned bunkers and Napoleonic forts in the winter, spending the whole day cycling through tiny lanes with my best friend, sitting on the sea wall eating fish and chips, watching the sunset. Then, as I grew older, I began to see the downside of living in such a small place. The familiarity, the sameness, previously so comforting to me, began to feel restrictive. In *The Devil's Claw,* I've tried to explore those contrasting feelings of freedom and confinement that living on an island can inspire.

Why did you include local folklore and legends?

My dad is a brilliant story-teller and constantly regaled my sister and I with local folk tales and legends, usually during our Sunday morning walks with the dog. One of my favourites was about the headless horseman at Fauxquets. Dad would tell us that the horseman galloped through the valley, dressed all in black, riding a black horse. We would walk quietly, so as not to disturb him, but secretly hope to catch a glimpse. Sometimes, as we crept through the trees, Dad would rustle a bush, or throw a stick into the undergrowth and my sister and I would run screaming and laughing until we reached the end of the path. The stories were endless; the Fairy Ring was a meeting place for the Devil and his cronies, goblins lived in the woods in St Saviour's, all the bunkers were haunted by German soldiers. I still can't walk down Pedvin Street in St Peter Port without a shudder, thinking about the witch who would put the 'evil eye' on me if she caught me making too much noise. According to my dad, every part of the island had its own ghost or witch or regular visit from the Devil. Some of these stories are recorded in local folklore books, others were pure invention, but they all stuck – for me, they are part of the fabric of the island.

You tell some of the story from the killer's point of view. Why did you choose this writing style?

I did a lot of research into real-life serial killers and was struck by how ordinary some of them had appeared to the outside world – they had families, respectable jobs, volunteered in the community, to all intents and purposes lived a 'normal' life. It was terrifying and, consequently, fascinating to me. I started to think about who the killer in *The Devil's Claw* really was, inside and out. What was his childhood like, who were his friends, how did he think? I wrote the first chapter from his point of view purely to satisfy my own curiosity, I never intended to include it in the book. But once I'd started to uncover the killer's past, I couldn't stop, I needed to know everything about him and I knew he had to be a central character. The difficulty then, of course, was how to keep his identity a mystery!

The book is filled with twists and turns. Did you know how the story was going to end? Or did it surprise you?

I had two scenes in my head when I started writing *The Devil's Claw*. One was a woman returning to her island home after years living away. The other was a dramatic showdown in a bunker. So the ending didn't surprise me, but I had absolutely no idea how I was going to get there!

You leave a few questions unanswered at the end of the novel. Will Michael and Jennifer return?

Yes. Michael and Jenny's characters evolved so much in the writing of *The Devil's Claw*. In Michael's case, he went from being a character on the sidelines to sharing centre stage. As for Jenny, she has only just begun to sort through the issues in her past. There are loose ends which need tying up, and some threads which have only just begun to unravel. And the location offers endless possibilities – Guernsey and its surrounding islands are perfect settings for mystery and intrigue. Michael is going to be kept pretty busy until his retirement. And as Jenny finds it impossible to ignore a good story, so is she . . .